The Road to Rowanbrae

by the same author

THE BROW OF THE GALLOWGATE

The Road to Rowanbrae

Doris Davidson

HarperCollins*Publishers*

I would like to thank my editor,
Rachel Hore, for all the help
she has given me with this book.

First Published in 1991
by HarperCollins Publishers,
77–85 Fulham Palace Road,
Hammersmith, London W6 8JB

9 8 7 6 5 4 3 2 1

BRITISH LIBRARY CATALOGUING IN PUBLICATION DATA

Davidson, Doris
The road to rowanbrae
I. Title
823′ [Fiction]

ISBN 0 00 223844 6

Phototypeset in Linotron Palatino by
Intype, London
Printed and bound in Great Britain by
Hartnolls Limited, Bodmin, Cornwall

Rowanbrae – 1984

Ewan Duncan had never been in trouble in all his twenty-four years, and had always intended to help the police by reporting anything he saw that seemed suspicious, but he couldn't bring himself to notify them about this. He could just imagine them asking countless questions he couldn't answer, and grilling him until he got so mixed up that he wouldn't know what was what. Then they'd start making enquiries and uncover any skeletons there were in the family cupboard . . . no, that was a bit too near the bone. Oh, God, he thought, rather hysterically, he had a one-track mind, not surprisingly in view of what he had just found, but how would he have reacted if he had found a whole skeleton? The skull was bad enough.

It lay grinning up at him as if defying him to disturb it, or perhaps it was ordering him to find out why it was there? It had been concealed too well for there to have been a natural death, but how long ago had it been buried? Whose was it? Was one of his long-dead – or not-so-long-dead – ancestors a murderer? Or was it one of his forebears who had been despatched to this ignominious grave? But they were all accounted for, as far as he knew. Wait! He vaguely recalled having heard, when he was very young, that someone had disappeared at some time and had never been seen again. Could this be why?

Ewan stood irresolutely, looking down. If he reported what he'd found, the extension would be held up for God knows how long, and Angie would be most upset if the house wasn't ready to move into by October. Deciding that it would be best to say nothing about it to his wife or to anyone else, he threw a shovelful of earth over the offending monstrosity.

Walking towards his car, it occurred to him that the deeds of the house had shown it to have been built some time in the 1930s on the site of the Duncans' croft, so it was more than likely that none of his ancestors had been involved in the secret burial. It was a comforting thought, but he had the strangest feeling that someone in his family *had* been responsible, and he knew that he couldn't leave the mystery unsolved. For his own peace of mind he would have to find out the truth.

PART ONE

Chapter One

1905

Setting another lump of peat on the fire, the girl watched the sparks flying up the chimney, her dark head – hair pinned up now that she was wed – bowed in despair. It was difficult to remember that she was Mysie Duncan now, not Mysie Lonie as she had been for sixteen years, but it was true, unfortunately. Jeems Duncan would not have been her choice if she'd had any say in the matter. Only three short weeks ago, she had been given an extra day off from her scullerymaid's position at Forton House to see the Turriff Show, an important agricultural event in the northeast of Scotland, and had trigged herself out in her Sunday best. The first person she had seen when she arrived was her father, who had apparently been drinking since the night before and was making the usual spectacle of himself. She tried to turn away without him noticing, but had only taken a few steps when the drunken fool spotted her.

'Mysie!' he shouted. 'Come here an' speak to your father.'

Knowing that he would follow her anyway, and afraid of what he would do if she disobeyed him, she walked reluctantly back, conscious of the amused stares of the people standing near.

Eddie Lonie put his arm round her, announcing to the world in general, 'She's my lassie. Is she nae a bonnie wee quine?'

He trailed her round the show rings where the farm animals were being paraded, and it was almost an hour before she managed to give him the slip.

She was wandering round by herself, stopping occasionally to look at the knick-knacks on the stalls run by the travelling people, when she became aware of the stranger. A big, broad man in a floppy bonnet, he was eyeing her as if she were a beast he was considering buying, and she walked away uncomfortably. He followed her for a good ten minutes, then her father appeared again from nowhere.

She was almost glad to see him, something about the stranger having disquieted her, though he had never uttered a word. Again, Eddie proclaimed that she was his daughter, and the other man gave a start. 'She's your lassie, is she?' he said, after a very slight hesitation. 'I was just thinkin' she was the best thing I'd seen so far.'

Her father cackled with delight. 'I've mair at hame just as bonnie, for us Lonies are blessed wi' good looks.'

From the stranger's expression, Mysie gathered that he didn't think much of her father's looks, and little wonder, for his face was mottled from the drink he had poured down his throat over the years. It crossed her mind that the other man had no claim to good looks himself. Well over forty, he had hairs sprouting out of the huge red nose in the middle of his fat red face, a mouth big enough to swallow the whole of the North Sea and still have room for a couple of lochs, and a pot belly that suggested he'd already done just that. Looking at his face again, she noticed that his eyes – fixed on her with an intensity that filled her with dread – were so light that they seemed colourless, though there was a hint of blue somewhere.

The man turned to her father again. 'I'm needin' a wife, an' your lassie's fair ta'en my fancy, so would you agree to lettin' me ha'e her?' He didn't see Mysie's expression of horror.

Always ready to grasp an opportunity, Eddie had found that a show of reluctance on his part often acted as a bit of a spur, and rubbed his chin thoughtfully. 'I'm nae so sure aboot that. You're nae the kind o' man I had in mind as a son-in-law.'

'I work Rowanbrae Croft in the parish o' Burnlea, an' I mak' a fair livin', enough to keep her an' ony bairns we ha'e.'

'A croft?' Eddie Lonie said, speculatively. 'But if I agree, I'd be lossin' my auldest lassie, so what . . . ?' Understanding how her father's mind was working, Mysie tried to protest, but he turned on her angrily. 'It's got naething to dae wi' you. It's just atween me an' this man.' After a pause, he went on, 'What would you gi'e me for her?' Taken aback, the other man scowled, then muttered, obviously averse to throwing away good money, 'Twenty pound?'

'Oh, Father, I dinna want . . . '

Ignoring his daughter, Eddie said, 'Mak' it forty?'

'Thirty!'

Mysie's heart plunged straight to her feet. Thirty pounds was a fortune to her father. 'What if I dinna agree to this?'

'Naebody's askin' you, so haud your tongue!'

She jumped back as his hand struck her, and rubbed her cheek as Eddie said, 'Weel, Mister . . . eh . . .?'

'Jeems Duncan, an' I'll bring you the money next week.'

'Weel, Jeems, she's worth a lot mair, but . . . och, weel, it's a bargain.' Eddie spat on his hand then extended it and they shook hands gravely.

Remembering, Mysie felt the same sickness again. She would never forgive her father for selling her like an animal, as she'd sobbed out to him on the way home that day, but he had yanked her along the road, grinning stupidly. When they reached the rather ramshackle house that had been her home until she'd gone into service, she ran to her mother and burst out, 'Father's sell't me to a auld man.' Jean Lonie – thirty-three, but looking much older because of her emaciated face and greying hair – turned round from her baking board. 'Sell't you? But what in God's name . . . ?'

9

'This man said he wanted me for his wife, an' he's goin' to gi'e Father thirty pound for me.'

'Jeems Duncan's got a croft in Burnlea,' Eddie said, proudly, 'so he'll be able to provide for her. Mysie'll be weel settled, an' that's ane less for us to worry aboot.'

'But, my God, Eddie, she's only fifteen, still a bairn.'

'She'll be sixteen afore the weddin', for the banns'll need to be cried, an' it's nae ilka day I can mak' thirty pound that easy. Noo, I'll hear nae mair aboot it, an' if she doesna dae what she's tell't, she needna expect to come back to my hoose.' He clambered into the box bed in the alcove in the kitchen and was soon snoring loudly.

His wife crossed over to the fireside, where their daughter was weeping silently. 'I'm sorry, Mysie. I'll try again the morn, but you ken what he's like when he's fu'.'

'Aye, I ken, but, Mother, I dinna like Jeems Duncan.'

'He'll maybe nae be so bad when you get to ken him, lass.'

All Sunday, Jean tried to make her husband see sense, Mysie adding her own sobbing pleas before returning to Forton House, but Eddie, still suffering from the previous day's drinking, was adamant. 'You ken fine the smiddy's nae payin' nooadays, an' thirty pound's aye thirty pound.'

Jean lost her temper at that. 'The smiddy would pay if you bade sober lang enough to work, but you canna keep awa' fae the drink. It's nae muckle wonder folk goes to Erchie Yule, for he mak's a better job o' shoein' a horse than you.'

'Is it ony wonder I drink?' Eddie thundered. 'A hoose fu' o' bairns an' a wife that nags fae morn to nicht? The bargain's made, an' nae even my ain lassie's goin' to mak' me br'ak it. She's lucky to get such a hard-workin' man.'

True to his word, Jeems Duncan came to Drumloanings Smithy the following Saturday to hand thirty sovereigns to Eddie, and the wedding took place in the manse two weeks later. Before the minister began the simple cere-mony, he drew Eddie aside. 'Are you sure your daughter knows what she is doing?' he asked, looking doubtfully at the bridegroom.

'Oh, aye, minister. Jeems Duncan's maybe nae a oil paintin', but he has his ain croft an' Mysie'll be weel enough there.'

The wedding proceeded, and they returned to Drumloanings to celebrate, Jeems providing the spirits to drink their health.

Give him his due, Mysie mused, he had just taken one glass himself, and she should be thankful that he wasn't a drinker. She had been betrayed for thirty pieces of gold, not silver, and her father had likely spent most of it before the wedding. If he hadn't drunk it himself, he had wasted it on his cronies, who had as big a thirst as his and congregated round any man with money to lash out. Wherever it had gone – and she was quite sure that her mother had never smelt a bawbee of it – Jeems had handed it over in all good faith and transported her away from Drumloanings in a rickety cart he had borrowed from the miller in Burnlea. Rowanbrae was nothing special, she had discovered, just a wee bit place with a few acres of land. The furniture was old – he had told her yesterday that it had belonged to his father and mother – but it was good, solid stuff, and should last Jeems and her for the rest of their lives, as well. A real china dinner service, delicate white with a dark red pattern, sat on the dresser shelves, but he had warned her that it was not for every day and had pointed to the using dishes – earthenware with just a plain blue band round the rim – which were kept on a rack nailed to the wall beside the back porch. The meal girnel in the corner looked a bit 'waur o' the wear', but it would serve the purpose, and the table would look better after a good scrubbing. The mantelpiece was nearly black with smoke from the fire, and would need a lot of elbow grease to take it back to its original colour, but, taken all in all, Mysie thought, brightening a little, she hadn't done too badly.

If only she could take to Jeems.

11

Last night had been much worse than her mother had led her to expect, and her body still felt sore from his muckle hands pawing at her. Should she chance telling him tonight that her time of the month had come, to save him touching her? But when it did come, he would know she had been lying to him, so it would be best just to put up with it. Sighing, she walked over to the girnel to get a handful of oatmeal for the pot, and by the time her husband came in for his breakfast the porridge was nearly solid. With trembling hands she put great dollops into the big bowl and waited for him to turn on her angrily, but after one spoonful, he looked up at her with what she supposed was intended to be a smile. 'It's nae bad, quine, but it would ha'e been better if you'd steeped the meal last nicht.'

Waiting at the fireside, she gave him the second helping he asked for, having to force the wooden spoon deep down into the grey morass to make it come out of the pot. 'If there's nae enough left for the morn,' he told her, 'put the rest oot to the hens. Feedin' them's your job, an' collectin' the eggs. Some lay ootbye fae the yard, but you'll get to ken where they'll be come time. An' you'll need to milk Broonie the coo first thing ilka day for I like fresh milk wi' my porridge, an' her udder'll be near burstin' by noo. I should ha'e tell't you last nicht, but . . . we'd other things to think aboot, eh?' He gave a lewd cackle that made her flesh creep. 'I dinna think you enjoyed it much, but you'll get used to it.' Mysie didn't think she would ever get used to *that*, but maybe a body could get used to anything.

Standing up, he said, 'I'm awa' to the well for the drinkin' water.' On his way past her, he gripped her buttocks for a moment. 'Aye, you've a broad enough backside on you, that's one good thing. The very dab for ha'ein' bairns, but they'll need to be loons, for there's nae room here for ony useless quines.'

Disgust surged up in her as she went to take the cow in from the field. They'd been wed for less than a day, and he was speaking about bairns already, but no doubt he'd be successful in that, as he was in everything else, from running this croft single-handed to bargaining for a wife. Her bed was made and she would have to lie on it, there was nothing else for it.

Her spirits lifted as the creamy liquid streamed into the pail. The cow was a lovely beast, a velvety black-and-white Friesian, with soft eyes which fastened on Mysie occasionally as if grateful for the gentle fingers, and her milk would make beautiful butter. When the steady flow became a trickle, she stopped pulling the teats and carried the pail into the dairy which Jeems had shown her last night, built on to the end of the house. At least everything here was spotless, she was glad to see, the wooden churn, the flat pats for shaping the butter, the press for squeezing the cheeses.

While she was feeding the porridge to the hens, she felt the touch of a hand on her back and jumped round, startled, to find a tall, well-built young woman regarding her with curiosity.

'I'm Jess Findlater, fae Downies, alang the road a bit. I thought you'd be needin' somebody to speak to, for your man can whiles be as dour as a fire kindled wi' damp sticks. You're awfu' young to be wed on Jeems Duncan, though, an' you'll need to stand up for yoursel'. I was just sayin' to Jake, that's my man, I hoped Jeems had picked a lass wi' a bit o' spunk in her, for he's needin' to be held in aboot a bit. He's been here on his ain ower lang, for it's aboot five year since his mother passed on, an' her man a good five year afore that, so he's got set in his ways.'

Noticing that her rigmarole had made the girl's mouth fall open, Jess gave a shrill laugh. 'Ach, I'm sorry. Jake says my tongue's as lang as the road to Timbuctoo, but he's a great ane for teasin', my Jake.'

Mysie smiled. 'I'm real pleased to meet you. I'm Mysie Lonie that was, an' my father's a blacksmith at Drumloanin's ootside Turra. Come into the hoose an' I'll mak' us a

13

cup o' tea.' As soon as Jess sat down, she said, 'Turra, you say? An' was that where Jeems met you?'

'Aye, at the Show. He gi'ed my father thirty pound to get me for a wife.' Mysie hadn't meant to tell anyone this degrading fact, but it was out before she thought.

Jess was impressed. 'Thirty pound? My God, Mysie, that's a fair bit.'

'That's what Father thought as weel, so they shook hands an' the bargain was made.'

'Weel, you didna get muckle o' a bargain,' Jess laughed, 'for Jeems has a face like a sow's erse, an' you'll ha'e your work cut oot settin' this place to rights, for a man doesna bother cleanin' up ahin' him. I'm aye tellin' Jake to lay things by when he's finished wi' them, but it's like water aff a duck's back. You'll need to let Jeems ken you've a mind o' your ain, right fae the start, or he'll glory on like he's aye daen.'

'Oh, I couldna say onything to him. I've never been able to stick up for mysel'.'

'If you dinna, you'll be makin' a stick to br'ak your ain back.' Jess took a gulp of tea. 'It beat me what ony lassie could see in him, but it was what your father saw, eh? Ach weel, it'll maybe turn oot a' right in the end. You'll maybe mak' a decent man o' the ill-mannered de'il yet.'

Mysie laughed. 'An' hens'll maybe lay duck eggs.'

Clapping her hands, Jess cried, 'Here's me thinkin' you'd naething in you, but that's the road, lass. Keep your he'rt up, an' mind, if you ever need a friend, you've only to come to me.'

'That's good o' you, Mrs Findlater.'

'Jess.'

'It's awfu' good o' you, Jess. I'll mind that.'

'I'd best get back to Downies, for Jeems'll nae be pleased if he sees me here.' Jess patted Mysie's shoulder sympathetically before she strode out, the wind flapping her black skirt and making wisps of her mousey hair fly in all directions.

Before Jeems came in again, Mysie had made the bed in

14

the other room, given the kitchen a tidy up, scrubbed the table and had potatoes and cabbage boiling at the fire. He lifted his spoon as she set his dinner in front of him, then disgusted her by wolfing the food down as though he hadn't seen any for days. It wasn't until he'd finished eating that he looked round the room appraisingly. 'Aye, it needed a real wumman aboot the place. I whiles had the miller's quine in, but she didna dae very much. Did you mind to feed the hens and milk the coo?'

'Aye did I, an' I had Jess Findlater in for a cup o' tea.' She deemed it best to tell him in case he found out.

'Jess Findlater has nae business comin' inside my hoose when I'm nae here,' he roared, his beetling eyebrows almost meeting over his bulbous nose. 'There's never been nae comin's an' goin's afore, an' that'll nae change though you're here.'

'You canna stop me takin' her in, Jeems.' Mysie held her breath – the retort had come out involuntarily – and, in the deathly silence that followed, she was afraid to look at him, but was thankful that he hadn't risen to strike her, as she'd been half afraid he might.

He gave a grunt, making her jump. 'Ho, so the little cattie's got claws, has she? You're nae the sharger I took you for, quine, but you're a' the better for that. You can ha'e Jess Findlater in for a cup o' tea noo an' then, but just her. I'm nae wantin' a' the weemen roon' aboot comin' in an' gawkin'.'

'I'll nae tak' naebody else in.' Mysie's thumping heart slowed down. 'Jess Findlater's a real kindly body.'

'She is that. Her an' Jake are good neighbours, nae like some o' the other nosey tinks that bide aboot Burnlea. Noo, you'll ha'e to milk Broonie again afore suppertime.'

Mysie sat down abruptly when he went out. She had stood up to Jeems and got away with it, but she might not be so lucky next time. It wasn't really fair, for she had always dreamt of meeting a young man, who would court her gently and treat her like a lady. He wouldn't have needed to be a rich man – that would have been expecting

15

too much – as long as his kisses made her swoon with love. Then, when he was sure of how she felt, he would have carried her away from Turriff on a white horse to a house where they would live happily ever after. He would have been handsome, with dark hair curling round his ears, and eyes that held smouldering passion in their depths. Oh, that was the kind of man she was meant for, not a dour forty-something-year-old with a face like a sow's backside, as Jess had so expressively described it.

Smiling, she rose to her feet and went to the back porch for an old rag to clean the smoke-blackened mantelpiece. Vigorous rubbing had no effect, so she moistened the cloth with water from the kettle, sprinkled on some salt, and within minutes she was rewarded by the emergence of a tiny area of deep reddish-brown. It would take time, she thought, but she was determined to master the house, and maybe lick her husband into some kind of better shape.

On Friday, Jess took Mysie to the general store in what was euphemistically called 'the village' by the residents – a small higgledy-piggledy cluster of run-down cottages. 'There's aye a puckle weemen in Dougal's on a Friday,' she had told the girl the previous day, 'so if you come wi' me, I'll introduce you. It's as weel to get it ower quick.'

The three customers in the shop turned to stare at them when they went in, and Mrs Mennie, behind the counter, lost track of the prices she was totting up. Highly amused by the impact they had made, Jess laughed. 'This is Mysie, Jeems Duncan's wife – Jean Petrie, her man's grieve at Fingask; Belle Duff, fae Wellbrae, the croft nearest the kirk; Alice Thomson, her man's the souter; Dougal Mennie an' his wife, Rosie.'

Mysie was embarrassed at the way the women were sizing her up, but she smiled a shy acknowledgement to each stiff nod, and was glad that at least the shopkeeper gave her a friendly smile in return. It was Mrs Petrie, the farm foreman's wife, ferret-faced and thin-lipped, who spoke first. 'We never thought you'd be so young, Mrs Duncan. You dinna look auld enough to be left the school.'

'I was in service in Forton Hoose in Turra for mair than twa year,' Mysie mumbled. 'I'm sixteen.'

'Sixteen? An' Jeems must be wearin' on for fifty, that's a big difference.' Jean was not famed for diplomacy, and the other women thought nothing of her observation.

Dougal Mennie, however, a rather stout man with bushy white hair and a pleasant, chubby face, felt obliged to intervene. 'That's none o' oor business, Mistress Petrie, an' dinna forget, there's mony a good tune played on an auld fiddle. I'm weel past fifty mysel', an' Rosie has nae complaints. Noo, if that's a' you're needin', I'll coont it up, for I've other folk to serve, as you can see.'

'Dinna put it on, then, for we're near the end o' the term an' there's nae muckle left in my purse.'

'I never charge mair than I should,' he said, sharply, for Mrs Petrie always rubbed him up the wrong way. 'Two shillings an' fivepence three farthings, if you please.'

She paid him and packed her purchases into her basket while Rosie Mennie handed change to Mrs Duff, and the two women left together. Mrs Thomson, the shoemaker's wife, dying to find out what her friends thought of the incomer, bought only two items and hurried out to join them, their heads going close together to discuss, Jess thought as she watched them, what Mysie could have seen in Jeems.

It crossed her mind that they would never guess, not in a month of Sundays, that he'd paid thirty pounds for his wife, and she smiled as she turned to lay her surplus butter, eggs and cheese on the counter. Mysie doing likewise, they soon came to an amicable agreement with the shopkeeper as to what they could have in exchange. The system of barter suited both sides. The crofters' wives could obtain such necessities as sugar, salt or paraffin without money having to change hands, and Dougal made a profit when he sold their fresh produce to retailers in the city. Luxuries like clothes had to wait until their husbands

17

sold potatoes and other vegetables when they went into town themselves.

Passing the little group outside, Jess remarked, 'If there's onything else you want to ken aboot Mysie, you've only to ask.' Glaring into their uncomfortable faces for a moment, she said, 'There's naething, is there? Weel, good day to you, ladies,' emphasising the last word with great sarcasm.

Mysie waited until they were out of earshot before she gave vent to her mirth. 'Oh, Jess,' she gasped, almost doubled up, 'what a terrible wumman you are.'

'It's just fun,' Jess giggled.

The clip-clop of horse's hooves behind them made them both turn round. 'It's the laird's carriage,' Jess said, importantly. 'His coachman tak's him into the toon, for he's got some kind o' business there.'

They both stepped nearer the ditch at the side of the road, and as the vehicle rumbled past, Jess gave a cheery wave, the blue-liveried driver inclining his head to her in a stiff nod, and the laird himself smiling broadly. 'He's a fine man, Mr Phillip,' she told Mysie. 'We hardly ever see his wife, though, for she doesna like mixin' wi' the common folk.'

'He looked awfu' young to be the laird,' Mysie observed, as they moved back into the middle of the road.

'He hasna been laird for very lang. It was his father when I come here first, but he died sudden, an' this ane fell heir. He hasna ony bairns yet, but nae doot they'll come. The gentry need sons to pass on their estates to.'

'Where aboot do the Phillips bide?'

'Burnlea Hoose – the drive up to the Big Hoose is between the kirk an' Wellbrae, the Duffs' place, but you canna see the hoose for the trees. The whole o' Burnlea, village as weel, belongs to the Phillips. Noo, what was we speakin' aboot?'

'We was laughin' aboot you sayin' yon to . . . '

'Oh, aye. They're gossipin' bitches that lot. Alice Thomson an' Belle Duff's nae quite so bad, but never tell Jean

Petrie ony o' your business, for she'll spread it roon' wi' that muckle added on you'll nae recognise it when it comes back to you.'

'I ken what you mean, for we'd a Jeannie Tosh at hame an' she was the very same. The biggest gossip on twa feet.'

'She wouldna beat Jean Petrie, she's the world's worst.'

Mysie giggled. 'I dinna think you like her.'

'I canna stand her, an' she'll be watchin' you like a hawk, noo, to see if you're in the family way, an' coontin' to see if it happened afore the weddin'.'

Mysie's face coloured. It was too early yet for her to be in that condition, but if her husband's nightly pounding into her was anything to go by, it wouldn't be long before she was. He started pawing and probing as soon as they went to bed, making her do things to arouse him and sickening her with his animal noises that grew louder and faster as his passion increased.

That night, when he rolled off her at last, he said, 'I ken you dinna like it, but I want twa loons so's I'll be sure there's somebody left to carry on here after I die.'

'Twa?' she murmured in some dismay.

'In case something happens to ane o' them,' he explained. Imagining what her life would be if she produced a string of daughters, Mysie came close to jumping up and running as far from Rowanbrae as she could, but she was bound to this monster by her marriage vows – and by the bargain he'd made with her father – and he would likely find her wherever she went. 'You ken,' Jeems went on, 'I never saw ony other lassie that I wanted to be the mother o' my bairns. I thought aboot Nessie White, the miller's lassie, for a while, but she's a bit saft in the head, an' when I saw you yon day at the Show, I thought, that's her. You'd a fine pair o' hips on you, an' twa grand paps, so I ken't you'd be a good breeder, though you'd nae beef on you nae place else.' Revolted by his coarse honesty, Mysie was thankful when his snoring told her that he'd fallen asleep, and she thought over what he'd said. He wanted two sons, so she would do her best, but

19

as soon as she produced them, she wouldn't let him touch her again if she could help it. Enough was enough of that.

At breakfast the following morning, Jeems said, 'I'll leave you to get the water the day, quine. Eck Petrie's wife's been lookin' at me queer this week, for it's aye the wives that go to the well, nae the men.'

'You should ha'e tell't me,' Mysie murmured, 'an' I'd ha'e went fae the first day I was here.'

'Ach weel, I've went mysel' for years, but there's aye some gossipin' weemen at it, an' they get right up my back.'

As Mysie was to find out, the well was used by several women with sources nearer their homes, but who made the icy purity of the soft spring water an excuse for meeting and gossiping with other wives in the area. As she drew nearer, she could see Jean Petrie – cottared at Fingask where pipes provided a tap in the yard as well as in the farmhouse – holding forth to Belle Duff – living at Wellbrae, she must be near a well – and Alice Thomson, who were hanging on to every word. A little apart from them, a buxom girl with a vacant expression was watching a fat, cheery-faced woman cranking up a pail, both apparently uninterested in the gossip. The woman, however, looked round and smiled when Mysie walked up. As before, Jean Petrie was the first to speak. 'So Jeems has made you come yoursel' the day, has he? I thought you might be ower genteel to carry water, seein' you come fae Turra.'

Mysie felt her hackles rising. 'I've daen a lot harder work in my time, but Jeems never asked me afore.'

Turning to her two henchwomen, Jean sneered, 'We'll need to excuse her, her just bein' wed for a week. It's nae wonder Jeems stopped comin', for the twa o' them must still be real tired in the mornin's, ha, ha.'

Alice Thomson laughed obediently. 'Aye, it's hectic nichts the first wee while, afore it tails aff.'

'My Rab never tailed aff,' sighed Belle Duff, 'but I dinna

20

ken aboot Jeems, though I wouldna fancy lettin' him touch me at a'.'

Setting her yoke on her shoulders, the fat woman turned to Mysie. 'It's you that'll need to excuse them, Mrs Duncan, for they've minds like middens. I'm Pattie White, fae the mill.' She held out a podgy hand, which Mysie shook gratefully, then attached her pails to the ropes swinging from her yoke. 'I'll likely see you again, but mind, lass, haud aff o' yoursel', or this three'll trample right ower you. Come on, Nessie.'

Followed by the girl, she moved away, her enormous rear end wobbling in her efforts to walk steadily so as not to spill her precious cargo, and Mysie, noticing that the other pails were already filled, went past Mrs Petrie to fill hers. Jean looked at her archly. 'Are you settlin' in a' right noo, Mrs Duncan?'

'Aye, fine.'

'We got a right shock when we ken't Jeems had ta'en a wife. Did you ken him lang?' Mysie set one pail on the ground and sent the other one down the well before she answered. 'A while.'

Addressing her friends, Jean said, 'I canna understand it, for Jeems was only awa' three times I ken o' – once to the Turra Show, an' he never let dab where he was the second Saturday, but twa weeks after that, he took hame a wife. In my coont, that's just three weeks after the Show.'

Nodding her agreement, Alice Thomson said, 'Lang enough to get the banns cried, that's a'.'

'So he'd arranged the weddin' the very day he met her.' Jean sounded as pleased as if she had solved the world's greatest mystery single-handedly. 'Weel, it must ha'e been Jeems that was in love, for I canna see ony lassie in her right mind bein' in love wi' him.'

Fully aware that she was being baited, Mysie concentrated on bringing her second pail up, but wished that Jess was there to put this woman in her place.

Jean turned to face her again. 'You didna ken him for a very lang while as far as I can mak' oot,' she accused.

Pretending not to hear, Mysie hooked both her pails on to the ropes dangling from her yoke, then straightened up slowly to take the full weight on her shoulders. 'You're awa', are you?' Mrs Petrie sounded disappointed that her snide remarks hadn't found their target. 'Weel, mind an' gi'e my . . . love to Jeems.'

Judging by their baying laughter, the other two found this highly comical, and Mysie walked away fuming inside but glad that she'd kept her temper. 'I felt like hittin' her,' she confessed to Jess the next day. 'Tryin' to nosey oot aboot me an' Jeems.'

'Weel, I ken for a fact that her an' Eck havena slept in the same bed since Effie was born, an' somebody tell't me it was him fathered Fingask's dairymaid's bairn three year ago, but folks is aye ready to spread dirt, an' I dinna really believe that, for you canna help likin' Eck.'

A little over two weeks later, Mysie recognised the first sign of pregnancy. 'I should ha'e started on Sunday,' she told Jess, 'an' it hasna come yet, so I must be awa' already.'

'You're only three days late,' Jess pointed out. 'It could start ony day yet.'

'No, I'm that regular you could use me for a calendar, but nae doot Jeems'll be pleased. He tell't me he's needin' twa sons to carry on Rowanbrae when he dies.'

'Me an' Jake's aye wanted a bairn,' Jess said, wistfully. 'A loon or a lassie, we wouldna care, but we've been wed ten year an' we havena been lucky yet.'

'Oh, Jess, I'm sorry. I didna ken you were wantin' bairns. Weel, if mine's a lassie you can ha'e her.'

'I ken you're only jokin', Mysie, but it's a nice thought. I wonder how lang it'll be afore Jean Petrie'll tummel to this?'

It was Jeems who was first to tumble to it. 'It's six weeks since I wed you, an' I've been on you ilka nicht, an' you were never bleedin' – except the first nicht, an' that's as it should be, for it let me ken nae other man had ever been at you. Are you nae turned a wumman yet, or are you . . . ?'

22

Lowering her head shyly, Mysie whispered, 'I changed when I was thirteen, so I think I'm goin' to ha'e a bairn.'

'Great God!' he roared, making her jump nervously and wonder what she had said wrong. 'You should ha'e tell't me as soon as you ken't, an' I wouldna ha'e touched you again, for I dinna want nae harm to come to my son.'

About to tell him that no harm could be done until nearer the time of the birth, it occurred to her that in his ignorance he would leave her to sleep in peace, so she held her tongue.

'The big gype,' Jess spluttered, when she was told about this. 'It just shows you how little men ken, does it nae? Weel noo, that's three o' us ken, an' I bet it'll be Jean Petrie next.'

Mrs Petrie tackled Mysie in the shop some weeks later. 'I think there'll soon be a little ane at Rowanbrae,' she smirked, looking the girl up and down with ill-concealed satisfaction.

Taken by surprise, Mysie was stung into retorting, 'How did you ken?'

A sneer crossed the woman's face. 'So I was right. I was near sure, for your face has been peely-wally for weeks.'

'Aye, you're right, an' there's nae shame to it.'

'Oh, no, I wasna meanin' that. How far on are you?'

'Just three month.'

'Aye, a first nicht bairn or maybe the nicht afore?'

Fortunately, Dougal Mennie stepped in. 'What can I dae for you the day, Mistress Petrie?'

Having learned all that she wanted, Jean turned to him, but Mysie could see Alice Thomson, Belle Duff and even Rosie Mennie assessing her figure, and suddenly found it very funny. 'You surely heard me tellin' Mrs Petrie I'm only three month,' she giggled, 'so you'll nae see onything yet.'

Dougal's eyes met hers briefly over Jean Petrie's head, and she could have sworn that he winked before he turned to fill a paper poke with salt for his most demanding customer.

Chapter Two

'I'm goin' to Aberdeen on Friday,' Jeems announced one bleak morning in November. 'I've some tatties an' neeps an' carrots to sell, an' I've to get binder twine an' things like that. The miller's goin' in wi' his horse an' cart, so me an' Rab Duff usually go wi' him.'

'When will you be hame?' Mysie would have been quite happy if he intended staying away for a week, but it wasn't likely.

'Och, I dinna ken. We whiles ha'e a puckle drams when we're there, so you can expect me when you see me.'

'What aboot your supper? What time will I . . . ?'

'I'll likely be that fu' I'll nae be needin' supper.' His face contorted into a toothy grimace. 'Forbye, we sometimes tak' something to eat in a restchuraunt. Dinna wait up for me, but I'll be hame afore risin' time on Saturday.'

Mysie was astonished to hear him talking so blithely about getting drunk. She'd hadn't realised that he was a drinking man, but she didn't know very much about him, after all.

It was almost two on Saturday morning when she was roused out of her slumbers by shouting and banging. Rising sleepily, she ran through to open the unlocked door, and her heart sank when she saw Andra White and Rab Duff supporting Jeems, who was roaring at the top of his voice. Smiling at Mysie rather stupidly, Rab said, 'He's fu', lass. What'll we dae wi' him?'

'You'd best tak' him ben the hoose.'

They dumped him unceremoniously on the bed, where he retched loudly then promptly vomited all over the pillows. 'He's been spewin' since we left the toon,' Andra informed her seriously, as he turned to go back to the kitchen. 'God kens where it's a' comin' fae.'

'We'd been in a puckle bars, of course,' Rab reminded him. 'We started aff in yon ane aside the Kittybrewster Mart, then the Butcher's Arms in George Street, then the Lemon Tree, an' we finished up in the Prince o' Wales. Was that a', Andra?'

'I canna mind nae mair, but it was in the Prince o' Wales he got fightin' mad, I mind that.'

'Fightin' mad?' A look of disgust crossed Mysie's face.

'Ach weel,' Rab sniggered, 'a silly bugger o' a toonser was makin' a fool o' him, and Jeems punched his guts, an' me an' Andra had to tak' him oot afore they got the bobbies.'

The miller grinned. 'You maybe didna ken, Mysie, but your man's got a helluva temper, an' if I was you, I'd leave him to sleep it aff. He'll nae mind naething when he's sober.'

Rab suddenly leered at her. 'God, you've got braw tits.'

Conscious of her nightdress straining against her swelling figure, Mysie folded her arms and smiled nervously. 'Goodnicht to you, an' thank you for takin' Jeems hame.'

Andra pulled at the other man's sleeve. 'Aye, come awa', Rab. You've a wife o' your ain at Wellbrae.'

'Belle's hardly nae tits at a',' Rab grumbled, as he followed the miller out. 'She's like a bloody stick. What pleasure is there in feelin' that?'

Closing the door behind them, Mysie burst out laughing, in relief that they were gone as much as at what Rab had said. Drunken fools, the three of them, she thought, and sat down to sleep in the chair for the rest of the night. There was no sense in taking any chances, though she doubted if Jeems could raise his head in his present state, never mind anything else.

Her husband rose at his usual time, and appeared to be none the worse for his escapade. 'We'd a grand time in the toon, Mysie,' he said when he came into the kitchen, 'but I canna mind on comin' hame.'

'I'm nae surprised,' she snapped. 'You was roarin'

25

drunk, an' Andra an' Rab wasna muckle better. It beats me how you could let yoursel's get in such a state.'

Looking slightly shame-faced, he said, 'Ach weel, it's nae very often.'

'I hope you'll nae mak' a habit o' spewin' in the bed. I've that to wash yet.'

The news had got round before Mysie went to the well, and Mrs Petrie was in her element. 'I'd ha'e thought Jeems Duncan had mair sense than get shit mirack an' thump somebody in a bar,' she flung at Mysie, who decided that silence was the best policy. 'If it had been my man, I'd ha'e been black affronted.'

The murmurs of agreement made Mysie forget to keep quiet. 'You never let your man aff the leash lang enough to get fu'.' Turning to Mrs Duff, she added caustically, 'An' your man wasna very sober himsel'.'

'Rab can haud his drink,' Belle retorted, smugly. 'I'm sure he would never punch another man in a bar.'

Looking at Belle's straight-up-and-down figure and recalling Rab's remarks about her, Mysie said, 'No, it's weemen he's mair interested in gettin' his hands on.'

There was a short pause before Belle said, in her very best dignified English, 'And what do you mean by that? My Rab has never looked at another wumman since me an' him was wed.'

The humour of the situation striking her, Mysie laughed. 'I didna mean naething. They were a' drunk, but I must admit – Jeems was worst.'

Somewhat mollified, Mrs Duff muttered, 'Weel, then,' as if to end the discussion, but Jean Petrie said, 'Andra an' Rab couldna ha'e been that bad. They got him awa' afore the bobbies come.'

Jess Findlater had a good laugh about it later. 'Jeems has an awfu' temper, so it's just as weel you didna sleep wi' him.'

'He wouldna ha'e ken't supposin' the coo had been sleepin' wi' him,' Mysie giggled. 'It was the other twa I'd ha'e needed to watch if they'd bidden muckle langer.'

'Oh, aye?' Jess looked interested.

'I was just in my goon an' they couldna keep their een aff my breasts. I ken they're growin' as big as balloons an' I was feared Rab Duff would put his muckle paws on them.'

'He wouldna ken what breasts was, for Belle hasna got ony – an' Pattie's that fat her breasts an' her belly's a' in ane.'

They were almost helpless with mirth when Jeems walked in. 'What are you twa laughin' at?' he demanded, truculently.

'We wasna laughin' at you,' Mysie spluttered, 'though I'm sure a'body else in Burnlea is.' His puzzled frown made her go on, although she hadn't meant to say anything to him in front of Jess. 'Do you nae mind what you did last nicht? You punched a man for makin' a fool o' you, though that wasna ill to dae, for you're the biggest fool on twa legs. You was lucky Andra an' Rab got you oot o' the bar afore the man got the bobbies.'

'Oh, God,' he moaned. 'I dinna mind naething aboot that.'

'Weel, I hope it'll be a lesson to you,' Mysie said. 'Jean Petrie tell't me I should be black affronted.'

'It's me should be black affronted.'

'Aye, so should you.'

James Duncan, junior, was born at twenty-five past six on a rainy morning in March 1906, three weeks premature. Jeems had gone for Jess at midnight, and the birth, although not easy, had been mercifully short.

'A lump come in my throat at seein' Jeems when he ken't it was a loon,' Jess told Mysie afterwards. 'He was near jumpin' his ain height, he was that prood. He's nae the only ane to be feelin' prood, though, for the laird's wife gi'ed him a son on Monday, so Rosie Mennie tell't me. It's his first, as weel.'

'Thank God I'd a loon,' Mysie said, with deep feeling. 'Jeems would ha'e went mad if it had been a lassie.'

'I'm thinkin' Jean Petrie'll ha'e something to craw aboot noo, though,' Jess observed. 'The bairn's early, so she'll be sayin' Jeems hadna waited till he put the ring on.'

Mysie pulled a face. 'I dinna care what she thinks. Jeems never had the chance to touch me afore the weddin', an' . . . I dinna ken aboot you, but I dinna like it ony road.'

Jess shot her a pitying glance, but left soon afterwards, and Mysie felt a touch of envy. Jess thought the world of Jake although she pretended to criticise him, and hadn't said she didn't like what he did. How would it feel to love a man like that and have him love her? Would that make any difference? Would that make her welcome a man inside her? Or could it be that she was unnatural? She must be incapable of love, and it wouldn't matter whom she had married.

A letter arrived for Mysie in June. It was postmarked Turriff and was addressed in her mother's laborious hand – Jean hadn't had the benefit of much schooling – but she laid it on the table apprehensively. Why would her mother be writing after nearly a year? If this letter was pleading with her to visit, she wouldn't bother answering it, for she could never go back to Drumloanings after what her father had done to her. But her mother surely wouldn't waste a stamp writing to ask what she knew was impossible? After dithering for a minute or two, Mysie picked up the envelope and tore it open.

It was short and to the point. 'Dear Mysie, Your father was coming home from Turriff last night and fell down the old well at Tinterty. The burial is on Saturday. Your loving Mother.'

Mysie read the few lines again, wondering what her father had been doing near the old well. Tinterty Farm wasn't on his way home from Turriff, but he'd likely been so drunk he hadn't known where he was going, and that didn't surprise her. What was more, she didn't care.

By the time Jeems came in at breakfast time, Mysie had

read the note three times, and handed it to him with a harsh laugh. 'Eddie Lonie died as he lived, drunk as a lord, an' I've nae sympathy for him, an' I'm nae goin' to the burial.'

Shocked by her callousness, her husband said, 'You'll need to go, it would look bad if you didna.'

'It would look worse if I did, for I would be laughin' mysel' sick when they covered him up.'

'My God, Mysie, that's an awfu' thing to say – he was your father, when a's said an' daen.'

'A father's supposed to provide for his bairns, but my mother had to work her fingers to the bone for us, for he drunk what he made an' hardly ever gi'ed her a penny, though she'd nine bairns by him. She'd to wash an' iron for the big hooses to get enough to feed us.'

Giving up, Jeems finished his porridge and went out without another word, but Jess Findlater gave Mysie the same advice when she called in. 'You'll ha'e to go to your father's frunial. What would folk say if you wasna there?'

'I dinna care what they say, I'm nae goin'.'

'Mysie, for your mother's sake . . .'

'My mother'll be as pleased as me that he's awa', if I ken onything aboot it.'

Shaking her head, Jess let the subject drop. 'How's my wee Jamie the day?'

'He was a bittie fractious through the nicht. Could it be his teeth already? He's hardly fower month auld.'

'Oh aye, he could be teethin', poor little thing, an' you're nae lookin' so good yoursel'.'

'I was feelin' sick when I rose this mornin', but I'm a bit better noo. It's likely the want o' sleep.'

'Has Jeems . . . eh . . . been at you again?'

'Aye, it wasna lang after the bairn was born.' Comprehending what Jess was hinting, Mysie burst out, 'You dinna think I'm awa' again, dae you?'

'I wouldna be surprised. You said he was set on twa loons, so he's nae wastin' nae time.'

'Oh, Jess, what'll Jean Petrie say if I am?'

'It's naething to dae wi' her, an' she canna say this ane's been conceived oot o' wedlock.'

Setting the table at dinnertime, Mysie decided not to tell Jeems until she was absolutely certain. Feeling sick one morning didn't prove anything. She let her mind turn to her mother's letter again, and a most unexpected surge of homesickness came over her – not for her father, who had got what he deserved, but for the couthy woman who had borne and raised her. Perhaps Jean Lonie wasn't expecting her eldest daughter to attend the funeral, but she might be glad to see her.

'I've been thinkin',' Mysie said, when Jeems came in. 'I'm nae carin' a docken aboot my father, for he didna care a docken for me, but I'd like to see my mother again. The only thing is, it's a lang road on trains wi' the bairn.'

'Aye, you'd ha'e to go into Aberdeen an' oot again.' After thinking for a few moments, he said, 'Maybe the miller would let me ha'e his horse an' cart for a day again. That would save the fares, as weel. Aye, I'll ask him.'

Mysie didn't want Jeems's company, but on thinking it over, she admitted that going to Turriff would be easier by cart, and it would let her take some butter, eggs and cheese to give to her mother.

The sky was heavily clouded on Saturday, the steady drizzle which began not long after they set out soon penetrating their clothes as the horse pulled the open cart across the windblown countryside where all the trees stood at the same peculiar angle. Mysie had taken an old oilskin coat and wrapped it round the sleeping baby. The twenty-two miles to Turriff took them over four hours, but when she ran into her mother's arms, she was glad she had made the journey.

After a few moments of emotional silence, Jean Lonie said, 'You're soakin', come in an' dry aff at the fire.' She took the infant from Jeems, removing the oilskin as she led the way in, and when she was satisfied that her visitors were near enough the heat, she turned to her daughter again. 'Oh, lassie, I'm right pleased to see you. I wasna expectin' you, kennin' what you thought o' your father.'

'It's nae for his sake I'm here.' Mysie glanced round the familiar room, drawing in her breath when she saw that the old cradle in the corner had an occupant. 'Oh, Mother, you havena had another ane?'

'Aye,' Jean Lonie said, wryly. 'Whatever else your father was, he was good at makin' bairns.'

The funeral was not until two o'clock, so after they'd had some broth, Jeems took the young Lonies with him when he went to see if there was anything in the smithy that would be of any use to him. Mysie sat down to feed her infant and fended off her mother's questions as to how she liked married life by describing Rowanbrae in glowing terms and praising Jeems for being so industrious, but Jean had something else to find out.

'I'm thinkin' your man's some like your father. Your face is pickit, though you're nae showin', so I might be wrang, but are you to be ha'ein' another bairn yoursel'?'

'Aye.' Mysie had been sick the past two mornings, but was surprised that her mother could tell so soon. 'Jeems's nae like Father, though, for he says he just wants twa loons.'

'That's maybe a' he's wantin', lass, but he'll likely mak' a lot mair if he's onything like Eddie.'

'But I'm nae goin' to let him touch me after I've gi'en him the twa loons, so . . .'

'He'll maybe nae tak' no for an answer.' Jean shook her head sympathetically then changed the subject. 'Mistress Gunn o' Tinterty has asked me to tak' on the cook's job, an' I'm to get the hoose her son had afore him an' his wife went to Canada. It's a lot bigger than this – three rooms forbyes the kitchen, an' a inside w.c. It's one good thing your father's daen for me, ony road, for Mistress Gunn said she was sorry for me wi' him meetin' his end like he did. If only she ken't. It's a blessed release I feel, after the purgatory he put me through. It's a awfu' thing to say, but I canna help it.'

31

Mysie had known that her mother had no high opinion of her father, but she was taken aback by Jean's forthright remarks. Fancy having to live with a man for . . . it must be seventeen or eighteen years, when she felt like that about him. But had it always been like that? 'Did you never . . . love him?' she asked, timidly.

Jean didn't answer for some time, having to delve deeply into her memory, then she gave a shuddering sigh. 'Eddie was the maist handsomest man I'd ever met. He was tall and straight an' his eyes looked into mine like they was turnin' me inside oot. When we was coortin', he tell't me I was the bonniest lassie he'd ever saw, an' there wasna a happier lassie than me the day he wed me . . .' Her voice broke. 'Oh, God, Mysie, I wonder what went wrang atween us? What was it made him tak' to the drink? Was it my blame?'

While her mother wept for a love which had foundered and sunk without trace, Mysie stood helplessly. Her father's back had been bowed for as long as she could remember, his face blotchy, his eyes bleary, his hair lank, but a vague picture was surfacing in her mind of a tall, laughing man, with bright eyes and thick fair hair, tossing her up in the air when she was a very small girl. She had forgotten about it until now, but how could a man change like that?

She would never be disillusioned about Jeems, that was one thing, for his looks couldn't get much worse. She hadn't liked him the first time she saw him and she didn't like him any better now, but he provided for her and wanted no more than two sons, so her life would surely never be as bad as her mother's. Instead of resenting her husband, she supposed she should be grateful for what he was. A little niggling voice inside her, however, told her that she had a right to be resentful. What of the dreams she had had, when she was younger, of a man who would sweep her off her feet, who would kiss her and make her love him as he would love her? And all she'd got was Jeems.

32

She looked round when her husband returned, and couldn't help hating his pudding face and big nose, and the way his thick dark eyebrows straddled across his forehead as if trying to reach each other. She hadn't even the doubtful consolation that he loved her, for, as he'd told her himself, he had just picked her to be the mother of his bairns.

The funeral was not well attended – some of Eddie's drinking cronies and a sprinkling of farm servants and their wives, there because convention demanded it – and the Duncans left soon afterwards. Mysie hugged her mother before she climbed up on the cart, but made no promise to return. How could she, when she would have two bairns in a few months?

On the way home, Jeems said, 'You're awfu' quiet, Mysie, but I suppose you'll be mournin' for your father noo?'

'I'll never mourn for him. It's my mother I'm mournin' for. She loved him once, for he was a real handsome man when he was young, an' it's terrible to think he let himsel' sink so low. What could ha'e drove him to the drink?'

'There's some men dinna need to be drove to the drink,' Jeems observed, quietly, 'it just comes natural, like.'

'Maybe. Em . . . Jeems . . . I'm goin' to ha'e another bairn.'

His head whipped round. 'Oh, quine, you should ha'e tell't me, an' I'd never ha'e let you come a' this distance. I hope you havena daen him ony harm.'

Angry that he thought more of the coming child than he did of her, Mysie said, huffily, 'It's me that might come to harm, wi' the soakin' I got.'

In the night, a prickling sensation started at the back of her nose, then she felt beads of perspiration running down between her shoulder blades. She had caught a cold, but it was no good telling Jeems, for he wouldn't care. Trying to cool herself, she let her feet rest against his, rough but icy, and it did help – she wasn't quite so bad in the morning. It was Jamie who was breathing heavily, his brow hot and clammy when she felt it. 'Oh,' she wailed, 'the bairn's got a fever.'

'You'll need to keep him in the hoose the day,' Jeems ordered, 'an' gi'e him some thin gruel to help his hirstly chest.'

When she picked up her son, his little body was so hot that she wished she had someone to advise her what to do for him. Jess wouldn't know, never having had any bairns, but Pattie White – their nearest neighbour on the other side from Downies – had Nessie and Drew, and although they were both in their teens now, she must have had to deal with something like this when they were younger, and she was a real motherly woman. A longing for her own mother filled Mysie's heart, for Jean had tended one sick child after another. What had she done for feverish colds like this?

Relief flooded through her when she remembered. Laying her infant in his cradle, she took an old flannel linder of her husband's out of a drawer and tore it into strips. Then she filled her yellow baking bowl with cold water and got a towel out of the press. Stripping the baby, she took him on her knee and laved the cold water over him, as she'd watched her mother do, and his grizzling stopped abruptly with the shock. After drying him thoroughly, she wound a strip of the flannel round his body and secured it with a safety pin. She could still hear the phlegm in his chest, though he felt cooler, but she dressed him and laid him down to make some gruel. He wouldn't feed from the spoon when she tried, so she bared her breast and drew her nipple across the tiny mouth, which fastened on like a leech, drawing steadily and strongly. By the time Jeems came in at dinnertime, Jamie was sound asleep in the wooden cradle, breathing more peacefully. The drastic cure had worked, though his nose ran for a few days. So did her own, but her pregnancy continued without a hiccough.

In January 1907, only ten months after her first son's birth,

Mysie produced a second, and Jeems was so pleased that he let her call the baby Alexander, after her mother's brother who had been lost in the Boer War. In contrast to the placid Jamie, Sandy disrupted the house from his very first day by crying constantly, except when he was sleeping or being fed.

'I'm that tired I can hardly keep my een open,' Mysie told Jess when he was about two weeks old. 'An' Jeems is that ill-tempered at nae getting slept, I feel like tellin' him I get nae mair sleep than him an' I've twa bairns to contend wi' day an' nicht, as weel as the other things I've to dae.'

Jess smiled sympathetically. 'If you like, I'll tak' Jamie wi' me to the shop to gi'e you some peace.'

'You can tak' him, but he's nae bother except for his chest whiles. He plays awa' on the rug wi' pot lids an' spoons and never a cheep oot o' him, but hardly a minute's peace dae I get fae Sandy, though to look at him sleepin' the noo, you'd think he was a angel.' A loud wail issuing from the cradle, she added, in some disgust, 'Ach! I spoke ower quick.'

Jess chuckled. 'You'll nae ha'e your sorrows to seek wi' that ane, I'm thinkin'. Weel, come on then, Jamie, I'll put my shawl roon' aboot us, an' we'll awa' to see Dougal an' Rosie.'

The new baby's face was scarlet from screaming by the time Mysie picked him up, his arms flailing about, his legs kicking wildly. Jess was right, she thought, ruefully – Sandy Duncan had a mind of his own, and he would be a problem when he was older, there was no doubt about that.

Chapter Three

1910

'Is there a clean sark in the hoose?'

'If you'd look instead o' just openin' your mooth an' lettin' your belly rummel,' Mysie began, then stopped, for Jeems lost his temper at the least little thing nowadays. 'You'll find ane in the top drawer o' the kist,' she finished, although she still felt impatient with him. Listening to him opening the drawer, she stirred the porridge fiercely, the spurtle cleaving through the grey mass like a plough through clogged earth. How had the man got on before she came here? He was a great useless lump, worse than a bairn. Young Jamie had far more sense at four years old, even wee Sandy at three.

She turned round to see her husband struggling with his huge hands to fasten his top button. 'Come an' dae it for me,' he ordered, 'instead o' screwin' up your face like that.'

As she closed the neck of his shirt, he growled, 'I'm scythin' the corn the day, an' you'll ha'e to bind the sheaves. An' muck oot the byre sometime, for it's sair needin' it.'

'Aye.' Mysie said nothing as she returned to the range. Her husband had changed since she had given him the two sons he wanted. Sandy had hardly been three months old when Jeems made her start working in the fields, yelling at her when she tried to protest one day, 'Nane o' your backchat, wumman. You didna dae very muckle afore, just the hens an' the milkin' – I've had a bloody poor thirty pound' worth oot o' you.'

'I didna ask you to buy me,' she had retorted, and he

hit the side of her head with such force that she reeled back against the wall. Now she knew to keep quiet.

Until Sandy learned to walk, she'd had to strap him to her back as she hoed, pulled turnips, gathered potatoes, and all the other things Jeems found for her to do. She hadn't that burden to carry round now, thank goodness, but her hands were calloused and her legs often buckled before she had done what was expected of her, so she had come off worse than he had in the stupid bargain. He even left her working outside on her own some evenings, telling her that he had to see Andra White about something, or Rab Duff, but she suspected that it was another woman he went to see, one of the maids at Fingask or Waterton, most likely. Not that she cared, for it meant that he didn't bother her so much. She had refused him as often as she dared, but, as her mother had once warned her, there were times – especially the times he came home drunk from Aberdeen – when he would not take no for an answer.

At that moment, the two boys burst in from the other room, Mysie and Jeems having had to sleep in his parents' box bed in the kitchen since Jamie was out of the cradle. 'We're awa' to the wee hoosie,' Jamie announced, as he went out through the back porch on his skinny legs followed by the chubby toddler.

'The wee hoosie' was how Mysie delicately referred to the structure in the backyard, where a wooden plank with a large circle cut out of it rested over the pail which Jeems emptied every night into the midden. The hole was meant for an adult backside, and she was always afraid that one of her sons would slip through, but it hadn't happened . . . yet.

Putting two large ladlefuls of porridge into the deep bowl, Mysie set it in front of her husband, who helped himself to a home-baked oatcake and some of the still-warm milk in the jug.

Sandy was back first, saying, as he clambered up on a chair, 'The futtret's got oot.'

'Losh be here!' Mysie was alarmed. A loose ferret could put her hens off laying again, and they had not long started after Sandy chasing them a week ago. 'You must ha'e left the cage open, my mannie, an' me aye tellin' you to mak' sure you put the sneck doon.'

'It wasna me.' The boy's eyes were round and innocent, but his mother wasn't fooled, and it was lucky for him that Jamie came in. 'I catched him, Sandy. He was coorin' doon ahin' the cage, near frozen stiff.' He produced the poor creature from under his nightshirt. 'We'll ha'e to put him in front o' the fire till he comes to himsel'.'

'You're nae putting nae futtret in front o' my fire,' Mysie exclaimed. 'You ken what futtrets are like, he'd ha'e the feet eaten aff me when I was makin' the dinner.'

Jeems let out a snort. 'Losh, wumman, what ideas you get. The beastie'll nae bite you unless it's feared. But put it back in the cage, Jamie. It's used wi' the cauld.'

'It wasna my blame it got oot, Mam,' Sandy insisted.

'Haud your wheesht an' sup your porridge.' She wanted peace to remember what she had to buy from the packman, for he only came one Wednesday in every three months. She had run out of little buttons for their shirts, her white thread was nearly done and she'd lost about half her hairpins. Sure that there was something else, she didn't look round when Jamie returned, nor when Jeems poked his head back round the door. 'You'll nae forget aboot the sheaves?'

'I'll be oot when I'm ready,' Mysie said, sharply, and added, hastily, 'I've to tidy up in here and feed the hens first, an' I'll need to wait till the packman's been.' As the door closed behind her husband, she turned to her sons. 'Get your claes on when you're finished and get ootside, but nane o' your tricks, Sandy. If you dinna ken what to dae, you can feed the hens for me, an' shift some o' the peat ower to the porch door.'

Washing the dishes, she tried to recall the elusive item she required – Auld Jockie was such a fine old body she liked to give him trade – but hadn't remembered when

Jess came in, on her way home from the shop. 'I've had right sair guts since I was here last,' Jess said.

'Are you ony better noo?' Mysie asked, solicitously.

'Aye, I took a dose o' castor oil an' that shifted me,' Jess grinned. 'An' how's things been wi' you?'

'Just the same. Jeems thinks I've naething to dae except help him, an' Sandy's still up to his tricks.'

'Aye.' Jess was of the opinion that Sandy did these things to get attention because Mysie always made more of Jamie, but she said nothing. Their mother should realise that herself.

'Auld Jockie should be here the day,' Mysie observed, suddenly.

'I'll swear Jockie kens a'body's business, but he never passes on nae gossip. I wish there was mair like him. Some o' the biddies roon' here spread stories whether they're true or no'.'

'Jean Petrie was sayin' Mrs Mutch o' Fingask was takin' up wi' young Gavin Leslie, an' her near twice his age. I just said I didna believe it, an' she wasna pleased.'

Jess looked thoughtful. 'I've heard that aboot Freda Mutch mysel', though, an' nae fae Jean Petrie. Do you think there's onything in it?'

'I wouldna think so, for she's got a' their men to pick fae – she surely wouldna bother wi' Gavin Leslie.'

'As my Jake sometimes says, weemen are kittle cattle, and you can never tell what they'll dae.'

'Weel, I wouldna ha'e Gavin mysel', an' that's sayin' something when you think on what Jeems is like.'

Jess gave a roar of laughter. 'Aye, Gavin Leslie's a soor bugger at times, but he's a fine strappin' loon, an' maybe it's what he's got under his breeks that tickles Freda's fancy, eh? Mind, her ain man's nae that bad lookin' – I'd nae say no to Frankie Mutch if she offered him to me.'

'Oh, Jess, what blethers you come oot wi'.'

'It's nae blethers, I'd fair like a change o' man. Jake's a' right, but . . . ach, weel, you ken. Changes are lightsome.'

'You shouldna say things like that.' Mysie was quite

upset. She had always thought that the Findlaters were ideally suited.

'I suppose no',' Jess admitted. 'If we'd had ony bairns, it wouldna be so bad, but we're that used to each other there's nae excitement in it noo.'

'You canna expect to ha'e excitement a' the time – an' look at me, I've never had nae excitement.'

Jess looked sympathetic. 'No, your Jeems wouldna exactly set the heather on fire, but you've had twa loons by him, so you must ha'e had a bittie excitement sometime?'

'If that was excitement, you can keep it,' Mysie said, dryly. 'I've had mair excitement shellin' peas.'

Jess went out chuckling, and Mysie lifted the hearthrug and took it outside. She was still banging it against the gable wall when she noticed Andra White's daughter cycling along the road. 'Aye, aye, Nessie,' she called, and was rather dismayed when the girl stopped and wheeled her bicycle over, because she had wasted enough time already.

'You're Jeems's wife, are you nae?' Nessie simpered. 'I like Jeems, he comes walks wi' me some nichts.'

'Jeems?' So it had been Nessie he had been seeing.

'Aye, we go ower the peat moss, an' roon' the auld quarry, an' there's a fine place at the far side that naebody can see us.'

Uncomfortably aware of what Nessie was working round to tell her, Mysie said, 'Are you awa' for a run on your bike?'

Nessie was not to be diverted. 'Me an' Jeems dae things. He lets me open his spaver an' tak' oot his . . . he says I havena to tell naebody, but I like what we dae.'

Mysie didn't care enough for Jeems to be jealous, but she was afraid that others might get to hear of it – this poor simple creature hadn't the sense to keep it to herself. 'I thought Jeems said you hadna to tell naebody.'

'I havena said a word to naebody else, nae even my ain Ma an' Da, but you're Jeems's wife, an' I thought he'd ha'e tell't you himsel'.'

40

Mysie sighed with relief. 'Dinna tell naebody else, though, Nessie, or Jeems'll stop goin' walks wi' you.'

She had hit the right note and Nessie's eyes clouded. 'You'll nae let on I tell't you, will you?'

'No, I'll nae let on. Noo, aff you go, for I'm busy.' Mysie went inside, quite sure that nobody else would hear of it from Nessie now, but praying that no one would ever see her husband with 'the daftie', as the older children called her. Suddenly realising the incongruity of her thoughts, she laughed out loud. If it kept her from having to suffer his crude pawings, long may Jeems continue to 'do things' with the miller's daughter.

About ten minutes later, the packman knocked. 'Good day to you, Mistress. Here I am again like the bad penny.'

'Aye, I was mindin' aboot you.' Smiling, Mysie held open the door. 'Come awa' in, Jockie.'

As she put the kettle on again, the old man put his pack on the table and opened it up. 'Razor blades, shavin' brushes, tie pins, collar studs . . .'

He rummaged through his goods until he found the three items she requested. 'Onything else? Ribbon, tape, safety preens?'

'I ken't there was something else. Safety preens, that's what it was. They aye come in handy.'

'Aye, that they dae. An' I've got some bonnie wheeling wool for knittin' socks or drawers for your goodman – lovat green or maybe a dark grey. I'm sure he's needin' . . .'

'Maybe next time.' Mysie was ashamed to tell him that she couldn't afford anything else, but Jockie likely knew, for most of the crofters' wives were in the same position.

Over a cup of tea, the packman said, 'The loons'll be ootside this bonnie day? Has Jamie's chest been botherin' him again?'

'A wee turnie noo an' then, but naething muckle.'

'Your littlest ane – I canna mind his name – but I hope he's weel enough?'

'Sandy never tak's onything, but he's a little de'il. He's aye in trouble, an' I whiles wonder what he'll dae next.

41

I'll be fine pleased when he starts the school, but it's twa year yet.'

'He keeps you on your taes,' Jockie smiled, 'an' that's what keeps you lookin' so young.'

'Och, you an' your havers.'

'I'm nae haverin'. If I'd been a young man I'd ha'e hung up my hat to you.' He laughed to show that he *was* joking, then said, 'Your goodman's keepin' weel, I hope?'

'Oh aye, I dinna think Jeems has ever had a day's illness in his life, though I some think he'd be a poor patient if he had.'

Swallowing the last piece of his buttered scone, the old man laid his empty cup on the table and stood up. 'Thank you for the tea, Mistress, but it's time I took the road again.' He waited until she paid for her purchases, then buckled up his pack and swung it over his shoulder. 'I'll see you in three month as usual, Mistress.'

He was a kindly old soul, Mysie thought, as she stood at the door watching him tramping along the road towards Downies. It must be a dreary life, walking round the countryside carrying that pack on his back, but he never grumbled and always had a cheery word for the bairns if they were in. She wondered if he'd ever had bairns of his own, but he never spoke about a family. Poor Jockie. Even if her own life was drudgery from morn to night she wouldn't change places with him or anybody else, for she had Jamie, with his dark curly head and his big blue eyes looking up at her full of love when she tucked him into bed. She hadn't the same feeling for Sandy, always up to things he shouldn't, no matter how much she scolded him.

When she went out to help Jeems, Sandy was balanced on top of the peat stack throwing lumps of peat at his brother, who was howling loudly. 'Stop that!' she shouted.

Sandy let his hand drop. 'Ach, I was only playin', Mam.'

'That's nae playin'! Did he hurt you, my lambie?'

'He got me on the lug.' Jamie clutching his injured ear, squeezed out a tear.

'Come, my dearie, an' I'll put a tickie butter on it.'

42

'Why is it aye me you pick on?' Sandy complained, as he slid down. 'Why dae you never rage Jamie?'

Her voice hardened. 'Nane o' your lip. If you was as good as Jamie, I wouldna need to rage you, an' if you havena cleaned up this yard afore I come back, you'll feel the weight o' my hand on *your* lug.'

Tenderly administering to her favourite son in the dairy, Mysie wished, not for the first time, that Jamie had been her only one.

Chapter Four

1913

'There's to be a meal an' ale up at Fingask on Saturday,' Jess observed. 'Are you comin'?'

'Jeems'll nae go.' Mysie had never pressed the matter when her husband refused, but now she felt resentful that he hadn't considered her before. It was over eight years since she had come to Rowanbrae but she was only twenty-four, and she wanted some amusement before she was too old to enjoy it. 'You ken, Jess, I dinna see why I shouldna go, an' Jeems can bide at hame if he likes.'

'That's the spirit,' Jess beamed. 'He's a cantankerous de'il an' he forgets you're nae as auld as him. Here's me an' Jake, we still ha'e a grand time at a meal an' ale, an' we're baith gettin' on for forty. But Jeems has never went, nae even when he was a lot younger.'

'He says it's just a excuse for the men to get drunk an' tak' up wi' somebody else's wife.'

'Weel, what's wrang wi' that?' Jess threw back her head and laughed. 'I've had a good puckle offers in my time, when Jake was that drunk he wouldna ha'e ken't what I was daein'.'

'Did you ever let . . . ?'

'I was sair tempted whiles, but something aye held me back. I didna object to gettin' a cuddle an' a kiss, though.'

'Was it onybody I'd ken that cuddled an' kissed you?'

'Weel, I once let the miller . . .'

'Andra White? But he's bald an' wizened.'

'He wasna so bald and wizened at that time, an', losh Mysie, I thought he'd ha'e the breeks aff me. I'd to kick his shins afore I could get awa' fae him.'

Picturing it, Mysie giggled. 'What did he say to that?'

'He roared oot, "You coorse bitch!" '

Jess imitated Andra's rather high-pitched voice, then winked. 'It wasna his shins that was hurtin' him, though, for my knee got him further up than that, so maybe that's the road he speaks so squeaky.'

'Och, Jess. What a wumman you are.'

'Another time, I let Rab Duff gi'e me a cuddle, but you've to watch yoursel' wi' Rab as weel.'

'I ken that.' Mysie could still remember the way Rab had leered at her in her nightgown. 'Was there ony mair?'

'The souter, once, an' I'm sure his wife would pee hersel' if she ken't what he tried to dae. Alice Thomson aye mak's oot she's a bit o' a lady, but if she lets her man carry on like yon in their bed, she's nae lady.'

'What did he dae?' Mysie leaned forward eagerly.

Throwing up her hands, Jess cried, 'What did he nae dae? God, his hands were in places I didna ken I had.'

'It's true what Jeems says, then?'

'There's never muckle harm daen, though. The men's just oot for fun, an' it's only them that's fu' that tries to go ower far. I've never let ony o' them get past the elastic in my bloomer legs though they prigged till they were blue in the face. I like to be tickled up a wee bit, but I dinna want to be served on a dung heap at the back o' a byre.'

'Do you think onybody'll want to tickle me up?'

'Nae doot, but if they try, keep your hand on your ha'penny, it's ower easy to get carried awa'.' Jess was rather regretting telling her friend so much, for Mysie was inexperienced in the ways of men and could easily find

44

herself in trouble, but it was done now. 'You say you're comin', but will Jeems let you?'

'I'll tell him he'll need to look after the bairns, an' he'll ha'e to like it or lump it.'

'You could easy tak' the bairns wi' you, there's aye a puckle runnin' aboot through folks's feet.'

'I dinna want to tak' the bairns wi' me,' Mysie said, her face clouding, 'but I will if Jeems'll nae look after them.'

'I wish I could see his face when you tell him,' Jess grinned. 'But stand back, for if he doesna hit the roof, he'll sure as hell hit you.'

That night, as soon as Jamie and Sandy were in bed, Mysie blurted out, 'I'm goin' to Fingask's meal an' ale wi' Jess.'

Her husband's eyes almost disappeared under his brows. 'I've tell't ye afore, you're nae goin' to nae meal an' ales.'

Her inside churning, Mysie said, 'It's nae use arguin', I'm goin', an' that's a' aboot it. You can bide wi' the loons.'

'Ha'e you gone clean daft, wumman? What'll folk think?'

'They'll be pleased you're lettin' your wife aff the chain for once, an' it's nae use hittin' me, for a'body'll see the bruises, an' what's mair, I'm nae stoppin' you comin' wi' me.'

He let his raised fists drop. 'What if I tied you to the bed and didna let you oot?'

'I wouldna put it past you, but I'd tell Jean Petrie on Sunday an' she'd let a'body ken.'

'Aye, she'd dae that, a' right.' Jeems fell silent, weighing up which would be the lesser of the two evils, then said, 'I'll ha'e to let you go, I suppose?'

'Aye.' Triumph shot through her at how easy it had been.

Mysie washed and ironed her Sunday blouse and skirt the next day, and checked that there were no holes in her stockings, for even if nobody would see them if there were any, she'd know they were there. She would have liked to have something new to wear, but there was no money for that, and Jess had told her that only the farmer's wife ever wore any finery.

Jeems watched but said nothing as Mysie prepared to go out on Saturday night, but when she was ready – her dark hair, shining and luxuriant, swept up in a loose knot on top of her head instead of dragged back into its usual plain bun at her neck, her blue eyes sparkling, her cheeks pink with excitement – he couldn't help feeling proud of her beauty. Not being the kind of man who could easily express his feelings, he merely stroked his big nose and gave a grunt. 'That's you ready, is it? I suppose you'll be for aff?'

'Aye,' she replied, not in the least cast down because he had passed no favourable comment on her appearance. Excitement coursed through her as she walked along the road between the Findlaters. 'Robertson o' Waterton never has a meal an' ale o' his ain,' Jess remarked, 'so maist o' his men'll be at Fingask the nicht, as weel.'

'The mair the merrier, eh, Mysie?' Jake nudged her.

When they arrived, there seemed to be hundreds of people in the huge barn, dancing in wild abandon – even Jean Petrie had her skirts kilted up and was hooching and kicking her legs in the air. Her husband, Eck the grieve, was rattling up his old accordion, unaware of her antics, or perhaps fully aware of them but glad that she wasn't miscalling their neighbours, as she was in the habit of doing at other times.

Half an hour later, disappointed that no one had asked her for the eightsome reel, Mysie spotted Andra White whirling Jess round, both screaming with laughter. Jake was standing at the improvised bar, drinking with the other men who were not up dancing, and looking as if he'd had more than enough already. His cheeks were scarlet, his hair, greying now and thinner, was sticking up untidily, but he was enjoying himself and his feet were tapping in time to the music. Standing next to him was Drew White, the miller's son, who was about the same age as Mysie herself, but his sister, Nessie, a year or so older, was skipping around, grinning and flaunting herself at any man who would look at her. Jeems had started something with his evening walks – or had Nessie always been like that?

Some small children were running through the dancers now, adding to the noise by yelling, and Kirsty Mutch, one of the farmer's daughters, was having a heated argument with Johnnie Thomson, Alice's youngest, both only six, but with fully-fledged tempers. Before they came to blows, Joe, Johnnie's father, dragged him away by the scruff of his neck, and Kirsty turned aggressively on the girl standing nearest her. She had picked on the wrong person, however, for Meggie Duff, six years her senior, gave her a shove that almost knocked her over.

Effie and Denny Petrie, thirteen and fifteen respectively, and Robbie Duff, fourteen, were huddled together in a corner, all of them looking as if they hadn't come to this social gathering of their own free wills. Thirteen-year-old Jinty Mutch, Kirsty's sister, was sitting forlornly on her own, her eyes riveted on something at the other side of the room, and when Mysie turned her head to find out what, she saw Gavin Leslie on a bale of hay with Freda Mutch, who was wearing a tight silky dress that had slid up so far as to be indecent – her very knees were showing. So Jean Petrie's story was true, Mysie thought, sorry for Jinty, who was likely embarrassed for her mother, for it was a terrible way for a farmer's wife to be carrying on.

'I see Mistress Mutch is busy.' Unnoticed, Jean Petrie had seated herself next to Mysie. 'I tell't you she was takin' up wi' Gavin, but fancy her bein' so brazen in front o' her man. Nae that he looks worried aboot it.'

Following the other woman's gaze, Mysie could see that Frank Mutch's eyes were also fixed on his wife and the youth, but he didn't seem to be jealous. Transferring her attention to the side again, Mysie saw that Gavin was pulling Freda to her feet, and although she put up a show of arguing for a few moments, she went outside with him willingly enough.

47

'Aye,' came Jean's low voice. 'I thought that would happen. He's a randy little bugger that ane, an' Freda's nae better.'

Mysie rose with the intention of moving away, but her way was blocked by a young man who had just appeared in front of her. 'Are you nae dancin', Mrs Duncan?'

'Naebody's asked me,' she replied, without thinking.

'I'm askin'.' He held out his hand to her and led her down the floor. 'I dinna ken what Eck Petrie's wife was sayin' to you, but you looked as if you needed some help.'

'Aye, I'm nae ane for listenin' to her nasty gossip.'

'I was watchin' you for a while, wonderin' who you was, an' it was Jake Findlater tell't me you was Jeems Duncan's wife. I'm Doddie Wilson, cattleman at Waterton for five year, but I've never seen you at a meal an' ale afore.'

'Jeems doesna like dancin', an' he would never come.'

'Is he here the nicht?'

'No, he bade at hame wi' the twa bairns.'

'He's nae feared to let you oot on your ain? You're such a bonnie quine, a' the men'll be after you.'

Blushing, she said, 'There's nae fears o' that.'

'I would, if I thought you . . . wouldna object.'

There was something in his dark eyes that made Mysie's heart skip a beat. He was everything she had ever dreamt about – tall and dark with twinkling eyes, broad shoulders tapering to narrow hips – and surely nobody could condemn her if she let herself enjoy his company?

Eck Petrie had been fortifying himself with a dram, but when the music started up again, Mysie allowed Doddie to take her into position for a strip-the-willow. Some of the men tried to birl her off her feet, and she found herself skirling like the other women, but it was great fun, and when she glanced round, she saw that Jess was enjoying herself every bit as much, not surprising when her partner this time was Frank Mutch.

At the end, Eck unstrapped his accordion and went to the bar for a large glass of ale to replace the sweat he had lost while his fingers had flown over the keys, and most of the other men did the same, ostensibly to get their breath back, but Doddie sat down beside Mysie. 'Your cheeks are flushed,' he told her, 'but it mak's you even bonnier. Oh, I wish you werena Jeems Duncan's wife. I could easy fa' in love wi' you.'

'You needna bother,' she laughed, but she, too, wished that she wasn't Jeems Duncan's wife.

The next dance was a Scottish waltz, and she could scarcely bear the thrill of being so close to Doddie; he was so gentle, so romantic, she wanted to stay in his arms for ever. When the waltz finished, he led her outside without saying a word, not that she would have said no if he'd asked first, but every dark corner they found seemed to be occupied, little squeals of girlish delight warning them not to go too near. By accident, they almost stumbled over the farmer's wife and Gavin Leslie, moaning in the last throes of ecstasy. It was like a death knell to Mysie, who hastily extracted her hand from Doddie's and said, firmly, 'We'd best go back inside, or somebody might see us, like we saw Freda Mutch.'

'Do you nae want to . . . ?'

'Aye, an' that's the trouble. I shouldna be feelin' like this when I'm wed on Jeems.'

'He'll never ken.'

'Somebody might tell him.'

'There's a lot o' men'll never ken what their wives are up to the nicht,' Doddie murmured, looking at her with unconcealed longing. 'Oh, Mysie, please?'

Torn between attraction to him and fear of her husband, she whispered, 'No, I canna.'

'I'll nae force you.' But he sounded disappointed. Inside, Mysie wondered if Jess had noticed her absence, but there was no sign of her, nor of the farmer. They were more than likely outside doing what she'd stopped Doddie from doing, and she wished that she'd let him, but it was too late now. He sat beside her again, telling her about himself, that his mother had died a few years ago and that his

49

father lived near Fyvie. And she told him about her father's death and her mother being cook at Tinterty. This made her remember that she hadn't had a letter from her mother for some time, and made her resolve to write to her the next day. But, occasionally, an electric silence fell, during which their eyes met and locked until the confused Mysie had to look away, alarmed by the depth of her feelings.

When the last dance was announced, Doddie looked at her in dismay. 'Will you come ootside wi' me again, Mysie?' he coaxed. 'I didna even get a chance to kiss you afore.'

She went with him eagerly, not caring who saw them, and this time, most of the other couples having gone inside, they found a secluded spot behind the dairy. By the time the Findlaters found them, Mysie was on the point of succumbing to Doddie's urgent pleading, and was almost angry at their interruption. Jake was swaying on his feet, but Jess met Mysie's guilty eyes without a blush. 'It's time we went hame, lass.'

Scrambling up, Mysie said, unsteadily, 'Thank you for . . . dancin' wi' me, Doddie, an' goodnicht to you.'

'Goodnicht, Mysie,' he answered softly. 'I'd best nae come alang the road wi' you,' he added to Jess.

'No, Jeems Duncan might see you an' start wonderin'.'

Jake's legs having developed a will of their own, the two women had to help him to walk, but after a few giggles at his expense, Jess said, 'Do you want to tell me onything, Mysie?'

'I've naething to tell, for Jake an' you spoiled it.'

'Maybe it's just as weel. Another man's kisses is aye mair excitin' than your ain man's, an' I'd a hard job nae to gi'e in mysel' but I'll tell you this, I wouldna really change my Jake for a dozen Frank Mutches.'

Mysie heaved a lengthy sigh. 'I'd change Jeems for Doddie the morn, if I got the chance. He treated me like a lady, an' Jeems whiles mak's me feel like I was dirt under his feet.'

'You'd best put Doddie oot o' your head, lass,' Jess said,

not unsympathetically. 'You're Jeems's wife, an' that's what you'll aye be.' Her tone became brisk. 'Noo, come on, we'll ha'e to get this man o' mine hame afore he fa's doon, for we'll nae be able to lift him, the big, daft gowk.'

When they reached Rowanbrae, Jeems was standing at the door, but when he saw Jake's condition, he came towards them. 'I'll gi'e you a hand to get him hame, Jess, an' Mysie, get inside in case the loons waken up.'

She pretended to be asleep when he returned, and spent the night remembering Doddie's tender kisses and gentle caresses, so different from her husband's rough maulings. Her body was aching for the young man, the man of her dreams, but she knew that it could never be. She was bound by law to Jeems, but at least he would never know what she and Doddie had been doing, for nobody except Jess – Jake had been too drunk – could have seen them.

Unfortunately for Mysie, someone else *had* seen, and her interlude with Doddie was common knowledge the following day, circulating in the district like wildfire. Jean Petrie, delighted to have some juicy scandal to pass on about Jeems Duncan's quiet young wife, made the most of it outside the door of the church. 'I seen her mysel' goin' oot wi' Doddie, though they didna bide lang, but they must ha'e liked it that muckle they went oot again later on an' never come back in.'

'Mysie Duncan an' Doddie Wilson?' marvelled Alice Thomson. 'I'd never ha'e believed that, for she's just a little moose, an' he's never looked at ony lassie afore.'

Mrs Petrie was puffed up with pride at surprising everyone. 'I was only jaloosin' what they were daein', but Meggie Duff tell't Belle she seen them lyin' thegither at the back o' the dairy, an' it was Belle tell't me.' Pausing for effect, she lowered her voice. 'We'll ha'e to wait a while afore we ken if onything comes o' it, but I think somebody should tell Jeems.'

Hearing this as she passed, Pattie White said, loudly, 'Keep your lang neb oot o' it, Jean Petrie. You're just jealous that naebody's ever ta'en you ootside to kiss you

51

or dae onything else.' She swept down the path like a battleship in full sail, but her outburst caused great hilarity amongst the other women and Jean closed her mouth, more determined than ever to inform the wronged husband at the very first opportunity.

On Sunday night, Mysie badly strained her ankle by stepping on a loose stone in the yard, and Jeems had to go to the well himself on Monday morning. He came storming back, his face dark and contorted with anger. 'What's this Eck Petrie's wife's sayin' aboot you an' Doddie Wilson?'

An iron band clamped round Mysie's heart. 'Oh! You ken she spreads terrible lees aboot folk . . . what was she sayin'?'

'Tell me the truth, if you dare, an' we'll see if she was tellin' lees or no'.'

'Me an' Doddie just went oot for a breath o' fresh air,' she murmured, but he cut her short.

'I'm nae daft, wumman. There's just one thing he'd ha'e ta'en you ootside for, an' I'm askin' you, did you let him?'

'No, Jeems, I swear to God I didna.' Her conscience, however, wouldn't let her stop there. 'I let him kiss me, that's a'.'

Setting the two pails on the floor with such force that the water slopped over, he leapt across the room and punched her in the stomach, making her double over, winded. He stamped out without waiting to see if she got her breath back. Doddie was in the big byre at Waterton when Jeems burst in. 'Aye, Jeems, what brings you here . . . ?' he began sociably, but the other man's scarlet face and wild eyes told him that this was not a social call.

'You ken fine what brings me here! What you an' my wife did on Saturday nicht, that's what brings me here. Christ, man, the whole place is speakin' aboot it, an' laughin' at me ahin' my back. Just kisses, she tell't me, but I'm bloody sure you didna stop at kissin' her, you horny bugger.'

Doddie met his furious eyes steadily. 'It was Mysie stopped at kissin'. I'd ha'e ta'en her in a minute, if she'd let me.'

Jeems's fist shot out and landed heavily on Doddie's mouth. 'You bugger o' hell! You tell me that to my face, dae you?' The second blow caught the young man on the side of the head, and when Doddie still didn't retaliate, Jeems roared, 'Oh, aye, you maybe think you're a great man wi' the weemen, but you're nae man enough to stand up for yoursel'.'

Wiping the blood from his mouth, Doddie said, quietly, 'You've a right to be angry. I shouldna ha'e kissed your wife, but I'd a puckle drinks in me an' she's the bonniest lass I ever saw. It's nae excuse, but it's the only ane I can gi'e you.'

Thwarted of a sparring match, Jeems struck out again, shouting, 'No, by God, it's nae excuse, an' I'll tell you this, if ever I catch you near her again, I'll kill you!' He made for the open door, then turned to issue one last warning. 'Nae man mak's a fool o' me an' gets awa' wi' it!' Watching him going out, Doddie took out his handkerchief to dab his face, and had the small satisfaction of seeing Jeems blowing on his knuckles to ease the pain in them.

Mysie looked up fearfully when her husband returned, his ugly face made even uglier by a sneer of victory. 'That's sorted Doddie Wilson oot,' he crowed. 'He'll nae kiss ony other man's wife for a lang time.'

'What did you dae to him?' she whispered.

'I punched him stupid, an' he just stood an' took it, the big jessie that he is.'

Mysie knew that Doddie was not a jessie – he had proved that by his passionate pleas and by his hardness against her, which she had felt even through the layers of clothing between them – but it would be wiser to let her husband believe that he had come off best. She was sure of one thing, though – her life would never be the same again now that she'd discovered what love was, for it must be love she felt for Doddie Wilson. Why else would her heart sing the way it did and her innards twist with desire as they had never done for Jeems?

Chapter Five

If only Sandy was more like his brother, Mysie thought – Jamie never tore his breeches, nor dirtied them like this. She had been nearly sick yesterday trying to scrub the same pair clean, and the little devil had fallen in the midden again as soon as he went outside after his breakfast this morning.

'Weel,' he'd pouted, when she raged him, 'there's a cobbly stane, an' I can never mind which ane it is.'

'But you shouldna be walking on the midden ony road.'

'I wasna walkin', Mam, I was runnin' alang the dyke to see how far I got roon' afore I coonted up to ten.'

Not feeling like arguing any more, loose stone or not, she'd said, 'It's a good thing for you it's the holidays, an' it's nae your school breeks you had on.'

She was not in a good mood today anyway. That letter from her mother had infuriated her. It was disgusting to think that a woman of her age was expecting and had to get married. It was bad enough that she had been carrying on with a man at all, but everyone in Turriff knew that Louie Gill had ill-used his first wife and was as big a drunkard as Eddie Lonie – one of his cronies, in fact. Not only that, he was as fat as a pig, with a beer-belly on him that hung down over the top of his trousers, and a pock-marked face that leered at any girl unfortunate enough to be near him. Of course, Mysie reflected as she scrubbed, it was years since she had seen him, since he had tried to paw her as she passed, but a man like that wouldn't have changed. How could her mother let him touch her? It was indecent. Well, that was the end. Even if she had the money for the fares, she would never go to see her mother again, and she was not going to answer this letter. Let the woman stew in her own juice.

Retching as she encountered a particularly nasty dollop of something she didn't dare to analyse, she became conscious that a man was standing beside her, and, put out at being found in such circumstances, she gasped, 'Oh, it's you, Jockie. I'd clean forgot you'd be here the day. Just gi'e me a minute till I get Sandy's breeks washed. He's aye up to something, gettin' worse ilka day, an' I'm at my wits' end wi' him. God kens what he'll be like when he's aulder.'

The old man smiled comfortingly. 'Och, Mistress, loons are better wi' a bit o' devilment in them. I mind when my . . .'

The abrupt stop made Mysie look up, but the wistful look she caught in his eyes was gone almost at once. 'Sandy's in the hoose,' she said, kindly. 'He's sittin' wi' a blanket roon' him, for he's only got his school breeks clean an' he's nae gettin' them on to play. Go in an' speak to him, I'll nae be lang.' She bent to her task again as he walked away. She had long since come to the conclusion that he was an old bachelor, but she was certain that he had almost told her about a son, or sons, when he caught himself, so he must have had a wife and family at one time. Maybe they had died, or he had walked out on them, or they on him.

After throwing the dirty water on the midden, Mysie laid the trousers over the hen run to be rinsed out later and went into the house. Sandy, who had been laughing, hastily assumed a peeved aura of injured pride, but she ignored him and spooned some tea into the teapot, filled it up, then turned to the old man. 'What like are you the day, Jockie?'

'I'm fine . . . no, I'm nae that good, really.'

'Oh, I'm sorry to hear that. What's . . . ?'

'It's my legs, they're ower auld to be travellin' roon'.'

'You're nae that auld.'

'I'm seventy come October.'

Sandy eyed him with interest. 'Seventy? That's awfu' auld.'

The man smiled ruefully. 'Aye, my loon, it's man's span on this earth – three-score year an' ten. I've been lucky to keep goin' as lang's this, but I ken't the time would come when I'd ha'e to hand my pack ower to a younger man.'

'Will you be a different packman the next time you come?'

Smiling at the boy's inconsistency, Jockie said, 'Aye, it'll be another man. It's mony a year since I'd a hame, an' I've nae idea where I'll be sleepin' noo. I aye got a bed in an oothoose at the last place ilka day, but that privilege'll go to the new man, once I find him, so I doot it's the workhoose for me.'

Mysie was horrified. 'Do you nae ha'e naebody o' your ain?'

'Nae a soul.'

The wistfulness was there again, and Mysie was more curious than ever about him, but she couldn't ask him anything as long as her son was there. 'Sandy, if you promise to keep awa' fae that midden, you can put on your school breeks an' go oot.'

'I'll nae go near the midden, Mam. Cross my he'rt an' hope to dee, cut my throat if I tell a lee.' He drew his forefinger across his neck before scampering into the other room.

He ran past her again as she made her purchases, but she waited until she poured the tea before saying, 'It's nane o' my business, but what made you start bein' a packman, Jockie?'

He took a dainty sip from his cup then laid it down. 'I've never tell't onybody, but I'm comin' near the end o' my days, an' I'd like fine to speak aboot it. I was a lucky man once, Mistress, wi' a good wife an' three fine sons. I'd a grand job at the mart in Ellon, an' a hoose that went alang wi' it, wi' three rooms, but . . . och, we're never content wi' what we've got, an' I hankered after mair. I started takin' money that didna belong to me, but I got found oot, an' the upshot was I lost my job, my hoose . . .

56

an' my wife an' bairns, for they disappeared the time I was in the jail.'

'Oh, Jockie, that was terrible. Did you nae look for them?'

'I looked a' ower, but I never found them. I think she must ha'e ran awa' wi' another man. I took to the drink for a while, an' I was at the end o' my tether an' wishin' I was dead, but it's only the good that die young. When I come to my senses, I wandered aboot lookin' for work, an' I come across this auld packman one day, lyin' at the side o' the road. I could see he wasna lang for this world, but he tell't me the places he went, an' I bade wi' him till he died, then I took his pack up and walked on to Mintlaw, an' I tell't the man in the shop where he was lyin' so somebody could bury him. I was feared to tell the bobbies, you see, in case they thought I'd killed him.'

'What a way to end his days.' Mysie's heart ached for the poor old man who had died without a friend.

'That was thirty year ago, but I dinna want it happenin' to me.' Jockie lifted his cup again, purposefully. 'Noo, how are you yoursel', Mistress?'

'I'm fine, just deaved wi' that youngest loon o' mine.'

'Be thankfu' you've got him. You dinna ken how lucky you are – twa bonnie bairns an' a good man.'

'Aye, it's just . . . ha'e you ever seen my Jeems?'

'Just fae a distance.'

'Weel, you'll maybe understand what . . .'

'You dreamed o' a young Lochinvar, maybe, at one time?'

'Aye, but he never appeared.' Remembering Doddie Wilson, Mysie reflected that her Lochinvar *had* appeared – too late.

'Have faith, lass. If the good Lord means it, you'll maybe find your true love yet.'

She gave a bitter laugh. 'Muckle good would it dae me when I'm wed on a great lump like Jeems.'

'We've a' got oor ain crosses to bear.' He hoisted his pack on to his shoulder. 'It's goodbye for ever this time,

Mistress. It's been a pleasure kennin' you, an' thank you for a' the cups o' tea you gi'ed me ower the years.'

'You were mair than welcome, Jockie, an' I'll be prayin' you find a decent place to bide.' As she held the door open for him and watched him limping away, Mysie wished that she was in a position to offer him a home, but she just had two rooms. Shaking her head mournfully, she went down to the burn to fill the tub again. 'We've a' got oor ain crosses to bear,' Jockie had said, and hers at the moment, and likely for the next few years, was Sandy. Taking his soaking breeches off the wire, she wondered where he was. Jamie was sitting against the byre reading a book he had been given as a prize at school, but there was no sign of his brother. 'Jamie, dae you ken where Sandy is?'

'He run after the packman, to keep him company a bit.'

'I hope he doesna go far.' Sandy could always surprise her, she mused, plunging his trousers into the clean water. His heart was in the right place, that was one good thing, but it would take a bone comb to find any sense in his head.

Sandy hadn't returned by twelve, when the rest of his family sat down to kale and mashed potatoes, and Mysie's irritation with him turned to anger. 'You'll ha'e to sort that loon oot, Jeems. He just does what he likes.'

Her husband took a large bite out of an oatcake before he answered. 'His belly should ha'e tell't him it was dinnertime.'

The crumbs flying out of his mouth infuriated Mysie, so she burst out, without thinking of the possible consequences, 'Ha'e you nae manners, man? Speakin' wi' your mooth fu' like that?'

'I was never a great ane for manners,' he growled.

'You dinna need to tell me that!'

'Mr Meldrum says manners maketh man,' observed Jamie.

'The dominie wouldna ken a man if he found ane in his

soup,' Jeems said contemptuously, 'the dried up auld maid that he is.'

Mysie's eyes flashed. 'Dinna speak like that in front o' the bairn. If you were a man yoursel', you'd be oot lookin' for Sandy, nae runnin' doon the dominie.'

'You watch your tongue,' he snarled, 'an' Meldrum would be a better a man if he'd ever had a wumman.' He took another big bite out of his oatcake. 'Sandy canna be far awa', let Jamie look for him. Aff you go, noo.'

The boy went out reluctantly, and, not daring to argue with her husband any more, Mysie finished her own first course and rose to dish up the curds and whey. She'd added rennet to the milk first thing in the morning to make sure it would be set firmly. 'Here's your yerned milk.' She set his plate down with a thump, 'an' there's nae mair bannocks, you've eaten them a'.'

'I just had three wi' my kale!' he roared. She tried to placate him. 'I'll be bakin' the morn again, but I just havena had time the day. I'd to wash Sandy's breeks an' the packman was here for a while.'

'You was speakin' when you should ha'e been attendin' to your jobs? Christ, I never thought you was such a lazy bitch.'

'I aye gi'e Jockie a cuppie tea,' Mysie said, nervously, for she could see that he was itching for a proper quarrel.

Jeems was ready to go back to work when Jamie burst in. 'I couldna see Sandy nae place,' he gasped breathlessly. 'I went right to Waterton, an' the packman was there gettin' some broth fae the cook, an' he said Sandy turned back at Downies.'

Jeems scowled. 'He should ha'e been hame lang ago, an' I'll skelp his erse when I get my hands on him.'

Mysie let this pass. 'I'm sure something's happened to him. Will you nae come wi' me to look for him?'

They had been searching the ditches at the side of the road for about twenty minutes when the boy said, 'I've just minded. Sandy tell't me he'd seen a martin's nest doon the auld quarry.'

Mysie was horrified. 'I've aye tell't the twa o' you to keep awa' fae there, it's a dangerous place.'

'Robbie Duff took him last week, but they couldna reach the eggs, an' Sandy said he'd try himsel' sometime.'

The old quarry was at the far side of the peat moss behind the mill, almost a mile off the road, and Jeems, having run off before Mysie could move, reached it well ahead of her. 'He's standin' on a stane a bit doon,' he said when she joined him, 'and God kens how we'll get him up.' A pitiful wail from Sandy tore at her heart. 'Thank God he's still alive,' she murmured, then, as her husband swung one leg over the edge, she cried, 'You canna go doon there.'

'Somebody'll need to go doon. No, wait! I'll haud Jamie by the feet an' let him doon slow, an' Sandy can get haud o' his hand, an' I'll pull them baith up.'

'Oh, God, is there naething else we can dae?'

Ignoring her, Jeems hauled off his jacket and handed it to Jamie. 'You'd best tak' that in case you canna stretch far enough. Noo, we'll baith lie doon, an' I'll haud you when you slide ower. I'll nae let you go, so dinna be feared.'

'Will I nae run to the mill?' Mysie implored. 'I could get a rope fae Andra.'

'There's nae time to waste, that stane could shift.'

Her hands at her mouth, she watched Jamie edging towards the drop, his father's huge hands round his ankles, but as the slim body disappeared over the edge, the weight made the man's face muscles tighten. 'You'd best haud my feet as weel, Mysie.'

Although she knew that she didn't have the strength to stop them falling if they slipped, she lay behind him and grasped his ankles, furious at Sandy for coming here when he had been told not to, and even more furious at Jeems for putting Jamie's life in jeopardy, too. For what seemed like hours, she clung on doggedly, then Jamie's strained voice floated up faintly. 'I still canna reach him.'

Groaning, Jeems made another strenuous effort, and

Mysie was certain that they were inching forward. She couldn't even be sure that her grip was holding, her hands were so numb, and was afraid that, when Sandy's weight was added to Jamie's, it would beat Jeems altogether.

Another eternity passed before Jamie shouted, 'He's got haud o' the jacket, Father! Pull us up!'

Jeems heaved and heaved, and with one last tremendous pull, he had Jamie up and was stretching out a hand to Sandy, but only when both her sons were lying safely on the ground did Mysie burst into hysterical sobs.

It was a long time before Jeems had enough breath to mutter, 'It was a near thing – I couldna ha'e held them ony langer.'

Jamie was first to move, but, as he went to give his father the jacket, he tripped over a hidden tree root. His arms beat the air for a split second, then, with a piercing shriek, and before any of the horrified watchers could do anything to stop him, he plunged straight down into the murky water at the foot of the disused quarry.

Chapter Six

Some thirty minutes earlier, when he'd come out at the door of the mill to smoke his pipe, Andra White had noticed three figures running across the moss – a man first, then, some way behind, a woman and a boy – but it had taken him some time to realise who they were and where they were heading, and longer still before the significance of their destination dawned on him. 'It was Jeems Duncan an' Mysie an' Jamie,' he told his wife, 'runnin' to the quarry like the devil was chasin' them. Surely Sandy wouldna ha'e fell doon the hole?'

'You'd best go an' see,' Pattie advised, 'an tak' a rope wi' you, in case the bairn's got stuck.' Her face grew grave.

'If he's went right doon, there's naething naebody can dae.'

When her husband came round from the outhouses carrying a coil of strong rope, she said, 'I'll come wi' you, Andra, for Mysie'll need a wumman body if . . .' She didn't finish.

Pattie, very stout and more breathless by the minute, lagged farther and farther behind Andra as he hurried across the bog, but when he caught sight of the group of three standing near the edge like statues, he turned his head and shouted to her, 'The laddie must be lost.' Drawing nearer, his growing concern turned to astonishment when he saw that it was Sandy who was with his parents, not Jamie, as he'd expected. Both Jeems and Mysie appeared to be paralysed with shock, but Sandy looked up desolately. 'I was tryin' to get a martin's egg an' I stretched oot an' slid ower, an' Jamie come ower to pull me up, an he's fell doon.'

Andra did not understand this garbled account, but he and Pattie took them to the mill, and it was there that he pieced the true story together. 'Oh, God, that's the worst thing I ever heard,' he muttered, when he took it in. 'To think you'd baith loons safe, an' . . .' He halted, appalled by the look on the other man's face as much as by the tragedy. 'Dinna blame yoursel', Jeems. You did what you thought was right, an' you couldna help what happened.'

Pattie, her arms round the still-silent Mysie, looked up at her husband and shook her head sadly. Andra noticed that the young woman's body was caved in, her eyes were blank in big, dark sockets, her face and lips as white as driven snow. She was scarcely breathing, and clearly had no idea where she was.

Pattie took matters firmly in hand. 'I'll best tak' Mysie up the stair to lie doon.' Helping the other woman to her feet, she led her out.

Remembering that the boy was still standing just inside the door, Andra said, kindly, 'Sit doon, my loon.'

Sandy had not said a word since they left the quarry.

He walked across the room unsteadily and perched himself on the edge of one of the chairs. There he sat, his fingers twining through each other, his eyes regarding the top of his father's head as Jeems sat bent almost double.

The miller, recognising the shame and appeal in the stare, wished he could take Sandy in his arms to reassure him, but it was Jeems's place to do that, or, even more so, Mysie's. The bairn was needing love at this time, but his mother and father were too wrapped up in their own guilt and sorrow to speak to him. It was a bad business altogether, Andra mused.

When Pattie came thumping down the stairs, she said, 'I'll mak' a cup o' strong, sweet tea for her.'

'Would you like a dram, Jeems?' Andra offered, hope-fully.

The bowed head lifted slowly. 'Thank you, no, I'll never touch strong drink again. Maybe this is God's punishment to me for nae bein' the man I should ha'e been, an' I swear, in front o' witnesses, that I'll . . .' Jeems's voice broke, and his head dropped again.

'You'll tak' some tea, then,' Pattie ordered. 'An' you, as weel, my lambie.'

The six-year-old jumped down from his seat and ran to her, bursting into tears when she sat down and took him on her lap. The sound triggered Jeems off, and Sandy glanced round for a moment in amazement at the loud, harsh sobs breaking from his father's throat, then he snuggled back against the miller's wife's ample bosom for con-solation. Just then, Nessie, in her furtive way, eased the kitchen door open, her eyes lighting up when she saw Jeems, but she withdrew, puzzled, when her mother lifted a hand and shooed her away.

They were still sitting, hushed now, when Mysie came down almost an hour later, ashen faced, but in complete control of herself. 'You should ha'e bidden up there,' Pattie scolded, shifting Sandy off her lap and moving across to the fireside to make the tea she had been prevented from brewing before.

Mysie's eyes, no longer blank, were deeply troubled. 'I want to go hame,' she whimpered.

Jeems stood up, still aching from the grief that had racked his whole body. 'You're right, we'd best get hame.'

'Aye, awa' you go.' Andra shuffled his feet. 'I'll report . . . what's happened, so dinna worry aboot that.'

Running forward, Sandy slipped his hand into his mother's. He didn't see the bitter look she gave him as they went out. It was Sandy's fault, she thought, as they trailed along the road, and she wished now that she'd had the courage to throw herself after her beloved son, but she had been too shocked to think clearly. How could she go on living when her Jamie was lying under all that water in a deep hole? If Jeems had let her get a rope, if he hadn't made Jamie go down, if they'd left Sandy...oh, she shouldn't be thinking that. When they entered their own house, her deep shame at her thoughts made her say, gently, 'Get to your bed like a good loon, Sandy.'

The pleading in his eyes told her that he was afraid to go through to the bed he had shared with his brother, which she could understand, for she didn't want to share a bed with his father. Sandy was only a bairn, and hadn't thought before he stretched down to the nest, but Jeems should have known better than do what he did. 'I'll sleep wi' you the nicht, my loon,' she whispered. Her husband's grief-stricken face made her feel fleetingly sorry for him. He, too, had lost a son. It did not occur to her that Jamie's death was not really Jeems's fault, because the boy could still have tripped and fallen even if her husband had let her go for a rope.

It was a long night for Mysie and Jeems, separately trying to forget Jamie's screams as he fell to his death, and Sandy was the only one to get any sleep, but he was so restless that his mother was tempted, several times, to rouse him from the nightmares that obviously troubled him.

Mysie rose well before her usual time, but Jeems was already dressed when she went through to the kitchen, his face white and haggard, his hand shaking as he lifted the teapot. She stepped forward to take it from him, but he laid it down and flung his arms round her. 'Oh, Mysie, I needed you last nicht.'

She stiffened. 'Sandy needed me, as weel.' She felt like screaming that he should have made sure both boys were away from the edge after he brought them up.

'I canna get it oot o' my mind, Mysie. I canna thole it.'

'You'll ha'e to thole it, the same as me,' she said, coldly.

'Oh, Christ! Oh, Christ!' He sobbed against her shoulder, shaking uncontrollably, but she made no effort to comfort him. When he calmed down, his tortured eyes looked at her piteously. 'Oh, I wish it was me that had went ower.'

Wishing that, too, she turned guiltily to Sandy as he came through. 'There's nae porridge made yet,' she said, sharply, but regretted snapping at him when she saw his pinched cheeks and huge, mournful eyes.

'I'm nae needin' ony porridge the day,' Jeems grunted.

'Either am I.' Sandy stood in front of his parents, his face expressing a wisdom far beyond his years. 'I ken it'll nae bring Jamie back, but I'm sorry it was my blame.'

'Maybe it was your blame in the first place, but it was my blame at the . . .' His father's voice broke, and turning on his heel, he walked out.

Feeling unable to cope with the boy on her own, Mysie said, 'Go oot wi' your father, Sandy.' As he moved away, head down, he reminded her of a dog that had expected kindness and been whipped instead. She had not loved him as she should, and, because it was through him that she had lost Jamie, she would never be able to love him now, though he was the only son she had left. How could she watch him growing and not think that Jamie would have been that bit taller, that bit more sensible, that bit more loving?

The wag-at-the-wa' ticked on relentlessly, but she remained sitting, unheedful of the chores she should be doing, unable to grieve properly for her dead son because

65

there seemed to be a lead weight where her heart should have been. She didn't even notice the daylight trying to stream through the curtain, and jumped nervously as the porch door burst open, but when she saw that it was Jess Findlater, welcome tears rushed to her eyes and she dashed across the room into the sturdy arms.

Jess rocked her to and fro, murmuring, 'I ken, I ken,' until Mysie pulled herself together. 'I'm sorry for lettin' go like that, but it's the first time I've grat since . . .'

'You've got to let it oot,' Jess soothed, 'or it would grow an' grow inside you till you went aff your head. Me an' Jake didna ken till Pattie sent Nessie to Downies on her bike to tell us this mornin'. I thought the daft thing was bletherin', but you never ken wi' Nessie, so we dropped a'thing an' run. Jake's speakin' to Jeems, an' . . . oh, God, I'm sorry, Mysie.'

'If only it hadna been Jamie.' Mysie dried her eyes with her apron, missing the odd look the other woman gave her.

'For ony sake, Mysie, dinna wish it was Sandy that was awa'.'

'I dinna, nae noo, but you ken Jamie was aye my favourite. I couldna help it, for Sandy plagues the very life oot o' me.'

'Dinna blame him though, an' try to show him you've nae ill-will at him for Jamie's death. The good Lord must ha'e meant for it to happen, one road or another.'

Completely taken aback at this, Mysie sat down. 'But why did He tak' Jamie? What had the bairn daen to be punished like that? He was a good loon, an' he aye did what he was tell't.'

'He was maybe ower good.'

Mysie gasped. 'I just minded. You'd think Jockie ken't what was goin' to happen, for he said it's only the good die young.'

'So it is, lass.' Jess rose to make another pot of tea.

Watching her, Mysie realised that it was this woman who was her strength, who would see her through, not her husband. He had a right to grieve, of course, but he could have tried to help her instead of pleading with her to help him. Without warning, she was struck by another thought and drew her breath in sharply. 'Was God punishin' me for what I did wi' Doddie?'

About to place a cup in a saucer, Jess halted with her hand in midair. 'But you tell't me you didna dae naething.'

'If you hadna found us, I'd ha'e let him tak' me an' welcome. I never ken't I could feel like yon aboot a man.'

Stumped for an answer, Jess set the cup down, then muttered, after a moment, 'But you didna let him, so . . .'

'But the Lord would ken what was in my mind, an' He'll ken I've been dreamin' aboot Doddie an' wishin' I could see him again.'

Jess lifted the teapot. 'I'm sure there's dizzens o' weemen ha'e dreams aboot a man that's nae their ain.'

'But they just dream,' Mysie said, bitterly. 'It was mair than dreams wi' me. I'd ha'e left Jeems in a minute if Doddie had asked me. I even . . .' Clapping her hand over her mouth, she stopped, ashamed at what she had admitted, and aghast at how close she'd come to saying that she wished Jeems was dead so that she would be free to go to Doddie.

Shrewd Jess, however, had guessed. 'Calm doon, lass. You're upset an' I ken you dinna mean what you're sayin'. Drink that tea, and I'll get the rest o' them in.'

When Jake came in with Jeems and Sandy, Mysie could see that he had had the same calming influence on them as Jess had on her, and was very grateful to them.

Over the next few days, both Duncans had even more cause to be grateful to their nearest neighbours. It was the Findlaters who helped them answer the questions asked by the police; who identified Jamie when his poor little body was dredged up by equipment loaned by Craigenlow Quarry; who made the funeral arrangements and saw them through the actual day.

When all the other people left, they sat down, their first chance to relax, and Jeems grasped Jake's hand abruptly.

'I dinna ken what I'd ha'e daen the day if you hadna been here, man. I'm sure I'd ha'e lost my reason.' Turning to Jess, he said, 'I've nae words to thank you for what you've daen for us.'

'I ken I've an awfu' tongue,' she said, seriously, 'but I can haud it when I like, an' buckle doon to what's got to be daen.'

'You've aye been a good freen' to me, Jess.' Mysie's voice was almost choked. 'An' I'll mind what you said,' she added, glancing at Sandy, who was sitting on the fenderstool in front of the fire, his white, drawn face turning pink with the heat.

Somewhat embarrassed, Jess said, 'It was good o' the laird's wife to send you that letter o' condolence when she's never even met you.'

Mysie gulped. 'A'body's been good, even Jean Petrie come an' tell't me how sorry she was, an' she really meant it.'

Jess stood up and looked at her husband. 'Come on, Jake, this folk's needin' their beds, but mind, Mysie, ony time you need me, just let me ken.' She laid a hand on the boy's head on her way to the door. 'Be a good loon to your Mam, Sandy.'

'I'll try,' he whispered as she went out.

Several minutes elapsed before Mysie leaned over and patted his hand awkwardly. 'Get awa' to your bed, my loon. You must be tired, for you've had a lang day.'

'Will you be sleepin' wi' me the nicht again?' She steeled herself against the appeal in his eyes. 'Nae the nicht. You'll ha'e to get used to sleepin' yoursel' noo.'

As Sandy trailed through to the other room, Jeems, stretching his arms above his head, gave a loud yawn and regarded Mysie hopefully. 'I'm fit for my bed mysel'. Are you comin'?'

'Aye, in a minute.' Like Sandy, she was loath to return to the old pattern, afraid that Jeems would demand the solace she couldn't give him. A few minutes later, she was shivering with disgust at his undressed figure. The long woollen drawers did nothing to hide the outward curve of his bandy legs; the tight linder emphasised his pot belly; the soles of his feet, as he clambered into the high box bed, were leathery and calloused.

Oh, God, she thought, in anguish, if he were Doddie she would be in the bed beside him like a shot, but she was tied to this ugly brute of a man for the rest of her life – or his – and she would have to try to forget the magic of Doddie's kisses, as she would have to try to forget the manner of Jamie's death. She was absolutely positive that she would never forget either the boy himself – or the man she loved.

Chapter Seven

'The new packman should be here the morn,' Jess observed.

Mysie nodded. 'I wonder what like he'll be?'

'He's bound to be younger than Jockie,' Jess grinned, 'but mind you, Jockie was a fine auld man – never a bad word to say aboot onybody. There's nae many folk like that nooadays.'

'No, an' he could mak' you feel as though you was his maist important customer.'

'I used to be sorry I couldna buy mair fae him,' Jess said, pensively, 'but he ken't I hadna the bawbees.'

'Aye, he never tried to mak' you buy ony mair than you asked. I aye took him in an' gi'ed him a cup o' tea, should I dae that wi' the new man?'

'You're auld enough to mak' up your ain mind aboot him when he comes.' Knowing Mysie's vulnerability with young men, Jess issued a warning. 'I wouldna gi'e him ower muckle rope to start wi', if I was you, though. It's best to go canny.'

Remembering that it was on the day of Jockie's last visit

that the tragedy had occurred, Jess wished with all her being that she hadn't brought up the subject, for Mysie hadn't got over Jamie's death yet. She'd carried on bravely from the day after the funeral, but her heart hadn't been in what she was doing, poor soul. It was really a good thing that it would be a new packman, for it wouldn't remind her so much.

Standing up, she said, 'I'll need to be awa'. See you the morn.' She had never missed a day going to Rowanbrae for the past three months, no matter how busy she was, and knew that her friend depended on her visits.

After Jess left, Mysie rinsed out the cups, thanking God once again for their friendship, deeper than ever since that awful day. She was gradually coming to terms with her loss, though she would never get over it completely, and the mention of the new packman had kindled her interest. In fact, she realised in some surprise, she felt quite excited about it, and she would likely have a big disappointment when she saw him. Even if he was young, he might be fat and greasy and sweaty and she just hated sweaty men. Sweat from hard work was a different thing. Jeems often came home sweating, but after he washed, he wasn't so bad, and Doddie Wilson had been sweating when he'd danced with her, but his sweat smelt different from Jeems's – sweeter, more manly. But she hadn't seen Doddie since the meal and ale four months ago, and there seemed little chance of ever seeing him again.

Sandy came home then, putting Doddie out of her mind, even making her forget her speculations about the new packman. He went straight to the pantry. 'Can I ha'e a scone an' butter, Mam? I'm that hungry I could eat a . . .'

'You'll get your supper in a wee while, just go an' change your claes, that'll tak' your mind aff your belly.'

'It'll nae dae that.' But he did as he was told, and was back in the kitchen with his old clothes on by the time Jeems came in. 'We got muppelication the day,' Sandy announced, when they were sitting round the table. 'I

70

canna mak' heads or tails o't, an' Meldie was ragin' me . . .'

Jeems scowled. 'The man's name's *Mr* Meldrum.'

'I ken, an' I put my tongue oot at him an' he saw me an' gi'ed me the strap, an' my fingers is still dirlin'.'

Although Jeems knew that the small, spare schoolmaster had an arm of iron that could wield the tawse to good effect, he jumped up angrily and dragged his son to his feet. Holding him by the collar of his jersey, he gave him a great thump on the back. 'That's for puttin' your tongue oot at the dominie!' Another two hard wallops followed. 'That's for lettin' him see you, an' that's for gettin' the strap.' He relaxed his hold so quickly that the boy almost fell. 'You behave yoursel' after this, Sandy, or I'll clout your lug ilka time he straps you, like my father did to me.'

Fighting back his tears, the boy put up a show of defiance. 'I wasna the only ane. He gi'ed Davey Dite fower on ilka hand for nae gettin' his lang division right, an' he's thirteen an' I bet he could thrash the guts oot o' Meld . . . Mr Meldrum if he got the chance.'

Knowing all the pupils in the one-teacher school, Mysie said, 'If it's David Robertson you mean, his name's nae Davey Dite.'

Without thinking, Sandy began to chant, 'Davey Dite sat doon to shite . . .' but stopped as his mother slapped his face. 'What's that for?' he asked, looking pained, although she hadn't hurt him as much as his father had.

'You ken fine what it was for. I'm sure you dinna learn that kind o' words fae Mr Meldrum.'

'What kind o' words?'

Jeems, who had almost smiled for a moment as he remembered the familiar doggerel, turned sternly again on his son. 'You should ken your mother's real pernickety. She doesna like you speakin' aboot shite at the table.'

'He shouldna speak aboot shite at a',' Mysie retorted, then looked at her husband indignantly. 'Now see what you made me say! You're worse than the bairn.'

71

When the boy went out, Jeems said, thoughtfully, 'He's got a lot mair spunk in him than Jamie ever had.'

Shocked that he could speak so disparagingly of their dead son, Mysie said, caustically, 'He's gettin' ower big for his breeches. Eh . . . do you ken the rest o' what he was sayin'?'

'It's just a rhyme. We used to shout it at Davey Linklater when I was at the school. A' Davids get Davey Dite, whatever their real names is.' Baring his teeth in a barbaric grin, Jeems recited, ' "Davey Dite, sat doon to shite, upon a marble stane. The wind blew, the skitter flew, into Davey Dite's een." Are you pleased noo?'

Taken aback at the vulgarity, Mysie burst out, 'That's awfu' things for loons to be sayin'.'

'Loons'll be loons to the end o' time, wumman, an' Sandy'll likely dae a lot worse things than that afore he's a man.'

Sighing, she rose to clear the table. Sandy had already done the most terrible thing she could imagine, so surely it wasn't likely that he could do anything worse? Nevertheless, right up until she went to bed, she felt a vague sense of foreboding.

Mysie had just come inside from churning the butter the next morning when someone knocked at her door. When she opened it, the pack on the man's back told her who he was, but she would never have guessed if it hadn't been for that. The packman wasn't much older than she was, very slim and tall, with coppery wavy hair and a big smile that disarmed her immediately. The warning that Jess had given didn't enter her head as she said, 'I aye took Jockie in an' gi'ed him a cup o' tea. Would you like ane?'

'That's good of you, Missus.' His English voice was deep and soft. 'I was hoping someone would offer.' He followed her into the kitchen. 'You're quite comfortable here.'

'It's nae bad,' she said, modestly. 'Jockie usually let me see his things the time the tea was maskin'.' Lifting his

72

pack from the floor, he laid it on the table and opened it up. 'This is the very best Valencian lace.'

'I canna afford to buy naething like that, for we're croftin' folk, an' I havena got naething to spare for fancy frills.'

He turned the full power of his magnetism on her. 'You don't need anything to set off your beauty, but let me show you.' Taking the roll out, he held a length of it against her neck, the touch of his fingers making her skin tingle. 'You're like a princess,' he sighed, his eyes coming to rest on her bosom.

She smiled nervously. 'You've never seen ony princesses.'

'You're just what I picture a princess must look like.'

She was fully aware that the flattery was to persuade her to buy, but it was good to be flattered, however insincerely. 'Weel,' she said, having asked the price, 'just gi'e me half a yard, that would be enough.'

'Enough to go round the neck of a nightgown,' he agreed, his hand brushing against her again as he took the lace away. 'I wish I could see you wearing it when you've sewn it on.'

'Och, awa' wi' you,' she giggled, quite embarrassed.

'Come closer and I'll show you what else I have.'

Unsuspecting, she moved nearer, and was startled when both his arms went round her, but the hypnotising entreaty in his dark eyes kept her from pulling away.

'What's your name, princess?' His voice was soft and low.

'Mysie,' she said, shyly, and was instantly ashamed of it. 'I was baptised May.'

'May suits you much better. Well, my little Princess May, how about a kiss now we're so close?' She shook her head weakly, but he kissed her anyway, a kiss that transported her to another world and made her forget her husband, her dead child, even Doddie Wilson. 'You must have been starved of love, Princess May,' he said, in a moment, 'but Larry Larry can put that right.'

'Is that your name?' She had never heard it before, but

73

he wasn't from round here, and the English had some funny ideas.

'I was christened Lawrence Lawrence, but I'm usually called Larry Larry, sometimes even Double Larry.'

Pulling her to him, he ran his hands up and down her spine while he kissed her, then, sure that the right moment had come, he turned her sideways to cup her breast, and Mysie, putty in his hands, didn't try to stop him. For some time, he took full advantage of her obvious naivety, murmuring sweet nothings as he stroked and fondled and kissed, until he judged that it was safe to proceed a little further. 'What a tiny waist you have,' he murmured against her neck. 'I can nearly span it with my hands, my lovely Princess May.'

She didn't understand that it was reaction to Jamie's death that was heightening the effect this man had on her, that and the emotions that Doddie had set loose at the meal and ale. She was grain ripe for harvesting, and Lawrence Lawrence from Yarmouth was more than willing to be the reaper. Manoeuvring her on to the hearthrug, he pushed her skirts aside, smothering her with kisses all the while to stop any protests she might make, but she was drowning in a sea of wonderful, unfamiliar sensations and had no inclination to try to save herself.

In the circumstances, the seduction practically amounted to rape, but, very shortly, Mysie Duncan knew an ecstasy she had never known before, and she didn't come to her senses until it was over. 'You shouldna ha'e daen that,' she gasped.

Larry Larry smiled. 'You didn't stop me, and you enjoyed it, didn't you? Tell the truth now, Princess May.'

Unable to meet his eyes, she scrambled up off the floor and straightened her clothing, but, recalling her ecstatic moans when her release came and the thrill of his fingers digging into her flesh when he reached his, she couldn't deny that she had enjoyed it.

Fastening his trousers, he got to his feet. 'I'll cut off your lace,' he said briskly, as if nothing had happened.

74

She was too embarrassed to look at him as she took out her purse and paid for the lace, but he grasped her hand and lifted it to his lips. 'Will that last you for three months?' His smouldering eyes told her that he wasn't referring to the lace, nor to the kiss on the hand, so she wisely said nothing. 'Have this sewn on before I come back,' he smiled, letting go her hand and passing over her purchase. 'I can hardly wait to see you in your nightdress.'

After he left, neither of them remembering the tea she had offered, she sank into a chair, her heart still pounding. She had committed a sin – adultery was one of the worst – and she should be deeply ashamed, but she wasn't, not one little bit. She felt . . . triumphant. Jeems had never taken her to the heights she had reached with Larry Larry, and she had learned that it was the man's place to coax the woman, not the other way round. It didn't matter if the young packman didn't love her – she was almost sure he didn't – for he had proved to her that she wasn't incapable of responding properly to a man, as she had once believed.

Chapter Eight

It was useless trying to pretend that it hadn't happened, Mysie thought, desolately; she couldn't fool herself any longer. There was no doubt that she was in the family way, and Jeems would know it wasn't his. He hadn't been at her for over six months, for poor, idiot Nessie White was more than ready to oblige him.

There must be something she could do to get rid of it, but Jess would be disgusted and wouldn't tell her even if she knew. It wasn't as if she had felt any real love for the man, just the need to be wanted, comforted, but he was due back tomorrow, and she would have to tell Jeems first. Having another man's bairn was a thousand times worse than kissing Doddie, and she was half afraid that her husband would kill her when he found out, but if he just threw her out, Larry Larry would have to look after her. It was all his fault, although she should have kicked his shins before he got as far as he did, like Jess had once done to the miller.

Deciding to say nothing until Sandy was in bed, Mysie stood up wearily and went to fill the wooden wash tub. The clothes she later hung on the lines had been scrubbed as they'd never been scrubbed before, the physical exertion helping her, but it was still an effort to appear normal at dinnertime. If Jeems had any suspicion that she was hiding something, he was likely to force it out of her, and she wasn't ready to confess.

When Sandy came home from school – his tongue wagging like the clapper of a bell in his haste to tell her that he'd fought with another boy about who could run faster – her apprehension of what might happen that night made her turn on him sharply. 'For ony sake, haud your wheesht. You should think yoursel' lucky you can run at a'. There's mony poor laddies that canna.'

'Dae you ken ony that canna?' Sandy's curiosity wasn't in any way dimmed by the steely glint in his mother's eyes.

'No, I dinna, but I've heard stories. Nae mair nonsense noo – shift oot o' your school claes an' tak' in some sticks for me. You're auld enough noo to gi'e me a hand.'

Jeems looked pleased with himself at suppertime. 'That's the far park ploo'ed, so I'll nae bother goin' oot again the nicht.'

Mysie nodded. 'Aye, you've worked hard this week.' If she kept him in a good mood, she reasoned, he might not lose his head so easily when she told him.

After they'd eaten, and the dishes were washed and laid past, she sat down to hear Sandy's reading, doing her best to keep calm when he stumbled over words he should have known. Then she asked him his spellings, but, seeing Jeems glancing at the wag-at-the-wa' and frowning, she knew that she could put the evil moment off no longer. 'That'll dae the nicht, Sandy,' she said, closing both primer and spelling book and putting them in his satchel. 'It's past your bedtime.'

'Can I nae ha'e a piece an' jam first?'

The boy made the slice of bread and jam last so long that Jeems barked, 'Go oot to the privy an' get to your bed.'

Knowing how quickly his father could pounce on him, Sandy went out, but made one last feeble effort when he returned. 'My throat's as dry as a board, Mam.'

'Bed!' Jeems thundered. 'I'll nae tell you again.'

As the door closed behind the boy, Jeems said, almost as if he were talking to himself, 'I used to say I was needin' twa sons in case onything happened to one o' them. Jamie wouldna ha'e been fit to tak' ower this place fae me, supposin' he'd lived, for he was never strong. Sandy's got mair in him. He's nae feared to try onything.' He yawned suddenly. 'Losh, I'm tired the nicht, I'll ha'e to go to my bed as weel. Are you comin'?'

'I'll just tidy up a bit first.'

She was conscious of him watching her from the bed as she pottered about, desperately trying to find the words to tell him, but eventually she lit the small lamp on the mantelpiece and turned out the big one on the table, the last thing she did every night.

'You've been awfu' quiet since suppertime,' Jeems observed, suddenly. 'Is there something on your mind?'

Her heart in her mouth, she looked straight at him. 'I'm goin' to ha'e a bairn.' She hadn't meant to come out with it like that, but couldn't think of another way. It obviously took a few seconds to sink in, and in other circumstances she would have laughed at the bewilderment on his face, but when it did penetrate, he flung back the bedcovers and sprang on to the floor, his face livid. 'I'll kill Doddie Wilson for this!'

'No, no, Jeems! It wasna Doddie! Please, Jeems, I'm tellin' you the God's honest truth – it wasna him!' It had never for one moment crossed Mysie's mind that he would think that.

'Who was it?' He came towards her menacingly. 'Another o' Waterton's men, or Fingask's, or do you nae ken which ane's the father? Were you whorin' among them a'?'

Taking a step back, Mysie whispered, 'I havena been . . .' She choked over the word.

'What would you say it was, if it wasna whorin'?'

'It was just once, Jeems, an' . . .' She broke off when his clenched fist cracked against her jaw.

'Tell me the bugger's name, damn you!'

Her hand clamped to her aching face, she muttered, 'You dinna ken him.'

'Tell me the bugger's name, you bitch!' he bellowed.

'What difference does it mak'?'

'I'll mak' the bugger o' hell wish he'd never been born!'

'An' what good would that dae? It'll nae put awa' the life inside me, an' it's me you should . . .'

'Aye is it, you worthless trash!' He punched her chest and watched with grim satisfaction as she reeled back, writhing in agony. 'An' dinna run awa' wi' the idea I couldna put an end to the life inside you, for I wouldna think twice aboot it!'

Doubled up as she was, Mysie couldn't resist taunting him. 'Go on, then! Kill my bairn – kill me, if you like!'

He came forward again, but stopped. 'No, no, my fine lady! You'll nae get oot o' it as easy as that! You'll ha'e the bairn, an' I'll let a'body ken it's nae mine, an' you can face up to the shame o' the whole place laughin' at you.'

'It's you they'll laugh at, for goin' to Nessie White.'

His anger flared up again at that. 'It was your blame I went to her, an' she gi'ed me what I needed, for you let me believe you didna like onybody touchin' you, though I can see noo it was just me you didna like. Weel, I'll mak' damned sure nae man will want to touch you again!' Grabbing her shoulders, he shook her until her teeth rattled. 'An' you still havena tell't me the father!'

'I tell't you . . . you dinna . . . ken him.'

He flung himself at her now, knocking her against the table, which teetered for a moment then fell over, the glass of the lamp shattering in smithereens on the floor. Her head snapped back with the impact of his knuckles on her eyebrow, making her cry out in pain, and with fear that he might go on until she had no life left in her. 'Oh, Jeems, stop, stop! I'll tell you! It was the packman!'

He stepped back in amazement, his mouth hanging open. 'I aye wondered why you was so anxious to see him. Christ, you must ha'e been desperate to let a auld man like him . . .'

'Jockie gi'ed it up a while back,' Mysie sobbed. 'It's another man that comes noo.'

'An' how mony times has he been, this other man? How often did you let him inside you . . . ?'

'He's only been here once,' she faltered, knowing that it made matters worse, and holding on to the back of a chair because her legs felt as if they might give way at any minute.

'Just once?' The chair was sent spinning when he lunged at her again. 'Jesus, you didna tak' lang to let him bed you.'

'I didna let him bed me,' she cried. Even although one eye was almost blinded with blood, she had to correct him on this. 'I'd never ha'e let him put me on the bed. I didna ken what he was goin' to dae when he put his arms roon' me first, but we ended up on the rug in front o' the fire . . .'

'That's nae such a sin, is it? An' was it better that way?'

Mysie couldn't help retaliating at the heavy sarcasm. 'Aye was it! He's a better man than you, an' he didna mak' me dae things to him like you did, for he was ready for me afore we lay doon . . . an' I was ready for him!' She clawed at his hands when he grabbed her hair, but he knocked her head against the mantelpiece until she was afraid that her skull would split, and she felt herself sinking towards oblivion. He stopped suddenly. 'I'd castrate that bugger if I could get my hands on him.' His eyes darted to the floor, where the drawer of the table had spilled out its contents, then he whipped round. Mysie's brain told her that she should get away from him as long as his attention was off her, but her whole body seemed to be paralysed.

When she saw him picking up the razor-sharp knife he used for skinning the rabbits he caught in his snares, she was sure that he meant to kill her. 'No, Jeems!' she cried out, but he twisted her arm behind her back and held it there until she sank to her knees, then, toppling her over with his foot, he threw up her skirts and lowered the knife slowly.

'The bloody packman'll nae want you when I've finished wi' you,' he roared.

Only then understanding what he intended to do, she begged, 'No, Jeems. Dinna cut me there, dinna, dinna!' Her desperate struggles hindered him a little, but she was no match for his brute strength, and he stared down at her with crazed eyes, forcing the knife inch by grunting inch between her tightly clenched legs. When the blade finally pierced her skin through her drawers, Mysie did sink into oblivion – her last thought being that she would be glad to die, to get away from this raving lunatic.

Chapter Nine

Wondering why she was lying on the floor instead of on her bed, Mysie tried to sit up, but there was a weight holding her down and the slightest movement was agony. Had she fainted? Had she banged her head as she fell? Oh, God, no! She remembered now – Jeems had been trying to mutilate her and she must have lost consciousness. Jeems? Was he still lurking somewhere, waiting to spring on her as soon as she came to? Turning her head warily from side to side, she could see no sign of him and gave a shuddering moan of relief. He must have gone out to let his temper simmer down.

She thought at first of lying there until she felt able to stand, but realised that she should try to get out before Jeems came back. She could hardly see, she'd been badly beaten up and felt very weak, but after frantically levering with her hands for several minutes, she did succeed in getting into a sitting position. Then she discovered why she had had so much difficulty. Her husband's legs were lying across hers, his trunk at an angle away from her and his head resting on a leaf of the overturned table. He must have fallen and knocked himself out.

Feeling her senses slipping away again, she struggled not to give in. She had to get away from here before Jeems came round. In an effort to get his legs off her, she bent over and gave his backside a push, then drew back in alarm as he rolled over, not realising, at first, that it was her push that had caused the movement. Her fluttering heart almost stopped in the next instant at what was now revealed, and she covered her face in horror. Great God! She hadn't done that, had she?

Slowly, she lowered her hands to make sure that she hadn't been imagining it, but it was true. The knife that he had been using on her was now stuck firmly in his own side, and what must have been a fountain of blood – judging by the amount on his linder – had dried up. She couldn't tear her eyes away, and her panic increased when she remembered that blood only stopped flowing when the heart stopped pumping. He was dead. He hadn't just knocked himself out – he was dead!

At last, as if drawn by some unseen force, her eyes travelled up his body and came to rest on his right hand, still holding his rabbit knife. His rabbit knife? She glanced down again, hopefully, but a knife handle was definitely protruding from his side . . . another knife! Her head swimming and her ears ringing with a deafening noise, she closed her eyes. She was going mad and she wouldn't

81

fight it. Gradually, however, she became aware of ordinary sounds; the ticking of the clock, the movement of the dying embers in the fire, the creaking of the thatch in the wind. Opening her eyes and mustering every last ounce of her strength, she staggered to her feet. She felt something trickling down her legs, but knew that however badly she was cut it would have to wait. She would have to think before she did anything.

Stepping back uncertainly, she stood with her right hand on her heaving chest, desperately trying to organise her confused thoughts. In her hysterical struggles, had Jeems let go of her long enough for her to get that second knife from the table drawer? But the cutlery had scattered over the floor when the table fell and he wouldn't have let her crawl around looking. Even if she had managed to get it, he wouldn't have given her a chance to use it. Oh, God, what had she done? She must have got the knife and thrust it at him, though she had no recollection of it, and surely nobody could do a thing like that and not remember? In any case, she couldn't have plunged it in right up to the hilt like that when she'd been at the point of unconsciousness herself.

But there was no one else it could have been – unless Jake Findlater had come to the house and seen what Jeems was doing to her? But he would have hit Jeems, not stabbed him. Could it have been Doddie Wilson? Had he come to get his own back on Jeems and arrived at the height of the quarrel? In the heat of the moment, he might have snatched up that other knife and . . . no, Doddie wouldn't have come here – would he? Forcing herself, she looked down at the rather pathetic body of her husband. She couldn't leave him lying there, and she wasn't fit to move him by herself, so what was she to do? She couldn't think properly, that was the trouble.

She'd forgotten her own injuries in the horror of the past few minutes, and now the pain struck her with the impact of a sledge hammer. Her nose was throbbing and so swollen that she couldn't see out of one eye, every inch of her was aching, her brain was spinning, her . . . Lifting her skirts, she felt around for the cut. It wasn't as bad as she feared – another fraction of an inch and it would have been a lot worse – but she would feel better if she cleaned herself.

Tearing off a bit of her apron, she dampened it with some hot water and held it to her nose, the heat helping a little, though it would be days before the swelling went down. She treated the rest of her face in the same way and dried it with a towel, then dabbed gently around the area of the cut in her groin and wiped the congealed blood off her leg. Slightly more composed now, she filled the kettle from the pail in the corner of the porch, set it on the fire and lowered herself gingerly on to a chair to wait until it came to the boil.

Twenty minutes later, she poured herself a third cup of tea. Her brain was addled, all she could think of was that Jess had said to come to her if she needed help, and even if it was only advice she gave, it would be something.

It was quite a while before Mysie stood up, keeping her eyes off the figure on the floor when she went to check that Sandy was still asleep.

Her son was lying as he always did, his body curled up, his head hanging over the edge of the bed, so peaceful that she thought for a moment that she had imagined the awful row there had been, but Sandy could sleep through an earthquake. Closing the door, she lifted her shawl from the hook on the front door and placed it round her shoulders. The frost nipped her tender face as soon as she went out, but, holding her head down, she stumbled along the unmade road, praying that the Findlaters would still be up. She had no idea of the time, though it felt like hours since supper, and crofters usually bedded early, for they had to rise betimes in the mornings.

There was no sign of a light when she reached Downies. She banged frantically on the door with both her hands, but it was a few minutes before Jake, in his underclothes, eased it open and held up a candle to see who had roused him from his slumber. 'Mysie! What brings you here at this time o' nicht?'

The deep voice comforted her. 'Oh, Jake, let me in so's I can speak to Jess.'

The agony in her low plea alerted him that something was far wrong, and he shouted behind him, 'Jess, come ben, will you? It's Mysie.' Taking her arm, he led her into the kitchen and touched the candle to the lamp on the table, then turned round and saw her face properly. 'Great God Almighty! Did Jeems dae that to you?' At her nod, he exploded. 'The bugger o' hell! I've a good mind to go an' gi'e Jeems what he deserves.'

Mysie grabbed his sleeve. 'No, Jake, no! He's got mair than he deserved already.'

Jess took charge now. 'Jake, go an' get your claes on, for me an' Mysie's got things to speak aboot.'

Understanding that she wanted him out of the way, Jake went into the other room. Jess guided the distraught woman to a chair, then pulled a stool over to sit beside her. 'Noo, lassie, tell me what happened.'

The gentle, coaxing voice snapping the fragile hold Mysie had been keeping on her emotions and she sobbed out her story. Although Jess's mouth fell open when she heard why Jeems had turned on his wife, she made no judgement and allowed Mysie to babble on. 'When I ken't I was goin' to ha'e a bairn, I was near oot o' my mind, for Jeems hasna . . . for a lang time . . . nae that I minded aboot that for I didna like . . . an' Larry Larry was gentle an' . . . och, I'm makin' excuses, an' there's nae excuse for what I did.'

She was too overcome to continue, but Jess said, 'An' how did Jeems find oot?'

Mysie gulped. 'I tell't him, for I thought he might put me oot, an' Larry's due back the morn, an' he'll tak' me awa'.'

Jess looked at her pityingly. 'Oh, Mysie, he'll likely say it's nae his. His kind tak' their fun, but they dinna provide for the poor lassie that's left to ha'e the bairn.' Waiting until Mysie wiped her eyes with her skirt, she said, 'Tell me, lass, do you love the man?'

'No, no, naething like that. Oh, Jess, I wish I'd jumped doon the quarry after Jamie, an' nane o' this would ha'e happened.'

Thinking it best to ignore this remark, Jess said, 'It's nae surprisin' Jeems lost his temper, Mysie, but he'll get ower it. Did he throw you oot after he struck you?'

'No, I come oot mysel'.'

'Weel, that's a good sign. Noo, you can bide here the nicht, an' I'll tak' you back in the mornin' an' try to mak' him see reason, for I'm . . .'

'No, no!' Mysie screamed. 'I havena tell't you the rest.'

Something clicked in Jess's brain. 'You said he'd got mair than he deserved? What happened? What did you dae?'

Even in her present state, Mysie knew that she'd have to be careful. If she said she was almost sure she hadn't stabbed Jeems, Jess might believe that it had been Doddie, for there was nobody else it could have been. She still wasn't sure in her own mind, but she didn't want anyone else suspecting him. 'Weel,' she began, very cautiously, 'Jeems got me doon on the floor, an' he took his rabbit knife up an' he said he would mak' sure the packman would never want to tak' me again . . . an' he lifted my skirts, an' . . .'

'Oh, my God, Mysie, he didna cut you there?'

'He near did, but when the blade touched me . . . I got some strength . . . I dinna ken . . . but we was strugglin' an' I got the knife oot o' his hand an' . . .' She stopped, appalled at what she was saying, but it sounded better than trying to make out that she had had time to get another knife. The horror on her friend's face made her carry on. 'I thought my last minute had come . . . an' I rammed the knife in him . . . an' he's lying dead on the rug.'

Jess's hand flew to her mouth. 'Oh, God, Mysie, you dinna mean to tell me you've killed him?'

'Aye, it was me that killed him.' The peculiar wording was to come back to Jess later, but she was too shocked to think anything of it at the time. 'Are you sure he's dead?'

'Aye, I'm sure.' Mysie looked at the other woman with deep appeal in her sunken eyes. 'Will you tell me what to dae?'

'Oh, lass, I canna tell you – I've never ken't o' . . .'

'You're the only ane I could ask. You'll ha'e to help me.' Staring at each other hopelessly, they both jumped when Jake came through, rubbing his cold hands together. 'Ha'e you got things sorted oot? I'm near frozen ben there.'

Jess sighed noisily as she looked up at him. 'Aye, Mysie's tell't me the whole story, an' I think we'd better ha'e a wee drap o' whisky. Me an' Mysie need it, an' you'll need it as weel, when you ken what's happened.' While they fortified themselves, Jess gave an account of what she'd been told – it sounded worse when somebody else said it, Mysie thought – and by the time his wife finished, Jake was looking as thunderstruck as she had done earlier. He turned it over in his mind for a little while, then shook his head. 'I aye ken't Jeems Duncan was a coorse bugger.'

Mysie, however, wouldn't let him slander the dead man. 'He'd good reason the nicht.'

'He'd nae reason to hit you like that, nor try to carve you up like a side o' beef.' Running his finger idly round the rim of his cup, Jake glowered into the fire, obviously trying to think of a way to deal with the situation, and the two women watched him anxiously. At last, he said, 'We'd best come hame wi' you, Mysie, an' shift Jeems oot o' the kitchen afore Sandy gets up an' sees him.'

'Aye.' She drew her shawl closer round her shoulders.

'You'll need to wait till I get on some claes,' Jess pointed out. 'I'll catch my death o' cauld in my goon.'

Holding on to the back of the chair she'd been sitting on, Mysie wondered, irrationally, if dying from the cold would be as bad as dying from the thrust of a knife and let out a high hysterical laugh. Jake grasped her shoulder firmly. 'You've had a helluva time, lass, but we'll dae what we can for you.'

When Jess was dressed, she and Jake led Mysie out, sweeping her along the road so quickly that she thought her lungs would burst and she had to fight for breath. When they approached her house, she felt herself shrinking back. 'I canna go in,' she panted. 'I'm ower feared.'

'If he's dead,' Jake said, 'he canna hurt you nae mair.' With these not altogether comforting words, he strode on ahead, and, Jess dragging her, Mysie tottered into her own kitchen a few seconds later. She had been half hoping, half fearing, that she had been wrong, that Jeems had got up after she went out, but he was still sprawled out on the hearthrug.

'He's dead, right enough.' Jake rose from his examination of the body and rubbed his chin, his fingers rasping against the dark stubble. 'We'll ha'e to bury him, Mysie. If onybody finds oot what you did, they'll tell the bobbies an' you'll be hung for murder. I'll ha'e a look roon' ootside for the best place.'

'Aye,' she agreed, her teeth chattering, her body shaking like a leaf in a gale.

Jess made Mysie sit down. 'Jake'll sort things oot. Dinna worry yoursel', lass.'

It wasn't long before Jake appeared again. 'I just minded. We canna put him in ony o' the parks, for he could be turned up wi' the ploo.'

'He finished the plooin' the day himsel'.'

'Somebody else'll ha'e to dae it again in the spring, though.'

It was only just into January, Mysie thought, and spring was a long way off, but Jake was right. Burying Jeems in one of the fields would only put off the day of discovery.

'I'd a look in the byre, though, an' it come to me – if we put him under the coo's stall, he'd never be found.'

The little spark of hope rising in Mysie was dashed away by her next thought. 'But when folk dinna see him goin' aboot, they'll wonder where he is. What'll I say?'

'We'll think o' something,' Jess soothed.

'I'll need a hand,' Jake observed, 'for the coo's tramped it doon solid. But there's some lime left in a bag – we could sprinkle it ower him to stop the stink and burn him awa'.'

They got spades and a shovel from an outhouse and laboured for the next three hours, Brownie's soft eyes regarding them curiously from the other side of the byre where they'd moved her, and her feet shifting about in agitation. When he judged that the hole was deep enough, Jake threw down his shovel and straightened up, rubbing his aching back wearily. 'We'd best tak' him oot, noo.'

In the kitchen, he lifted the dead man's shoulders while the two women each took one of his legs. They hadn't expected the body to be so heavy, but they staggered out with their burden until Jake set his end down and Mysie and Jess thankfully lowered theirs. 'We can trail him the rest,' he puffed. 'The bairn'll nae hear us oot here.' They laid the body at the side of the grave, and Jake mopped his perspiring brow with his sleeve. 'You could tell folk he just left you, Mysie – they'd believe that, he was a queer de'il – but we'll need to bury a' his things wi' him. Jess, you go an' help her, an' I'll get the lime ready.'

Mysie took a reluctant look at her dead husband, shuddering as she saw that his linder and drawers, clean on when he rose, were soiled from being hauled over the ground, but the darker stain, deep brown now, told its own sordid story, the truth of which was still unexplained to her.

'Come on, lass.' Jess urged her towards the house again.

When all Jeems's belongings – his spare set of underwear, his working clothes and Sunday suit, his razor and strop, socks, collars and collar studs – were in the grave, Jake flung a shovelful of lime over them before he toppled in the body and did the same to that. 'We'll ha'e to cover him up noo.'

Mysie turned her head away after her first scoop of earth went in, but the hole was filled in much quicker than it had been dug out, and Jake trod it well down with his boots. When Jess replaced the straw to cover their handi-work, the cow was timid about returning to her stall, but a few gentle pushes from behind were enough to reassure her. When they went inside, the Findlaters eliminated all signs of the earlier struggle, Mysie watching like a detached outsider. Jake set the table and chair on their legs again, put all the cutlery back in the drawer, then picked all the shards of the glass lampshade from the hearthrug before Jess went down on her knees to scrub out the bloodstains.

The kitchen restored to its normal, spotless state, they sat down to have a cup of tea, only then fully comprehend-ing the enormity of what they'd done. Each avoided the others' eyes, ashamed of the part he or she had played.

Jake cleared his throat noisily. 'It was the only thing we could dae, Mysie, though I'm sure naebody could blame you for killin' him after what he was tryin' to dae to you.'

'They'd blame me for what I did wi' the packman, though.'

'But they'll think it's Jeems's bairn you're carryin',' Jess pointed out, 'an' naebody'll ever ken different.' Looking at the clock, she stood up. 'It'll nae be lang till risin' time, we'll need to get hame. If Sandy sees us, he'd wonder what we was daein' here, but I dinna like leavin' you like this, Mysie.'

'I'm a' right. Awa' you go, an' . . . thank you for a'thing.'

On their way out, Jess paused. 'I'll be back afore that bugger o' a packman comes, for I'm feared you let a'thing oot to him, an' it'll gi'e me the chance to tell him to bide awa' fae you.'

After they had left Mysie didn't move. What was the use of going to bed? She wouldn't sleep anyway. She didn't think she would ever be able to sleep again. Every time she closed her eyes, she would see Jeems lying on the floor with the knife in him, and she would never forget her last glimpse of him as she had flung the earth over him, his face almost hidden by the leg of his Sunday trousers. A cold hand clutched at her heart. When Jake flung the body in, the trousers must have whipped round the head. Had it not been limed, after all? Had Jake been in too great a hurry to make sure? Had there not been enough lime in the bag?

At first, Mysie paid no attention to the deep ache which had started in the pit of her stomach, thinking it was still the effect of the body-blows Jeems had given her, but, as it grew worse, it dawned on her that she was miscarrying. Her womb was ejecting the packman's child, and all the pain and mental anguish she had suffered that night had been unnecessary.

Chapter Ten

The crowing of the old cockerel in the back yard made Mysie start up in bewilderment, then the awful memories crowded in, like a nightmare returning to haunt her. But it was over now. It was all behind her. There was nothing more to worry about.

Standing up, she felt the unaccustomed bulk between her legs and bent down to remove the blood-saturated sheeting she had packed there when she aborted. She gripped it together, not looking at it, and flung it into the heart of the fire. Then she took the tin bath out of the porch, filled it with water from the kettles sitting by the fire, stripped off her clothes and stepped in. She scrubbed until she felt cleansed of shame, both inside and out, and had just dressed herself when Sandy came through from the other room.

'Get yoursel' washed,' she ordered, 'for you'll ha'e to get a pail o' water fae the well for me afore you go to school.' His puzzled eyes resting on her face made her wonder how bad her injuries were, so she went over to the looking-glass at the back of the dresser. The skin around both eyes was badly discoloured, dark bruises were beginning to creep down her cheeks, and her nose was twice its normal size. Turning to the gaping boy, she tried to excuse her appearance. 'I slipped on the ice last nicht when I went oot to the wee hoosie an' I fell against the midden wa'. Noo, get on and dae what I tell't you.'

When he came through again, she said, softly, 'You'll get your breakfast when you come back, an' dinna fill the pail ower fu', or you'll nae be able to lift it.' When he had run off, Mysie went outside to mash some turnips for Brownie before she milked her. Her heart hammered when she neared the byre, and she half expected to see Jeems looming up at her out of the darkness when she opened the door, but only the cow moved, turning her head placidly as she munched her hay. Sitting down on the milking-stool, Mysie felt her eyes drawn inexorably past the bulging udder to the straw-strewn floor below. Astonishingly, it looked the same as usual. Nothing showed of the terrible secret it now concealed.

It seemed only a few minutes before her son returned. 'Are you back already?' she asked, in some surprise.

His face suffused with pride. 'I run there an' back. I could milk Broonie for you, Mam, if you show me what to dae.'

She gave a few sharp tugs on the teats to demonstrate. 'It's easy when you ken. Come on, then, loon, ha'e a try.'

They changed places, but the strange fingers made the beast moo in protest, and Sandy jumped back, squealing in disgust. 'Ach, Mam, her sharny tail near went in my mooth.'

'Keep it shut, then.' A ghost of a smile crossed her face.

The first few jets of milk landed on the floor and on the boy's trousers, but he was soon aiming expertly at the pail. Watching him, it crossed Mysie's mind that it was lucky he was old enough to help her, though he was only seven; some wives had to run their crofts single-handed if they were left without a man. With a sickening lurch in her stomach, she remembered that she still had to explain his father's absence to Sandy, but she would leave it for now. 'Watch an' nae mak' yoursel' late for the school,' she warned as she left the byre. Inside she poured boiling water over some oatmeal – she had been in such a state last night that she'd forgotten to soak any for porridge – and when he came in, she waited until he supped the brose then said, very quietly, 'Your father'll nae be in, for he's went awa' an' left us, but dinna tell naebody.' Sandy was obviously surprised, but after a moment's thought, he said, 'Me an' you'll manage oorsel's twa, Mam, will we nae?'

'Aye, we'll manage fine.'

The boy had just left for school when Mysie heard a knock at the door and opened it without thinking. 'Good mornin' to you, lass, I hope I'm nae ower early for you? Will you be needin' onything oot o' my pack the day?' Her shock at seeing a strange face made her grab the jamb of the door, and the man stepped forward anxiously. 'Are you a' right, lass?' Helping her inside, he made her sit down.

'I'm sorry,' she muttered, 'I dinna ken what come ower me.'

'You maybe jumped up ower quick to answer the door, but sit there till you feel better, an' I'll open my pack, though you're maybe nae needin' onything the day?'

Mysie's thoughts were so confused that she couldn't answer. Jess had said she'd be there before Larry Larry came, but she hadn't appeared yet and it wasn't him anyway.

'You'd had a different man roon' the last time?' The man had taken her silence to mean she didn't want to buy, and laid his pack unopened on the floor. 'He was an awfu' lad, yon. He tell't me he was a trawlerman, but he'd missed his boat aboot four month afore through him bein' drunk. Weel, he said he'd been drunk, though it wouldna surprise me if he'd been bedded up wi' ane o' yon weemen that hang aboot the Aberdeen harbour. God, I've got my een open since I took ower fae him. Near ilka young wife I've

92

been seein' tells me he'd tried to . . .' Mysie's gasp made him glance round at her – he had purposely avoided letting his eyes rest on her bruised face before. 'Oh, lassie,' he said, sorrowfully, 'I hope you didna let him.'

Keeping a tight grip on herself, Mysie said, hastily, 'No, no.'

'I'm pleased to hear it, but you're nae looking very weel.'

She stood up shakily. 'I'll mak' some tea.'

'I'd best introduce mysel',' he said, as she filled the teapot. 'The name's Peter Lamont, an' I'm fifty-nine year auld. My wife died eight month ago, an' I lost interest in things for a good while. I gi'ed up my job – I was a linesman on the railway – but I went doon to the harbour one day to . . .' He paused and shrugged. 'Weel, I suppose I was goin' to throw mysel' in, I was that low, but this English lad come up an' said he was wantin' to sign on a boat, an' he wanted me to tak' his pack. You see, when he was oot o' a job, he'd met this auld packman that said he was gi'ein' it up, and the lad had agreed to tak' ower his round, seein' he'd naething else to dae. But he tell't me he missed the sea something terrible, and near forced his pack on me so's he could get awa'.'

'How do you like bein' a packman?' Mysie asked, faint with relief that she would never have to face Larry Larry again.

'I feel as free as the birds in the air when I'm oot on the open road. I'm happier than I've been for a lang time.'

When he had drunk the tea, he stood up. 'Dinna worry aboot nae buying onything,' he said, kindly. 'I can see you're nae yoursel', an' I'll be back in three month again.'

Stunned by what he had told her, Mysie sat on until, about fifteen minutes later, the door was flung open. 'It wasna the same packman,' Jess burst out, 'an' he was a lot earlier than Jockie or the other ane. I hope you didna say onything. Losh, Mysie, you look worse than you did last nicht.'

'I'm feelin' better, though, for *he's* awa' on a boat, so

he'll never be back – an' the bairn come awa' after you went hame.'

'Thank God! You'll nae need to worry nae mair aboot that.'

'But if it had come awa' quicker, I wouldna ha'e had to tell Jeems aboot it, an' . . . och, you ken what I mean.'

'It was likely the shock o' a'thing that did it, Mysie.'

'Aye, I never thought on that. I was in a awfu' state.'

'Weel, as my mother used to say, "Ilka cloud's got a silver linin' ", an' you'll nae ha'e a ill-begotten bairn to remind you. Did Sandy say onything when he saw your face this mornin'?'

'I tell't him I fell last nicht, an' he was awfu' good. He went for the water, an' milked the coo for me.'

'Did he nae ask where Jeems was?'

'I tell't him his father had went awa' an' left us, an' he just said the twa o' us would manage fine oorsel's.'

'He maybe heard you fightin' and he'll be thinkin' that's the reason Jeems went awa'.'

'No, he hadna heard naething, for he was sleepin' sound when I looked ben at him afore I come to you.'

'Och, weel, you'd best leave it like that. I'll never tell a soul, an' Jake'll keep his mooth shut, as weel. Try to forget aboot it, for what's by is by.' In an effort to help Mysie to put it out of her mind, Jess chattered about whatever came into her head until she went home to make Jake's dinner .

On Thursday morning, Mysie discovered that she had run out of tea and paraffin and braced herself to go to the shop. Dougal averted his eyes as he served her, but when Rosie came through, she burst out, 'God preserve us, Mysie. Your face is a awfu' mess an' you've twa right blue keekers. Did Jeems dae that?'

'Aye, but he'll nae dae it again.' It was out before Mysie thought, but she covered her slip with an ease that would not have shamed a practised liar. 'He's left me.' It didn't occur to her that, by early afternoon, wild speculations would be going on in the village about which man had been at the back of it, and by evening, even veiled suggestions that something sinister had taken place at Rowan-brae.

As Dougal observed to his wife when they went to bed, 'Jeems Duncan wouldna walk oot an' leave his croft like that. It's been in his family for generations, an' he used to say his sons would get it after him.'

'But Jamie's nae here noo,' Rosie pointed out.

'I ken that!' Dougal was still annoyed with his wife for telling the customers what Mysie had said. 'But Sandy is, an' he's nae auld enough yet to tak' it ower. No, there's mair to this than Mysie's lettin' on.'

'There was aye something queer aboot Jeems, though.'

A similar conversation was taking place in the mill. 'I can believe Jeems punched Mysie,' Andra said, thought-fully. 'I've thought afore that she'd bruises on her, but for him to walk oot on her . . . weel, that's harder to believe.'

'Mysie would never tell lees.' Pattie didn't really know what to think, but she didn't doubt that Mysie had told the truth, or the truth as she saw it. 'Maybe Jeems went aff his head – he's never been the same since poor Jamie was lost, an' his father was dottled afore he died.'

'Auld Duncan was dottled wi' age, that's a different thing, an' Rowanbrae was Jeems's whole life. No, I canna understand it. There's something damned fishy aboot the whole business.'

Jess Findlater was bombarded with questions when she went to the shop the following morning, but parried them by saying that Mysie was well rid of Jeems and it was nobody's business but theirs what had happened between them.

Jean Petrie tried to shed some light on the matter. 'They'd fought aboot Doddie Wilson, likely. He could ha'e been goin' to Rowanbrae on the sly, for a' we ken, an' Jeems found oot.'

The murmurs of agreement incensed Jess. 'Doddie has never been near Rowanbrae. I ken that for a fact.'

Bridling, Mrs Petrie sneered, 'Oh, aye, so she tells you,

but she could easy ha'e been meetin' him some place else. She's a deep ane, Mysie Duncan.'

Jess could take no more. 'You're nae deep, ony road, Jean Petrie, for you blab oot whatever comes into your empty head, an' you've a mind like a shitehoose.' She stamped out, leaving Mrs Petrie gaping after her and the other people in the shop trying to hide their amusement that she had been bested.

Jess's anger wore off as she strode home, sparks flying from the metal sprigs in the heels of her boots. She was halfway home when Mysie's words came back to her, 'Aye, it was me that killed him.' It was queer her saying that when she had already admitted it. Was it somebody else's hand that had wielded the knife? Had she and Doddie been meeting on the sly, like Jean Petrie was trying to make out? Could it have been his bairn she'd been carrying, and had she blamed the young packman to save any suspicion falling on Doddie? Surely she wasn't as daft about him that she would confess to murder to shield him? But Doddie would never have let her take the blame for him, and the packman had sailed away ages ago, so it couldn't have been him, either.

For the very first time since Jamie's death, Jess went past Rowanbrae without going in. She had to get things figured out before she could face Mysie again. If it wasn't Doddie, nor the English lad, there must have been another man in Mysie's life, though there had never been any word of it – not even from Jean Petrie, who was generally first to uncover anything like that – and sooner or later, unlawful couplings were always found out, no matter how carefully they were conducted. But maybe Jeems *had* found out. Maybe that was why he was lying stone cold under the floor of his own byre? Well, whoever the man was, he would come back to Mysie, easy in his mind now that he'd sent her man to kingdom come, and with the coast clear, he'd likely move in with her come time. Then, Jess thought, with satisfaction, she would know exactly who had committed the foul deed, for she was positive it hadn't been poor Mysie.

Over the next few days, Mysie refused offers of help from Rab Duff, Andra White, even from Jake Findlater, considering that they had enough to do on their own places. She was taken aback when Doddie Wilson turned up one night, but told him, as she had told the others, that she was managing fine. 'Sandy's a big help, an' it lets me dae the things . . . Jeems did.'

Doddie regarded her sympathetically. 'But there's jobs you'll nae be able to tackle. There's surely something I can dae?'

Mysie could see that he was disappointed by her refusal, and, being a farm servant, he didn't have a croft or a mill to run. What would be the harm in letting him do a few jobs? 'Weel,' she murmured, 'the palin' at the far side blew doon last week, an' I'd be obliged if you'd fix it for me.'

His smile made her blood turn to water, and, as she closed the door, she longed for the comfort of his arms around her, but she had forfeited all hope of that by her wickedness.

When she told Jess that she'd accepted Doddie's help, Mysie thought that her friend seemed a bit put out, and added, 'But I never let him inside the hoose, so naebody can say naething.'

'No, naebody can say naething,' Jess agreed, but she still didn't look any happier about it.

From the peculiar looks she received at times, Mysie knew that there were still doubts in some minds about Jeems leaving his croft so suddenly, but as time went on, she felt easier in her mind. No one could prove that he hadn't just walked out as she had said. Doddie came twice a week now to carry out whatever task she set him, and it was good to see him, even for the few minutes he stood at the door, although she knew that nothing could ever come of it.

'You look different, Mam,' Sandy observed, one morning.

'What kind o' different, my loon?'

'I dinna ken, just different. Happy, like.'

'I am happy. We're gettin' on fine, wi' Doddie helpin'.' His eyes clouded as he went to walk the two miles to school, and Mysie felt deeply sorry for him for a moment. He was likely missing Jeems and couldn't understand why she was so cheerful.

When Doddie knocked at the door that evening to say that he was going to repair the thatch, she exclaimed, involuntarily, 'You canna work on the roof in this weather, it's ower cauld, but come in for a cup o' tea.' She hadn't meant to ask him in, but it was done now and she could hardly say she had changed her mind. He seemed reluctant, so she coaxed, 'It'll nae tak' a minute to mask.'

Pulling off his flat cap as he went through the door, he sat down on the edge of a chair and watched her filling the teapot. 'I canna understand Jeems leavin' you,' he said, after a while. 'I ken I've nae right to ask, but did you an' him ha'e a fight?'

'Aye.' Her happiness was turning to unease now.

'I'm sorry, it's nane o' my business.' Doddie sat back in his seat. 'This is the kind o' place I aye fancied, but I'm nae bad at Waterton, I suppose. Robertson's a good enough man to work for.' He hesitated briefly. 'I'll dae the plooin' for you, if you like. It's nae trouble, an' I could plant your seed tatties an' sow your grain as weel.'

He fell silent as she passed over his cup, and she wondered if he felt uncomfortable in the house. At the meal and ale – it seemed so long ago now – it hadn't bothered him that she was married, but it was different here. If only she could tell him that Jeems would never be back . . . but it was safer not to, for she couldn't tell him why. But maybe he knew? Maybe his had been the hand that struck Jeems down?

Mysie had tried to push that traumatic night from her mind, but the suspicion was still there. If she hadn't done it – and she was practically certain that she hadn't – it must have been Doddie, and he would be wondering where the body was. If she told him, he would be pleased that it was safely hidden, but it might be better to let sleeping dogs lie.

When Jess walked in a little later and saw Doddie, her smile vanished. 'I'm sorry, Mysie, I didna ken you'd ony-body here.'

His weatherbeaten face a deep crimson, Doddie mumbled, 'I come to gi'e her a help, an' she asked me in . . .'

'He was to be mendin' the thatch,' Mysie explained, hastily, feeling guilty for no reason, 'but it was ower cauld, so I took him in for a cup o' tea.'

Rather stiffly, Jess said, 'I thought you'd be glad o' some company, but I can see you'll nae be needin' me the nicht.'

Her expression was innocent enough, but a shiver of fear ran through Mysie. Jess surely didn't think that she'd asked him to sleep with her – that had never crossed her mind. She was greatly relieved, therefore, when Doddie drained his cup and stood up. 'I was just leavin', Jess, so you can bide.'

'No, I'd best get back. I'll walk alang the road wi' you, though, if you've nae objections?'

He smiled. 'Nane at a'. I'll be back on Friday, Mysie.'

Pouring herself another cup of tea, Mysie wondered why Jess wanted to get Doddie on his own. Was she going to tell him about the packman? Or, worse still, what they had done with Jeems? If Doddie hadn't killed him, he would think *she* had, and he would never come back. Frantically turning it over in her mind, she decided that it must be a guilty conscience that was making her so nervous. Jess had sworn solemnly never to tell a soul, and she wouldn't break her promise, for she was a good woman – the very best.

The good woman was struggling with her own conscience. She had said that she would never mention that terrible night to anybody, but she had a duty to Mysie. If Doddie had killed Jeems, he was a poor man to leave the lassie to dispose of the body and take the blame. He should realise that working a bit on her croft was scant recompense for the ordeal he had made her suffer. If only she could be certain, Jess thought. Doddie might be quite innocent, just trying to help, as he had said, so it would be best to wait for further developments before she tackled him. But she could put out a feeler. 'Mysie was in a awfu' state the nicht Jeems . . . walked oot,' she began, studying his face for any sign of guilt.

'Aye, she must ha'e been, poor lass.' There was nothing in his expression except sympathy, but she persevered. 'She come runnin' to Downies, an' me an' Jake had to quieten her doon, an' tak' her hame.'

'She's lucky she had you. You ken, Jess, I think a lot o' Mysie, but she's still Jeems's wife. If he'd died, instead o' just walkin' oot, I'd ha'e been free to court her an' . . .' He drew in his breath sharply. 'Ach, I dinna ken what you must think o' me, Jess.'

She couldn't make up her mind what she thought. He could be telling the truth, but he was the only man Mysie had allowed to help her, and how often had he been in the house? 'I dinna think Jeems'll ever come back, Doddie,' she said, slowly.

'If he doesna, Mysie'll ha'e to work that croft on her ain for the rest o' her days, an' . . .'

'Sandy's aye growin' aulder, though, an' once he leaves the school, it'll be easier for her. He'll be able to dae a' the heavy jobs.'

'I suppose so, but . . . oh, Jess, I might as well tell you. I love Mysie wi' a' my he'rt, an' I'll never be able to wed her, nae wi' things the way they are.'

Had she misjudged the man? Was he as straightforward as he sounded? She'd heard of men who could swear the moon was blue and have everybody believing it, but she couldn't help feeling that Doddie wasn't one of them. 'It's a nasty business,' she agreed. 'I can see you're in a bad position, but you'll just ha'e to put up wi' it. You'd baith be the speak o' the place if you went to bide at Rowanbrae.'

'I ken that. Maybe I should look for another fee, though it would br'ak my he'rt to leave her.'

Jess, having made up her mind about his honesty, wished that she could let him know that Jeems *was* dead, but it might shock him to know that Mysie had claimed to be responsible.

When they reached Downies, Doddie grasped her hand. 'Thank you for listenin' to me, Jess. I ken you'll nae tell onybody what I've been sayin'.'

Compassion for him welled up inside her. 'Would you like to come in an' ha'e a word wi' Jake? He'd be glad o' a man body to speak to for a change.'

'I'll nae come in, if you dinna mind. I've said mair than I should already, an' I'm nae feelin' very sociable.'

Jake looked up when his wife went inside. 'You didna bide wi' Mysie very lang.'

'Doddie Wilson was there.'

'Weel, he's a fine lad, Doddie, an' I'm sure he thinks a lot o' her. He'll be good for her.'

'He would that, but he wouldna bide, an' I wanted to get him on his ain. I've aye wondered if it was him that killed Jeems, for I never thought it was . . .'

'Oh, no, Jess, nae Doddie. He's a decent man.'

'I'm sure o' that mysel' noo, just as I'm sure it must ha'e been some other man that did it.'

'Did you nae believe what Mysie tell't you?'

'Did you?'

Jake considered for a moment. 'Weel, aye, I did. She was feared Jeems was goin' to cut her, kill her, an' she tried to stop him, an' it could ha'e happened like she said.'

'It could, though I'm near sure it didna. But the terrible thing is, Jake, Doddie loves her an' he'll dae naething aboot it, for he thinks Jeems might come back.'

'A lot o' folk still think that.'

'I was that sorry for him, I near tell't him Jeems was dead, but I managed to haud my tongue.'

'That's something new.' Jake gave a short, snorting laugh, then said, gently, 'Leave it alane, Jess, there's nae sense in meddlin'. Let things tak' their ain road, that's the best way.'

Chapter Eleven

'They say Doddie Wilson's workin' a lot at Rowanbrae at nichts.' Jean Petrie looked very pleased that she'd been right.

Jess shrugged. 'She needs a man aboot the place.'

'We a' need a man aboot the place, but we're decent weemen an' stick to the man we're wed on.'

'Mysie's a decent wumman, a better wumman than you, wi' your nasty mind. It's near six month since she . . .' Jess caught her runaway tongue and went on lamely, '. . . six month since Jeems walked oot on her, an' he'll nae be back . . . noo.'

Like lightning, the sneer on the woman's face changed to a fawning smile. 'I'll let you go in front o' me, Jess.'

Dougal Mennie sighed. Mrs Petrie was the bane of his life, and he had thought she would be leaving his premises in a few minutes, but he put on a smile for Jess. 'What can I dae for you the day, then, Mistress Findlater?'

Jess made her purchases and left, but as soon as she went out, Jean Petrie leaned over the counter to Rosie. 'What did you mak' o' that?'

'Mak' o' what?' Mrs Mennie was as mystified as the other two customers, who were listening eagerly.

'Jess said it was six month since Mysie did something. She stopped hersel' and said it was six month since Jeems walked oot, but I'm near sure she was goin' to say something else.'

The shopkeeper's wife raised her eyebrows. 'Like what?'

'Like Mysie had *put* him oot, maybe. Would it have been Jeems that had been takin' up wi' another wumman?'

Rosie shook her head. 'A'body ken't aboot Jeems an' Nessie White an' I dinna think Mysie cared.'

Tutting impatiently, Jean said, 'I didna mean Nessie – I meant a right wumman.'

'Nessie's never been particular what man she lies doon wi', but nae other wumman would look at Jeems Duncan.'

'Mysie did.'

'Aye, but my cousin in Turra tell't me he'd made a bargain wi' her father, an' she'd nae say in it.'

'Oh, d'you tell me that?' This was obviously news to Jean, who chewed it over for a few moments before going on. 'Jeems must ha'e been takin' up wi' somebody, for if he'd found oot that Mysie was seein' Doddie, he wouldna ha'e went awa' an' left them free to carry on like they're daein'.'

Rosie nodded. 'He'd mair likely ha'e punched her . . . oh! Her face was black an' blue that day she tell't me Jeems had left her, an' she said he'd hit her.'

Jean's eyes narrowed speculatively. 'You see? He'd found oot aboot her an' Doddie, an' he'd punched her an' walked oot.'

Dougal jumped in at her slight pause. 'It's nae oor business what Jeems did, or what Mysie an' Doddie are daein'. Will you be needin' onything else, Mistress Petrie?'

'No, that's the lot.' Somewhat abstractedly, she paid him and left the shop.

Looking across the fireside at Doddie, Mysie wondered why he always shied off saying anything personal. For weeks now, she had given him a cup of tea after he had done the work he came to do, and he always thanked her, but he had never once paid her a compliment. He was friendly, like he would be with any woman he knew, but that was all. Sometimes, when they were saying goodnight at the door, she thought that he was on the point of kissing her, but he always sighed and walked off.

Tonight, however, it seemed that he was trying to make up his mind to say something, and she wished that he would come out with it, whatever it was. She hoped he wasn't going to tell her that he'd taken another fee and would be going away, but if he did, she could do nothing about it. She had no claim on him, he was free to go wherever he wanted, and it might be as well if he did leave Burnlea, for Jeems, even though he was dead, would always be between them.

'Mysie.' Doddie had obviously made his decision.

'Aye?' Her spirits lifted at the softness of his voice.

'It's a damn shame you bein' here on your ain, an' me . . .'

'I've got Sandy.' She didn't want him to feel sorry for her, but her heart was fluttering at the thought of what he might be intending to say.

'Aye, you've got Sandy.' He fell silent again.

Angry at herself for interrupting him, she waited for him to continue, but he said no more and stood up in a few minutes. 'It's time I was gettin' back to Waterton.'

She could hardly hide her disappointment. 'Aye.'

After seeing him out, she sat down and leaned back in her chair. If he had meant to ask if he could move in with her, she had spoiled it, and being the kind of man he was, he would never ask again. Not that she would agree if he did, for there were too many people waiting for him to do just that, waiting to point a finger at her for committing adultery, and she could never tell them that they were wrong.

She didn't hear the door opening quietly, and jumped to her feet when he said her name. What he saw in her eyes made him go straight across to her. 'I couldna go awa' withoot tellin' you what I come to say . . . I love you, Mysie. I ken we can never be wed, but would you let me come an' bide at Rowanbrae?'

'It would set a lot o' tongues waggin'.'

'A' the tongues in the place can wag till they fa' oot, as lang as I ken you love me.'

'I love you, Doddie, an' I'd be happy for you to bide here.'

'I'll ha'e to go back the nicht, for they're expectin' me, but I'll tell Robertson in the mornin' that he'll need to look

104

for another cattleman, though I'll likely need to work for him till the end o' the term.'

When he had left, Mysie undressed and went to bed, her spirits soaring, until she began to think. How could she find out if Doddie knew that Jeems was dead? If she were to tell him that she had stabbed her husband, he might ask why, and she could never tell him about the young packman. Hopefully, though, he might admit that it was he who had done the killing, but if he didn't, she would never know for sure. It was best to leave things the way they were. They would be happy together – as good as married – and he wasn't the kind of man to let gossip worry him. He loved her as much as she loved him, and nothing could happen to spoil that.

Jess could see that all the wives were anxious to know, but, as usual, Jean Petrie was spokeswoman. 'Doddie tell't Robertson he'd be leavin', an' he's nae sleepin' in the bothy, an' he took his claes awa', so . . .' she looked round triumphantly at the other customers, 'so he must be bidin' at Rowanbrae.'

'What's wrang wi' that?' Jess demanded angrily.

Jean made a face. 'What's wrang wi' that, she says? An' Mysie still wed on Jeems Duncan?'

Having almost forgotten that this was what most people would still believe, Jess racked her brains for a way to justify the situation. 'Jeems walked oot on her, dinna forget, so he canna expect her to . . .'

'Thou shalt not commit adultery,' quoted Mrs Petrie, shaking her head reprovingly. 'An' if Mysie's nae committin' adultery, I'm a Dutchman.'

'You're nae a Dutchman,' Jess burst out, 'you're a narra'-minded hypocrite. You're just jealous, the lot o' you, for nane o' you would turn Doddie Wilson awa' if he come knockin' on your door.' As she moved away, she added, 'Nae mair would I.'

Calling in at Rowanbrae, she told Mysie what she had said in her anger, and when Mysie passed it on to Doddie that evening, he burst out laughing. 'Weel, I'll ken to go to Downies for comfort if you ever tire o' me, lass.'

Mysie didn't feel like laughing. 'Oh, Doddie, I'll never tire o' you, but does it nae worry you, folk sayin' that?'

'De'il the bit.'

Her own conscience was clear as far as this was concerned, for how could she be committing adultery when her husband was dead and buried? But no one else, except Jess and Jake, and perhaps Doddie himself, was aware of that.

The outbreak of war against Germany took all Burnlea minds off the scandal at Rowanbrae for a short time, even Jean Petrie's vituperous outpourings being directed solely at the Kaiser. Mysie was happier than she'd been in her whole life, though she sometimes felt guilty that it was because of a war that she was being left to live in peace, and it was Sandy who shook her out of her euphoria one morning. 'Doddie's nae goin' to be bidin' here a' the time, is he, Mam?'

'Aye is he, my loon.' The dimming of the bright eyes in the innocent young face made her say, sharply, 'He's a fine, decent man, Sandy, an' I wouldna manage withoot him.'

'But I dinna want him here.' He regarded her mournfully. 'We was a lot better when we was just oor ain twa sel's.'

'I thought you liked him.'

'I liked him weel enough afore he come to bide, but . . .'

'You're nae used to him yet, an' you'll feel better aboot him once you get to ken him right.'

The unhappy expression on his face as he trailed out warned his mother that there would be trouble once Doddie took over the running of the croft full time, but she couldn't understand what Sandy had against him. It wasn't as if the boy had loved his father – Jeems had been hard on him though he had thought a lot of him – but things would surely work out come time.

*

Mysie was sorry for Doddie, who was trying hard to make Sandy like him. He had shown the boy how to do various jobs about the croft, telling him why they had to be done and praising him if he did them well, but the boy remained dour. Even when Doddie helped him with his home lessons, patiently going over again and again anything he couldn't understand at first, her son was uncommunicative. She was certain that he had learned more in the past two months than he had done in the whole of his time with Mr Meldrum, but his manner towards her lover was still as distant as ever.

That night, as usual, Doddie proved his love to her in bed, but when, also as usual, he pulled out of her abruptly, she murmured, 'I wish you would let me gi'e you a son o' your ain.'

A few seconds elapsed before he answered. 'I canna let you dae that, Mysie, an' if you think aboot it, you'll see I'm right. He would be a bastard, an' you wouldna want him to go through life wi' that hangin' ower him.'

'But he wouldna . .' She stopped, appalled at how closely she had come to telling him that Jeems was dead. What Doddie said was true, in any case. She wasn't married to him by law, could never marry him with people believing Jeems was still alive, so any child they had *would* be a bastard.

Doddie stroked her hair. 'I feel as tied to you as though I'd put that ring on your finger mysel', an' I consider we're wed in the eyes o' God, but other folk wouldna . . . I would gi'e onything for you to ha'e my son, lass, but it would likely set Sandy mair against me.'

The following morning, when Doddie carried in the two pails of water – he hadn't let Mysie do it since he came – he said, 'Pattie White was sayin' Andra an' Rab's goin' in to the toon the morn, an' I said I'd go wi' them. I'll be plantin' next week, an' I'll ha'e to get grain an' a puckle mair seed tatties.'

'See an' nae come hame fu', then.' Mysie could have kicked herself for saying it. No doubt he had heard that

Jeems had always come home drunk from Aberdeen, and she hated reminding the man she loved about the husband he probably thought was still alive. Doddie, however, was supping his porridge with the same zest as usual.

When Sandy came through on his way to school, he held his head down. 'I'm awa' noo, Mam.'

Doddie looked pensive when he'd gone. 'He never says a word to me, but I suppose he thinks it's Jeems should be here, nae me. It's only natural, for he must miss his father.'

Mysie was vaguely uneasy, but she told herself she was being stupid. Doddie was only trying to find an explanation for Sandy's behaviour, nothing else, though he must wonder sometimes about the suddenness of her husband's departure.

That night, Sandy's rejection of him made Doddie show his hurt for the first time. Laying down the school book he was holding, he stood up. 'There's nae much point in me tryin' ony mair, is there? You've made up your mind you dinna like me, an' I admire you for stickin' to your guns, but I wish you'd understand I'm nae trying to tak' your father's place. He left you an' your mother, an' I'm here because I wanted to help an' because I love you an' her baith. She loves me, but if you canna bring yoursel' to even like me a wee bit, weel, that's it. I'll nae force you.'

Mysie was very angry at her son. 'After what Doddie's done for us, it's terrible that you . . .'

'Leave it be, lass,' Doddie sighed. 'You'll only mak' things worse. I'd best get some sleep, for Andra wants to leave early in the mornin'. I'll likely nae ha'e time to fill the lamps for you afore I go, but you'll manage yoursel'?'

Sandy looked up at his mother hopefully. 'I could fill the lamps for you the morn, Mam.'

'You're nae auld enough for that, and' I'll manage fine. It's time you was in your bed, as weel.'

Doddie having left at the crack of dawn, Mysie had to go for water herself the following morning, and her heart sank as she neared the well. Jean Petrie and her two bosom friends were standing talking, but stopped when they spotted her, and she was sure they'd been speaking about her and Doddie again.

'So you're here yoursel' the day?' Jean was at her most sarcastic. 'Has Doddie Wilson walked oot on you noo?'

With great difficulty, Mysie kept her temper. 'He's awa' to the toon wi' Andra an' Rab to attend to some things.'

'He's a great ane for attendin' to things, especially other men's wives.' The thin face twisted into a huge smirk.

Mysie kept every muscle in her face under tight control. 'I consider mysel' lucky he's helpin' me oot at Rowanbrae.'

Jean's mouth pinched briefly. 'You've only twa rooms in your hoose, Mysie, so does he sleep wi' you or wi' Sandy?'

'It's nane o' your business,' Mysie said, sharply, 'but I'm nae ashamed to say he sleeps wi' me, as you ken't withoot askin'. Can you blame me if you think back on what Jeems was like?'

Unabashed, Mrs Petrie said, 'Aye, weel, but you took Jeems for your wedded husband an' had twa bairns to him . . . or maybe they're Doddie's, for a' we ken?'

'You ken fine I never met Doddie till yon meal an' ale, an' you took good care to tell Jeems aboot that.'

A look of shocked indignation covered the woman's face now. 'Och, noo, Mysie, if it hadna been me, somebody else would ha'e tell't him, for a'body in the place ken't. You canna hide a thing like that.'

Ignoring her, Mysie pushed past them and hooked one of her pails on to the cable in the well.

'Far be it fae me to cause trouble,' Jean Petrie continued, 'but I think you should ken what Sandy's been sayin' to some o' the other bairns in the school playground.'

Her curiosity getting the better of her, Mysie turned round as she let the pail down. 'What's he been sayin' noo?'

'He was blawin' that you'll nae need Doddie at Rowanbrae when he's bigger, for he'll dae a'thing himsel'. I think he doesna like your fancy man very muckle.'

109

Mysie, nauseated by the woman's nerve, concentrated on what she was doing, but the insinuating voice behind her carried on. 'Of coorse, he's only a bairn, an' maybe his father'll be back afore he grows up, an' Jeems'll put Doddie oot on his lug.'

Hooking the two full pails on to her yoke, Mysie walked away, her cheeks flaming and her mouth set in a thin straight line, furious at Sandy for providing Jean Petrie with the fodder to feed her vicious tongue. Her mind was so preoccupied that she almost bumped into Jess Findlater who was making for the shop early, having run out of yellow soap.

'My God, Mysie! What's up wi' you this mornin'?'

'I'm sorry, Jess, I didna see you, I'm that mad.'

'Mad? You'd best tell me aboot it, lass, for a trouble shared is a trouble halfed, as they say.'

Laying down her pails, Mysie told her, including also what Sandy had said to her about Doddie months earlier and the way he treated him now.

'Ach,' Jess said, 'you shouldna tak' ony notice o' that bitch Petrie, an' Sandy's likely jealous o' Doddie, for he had you to himsel' for a while and he'll think his nose is oot o' joint. He'll grow oot o' it, so dinna say onything to him, or Doddie either, it'd only mak' things worse. I'll maybe gi'e you a cry in on my road hame to see if you've calmed doon.'

'I've calmed doon already, just speakin' to you,' Mysie said, earnestly. 'I dinna ken what I'd dae withoot you, Jess.'

In her own kitchen, Mysie laughed at herself for letting Jean Petrie get under her skin, but she was dismayed at how serious Jess was when she called in on her way home. 'I was thinkin', Mysie, but I dinna ken if I should tell you.'

'You'd best tell me, whatever it is.'

'Weel, I ken I promised never to speak aboot this again, but would Sandy think Doddie had something to dae wi' Jeems . . . eh . . . goin' awa'?'

Mysie kept her voice steady. 'No, I'm sure he doesna.'

'Och weel, if you're sure that's nae what it is, it'll just be jealousy right enough.'

Jess chattered on, but for the first time since she'd known her, Mysie was glad when her neighbour left and she had peace to consider Sandy's behaviour. There was no reason for him to think that Doddie had anything to do with Jeems's disappearance, not unless . . . She put her hand on her chest as the thought struck her. *Had* Doddie been there that night, as she half suspected, and had Sandy heard him? Worse, had he seen him stabbing Jeems? Was that why the bairn was so against him? But Sandy couldn't have heard or seen anything; he had still been sound asleep when she looked in at him before she ran to Downies. It must be jealousy – he must realise that she loved Doddie best – and she would have to show him more affection.

When the boy came home from school, she helped him with his home lessons and was as patient as she could be, then, as they sat down to have supper, she patted his hand. 'It's just me an' you the nicht, Sandy.'

He looked away, shifting his hand. She couldn't make out why he was behaving like this – he couldn't know that she'd been told what he was saying at school – and she was alarmed to see a slyness in his eyes, like he was contemplating doing something he knew was wrong. Her mind eased when he went to bed – tomorrow was another day, and Sandy's moods had always been like quicksilver, changing from one minute to the next.

At nine o'clock, she undressed and went to bed, tired out with the additional work she'd had to do with Doddie away, and, being safe in the knowledge that he wouldn't come home drunk, she fell into a sound sleep almost at once.

Lying awake, Sandy heard the bedsprings creak as his mother lay down, and felt his heart thudding against his ribs. He had planned everything out, but now that the time had come, he was almost afraid to go ahead. What if she woke up and saw what he was doing? No, he would be as quiet as a mouse, and she wouldn't know what he'd done until the morning. Then she'd see that she didn't need Doddie Wilson – or anybody else, except him. He would prove to her that he was as good as any man.

He waited for a long time, then slid his feet on to the floor and lifted his breeches to take out the box of matches he had got from Robbie Duff that afternoon. Then he lit his candle and, easing his door open, tiptoed silently across the kitchen to the table and set the candle down beside the new lamp that Doddie had bought some months before. It was beautiful, brass with a glass globe on top of the part that held the paraffin, and he wished that he'd watched when Doddie filled it, but it should be easy enough if he was careful.

He couldn't go out the back way for fear of disturbing his mother – her bed was on that wall – but she wouldn't hear him if he went through the front porch. Once outside, he ran round the house to the yard. The can of paraffin was kept at the end of the hen run and was very heavy, but he only had to lay it down twice before he got it inside.

The next bit was the tricky bit. Unscrewing the cap of the can first, he took off the stopper on the lamp then tried to lift the can far enough up to pour in the oil. After a long struggle, he realised that it would be easier if the lamp was on the floor and moved it down. When he tipped the tin over, the paraffin gushed out over the foot of his nightshirt and the rug, but his determination made him persevere. On his next attempt, the liquid spurted all over the lamp, but eventually he got the hang of it, and poured it straight into the hole. A second later, the lamp over-flowed – it hadn't needed filling, after all, or else his mother had done it during the day – and he sat back on his heels, disappointment almost choking him.

But she would be pleased that he'd been able to do it, he thought, cheering up, and she would let him do other jobs she hadn't let him do before. She wouldn't be very pleased about the wet rug, though, so he'd better clean it

112

before he went back to bed. First, he'd have to put the lamp up on the table again, and take the can back to where it belonged.

As he turned towards the door, he remembered having seen his father using a funnel to fill the old lamp, and wished that he had remembered earlier. The tin was much lighter than it had been when he took it in, and having replaced it, he thought he had better go to the 'wee hoosie' as long as he was outside. A high wind had sprung up, but even the cold blast around his legs didn't lessen his jubilation at having proved how clever he was. His mother would see that there was nothing special about Doddie, and she would give all her love to her son now.

Alas, as Sandy might have known if he had been older, pride always comes before a fall – another gust of wind had whirled through the open porch door and blown his candle over. When he came over the threshold, only minutes later, he stopped in horror at the sight of the fire snaking over the table towards the lamp, and down the side leaves where some of the paraffin had splashed. Then he ran forward, screaming, 'Mam! Mam!'

At that moment, the flames reached the saturated rug, and this explosion was followed by another as the fire penetrated the container of the lamp. Within seconds, the whole kitchen was a blazing inferno.

Chapter Twelve

As the horse plodded home, unguided in the darkness, the miller and Rab Duff were roaring out verse after bawdy verse of 'The Muckin' o' Geordie's Byre', followed, just as unmelodically, by an even bawdier version of 'The Ball o' Kirriemuir', then, their mood changing, 'The Dying Ploughboy'. This left them somewhat maudlin, and

Doddie Wilson was glad when they fell asleep, for at long last he had time to think about what he had done.

It wasn't that he didn't love Mysie – he loved her with all his heart – but it was quite obvious that it would be a long time before Sandy accepted him. He wasn't really a part of her family, not legally, and it looked as if he never would be. He could never marry her as long as she still believed that Jeems Duncan was still alive, and he couldn't go on the way things were. That was the reason he had taken the King's shilling that forenoon.

He half regretted it now, but he had committed himself and couldn't back out; besides, he needed to get away. Maybe, by the time the war ended, he would feel differently – not about Mysie, for his feelings for her would never change, but about the whole situation – and maybe Sandy would feel differently. The boy would surely think more of a soldier returned from the war, and they could all go away together and make a new start where nobody knew anything about them.

The cart was about five miles from Burnlea when a glow in the sky caught Doddie's attention. It was likely a barn on fire, he thought, but, trying to figure out from the direction which was the unlucky farm, he realised, in deep alarm, that it was neither Fingask nor Waterton, but somewhere in between. In sudden panic, he grabbed the reins from Andra White's inert hands, and urged the horse on, faster and faster.

The miller woke up as they jolted over a large stone. 'My God, Doddie, what's your hurry, man?'

Rab Duff opened his eyes, and murmured, sleepily, 'You surely canna be that desperate to get back to Mysie? It would suit me fine if I never saw my Belle again, for she's . . .'

'There's a fire!' Doddie shouted. 'I'm nae sure if it's Jake Findlater's place or Mysie's, but . . .'

'God, aye.' Andra focussed his eyes on the conflagration. 'That's some blaze. It's ower near Waterton to be the mill, thank God, but it could be Downies or Rowan-brae.'

His heart sinking lower as they drew nearer, Doddie became sure, at last – it was Rowanbrae! The thatched roof, tinder dry, had already fallen in, and if Mysie and her son were still inside, there was no hope for them. Pulling on the reins when they reached the fire, he jumped down from the cart and raced towards the house, but was beaten back by the heat and smoke. Followed by Andra, he ran round to the yard, but there was no sign of anyone there, so he made for the back porch.

'You canna go in there, Doddie,' Andra shouted, drag-ging him away. 'Mysie an' Sandy must be at Downies, so get back up on the cart. There's naething we can dae here.'

'But I'll ha'e to mak' sure Mysie's nae inside.'

'It's nae use, lad. I'm he'rt sorry for you, but I think we should see if she's wi' the Findlaters. If she's nae . . .' He stopped and held out his hand to help Doddie up beside him, then smacked the horse's flank with his whip and yelled, 'Gee up, Star, for a' you're worth.'

As the tired horse trotted off, Doddie held his head between his hands hopelessly, and Rab Duff spoke into his ear. 'They must be at Downies. They'll be a' right, man.'

Doddie didn't answer. Mysie couldn't have gone to Downies, for if she had, Jake would have known Rowan-brae was burning, and he would have been there fighting the fire.

It was the miller who roused the Findlaters. 'Is Mysie an' Sandy here?' he shouted, when Jake opened the door.

'No, they're nae.' The anxiety in Andra's voice made Jake feel sick. 'Are they nae at hame?'

'Rowanbrae's burnt doon.'

'God Almighty! I never ken't naething aboot it. Wait till I get my claes on, an' I'll come back wi' you to gi'e you a hand to look for them.'

Jess had appeared seconds after her husband. 'What in God's name could ha'e happened to them?'

Casting a surreptitious glance at Doddie, Andra whispered, 'We thought they'd come here, but . . . I doot . . .'

'Oh, my God!' Jess gasped, clutching at her heart. 'I canna believe it. Nae Mysie an' Sandy?'

Jake joined the men on the cart in a few minutes, and by the time they arrived back at Rowanbrae, the fire had practically burned itself out. A thick pall of acrid black smoke still hung over the shell of the house. Jake ran round the back, but Doddie took off his jacket and held it over his face as he stepped through the smouldering doorway. Andra kept close behind him, afraid that what they might find would unhinge the young man's mind altogether. But they saw nothing except charred, smoking beams littering the floors of both rooms.

'Where'll they be?' Doddie shouted, his eyes sweeping wildly from side to side in his distress.

Andra took a firm grip of his shoulder. 'They must ha'e got oot. They'll be aboot here some place, an' we'll ha'e to look for them, for they'll be in a sorry state, wherever they are.'

As they staggered out, Jake came charging round the side of the house. 'I found them, Doddie, oot in the nearest park.'

The woman and the boy, their smoke-blackened faces blank, their nightclothes singed, didn't look up as the men raced towards them, but Doddie gathered them into his arms, moaning, 'Mysie, Mysie, my ain true love. I thought I'd lost you. I thought I'd lost you baith.'

At last, Jake stepped forward. 'We'd best tak' them back to my place, Doddie. They're in nae fit state for onything.'

At Downies, Jess tended to their burns and forced them to drink some tea. 'Go an' plump up oor pillows, Jake, an' spread up the blankets, for they'll ha'e to go in oor bed.'

Andra stood up. 'Come on, Rab. We're just in the road here.'

Doddie lurched to his feet, too. 'Thank you for what you did. I'd ha'e went aff my head if you twa hadna been wi' me.'

The miller smiled sadly. 'If there's onything mair we can dae, you've only to let us ken.'

Rab followed him out and they mounted the cart to go home, their shock at what had happened tempered by the anticipation of being first to break the news to the rest of the community.

After undressing her charges in the other room, Jess slipped one of her nightgowns over Mysie's head and an old shirt of Jake's over Sandy's, then helped them into the wide, high bed, crooning, as she covered them up, 'You'll be a' right noo, my dearies, just cuddle doon.' When she joined Jake and Doddie, she said, 'Poor Mysie. I suppose it'll be a lang time afore she can bide at Rowanbrae again?'

Jake heaved a deep sigh. 'She'll nae be able to bide there ever again, Jess. It's gutted.'

'But could you nae sort it, you an' Doddie?'

The young man lifted his head slowly. 'I'll nae be here, Jess, even if it could be sorted, though I dinna think it can.'

Frowning in puzzlement, Jess said, 'Where'll you be?'

Jake, noticing the other man's discomfiture, stood up hastily. 'Would you like a dram, Doddie?' Getting no reply, he went to the dresser and filled two small glasses. 'Here you are, man,' he said, handing one over. 'Dinna ha'e me drinkin' on my ain.'

Doddie accepted the whisky and said, dully, 'I enlisted when I was in the toon the day.'

Jake stared at him in amazement. 'You never said . . .'

'I'd never thought aboot it, but I couldna stand biding wi' Mysie when we couldna wed, so I was goin' to ask ane o' the farmers at the Mart if they'd a job for me, but twa recruitin' sergeants fae the Gordons was there. Afore I ken't what I was daein', I'd signed up and ta'en the shillin'.'

A deathly silence fell, both Jake and his wife wondering what this would do to Mysie, but at last Jess said, 'Maybe it's just as weel, for you've nae place to bide noo.'

His face crumpling suddenly, Doddie burst into noisy

117

sobs, and she rose to comfort him, holding him against her bosom and patting his back until he drew away. 'I'm sorry, Jess. I've been greetin' like a bairn, but I love them – baith o' them – an' I didna want to hurt her.'

'At least you had a wee while thegither,' she soothed.

'Aye, I'll be thankfu' for that for the rest o' my life. Oh, God, I dinna want to leave her, nae noo, nae when she's lost everything she had.'

'You'll get ower this, Doddie. You'll nae think that this very minute, but you will, an' so'll Mysie an' the bairn. They can bide here till she mak's up her mind what she's goin' to dae, but we've only the one bed, an' . . .' Jess cleared her throat and moved over to the range. 'I'll mak' some fresh tea. This pot's been standin' that lang it must be stewed.'

When she had poured out three cups, she said, 'Do you want me to tell her aboot you enlistin', Doddie?'

'No, I'll tell her mysel' when she wakens up, but, oh Jess, I wish I'd had mair sense.' He tipped his whisky into his tea.

'It's ower late noo for regrets. What's done is done, as the sayin' goes. I think we should a' try an' get some rest, an' maybe things winna look so black in the mornin'.'

'Maybe no'.' He gulped down his laced tea.

Settling back in their chairs, the Findlaters soon dozed off, but Doddie's troubled thoughts kept him awake. He still had to tell Mysie what he had done and why, and it was so painful to think about that he gave up and turned his mind to the fire. How could it have started? A spark from a stick or a bit of peat would have smouldered for a while, and the smell of smoke would surely have wakened Mysie and given her time to dowse it before the whole place went up in flames like that. It must have happened very quickly, for she and her son had been slightly burned before they got out. There was something damned queer about it.

Jess looked up as he moved his feet in agitation. 'I ken

you're upset, Doddie,' she whispered, 'but things'll work oot for you in the end, I'm sure. Try an' get some sleep.'

He closed his eyes obediently, and was astonished when he woke up some time later and saw Jess standing beside the range stirring a pot. 'What time is it?' he murmured, drowsily.

'Near seven already. Jake's awa' to Rowanbrae to see aboot the coo, but Mysie an' Sandy's still sleepin', poor things.'

Having been so concerned about Mysie, Doddie had forgotten about Brownie. 'You should ha'e wakened me, Jess.'

'You was dead to the world, an' I hadna the he'rt. Ony road, Jake was wantin' something to dae. He was awfu' annoyed at himsel' for nae kennin' aboot the fire in time. Ah, there you are.' She turned as her husband came in.

'It's a good thing the wind was blawin' awa' fae the byre last nicht,' Jake observed. 'Mysie's coo wasna touched, an' I've put her in the park aside oor Betty. I'll leave you to milk her, Jess.'

'Aye, after we've had oor porridge.'

When they sat down at the table, Doddie said, 'I'd best tak' the hens here, as weel, Jake, if you dinna mind?'

Jake agreed and scratched his head. 'There's a puckle things lyin' aboot ootside, an' if we asked Andra for a lend o' his cart, we could shift a'thing here that's ony use. I'll see to them till you come hame fae the war.'

'Aye, that's the very thing,' Jess chipped in, 'for Mysie'll nae ha'e nae place to put them.'

At that moment, Mysie came through from the other room, her eyes dull and sunken, her pinched face still pink with scorch marks, and Doddie jumped up. 'How are you feelin', lass?'

'Oh, Doddie,' she burst out, 'I dinna ken how the fire started, but I'd ha'e been burned alive in my bed if it hadna been for Sandy. He must ha'e smelt it and shouted at me, but we'd an awfu' job gettin' oot. A'thing was blazin' roon' aboot us.'

Feeling that his heart was being compressed in a vice, he held her gently in his arms. 'Thank God you're a' right.'

Jess, whose own heart felt constricted with emotion, was glad when Sandy came through, and filled a bowl for him. 'Here's some porridge,' she said, rather brusquely, brushing her eyes with her hand. 'Sit doon an' sup it afore it's cauld.'

Sandy sat down but made no attempt to eat, and realising how shaken he must be, she shook her head sorrowfully. 'Come oot wi' me to gather the eggs, my loon, an' Jake, you've your work to dae.'

Aware that she had left them to talk in private, Doddie said, 'Mysie, I've something to tell you.'

His grave expression alarmed her. 'What is it, Doddie?'

'Weel, it's like this . . . oh, Mysie, I canna think o' a easy way to tell you. I enlisted in the Gordons yesterday when I was in the toon.' Her stunned face made him hurry on. 'I just couldna go on like we were, lass. I wanted you to be my wife, an' as lang as we dinna ken where Jeems is, we can never be wed. I've to report at the Barracks on Wednesday, but I'll come an' see you when I get leave, an' when the war's finished, we'll go right awa' fae Burnlea an' tak' a croft some place where folk dinna ken us, an' they'll think we're man an' wife.'

Still slightly in shock, Mysie said nothing for a minute. If she told Doddie now that Jeems was dead, would he tell her the truth? Would he admit to having killed him? If it hadn't been him, though, he would want to know how Jeems died, why they had been fighting, how she had come to be carrying a bairn that wasn't her husband's. Oh, God, what a mess her life was, and she couldn't even be sure of Doddie. The only thing she was sure of was that she loved him, no matter what. At last, she looked at him longingly. 'Oh, I wish we *could* go right awa' fae Burnlea an' live as man an' wife.'

'We can, Mysie, once I come hame again. We'd be wed in the sight o' God, and we'd be a real family, you an' me an' Sandy, an' ony others that come.'

A faint ray of hope appeared in the lack-lustre eyes. 'Oh, I love you, Doddie.'

'An' I love you, mair than I can ever tell you.' He crushed her to him, then remembered something else he should have told her, and said, rather shamefacedly, 'I near forgot, though. I didna like to tell the recruitin' sergeants aboot us nae bein' wed, an' I put my father doon as my next o' kin, so you'll nae get an allotment. I'm sorry aboot it, Mysie, but . . .'

'I dinna care, Doddie,' she assured him, then added, ruefully, 'I dinna suppose I'd ha'e got onything if you *had* tell't them aboot me. They wouldna gi'e onything to a fancy woman.'

'Oh, Mysie,' he groaned, 'you're nae my fancy woman. You're my wife, nae matter what other folk think. Dinna forget that.'

Realising that she had hurt him, she kissed his cheek. 'I'll never forget it, Doddie, dinna fear, an' I'll be your wife for as lang as we baith shall live.'

Outside, Jess said, 'Sandy, you go on wi' the basket, for I want to speak to Jake for a minute.' She turned to her husband when the boy moved away. 'I canna help thinkin' it's a good thing Doddie's leavin'.'

Jake's eyebrows rose. 'Are you nae sorry for Mysie?'

'Aye, I'm sorry for her, just when they'd got thegither an' were happy, but she hasna got Rowanbrae noo, an' she'll need to get things sorted oot. Her an' Sandy canna bide wi' us till Doddie comes back fae the war, for we've only got the one bed.'

'Somebody would maybe let us ha'e the lend o' a bed,' Jake suggested, hopefully, 'an' we could sleep in the kitchen.'

'But we canna feed twa extra mooths, an' she'll ha'e naething comin' in to pay for their keep. It's nae that I dinna want them here,' she added, sensing her husband's displeasure, 'but it's just the way we're placed an' . . . och, you're right enough, Jake. I couldna put her oot, for she's been like a sister to me ever since I ken't her.'

'She hasna had muckle good oot o' life,' Jake observed, sadly. 'Gettin' sell't to a man auld enough to be her father, lossin' her auldest bairn doon the quarry, an' yon bugger o' a packman landin' her wi' a bairn. What's mair, Jeems turned on her when she was needin' a' the comfort she could get. Nae wonder she lost her head an' . . . did what she did.'

Jess said nothing to this, still quite sure in her mind that it had not been Mysie who killed Jeems although she had never come up with another solution. She didn't think it had been Doddie, either, yet who else was there? Giving a long sigh, she crossed the yard to help Sandy collect the eggs.

When they went inside, Doddie and Mysie were sitting at the fireside, silent and morose, so Jess said, brightly, 'Awa' you go oot to Jake, Doddie. He's needin' a hand wi' a palin' post.'

'But him an' me was to be goin' to the mill for . . .'

'You can go later on. There's nae hurry. You'd best go oot, as weel, Sandy, an' see they put the post in straight.' Waiting until they had gone, she said, 'I suppose Doddie's tell't you, has he, Mysie?'

'That he's enlisted? Aye, he's tell't me.'

'It's maybe for the best, lass. He wouldna be able to bide wi' you, ony road, noo Rowanbrae's doon. You an' Sandy can bide here for as lang as you like, lass, but we havena room for . . .' Jess was interrupted by a loud knock and when she went to the door and brought in a policeman, Mysie's terror almost stopped her heart beating.

The sergeant, Wullie Milne from Inverurie, spoke to them in an officious tone of voice. 'Mr Mutch of Fingask telephoned to the station early this morning to tell us about the fire, and I have just come from Rowanbrae. Which one of you ladies would be Mistress Duncan?' His eyes regarded them sternly.

'Me,' Mysie whispered, faintly.

'I was glad to hear you and your son was safe. Was anybody else in the house at the time?'

122

'No, Doddie wasna there.'

'Doddie?'

'Doddie Wilson. He . . . he bides wi' me.'

'Could it have been him that set fire to the place?'

Mysie was stunned by this assumption, but Jess said, 'Doddie went to the toon early yesterday wi' Andra White an' Rab Duff, an' Rowanbrae was burnt doon afore they come back.'

'Oh, weel, then,' the sergeant muttered, slightly disappointed, 'it hadna been him. I just asked, for you never ken; some men dae some awfu' things.' Realising that he had lapsed into his off-duty language, he corrected himself. 'I take it the boy and you were in your beds? Have you any idea how it started?'

Mysie found her tongue again. 'That's what's been puzzlin' me, an' I canna tell you.'

'It's none of my business why Mr Wilson was biding with you,' Wullie said, looking embarrassed, 'but your man will have to be informed that the croft has burned down. We have notified Mr Phillip of Burnlea House, and he told us Mr Duncan is still the rightful tenant. Now, if you will just tell me where I can get in touch with him . . .?'

Mysie cast a glance of appeal at Jess, who said, with more confidence than she felt, 'Jeems Duncan walked oot on her mair than a year ago, an' naebody kens where he is.'

Screwing up his face for a moment, the sergeant looked at Mysie sympathetically. 'You didna report him missing?'

'She doesna want to ken where he is,' Jess declared, before Mysie could say anything, 'an' she's better aff withoot him.'

'Aye, but we still have to find him – it's a matter o' the law – and I'd like a word wi' Mr Wilson. Is he aboot?'

'He's ootside wi' my Jake.'

'He'll likely not be able to tell me nothing, but . . .' Wullie Milne sighed. 'I can't find out how the fire started, and I'll be reporting it as a accident.'

When the sergeant went out, Mysie collapsed against the back of her chair. 'Oh, God, Jess, this is awfu'. What am I goin' to dae? If they start lookin' for Jeems, they'll maybe find him an' start askin' a lot o' questions, an' I'll get a' mixed up, an' I'll maybe tell them that it wasna . . .' Her hand flying to her mouth, she stopped abruptly.

Curious as to what Mysie had been about to say, but afraid that she could blurt everything out to the policeman in her present state, Jess gripped her shoulder. 'Naebody's goin' to find Jeems, lass, nae unless you tell them where he is.'

Jake poked his head round the door in a few minutes. 'That's the bobby awa', an' he says we can tak' whatever we want oot o' Mysie's place, for he's satisfied there was nae arson. So me an' Doddie'll get aff to the mill to ask Andra for his cart.'

Jess sat up. 'Ask him if he's a spare bed when you're there.'

Andra White was quite willing when Jake asked for the loan of his horse and cart, but had no bed to give them. 'I can let you ha'e an auld mattress, though, an' seein' Doddie'll be awa' on Wednesday, he can sleep on oor couch – as lang's he watches himsel' wi' oor Nessie, for she's an awfu' case for the men.'

This agreed upon, Jake and Doddie went back to Rowanbrae in the cart, and spent the rest of the forenoon loading it. There was nothing worth salvaging in the house itself, but they took the hand plough and most of the other implements from the big shed, and all the bales of hay and straw.

'You can use oor tatties fae the pit,' Doddie said, 'an' the carrots an' neeps. If you've plenty o' your ain, you can gi'e them to Dougal to sell, for it's a shame to waste them.'

Jake shook his head. 'I'm helluva sorry aboot a' this.'

Swallowing, Doddie said, 'If only I hadna been awa' . . .'

'You canna change things.'

They shooed the hens into the crate Andra had lent

124

them for the purpose, Doddie saying, 'The run's nae worth takin'. I did buy nettin' wire yesterday to mak' a new ane, but it was left on the cart wi' the rest o' the stuff, so I suppose Andra's got it. Oh, you might as weel tak' this paraffin. There's nae sense in leavin' it here.' He lifted the two-gallon tin, then laid it down with a hoarse cry. 'It's near empty!'

'It doesna matter.'

'Aye, it does. I bought it fae Dougal last Tuesday, an' I just used it once, to fill the lamps on Tuesday night.'

They stared at each other in astonishment, then Jake said, 'You must ha'e used it for something else. Think, man.'

'I suppose Mysie filled the lamps again when I was in the toon, but she wouldna ha'e used as muckle as that.'

'But naebody else would ha'e used it.'

'Somebody else must ha'e used it, aboot a gallon an' a half o' it, but what for?' Doddie's face darkened. 'It could ha'e been the bugger that set fire to the place.'

'For God's sake, man, naebody would set fire to Rowanbrae. Your brain's turned, an' you'll mind later on what you used the paraffin for. Or maybe Mysie used it to wash something doon.'

'I never thought o' that.' Doddie's anger was slowly fading, but there was still a trace of doubt in his voice.

After the can was loaded, well away from the old mattress, they mounted the cart and Jake took the reins. 'I wouldna say naething to Mysie aboot this, if I was you, Doddie,' he said, as the horse set off. 'She's got enough to worry aboot as it is, withoot thinkin' somebody set fire to her place.'

From the expression on the other man's face, Doddie could see that there was doubt in his mind, too, but, by common consent, the subject was not mentioned again. Mysie and her son were safe, and that was the main thing.

The fire, of course, was the main topic of conversation in the area that day, and although no one could shed any light on how it had started, it was generally accepted that a piece of stick or peat had fallen on to the hearthrug.

Jean Petrie had voiced her opinion to Belle Duff and Alice Thomson when they met at the well. 'It's a judgement on Doddie an' Mysie, that's what it is. The good Lord doesna tak' kindly to them that br'ak his commandments, an' I darena think what Jeems Duncan'll say aboot it when he comes hame.'

Regarding her warily, Belle muttered, 'I dinna think Jeems'll ever come hame.'

Rather taken aback by this uninvited, and most unexpected, contradiction, Jean said, 'What mak's you think that?'

'Weel, the day after young Jamie fell doon the quarry, the miller's wife tell't me Jeems blamed himsel', an' my Rab says he was a changed man right up till he disappeared, awfu' quiet, an' if he'd been broodin' aboot it, weel . . . he was aye a queer man, nae very stable, nae wi' a temper like yon . . . an' maybe he did awa' wi' himsel' . . . maybe he jumped doon the quarry?'

This had never occurred to Jean Petrie, whose mouth fell open as wide as Alice Thomson's in surprise. For at least twenty seconds, the three women pondered silently over this dreadful possibility, then Jean said slowly, as if it hurt her to admit it, 'You ken, Belle, I think you're maybe nae far wrang.'

She could hardly wait to tell Eck, and refused to go in with Alice for her usual cup of tea in order to get home as quickly as she could. Leaving her two pails at the door of her cottar house, she carried on to Fingask, where her husband and the farmer were debating the need for new drains.

Eck looked up frowning, annoyed at his wife for interrupting so important a discussion. 'What are *you* needin'?'

'Belle Duff thinks Jeems Duncan did awa' wi' himsel',' she burst out, his ill humour going straight over her head.

'Belle Duff's aye got some queer notion or other.'

Frank Mutch scratched his nose. 'It's funny she should

say that, though, for I've been thinkin' the same thing mysel'.'

As far as Jean was concerned, the oracle had spoken, and by that afternoon it was widely known that Jeems Duncan was lying at the bottom of the old quarry. No one, however, thought of informing the police – they had to do their own dirty work – but it must be true enough, for Eck Petrie's wife had got it from Frank Mutch himself.

With the mystery of Mysie's husband's departure now solved to their satisfaction, the women cast no further aspersions on her association with Doddie Wilson. She was a widow and was free to take another man if she wanted . . . but for the sake of decency, she might have waited a while longer. Only a few of the women, less gullible than the rest, kept their opinions to themselves – it was too easy to jump to conclusions.

After suppertime, when Sandy was in bed and Mysie and Doddie went outside for a walk, Jess again voiced her suspicions to Jake. 'I'm sure Mysie near tell't me the day that it wasna her that killed Jeems. I've aye said she was shieldin' the man that did it, but you aye tell't me I was daft.'

'There was never nae signs o' another man,' Jake pointed out, 'except yon bloody packman, an' he didna care a docken for her, so he'd nae reason to kill Jeems.'

'I suppose no'.' But Jess was still troubled. Even allowing for the situation that night, and the circumstances that had built it up to a powder keg ready to explode, she just couldn't imagine Mysie acting so violently. It wasn't like her, and a woman couldn't act against her nature, no matter what had gone before. No, there must be something that hadn't come out yet, something to prove that a third person had been in the kitchen at Rowanbrae, the man who was really responsible for the death of Jeems Duncan.

Jake had also been thinking. 'Mysie said she managed to get the knife fae Jeems, but he was a hefty man . . . though fear could ha'e gi'en her the strength to . . .'

Jess's cry stopped him. 'That's it, Jake! I aye ken't there was something we was forgettin'. Jeems still had the knife in his hand! It was another knife that killed him.'

Fully half a minute elapsed before Jake said, 'Aye, I mind noo. There *was* twa knives! I flung them baith doon the quarry the next day, when I was at the moss cuttin' peat. We was that worked up that nicht, we werena thinkin' straight.'

They looked at each other for a moment, then Jess whispered, 'So there *was* somebody else there.'

Jake rubbed his nose. 'I suppose Mysie *could* ha'e picked up the other knife? The drawer was lyin' on the floor.'

'An' her near senseless wi' what Jeems was daein' to her? No, Jake, that'll nae haud water. It was somebody else, an' I'm sure it wasna Doddie.'

'Och, Jess. Let it be. It was a sorry business fae start to finish, but it's a' ower, an' though we'd a hand in it, we did what we thought was best at the time. There's nae good'll come o' bringin' it a' up again.'

Sandy had hardly uttered a word since the fire, and Mysie was quite worried about him. He was taking too long to get over it, and maybe she had done wrong keeping him off school. She broached the subject to Jess on Tuesday afternoon. 'What do you think? He's been wanderin' aboot lookin' lost. Would he be better among the other bairns?'

'It might tak' his mind aff it, poor wee lambie. Sometimes you need to be cruel to be kind. An' he's got the claes Belle Duff sent alang, so you dinna need to worry aboot that.'

When Sandy was told that he would have to go back to school the next morning, there was no adverse reaction – no reaction at all – so, on Wednesday, Mysie supervised him washing and dressing, then stood at the door watching as he walked slowly along the road, his head down, his hands in his pockets. 'I hope he'll be a' right,' she said, when she went back into the kitchen. 'He looks that miserable.'

128

About half an hour later, Jess having made herself scarce, Mysie clung desperately to Doddie when he came to say goodbye. 'Dinna greet, lass,' he murmured, against her face. 'I'll write to you, an' I'll be back when I get leave.'

'Oh, I'll miss you sair,' she sobbed.

'I'll be thinkin' aboot you every minute I'm awa'.'

His parting kiss was short and rough, as if he couldn't trust himself to linger over it, then he tore himself away from her and strode through the door. She longed to run out after him, to watch him going along the road, too, but he had made her promise to stay inside, so she sat down with her head bowed until Jess came in again. 'He's awa',' she murmured, brokenly.

'Aye, I saw him. Listen, Mysie, Jake's needin' me to haud some nettin' wire till he nails it to the posts o' the palin', an' I'll nae ha'e time to make ony butter, so would you feel up to daein' it for me?'

'Aye, I'll easy manage that.'

Mysie knew that Jess was keeping her occupied to stop her brooding, and was grateful to her for trying, but her brain was still active as she turned the handle of the wooden churn. She couldn't expect the Findlaters to keep her and her son for much longer, but she had nowhere else to go. If she didn't have Sandy, it wouldn't be so bad, but the poor bairn needed a home – he'd been through an awful lot lately – and how could she provide that? Maybe Jess would be willing to keep him to let her go into service? It seemed to be the only solution and she would sound Jess out later.

She had just returned to the kitchen when the laird's brougham drew up outside and she flew to answer the door. Her curiosity became astonishment when the driver handed over an envelope addressed to her. 'I've to wait for an answer,' he said, as Jess ran round the side of the house to see what was going on.

Opening the letter, Mysie read it and handed it to her friend in a flurry of excitement. 'It's like the answer to a prayer, but are you willin' to keep Sandy if I get the job?'

129

'Wait till I read it, till I see what you're speakin' aboot.' In less than a minute, Jess was just as excited as Mysie. 'It's providence, that's what it is. Aye, me an' Jake'll keep Sandy, so tell the man the answer's yes.'

Jake joined them as the carriage moved away, and had to be told the good news. 'The laird's wife's asked Mysie to go an' see her aboot a job,' Jess began.

Mysie took up the explanation. 'She's needin' a cook, an' she kens Rowanbrae's burnt doon, an . . .'

'She's to go to the Big Hoose the morn at ten,' Jess butted in, 'an' if Mrs Phillip likes her she'll get the job.'

Jake took the letter to find out for himself, holding it well away from him because his spectacles were sitting inside on the dresser. 'It's what it says, right enough.'

Jess laughed with delight. 'You'll nae be far awa', Mysie, an' it's nae as though you hadna been in service afore.'

'I was only a scullerymaid when I was at Forton Hoose, an' that's near ten year ago. Forbye, I'm nae that sure if I could dae the kind o' cookin' the gentry would be expectin'.'

Jess gave a loud laugh. 'Aye, could you, for they like plain fare, an' it just couldna ha'e worked oot better. Sandy'll bide wi' me an' Jake, an' you can come an' see him on your days aff.'

The thought of only seeing her son occasionally made Mysie realise with a shock how fond of him she had become since Jamie died. It would be best not to tell him anything yet, for the laird's wife might not think she was suitable for the cook's job, and he would be all upset for nothing.

Unable to sleep for worrying about the interview, Mysie was ready long before the carriage came to collect her next day, but the minute she saw Mrs Phillip, tall and matronly, with a large white apron on and her hair protected by a cotton cap, she was sure that her worries had been for nothing.

The woman smiled at her kindly. 'I'm so glad you could come, Mrs Duncan. I was at my wits' end, but when I

130

learned about your misfortune, I thought that we could do each other a good turn. I need a cook, you need a home, and my husband agreed that I should write to you and offer you the position.'

'I've never daen ony fancy cookin',' Mysie said, shyly.

'I don't expect any fancy cooking, as long as it is palatable. My last cook was not very satisfactory, but I put up with her to save myself the trouble of finding someone else. However, she took umbrage at me for criticising her soup, and left on Saturday without giving me notice. I've been doing the cooking myself since. I quite enjoy it, but Mr Phillip insists that I stop. I am sure that you will be an improvement on Mag, and I hope that you will be happy with your room. There is a double bed, but you will not mind your son sleeping with you?'

'Oh! You ken't aboot Sandy? I thought I'd ha'e to leave him wi' the Findlaters.'

'Not unless you want to. He is very welcome here.'

'Oh, thank you! I'm sure he'll be pleased aboot that.'

'Good. Now, when can you start work?'

'I'll ha'e to wait till Sandy comes hame fae the school, but we could come back the nicht.'

Beaming, Mrs Phillip said, 'Splendid! Maitland will take you back to Downies, and call for you again at . . . six? Will that give you time to pack all your clothes?'

'I've naething to pack, Mrs Phillip, for I lost a'thing in the fire. This is Jess Findlater's auld blouse an' skirt I've got on, an' Sandy's been wearin' things folk gi'ed him.'

'I'm sorry, I should have realised. I will look out some of my old clothes for you. They will be far too big, but you can take them in, and they will do until you can buy some of your own. How old is your son?'

'Sandy's eight.'

'Some of the things my Bobby has outgrown may fit him then. Bobby is nine – he's a weekly boarder at a school in Aberdeen – and Sandy may be able to keep him out of mischief during the weekends and the school holidays.'

Mysie's heart sank, but it was better to be frank. 'I'm nae so sure aboot that, for Sandy can be a little de'il himsel'.'

'In that case,' Mrs Phillip said, wryly, 'we will have to keep our eyes on them. Now, off you go with Maitland, and when you come back at night, Meggie will show you your room.'

On being told the arrangements, Jess said, 'I'm right pleased Sandy'll be wi' you, nae that I wasna wantin' him here, but he needs his ain mother, especially just noo.'

When he came home from school, Sandy went round the back to speak to Jake first, and came into the house minutes later, more animated than he had been for some time. 'Is it true, Mam? Jake says we're to be bidin' at the Big Hoose?'

'Aye, I'm to be cook to Mrs Phillip.'

Mysie did her best to control her son's excitement until six o'clock, but she didn't even attempt to make him do his home lessons. When they were leaving, Jess and Jake went out to see them off, and Mysie's eyes filled with tears as she waved to them through the rear window of the carriage.

Sandy turned to her as she sniffed. 'What are you greetin' for, Mam? Do you nae want to go?'

'I was just bein' daft, my loon. We'll ha'e oor ain room, just the twa o' us, an' we'll be happy there, I'm sure.'

Meggie, the fourteen-year-old daughter of Belle and Rab Duff, let them in by the servants' entrance, and on the way up the back stairs, she said, 'Mrs Phillip's good to work for, Mysie. Mag, her that was the cook afore you, didna like her, but that was only through the mistress complainin' aboot her cookin'.'

'I hope she doesna complain aboot mine,' Mysie muttered.

'I dinna ken what made Mag ever think she could cook, for even the very dog wouldna eat the leave-owers.'

Sandy's eyes brightened further. 'What kind o' a dog?'

'He's a saint something, a great muckle soft lump.

132

Brutus, his name is, but onything less like a brute you couldna find.'

Mysie thought that she had better issue a caution. 'You're nae to start tormentin' it, mind, Sandy.'

Having reached the top, Meggie swept a pointing finger round the landing. 'That's my room, I'm your kitchen-maid, that ane's Chrissie an' Janey's, they're first an' second hoosemaids, an' this ane's yours.' She flung the door open and went across to light the lamp from her candle. 'It's a lot bigger than mine.' As she turned to go, she said, 'Oh, an' dinner's at seven, but the mistress made it earlier on an' I've just to put it in the oven for half an 'oor, then serve it. Come doon an' get yours when you're ready.'

'Jess Findlater gi'ed us oor supper,' Mysie told her, 'but I'll come doon an' help you, if you want.'

'The mistress says you've nae to start work till the morn, but you can come doon an' sit in the kitchen if you like. It's a lot warmer there than it is up here.'

Mysie considered for a moment. 'I think we'll bide up here for a while till we get oor breath back.' She waited until the girl shut the door, then said, 'Sandy, get your home lessons daen, or Mr Meldrum'll be ragin' you the morn.'

'Ach, Mam, I've only six sums, an' they're that easy I could dae them standin' on my head.'

'You'll dae them better sittin' on your behind,' she told him, relieved that some of his spirit had returned.

While her son worked out the answers to his sums on top of the square wooden trunk under the skylight, Mysie sat down on the bed to take stock of her surroundings. The room was much larger than the kitchen at Rowanbrae, and had a cupboard for hanging clothes, a chest of drawers with an oval cheval mirror on top, as well as a ewer and basin and the lamp Meggie had lit. There was also a straight-backed, uncushioned chair at each side of the bed, which, she was pleased to find, had a horsehair mattress. It was much firmer than the lumpy chaff bag she'd been used to, and wouldn't have to be filled every year to keep it fresh.

It was all fairly spartan, Mysie mused, but it was home to her and Sandy now – at least, until Doddie came back from the war to take them away.

Chapter Thirteen

1915

Unsure of her capabilities as cook, Mysie had been even more apprehensive on her first morning when her employer handed her a menu for the day. 'Oh,' she gasped, 'I've nae idea what half o' that means. I've hardly never cooked meat, just a rabbit or a hen whiles, an' never nae fancy puddin's.'

Mrs Phillip had laughed. 'I thought as much, so I will give you an old recipe book of my mother's. I was using it myself before you came, and it is easy to follow. I have ordered for today and tomorrow, and when the butcher delivers – the van comes from Inverurie – you can order for the weekend. Look through the book and choose whatever you think is easiest for you – there is nothing that either my husband or I dislike.'

Mysie had opened the book in trepidation, and, though the recipes had looked simple, she was still surprised when the laird's wife congratulated her after luncheon, as she called it.

Now, three months later, she scarcely consulted the book at all, and Mrs Phillip seemed to be satisfied with everything she made, especially if she improvised a little, or experimented, as she had taken to doing once she felt confident. She didn't tell Doddie, when she wrote, about the meals she cooked. His letters were brief since he'd

134

been sent over to France, and she could imagine the awful hardships he had to face.

Anyway, she had plenty to tell him – the things Sandy said, the gossip she heard from Jess on her days off, the tidbits Meggie Duff came out with after she had been home. Mysie had grown fond of her little kitchenmaid, though she couldn't help laughing at her sometimes. Meggie's fine, fair hair was always escaping from her cap, no matter how often she pushed it back; her aprons were for ever coming undone and flapping in front of her. She was still a child at heart, even at fourteen.

'Is Doddie your lad noo Jeems is awa'?' she'd asked when his first letter arrived addressed care of Burnlea House, and had been so interested in every one that Mysie had started reading bits of them out loud. It was good to have someone to confide in, someone who didn't know the truth about her, and she even forgot herself, sometimes, that Jeems hadn't just walked out.

The two housemaids – Janey Paterson, tall and ungainly, and Chrissie Grant, a dainty wee thing – were often to be found giggling in corners about the lads Chrissie met at the dances she cycled to, and the coachman – Maitland, who was also the handyman and whose Christian name Mysie had never heard – was too busy teasing them to pay much attention to the cook and the kitchenmaid, which suited them fine. There was only one other person on the staff – McGregor, the gamekeeper-gardener, a quiet old man who didn't bother anybody.

Sandy had been very good since they'd come here in February, pushing three-year-old Beatrice carefully on her swing when he came home from school, or taking Brutus, the St Bernard, out for long walks. At the table, his manners were impeccable; no speaking with his mouth full, no gobbling as if there would be no tomorrow. Bobby Phillip, at a private school in Aberdeen, just came home at the weekends, and he and Sandy had taken to each other from the first. They played football, they stalked imaginary wild animals in the gardens, they amused themselves and were no trouble, even in the Easter holidays. During the next school break, they spent each long summer day together, and Mysie only saw her son at mealtimes, sometimes not even then. But it was too good to last, as she found out.

'Oh, I was black affronted,' she told Jess, the next time she went to see her. 'They'd eaten maist o' the strawberries in the garden, an' they were baith sick.'

'Served them right,' said Jess. 'What did Mrs Phillip say?'

'She gi'ed Bobby a good wallopin'.'

'I didna think the gentry would wallop their bairns.'

'She took him ower her knee an' laid into him, so I did the same to Sandy, an' they were baith howlin'.'

'So that'll ha'e stopped their tricks?'

Mysie grimaced. 'No, it didna stop them. The very next day, they swung wee Beatrice that high on her swing, *she* was sick when she got aff. But the mistress blamed Bobby for that an' sent him to his bed. I gi'ed Sandy the edge o' my tongue, though, for he could ha'e stopped him.'

'You didna bring him wi' you the day?'

'I was goin' to, but Mr Phillip was takin' Beatrice an' Bobby to the beach at Aberdeen, an' he said Sandy could go wi' them. I just hope he behaves himsel'.'

Jess leaned forward. 'What's he like, the laird? I've never seen him up close.'

'I dinna see muckle o' him, but he's real nice. He's fatter than I thought he'd be, an' he's aboot the same height as her, an' you can tell he loves her. It's nae surprisin', though, for her face minds me on a picture o' Helen o' Troy I once saw.'

Mysie's sigh made Jess feel quite tender towards her. 'Ha'e you heard fae Doddie lately?'

'I'd a letter last week, but I wish he could get hame. The only thing is, he'll nae ha'e nae place to bide, an' I'll be tied up at the Big Hoose, so he'll likely go to Fyvie to his father.'

Jess frowned. 'Write an' tell him he can sleep here. We've still got that auld mattress Andra White gi'ed us.'

'That's good o' you, Jess. I'll tell him next time I write.'

'Speakin' aboot Andra, his Drew's enlisted, as weel. Poor Pattie, she's enough on her plate wi' Nessie withoot that. D'you ken what that daft bitch did? She wandered awa' one day an' fell in wi' a sodger fae the camp at Cairndoon, an' you ken what she's like for men, so she's in the family way noo. The only thing she can tell them is it was a man wi' a kilt. God, they're a' kilters at Cairndoon.'

'Poor Nessie,' Mysie murmured.

Jess gave her a calculating look. 'She's just a penny to the shillin', of coorse, but did you nae ken aboot her an' Jeems?'

Mysie didn't want to think about Jeems, but she said, 'Aye, I ken't, an' she was welcome to him.'

'Aye, weel, but it surprises me she hasna been catched afore, for I'm sure she's had near a' the men roon' here at her.'

'Even Jake?' Mysie couldn't resist it.

'Like enough. What man would say no if a wumman walked up to him wi' her skirts lifted up? That's what Nessie does, you ken, an' her whiles wi' nae bloomers on.'

Mysie laughed. 'Och, Jess, you're bletherin'.'

'It's true, as sure as I'm sittin' here, an' she's a bonnie enough quine, though she's soft in the head.'

Mysie left soon afterwards, remembering, as she cycled past the empty shell of Rowanbrae, how happy she and Doddie had been there, and when she came to the mill, she wondered if Nessie had tried to tempt Doddie when he'd slept there before he went away. It was too awful to contemplate and she was glad when she met Jean and Eck Petrie, on their way home from a walk.

'Hey, Mysie!' Jean shouted. 'You've time to speak a minute?'

'Just a wee minute.' She stopped and dismounted.

'How are you likin' being' a cook?'

'Fine.'

'Ony word o' Doddie comin' hame?'

'Nae yet.'

137

'Jess'll ha'e tell't you aboot Nessie White? It's a good job Jeems is awa', or we'd ha'e been thinkin' he was the father.'

Mrs Petrie's eyes were glinting with the satisfaction she got from casting slurs, and Mysie couldn't help laughing. 'I ken't aboot her an' Jeems, Jean, an' I dinna suppose you refused her either, eh, Eck?' It came out before she thought and there was a brief moment of shock all round.

'No, Mysie,' Eck said, quietly. 'A man doesna refuse what's cocked up in front o' him, especially when his ain wife keeps him oot o' her bed.'

Mysie had forgotten that, and was so ashamed of what she'd said that she cycled off without another word, but heard Jean loudly berating her husband. 'Did you need to tell her that, Eck Petrie? An' admittin' you took that daftie? I'll never be able to look her in the . . .' The rest was lost.

Mysie reflected guiltily that she'd got her own back on the woman for all the nasty things she'd said in the past, but it didn't make her feel good. When she got back, she put Meggie's bicycle in the shed and went to make sure that the girl hadn't let the stew burn. 'Is Mr Phillip an' the bairns hame yet?' she asked, and was relieved to learn that they weren't.

When Sandy ran in ten minutes later, he chattered on about what Mr Phillip had said, what Mr Phillip had given them in the way of sweets, what Mr Phillip had let them have turns on at the carnival, and Mysie listened with only half an ear as she filled plates for both upstairs and downstairs. He only stopped speaking when he sat down to eat, and she seized the chance to ask, 'Did you behave yoursel'?'

'Mr Phillip said I behaved better than Bobby, Mam.'

'As lang as you didna disgrace me. Noo, it's up that stair to your bed the minute you've finished your supper.'

'It's a man's hand he's needin',' she confided to Meggie while they were tidying up. 'He was good as gold wi' Mr Phillip, an' once Doddie's oot o' the Gordons he'll keep him in aboot.'

When Meggie returned from visiting her parents the following week, she said, 'Denny Petrie's enlisted, an' Ma says Jean's goin' aboot tellin' folk that him an' Drew White are the only real men in Burnlea. Oor Robbie's wantin' to go, but Da'll nae let him, for he says he's mair needed at hame.'

Doddie had been first to enlist, Mysie thought, sadly, but after what she had said to Eck she wasn't surprised that Jean Petrie had slighted him by not mentioning him, although it was really her that the besom was trying to slight.

Bobby Phillip and Sandy did nothing really outrageous before the summer holidays were over – just irritating things, like tearing their clothes climbing trees, and throwing pails of water over each other when it was unbearably hot. The only time Mysie had been really angry was when Bobby found a tin of whitewash – Maitland had forgotten to put it out of harm's way after he'd been using it – and painted Sandy from head to foot. Meggie had been nearly scared out of her wits when the white apparition had appeared at the back door, but Mysie took one look at the naked boy and gave him a walloping he wouldn't forget in a hurry.

'It wasna my blame,' he sobbed, as she scrubbed him until his skin was almost raw.

'Naething's never your blame,' she scolded, but was thankful that he'd had the sense to take his clothes off first. He was almost back to normal again, although there were times when he was very quiet, perhaps brooding over the old days and wondering what had happened to his father. He never asked any questions about Jeems, though, nor made any mention of the fire, and it usually wasn't long before he came out of his queer mood.

When the schools resumed, the whole household heaved a sigh of relief, but the folk in the Burnlea area had other things to trouble them. Every week, Mysie learned of another family's son leaving, and several of the single farm servants, from both Fingask and Waterton, felt the urge to

139

go and fight for their country. As Jess said, 'The place is emptyin' quicker than the school at four o'clock.' Maitland, twenty-five and also single, felt obliged to tell everyone that he had flat feet and the army wouldn't want him anyway, so he needn't bother offering his services. Chrissie, despondent at losing so many of her lads, found admirers galore at Cairndoon camp, and discovered, to her delight, that they were more fun than the locals.

Doddie's letters were like gold to Mysie, and just as scarce, but she wrote to him faithfully each week, and life went on in the usual way – hard work and little leisure.

When Mrs Phillip came into the kitchen one afternoon at the beginning of December 1915, Mysie wondered if Sandy had done something he shouldn't, but it was nothing to do with Sandy.

'My brother will be home for Christmas,' her employer smiled, 'so I thought I should give a small dinner party, just family. My mother died some time ago, but I will invite my father and his sister Beatrice, as well as my brother, also Mr Phillip's parents and his sister and her husband. That will make nine adults, and the children.'

'How mony children, Ma'am?' Mysie asked, trembling.

'Just our two,' Mrs Phillip smiled. 'Don't worry about it, Mrs Duncan. Just traditional Christmas fare, turkey and all the trimmings, and plum pudding, of course.'

Mysie had no idea what the 'usual trimmings' were, but nodded wisely. There was a section headed 'Special Occasions' in the old recipe book although she'd never looked at it, but provided that it was as simple as the rest of the book, it should be easy enough to follow, and she had three weeks to study it.

When next she went to Downies, she told Jess all about the dinner. 'The Christmas menu in the recipe book says cream of asparagus soup to start wi', but I'm goin' to gi'e them broth, for it's the only thing to keep the cauld oot. Then it says roast turkey an' cranberry sauce, though that's a funny thing to be eatin' wi' turkey, an' brussel sprouts an' carrots an' peas, an' roast tatties an' chestnut stuffin'.'

'Chestnut stuffin'?' Jess seemed surprised.

'I wouldna fancy it mysel' an' I thought, if I made skirlie an' said it was oatmeal stuffin', it would be a change for them. I've made the puddin' already, for it says it should be kept for twa month, but it would be mouldy by that time, an' Mrs Phillip didna tell me early enough, ony road. I've nae idea what it'll taste like, for I'd to put brandy in, an' I've to pour mair brandy ower it when it's served, an' set a match to it. It sounds queer, but that's what it says in the book. An' I've still to mak' the Christmas pies for ha'ein' wi' their coffee.'

'You wouldna think there was a war on,' Jess observed, having waited patiently to tell her piece of news. 'Drew White's been wounded, an' Nessie's bairn died, though that's maybe a good thing. Pattie says she goes aboot the hoose lookin' for it, an' it wouldna surprise me if she lost the rest o' her wits, noo. She'll nae be so ready to let a man tak' her again, though I doot if she kens that's how the bairn got in her to start wi'.'

'She's a poor thing,' Mysie agreed, 'but what aboot Drew?'

'Pattie says it was shrapnel in his leg, but he's nae bad enough to be sent hame.'

'I hope Doddie never gets wounded.'

Little of the Christmas dinner was sent back to the kitchen, and further proof of its success came when Mrs Phillip went downstairs the next morning. 'All my guests thought that the meal was just perfect, Mrs Duncan, and Gregor, my brother, even said that the oatmeal stuffing was a heaven-sent inspiration. He was always something of a gourmet, so that was indeed a great compliment, and I think you could consider yourself a fully-fledged cook now.'

Mysie felt very proud, but as soon as her employer went out, she turned to her kitchenmaid, who had prepared most of the vegetables and even helped with the dishing-up. 'I'd never ha'e managed withoot you, Meggie.'

The girl glowed with pleasure. 'I'd like to learn to be a cook, though. Would you show me, sometimes?'

'Aye, once Hogmanay's past.'

Hogmanay passed uneventfully. Maitland had gone to see his parents, and old McGregor saw the New Year in quietly with the cook and the kitchenmaid. There were none of the wild parties Mysie had imagined the gentry holding, and if the laird and his wife did take a few drinks, they had kept it very quiet.

On the fourth of January, a letter from Doddie made Mysie sit down and weep, and Meggie, coming in from the scullery, ran across to her full of concern. 'What's wrang?'

'Doddie's comin' hame on leave,' Mysie sobbed.

'You should be happy, then.'

'I am happy, it's just that I havena seen him for near a year an' . . . oh, I'm just bein' daft.'

'Aye are you.'

At Downies, Mysie's good news was rather blunted when Jess told her that Davey Robertson, the eldest son of the farmer at Waterton, had been killed.

'Oh, that's terrible,' Mysie exclaimed. 'He surely wasna auld enough to be in the war?'

Jess shook her head. 'He cheated his age when he enlisted, an' I'm near sure he's nae even seventeen yet.'

'I dinna ken his mother and father, but I'm sorry for them.'

'They never mixed muckle, thought themselves a bit above the rest o' us, but death comes to us a', rich or poor.'

'But nae so often when folk's as young as Davey Robertson.' Mysie's heart cramped suddenly. 'I hope naething happens to Doddie afore he comes hame.'

'He'll be here, dinna fret, lass.'

Perking up a little, Mysie said, 'He'll likely come to Downies first, so tell him to come to me as quick as he can, for I'm desperate to see him.'

Going back to Burnlea House, she didn't even glance at

the blackened walls of Rowanbrae as she cycled past, she was too intent in praying that Doddie was safe.

Chapter Fourteen

1916

Early on Tuesday afternoon, a loud rap at the servants' door sent Mysie running to answer it, almost sending Meggie flying in her haste. Flinging the door open, she felt herself go weak at the knees and stood for a second drinking in the familiar features of the man she loved. He looked older – there were lines on his face that hadn't been there before – and paler, more serious . . . but he was still . . . 'Oh, Doddie!'

He had been waiting uncertainly, but now the khaki arms went round her, holding her as if they would never let her go, and while they stood locked together, he murmured her name against her cheek. 'Mysie, my ain dear Mysie! I can hardly believe I'm wi' you again. It's been such a lang time.'

Meggie was weeping unashamedly at the emotional reunion, but after a moment – a very long moment – she said, 'Look, Mysie, I'll bide in the scullery an' you can tak' your lad into the kitchen an' shut the door.'

Few sensible words were spoken over the next quarter of an hour, embraces and kisses being sufficient to show how much each had missed the other, but at last they broke away. 'Oh, Mysie, I love you mair than ever,' Doddie breathed, sitting down at the side of the large range. 'I've thought aboot you every day, an' pictured your bonnie broon hair an' blue een.'

'I must look a mess,' she protested. 'I've still on my auld apron an' cap.'

'You could never look a mess,' he told her, devouring her with his eyes. 'I'd forgot how bonnie you really were.'

Love for him overcoming her, she sat on his knee to kiss him again, a kiss which kindled long-denied desire in both of them, and Doddie's caresses were growing quite passionate when Mrs Phillip came in. Mysie jumped up, her face scarlet. 'Oh, I'm sorry, Ma'am, but Doddie's new hame on leave . . .'

Her employer smiled indulgently. 'You should have told me he was coming, and I'd have arranged some free time for you, but if you prepare dinner before you go, Meggie can dish up, so you may have the rest of the day off – provided that you do not stay out too late.'

Romantic Meggie was more than willing to see to the dinner and to supervise Sandy when he came home from school, but it was almost an hour before Mysie was satisfied that she had done all she could to leave the kitchen-maid as little work as possible, and she felt able to leave the house with Doddie.

When she first saw him, she had been shocked at the change in him and couldn't get over how thin and drawn his face was, how dull and deep-set his eyes. It was difficult to remember how handsome he had been when he left, rosy cheeks shining with good health, eyes clear and bright, and she was anxious for him to tell her what had wrought the change.

Strolling so slowly between kisses that a snail could have overtaken them, it took them over thirty minutes to walk down the avenue. The grass was too wet to sit on – sleety rain had been falling steadily since early morning – but everything they passed seemed beautiful to them, even the rusty, creaking gate on to the road when they finally came to it.

'We'll just ha'e to go to Downies, there's nae place else we'll get a seat.' Mysie was bitterly disappointed that love-making was out of the question, but at least they were together, and there would be other days.

As they walked, she told him about Nessie White's baby,

about the men who had enlisted after him, about Drew White's wounded leg, about the Christmas dinner, but not about Davey Robertson. Death was a subject that shouldn't be brought up to a serving soldier who would have to return to the front line. At last, with him telling her nothing about the war, she said, 'You must be tired listenin' to me goin' on an' on.'

'I could listen to you for ever.' He squeezed her arm. 'I'm storin' it up in my mind, so when I go back I can picture the kind o' things you'll be daein', an' a' the folk I used to ken. Weel, that's if I get ony peace to think. There's whiles we dinna even get a chance to sleep.'

'Is it awfu' bad ower there, Doddie? Is that why you havena tell't me onything aboot it?'

'Aye, it's bad, lass.'

'Tell me aboot it. I want to picture you when you're awa', like you'll be picturin' me. I want to ken the places you've been an' what happened to you.'

'Mysie, I want to forget it.'

'Please, Doddie?'

'It's naething but trenches an' shells an' . . .' He turned towards her, sighing. 'A' right, I'll tell you. It'll maybe dae me good, for it eats awa' inside me sometimes, an' I swear I'll never forget some o' the things I've saw. When I went ower first, we was in a place called Neuve Chapelle. That wasna so bad, for we had a twelve-day tour o' duty – two days in the trenches, two oot, two in, two oot, an' so on, then six days rest in reserve. Even though, a lot o' the men were killed or wounded. When we were pulled oot o' there, we were marched to St Julien, just a little place nae much bigger than Burnlea, an' a' we saw was dead horses an' men lyin' aboot. The shell-fire was the worst we'd had, an' one o' the Canadian divisions wi' us was near wiped oot.'

Mysie, absolutely horrified by what he was saying, let him carry on, knowing that if she interrupted, he would clam up. 'The nichts was the worst, white flares goin' up a' the time, an' machine-guns you couldna see though you

145

ken't they were there for there was lang bursts o' firin' whiles, an' shells whistlin' ower your head – if you was lucky. But the worst place, for me ony road, was Loos. A terrible battle was ragin' afore we got there, an' the Northumberland Fusiliers were goin' in for the attack. Nae very mony o' them survived.' He halted there, overwhelmed by the memory of it. 'Oh, Mysie, I shouldna tell you things like that – I didna mean to tell you onything.'

'I wanted to ken, Doddie. Will you be goin' back to Loos?'

Full of remorse for what he had already said, he felt obliged to reassure her. 'No, I shouldna think it. We've daen mair than oor share.' He knew perfectly well that he would be back in the front line soon, but it was best that she didn't know.

When they arrived at Downies, Jess said, 'You're blue wi' the cauld, baith o' you, sit doon at the fire. The supper's in the oven, but Jake wants me to help him wi' . . .'

Standing up, Doddie cried, 'No, let me help him. You sit doon an' speak to Mysie.'

Jess pushed him back into his seat. 'Mysie's seen me every second week since you went awa', an' it's you she wants to . . . speak to. Tak' the chance when you've got it.' She marched out, smiling broadly.

'I thought I'd best offer to help,' he told Mysie, 'though I didna want to leave you. Ony road, I can help Jake the times I canna see you. I must work for my keep.'

'Aye,' she murmured, shy now that they were alone inside, and still recovering from the horrors he had described, although she suspected that it had been much worse for him than he had told her.

Her slight blush made him feel like sweeping her up in his arms and carrying her through to the Findlaters' bed, but that was impossible, so he drew his chair up next to hers and took her hand. 'I've dreamed aboot this for months, Mysie. I used to think aboot you when we was on guard duty, or back aff the line for a rest, and I sometimes planned what we'll dae when we're in oor ain place.'

146

They were still planning for their own small croft – Mysie even saying she wanted honeysuckle round their porch – when Jess came in again, stumbling intentionally over the back step to warn them. 'He looks real good in the kilt, doesn't he?'

Mysie nodded. 'Aye, does he.' Doddie *was* an exceptionally fine figure of a man in the kilt, she thought, his legs firm and sturdy, his back so erect that the pleats fell straight down to his knees, but his khaki jacket was hanging loosely on him. Had it always been like that, she wondered, or had he grown that much thinner since it had been fitted? Maybe they didn't fit them, though. Maybe they just handed out whatever sizes were available.

After supper, they all sat round the fireside talking, Jake stepping in to fill any awkward gaps in the conversation, but Doddie couldn't stop himself from looking frequently at Mysie, his eyes telling her that this was not how he had envisaged them passing their precious time together. The evening was well advanced when Mysie noticed the time and gasped. 'Oh, I should ha'e been awa' ages ago.' Standing up, she felt ashamed that she had never given one thought to Sandy for hours, nor to how Meggie Duff was coping on her own.

Doddie held her coat up for her. 'I'll walk you back.'

'But you'll ha'e to walk back here again.'

'I'd walk to the ends o' the earth for you, Mysie,' he told her earnestly, not caring that Jess and Jake would also hear.

It was far too cold now to linger on their journey, but it was after ten before they arrived at Burnlea House. 'I'm goin' to Fyvie the morn, to see my father,' Doddie said at the door, 'but I'll come for you on your next time aff.'

'I've got the afternoon on Thursday, but I havena a whole day till the Sunday the week after.'

'That's the day I've to leave,' he said sadly. 'Oh, weel, it canna be helped. What time will I come on Thursday?'

'I could maybe manage half-past one, an' I've to be back at six, for their dinner's at seven.'

'Half past one, then.' He kissed her and hurried away.

Mysie went through her kitchen and ran up the back stairs. Meggie was in bed, but not asleep. 'I got on fine,' she said, proudly, 'an' Sandy was as good as gold, so I could let you oot ilka nicht Doddie's here, if you like?'

'But Mrs Phillip wouldna . . .'

'If you wait till the dinner's past she's nae needin' to ken. She never comes doon the stair at nicht, you ken that fine.'

Mysie longed to accept the offer, but wasn't too sure about it. 'We'll see. Doddie's goin' to Fyvie the morn, an' I'll be aff on Thursday afternoon ony road, but maybe on Friday.'

With having nothing to look forward to on Wednesday, Mysie was all the more irritable with Sandy when he did not eat his breakfast. 'Wastin' good food like that! Get it doon you!'

It was not until he said, 'When will Doddie be goin' awa'?' that she realised what was wrong with him. 'He's to go back a week on Sunday,' she told him, her voice much softer.

'I didna ken where you were when I come hame fae the school yesterday, nae till Meggie tell't me.'

'I didna ken mysel' that I'd get oot. Oh, Sandy, you're nae angry that I was wi' Doddie, are you? I thought you was big enough for me to leave you a while, an' Meggie was there.'

'I am big enough, I'm nae a baby.' He lifted his spoon and began to sup his porridge, in an effort to show her that her short desertion had not upset him.

'I dinna ken what to dae aboot Sandy,' Mysie told Meggie when they sat down at half-past ten to have a cup of tea. 'I think he's nae very pleased at me goin' oot wi' Doddie.'

The kitchenmaid pushed a strand of hair away from her eyes. 'He didna say naething last night.'

'No, but maybe I should tell Doddie I canna get oot . . .'

'Dinna be daft, Mysie! Sandy an' me got on fine, he's just puttin' it on wi' you.'

'I suppose so.' Mysie had too much work to do to worry any more about Sandy. He was only a bairn and he would soon get over it, and it wasn't as if she was doing anything wrong.

On Thursday afternoon, she and Doddie meandered round the grounds of the house, stopping to kiss behind a tree every now and then, and she would willingly have let him make love to her standing up if he had tried. They were almost back at the house when he stopped once more and looked at her earnestly. 'Mysie, maybe you think I dinna want you, but I just canna tak' you like a beast, though I'm desperate for you.'

'I wouldna mind, Doddie,' she whispered, shyly.

'No, lass. I love you mair than ever I did, but I dinna want to spoil things atween us. I would feel as if I was treatin' you like a whore, an' it's nae just for that I love you. Can you understand what I mean?'

'Aye, I can, an' I suppose you're right.'

'If only we had some place to go . . . och, Mysie, I'm bein' selfish. I can wait.' He drew her into his arms again, his kisses showing how much he wanted her, but in no time, he drew away abruptly. 'I'll nae be able to wait if we go on like this. Afore you go in, will I see you again?'

'Meggie says it should be a' right if I took an hour or so aff ilka night, so come at the back o' seven the morn's nicht.'

For the rest of Doddie's leave, Mysie closed her eyes to her son's pique, and allowed herself some time off every evening. Unfortunately, the weather was against them, it being January, but even the snow and hail beating down on them didn't lessen their happiness at being together.

All too soon, the day of his departure came, and at eleven o'clock on Sunday forenoon, she sat tearfully in Downies with Jess, Jake and Sandy, trying not to let them see that her heart was breaking. Of course, she had to carry on as usual when she returned to the Big House, and, within a week, it was as though Doddie had never been home.

Mrs Phillip's father died unexpectedly in Aberdeen in May, so everyone crept about sadly for a few days, but Mysie was more upset when Jess told her that Denny Petrie had been killed. For as much as she had disliked Jean, she wouldn't have wished that on her, and it made her more concerned for Doddie – two deaths connected with the place already, there was bound to be a third, sooner or later.

Before she knew it, the school summer holidays were on them and Bobby Phillip and Sandy were on the loose again. Little Beatrice knew to steer clear of them, but they still got into scrapes. Finding the mower McGregor had left out while he had a mid-morning cup of tea, they ran around the lawn with it, pushing it off the grass eventually and decapitating a whole row of colourful dahlias. Being threatened with confinement to the house if they went near the gardens again, they dared each other to climb one of the stately oaks that lined the curved avenue, and, sitting on a slim branch which snapped under the combined weight, they ended up with a broken leg apiece.

'It's lucky for you Maitland had been into the toon,' Mysie scolded her nine-year-old son afterwards. 'You could ha'e lain there for lang enough withoot onybody kennin'.'

'Och, Mam,' Sandy protested. 'Was you never young?'

No, she thought, ruefully. She had never been young, not in that way, for she'd had the responsibility of looking after her younger brothers and sisters until she'd gone into service, and when she was newly sixteen, her father had forced her into a loveless marriage. Her mind sheered off her marriage. It was Doddie she wanted to see again, Doddie she wanted to share a new life with in a new home, but that day would come, and they would look back on their time apart as a bad memory.

The accident forced confinement on the boys after all,

and the holidays were almost over before they were fit to go out to play again. Their experience had had a sobering effect on them, however, so they got up to no further escapades.

Mrs Phillip presented another challenge to Mysie towards the end of November. 'I am giving a ball in about three weeks. Some officer friends of my husband's and their wives, also some relatives and perhaps the farmers and their wives. I do not care for Mrs Mutch, but . . .'

'How mony'll be comin'?' Catering for a large number didn't worry Mysie any more, but she would have to know exactly.

'Prepare dinner for fifty, that should be enough . . . or is that too many for you?'

'No, no, I'll manage that. Will you be makin' oot a list o' what you want served?'

'I'll leave it to you, but I'd like to see the menu once you have decided. I had better hire two waitresses. Meggie will be needed to help you, and neither Chrissie nor Janey would be very suitable, but they can lend a hand with the washing up.'

Mysie couldn't help smiling as she imagined seventeen-year-old, gawky Janey Paterson carrying trays of plates – they'd be sure to land on the floor – and Chrissie Grant, although she was bold enough for her sixteen years at times, would run a mile if one of the gentry as much as looked at her.

'By the way,' Mrs Phillip continued, 'I'm sorry to give you more work, but some of the guests will be staying on for a day or two, so . . .'

'That's a' right, Mrs Phillip, if you let me ken how mony folk there'll be for every meal.'

'Yes, of course.'

The next three weeks passed in a flash. Mysie studied the 'Special Occasions' section of the old cookery book, choosing recipes for meat, fowl and game which she thought would give a wide enough selection to suit all

151

tastes, and wrote out a menu to show her mistress, who gave it her approval. Then she made a list of what she would have to order, and washed all the utensils and dishes she would need in the preparations.

Meggie, still hoping to be a cook some day, hung on to her every word, watched her every movement, and Mysie was quite happy to instruct her. The girl was quick to learn, and turned out to have a natural hand for pastry and sponges. Everything that could be prepared beforehand had been set on the marble shelves in the coolest pantry, covered to keep flies off. The pheasants, quails, wood-pigeons and hares supplied by the old gamekeeper had been hung for two weeks and were now ready to be plucked, or skinned, and gutted before cooking; the beef, pork and lamb were marinating in large bowls.

The rest of the staff were also kept busy. The housemaids had to make bedrooms ready for guests who would be staying. Maitland cleaned and polished the motor car – a big Daimler – which had recently been bought by Mr Phillip, raked the gravel on the drive and made sure that the front of the house bore no signs of birds' droppings, while McGregor occupied his time by keeping the gardens looking their best.

On the day of the ball, Mysie rose at three in the morning, determined that everything would be ready in time, and young Meggie joined her at four, also anxious that there would be no hitches. They worked silently, preparing vegetables, basting, stirring, seasoning, tasting. When Sandy came down at seven, he was handed a large sacking apron and told to buff up the silver cutlery which Meggie had already rubbed vigorously with bathbrick. A cold luncheon was sent up to the dining room at half-past twelve, but little was eaten in the kitchen.

When the two waitresses arrived late in the afternoon, their faces were almost as forbidding as their stiff black dresses and starched caps and aprons, giving Mysie a moment's panic. What would these women think of her efforts? They were professionals, used to large functions.

152

Had she garnished the dishes properly? Did they look attractive enough? But she hadn't time to dwell on it, and the waitresses did not look at all critical or amused when everything was laid out on the large table ready to be carried upstairs to the dining room.

As time went by and the first trays of dirty dishes were taken down, Meggie, Janey and Chrissie set about washing and drying them, leaving Mysie to concentrate on having the following courses ready. It was only when the empty coffee cups came back that Mysie relaxed, sinking thankfully into the wooden armchair beside the range. Long strands of her dark hair, damp with perspiration, were straggling out from under her cap, her apron was dotted with the multicoloured stains of gravy and juices, her feet were throbbing, but she felt a sense of achievement such as she had never experienced before. The waitresses had said that most of the guests had sent her their compliments, and her hard work had not been in vain.

The fine china washed, Meggie set the scrubbed kitchen table with earthenware plates, and the staff sat down to finish off most of what had been left over. The two waitresses proved to be quite human after all, amusing the others with tales of the catastrophes at previous dinners they had been hired for, and old McGregor unbent enough to describe the peculiarities of the gentry who had employed him over the years.

Mr Phillip had engaged a quartet for the ball, and, as Mysie supervised the laying past of crockery and cutlery, the strains of music filtering downstairs made them all feel less tired. The young maids were desperate to find out what was going on in the ballroom, so Mysie let them go up, one at a time, to have a peep through the open door before they went to bed, and then went up herself for a few minutes. She was amazed that the dress uniforms of the officers almost outshone the colours of the ladies' dresses, and would have liked to watch longer, but was scared that she'd be seen. In any case, she was ready for bed. It had been a long, hard day.

It was after ten the following morning before Mrs Phillip came to the kitchen, accompanied by a tall, gaunt officer in the uniform of the Scots Guards, but her beaming face showed that everything had run smoothly the evening before. 'This is my brother,' she told Mysie, 'Captain Wallace. Everyone said the meal was the best they had ever tasted, but he wanted to see my marvellous cook for himself.'

'I'm impressed,' her brother said. 'I expected a fat old lady, rather like a bolster tied in the middle, but I find a beautiful girl who can't be more than seventeen, with a figure that would outshine the Venus de Milo.'

Blushing, Mysie looked away. 'I'm twenty-seven, sir.'

'Oh,' he said, his eyes dancing although she didn't see them, 'I suppose you think that's really old? Well, since I am forty, you must think I am in my dotage.'

'Stop teasing, Gregor.' His sister registered disapproval. 'You will be turning Mrs Duncan's head. Come away and let her get on with her work, otherwise there will be no luncheon.'

When they went out, Meggie, who had been standing with her mouth open, said, 'He's nae very good-lookin', is he? An' he's naething like his sister, though he's got her een.'

'I never noticed.' Mysie had been so overcome by the praise and flattery that she hadn't been able to look at him after the first glance, but he had a sweet tongue, that was sure, telling her that she only looked seventeen.

Gregor Wallace came into the kitchen after breakfast next day, sitting on the arm of a chair and chatting to Mysie as she worked and making her as flustered as Meggie. It was true that he wasn't very handsome, but there was an attractiveness there – his eyes, his smile, she couldn't put her finger on it. His lean upright body had the stamp of a soldier, his hair was the colour of treacle candy, his small, neat moustache just a fraction lighter, with a touch of gold through it. She couldn't help liking him, although he was teasing her a bit.

'I wish I could take you back with me to cook for us,' he smiled. 'You'd be a real treasure, but all the other men would go wild about you, too.'

'Och, you're bletherin',' she said, embarrassed.

'I'd fight them off, though. Captains have first pick of all the beautiful girls, and I would lay claim to you.'

His admiration made her uneasy. She didn't mind when he was just talking, but she wasn't used to this kind of joking. When he went out, she turned sharply on the grinning kitchenmaid. 'Stop your laughin', Meggie. Men like him flirt wi' ony woman they come across, an' think servants are fair game to them.'

On the following morning, the Captain came into the kitchen again. 'I had to come to see you, my fairest,' he murmured, slipping his arm round her waist. You haunted my dreams and made me desperate.'

Mysie extricated herself as firmly as she could, wishing that she could stop the hot flush that she could feel coming into her cheeks. 'Excuse me, Captain Wallace, but I must get on.'

'Can you not spare a minute to say goodbye to a poor soldier returning to battle?' Laying his hands on her shoulders, he turned her round to face him, then placed one finger under her chin to tilt her head up. 'Ah, you are blushing. Does that mean what I hope it means?'

His lips were within half an inch of meeting hers when Mrs Phillip opened the door. 'Gregor! I will not have you acting like this with any of my servants! Please go.'

Seemingly unabashed, he dropped his hands. 'Margaret, if you employ such a lovely cook, you can't blame me for . . .'

'That is enough. Leave the kitchen at once.' She waited until he closed the door, then rounded on Mysie. 'As for you, Mrs Duncan, I did not think you would encourage him, and in future, please remember to keep your place.'

'I'm sorry, Ma'am,' Mysie mumbled, her cheeks deep crimson now, 'but I didna encourage him.'

'I am quite sure that you could have stopped him.'

155

Mrs Phillip flounced out, leaving Mysie almost in tears, and Meggie, having seen everything from the scullery, came through to sympathise. 'It wasna your blame, an' what a way for a man like him to be carryin' on. It mak's you wonder.'

Feeling guilty although she had done nothing wrong, Mysie said, 'I tell't you. The gentry think servants are fair game.'

Only half an hour later, the Captain poked his head round the kitchen door. 'Margaret is busy,' he told Mysie, who had stepped back in alarm. 'I'm sorry she caught me, but I'm not sorry for what I did. Don't be afraid, though, I am not coming in. I just wanted to let you know that I have to leave this afternoon. I wish I could stay here for ever to be near you, Mrs Duncan, but the war still has to be won.'

'Aye,' Mysie said, nervously. 'My Doddie's in France wi' the Gordons, but he's goin' to get his ain place when the war's finished, an' Sandy an' me'll be leavin' here.'

'Oh.' He sounded quite disappointed. 'I thought you were a widow. I didn't realise that your husband was in the army.'

She didn't correct him as he closed the door. It was best to leave him thinking that she was married to Doddie, and, in any case, she was, in everything except name.

Chapter Fifteen

Life at Burnlea House had returned to normal after the last guest left – although even Mrs Phillip had admitted that she felt flat for weeks – and the months rolled past relentlessly.

In April, 1917, Meggie returned from a visit home with the news that her brother Robbie had been conscripted. 'Da tried to get him aff, but it was nae use.'

'What a shame.' Mysie was sorry for Rab Duff, who would be left to work Wellbrae on his own now. He was not a robust man and Belle wouldn't be much help to him.

Shortly afterwards, Mysie learned that both Frank Mutch of Fingask and David Robertson, senior, of Waterton had gone to tribunal to plead against the conscription of their labourers. 'Gavin Leslie's awa',' Jess told her, 'an' the horseman as weel, an' Frankie said he wouldna manage wi' just Eck Petrie an' the young loon, but they just said the other three had to go. They werena so hard on Robertson, for he's lost one son already, an' he's nae very weel himsel', so they've left him wi' three men.'

As Mysie cycled back, she wondered if the war would ever end. It was coming up for three years since it had started, and Doddie had been away for over two of them. She couldn't bear the thought of him being away much longer, but surely he would be home on leave again soon – it was a year past January since she had seen him.

His letters were still coming, very occasionally, and she read them out proudly to Meggie, who sighed with envy at the things he wrote. 'I dinna think naebody'll ever tell me he can hardly live withoot me,' she moaned one day.

'You're young yet,' Mysie soothed. 'You'll meet the lad for you ane o' these days.'

On Mysie's next day off, Jess Findlater told her that some of Doddie's most affectionate phrases were being bandied about in the village. 'I'm surprised at you for tellin' Meggie what he writes, for she tells her mother an' Belle goes right to Jean Petrie wi' it, you ken how close they are. You'd be as weel gettin' his letters printed in the Press & Journal. I thought Jean would simmer doon a bit after Denny was killed, but she's as bad as ever, if nae worse.'

Mysie could picture both Jean and Belle sniggering over what Doddie had written, but she didn't care. 'They can laugh as muckle as they like, for he's takin' me an' Sandy awa' wi' him when the war's finished.'

Jess eyed her pityingly. 'They're sayin' he'll nae come back here to you, Mysie, noo he's had a taste o' freedom.'

'He will so come back to me,' Mysie declared, confidently, 'an' I'm surprised at you for listenin' to them.'

'I'm only tellin' you what's bein' said, lass, but I'm sorry if I've upset you.'

'I wouldna let onything Jean Petrie said upset me.'

'Aye, weel.' Jess sighed, then asked, 'An' what mischief has Bobby Phillip an' Sandy got up to since I saw you last?'

Mysie launched into an account of the latest prank. 'They sneaked oot ane o' Mrs Phillip's frocks an' a hat, an' you'll never guess what they did?'

'What would twa laddies be wantin' wi' a frock an' a hat?'

'Weel, I was choppin' parsley when the kitchen door opened, an' I thought it was Sandy, so I says, "I've new washed that floor, so clean your feet." He never answered, an' I looked roon' an' near chopped my finger aff. Here was this muckle dog wi' the frock an' hat on, an' lookin' up at me wi' his great een like he was pleadin' wi' me to help him.'

'Oh, God save us.' Jess held her sides as she laughed, and Mysie, rather belatedly, saw the funny side, too.

'They'd even put a pair o' her bloomers on him, an' he was that pleased when I stripped him, poor Brutus, he licked a' ower my face an' near knocked me ower. I never ken what that twa loons'll get up to next.'

'There's naething wicked in them, though.' Jess wiped her streaming eyes. 'It's just fun.'

It was almost eleven o'clock at night and Meggie hadn't come back from her day off. It wasn't pitch dark yet, being August, but Mysie was beginning to worry that she'd had an accident on her bicycle when she burst in, her face radiant.

'I was bikin' back, an' I sees Drew White – you mind him, the miller's loon? – an' I shouts, "You'll be hame on

158

leave, Drew?" an' he says, "Stop a minute, Meggie," an'
I didna need twa tellin's, for he's awfu' good-lookin' in his
kilt. I gets aff my bike, an' he says, "Put it doon on the
grass." So I laid it doon an' he sits doon an' pulls me doon
aside him.'

Mysie's face had darkened. Drew White was far too old
for Meggie – twenty-seven to her sixteen – and what had
he done to her to make her look as happy as this? 'Go on,
then,' she coaxed, reluctant to issue any warnings unless
she was certain that they were needed.

'Weel, we sits an' speaks for a while, an' he tells me
he's been awa' to the toon to meet some o' his sodger
chums, then he says, "I've to go back to France in fower
days, so you'll nae refuse me a little kiss, will you,
Meggie?" Weel, I couldna say no when he's goin' back to
the trenches, an' ony road, I wanted to see what a kiss
would be like.'

'An' did it live up to your expectations?'

'Oh, aye, an' once he started, he wouldna stop, nae that
I wanted him to stop, for my he'rt was bangin' against my
ribs, an' I thought it would burst ony minute. Is that love,
Mysie?'

In spite of her misgivings, Mysie had to laugh. 'I couldna
tell you that, Meggie, you should ken yoursel'.' She sobered then. 'It was love for me an' Doddie wi' the first kiss,'
she admitted, after a moment.

'Weel, I'm near sure I love Drew, an' he wouldna kiss
me like that if he didna love me, would he?'

'A man that's been awa' fae lassies for as lang as him
would kiss a coo an' think naething aboot it.' Mysie regretted her flippancy as Meggie's face fell. 'Did he dae onything else to you, besides kissin'?'

'He tell't me I'd grown up into a bonnie quine, an' he
near squeezed the breath oot o' me.'

A little relieved, Mysie said, 'Did he ask to see you
again?'

'He said he'll come up here the morrow nicht at eight,
if I could get oot. Will you let me, Mysie?'

Mysie couldn't refuse the pleading eyes, and the girl had let her go out when Doddie was on leave. 'A' right then, but watch yoursel'. You're nae wantin' to land wi' a bairn, are you?'

'I'm sure Drew wouldna dae onything he shouldna, an' I'm nae as green as I'm cabbage-lookin'.'

Mysie was still laughing when she went upstairs, but as she undressed, she recalled how easy it was to be carried away by a man's kisses, even a man you didn't love.

For the next two nights, it was late before Meggie came in, her face flushed but her starry eyes meeting Mysie's frankly. On Drew's last night, however, as Mysie had been half fearing, there was a new maturity in them. The girl coloured and gave a nervous laugh. 'I couldna help mysel', Mysie, an' it wasna Drew's fault, for he didna want . . . nae to start wi', but a' at a sudden, his hands were a' ower me me, an' . . .'

'You needna tell me ony mair. I ken a' aboot that.'

'Was it the same wi' you an' Doddie? Oh, Mysie, there's nae another thing in the world could mak' a lassie feel like that.'

Mysie stood up. 'I only hope you'll feel as happy in another month or twa. Get awa' to your bed an' let me get to mine.'

On her own day off, she didn't tell Jess about Meggie and Drew White. She knew what it was like to be talked about and wanted to shield the girl from the pain of that for as long as she could, although nothing would hide the mating if anything did come of it. It wasn't the poor girl's fault anyway, for Drew should have known the possible consequences of his act.

Jess had her own piece of news to impart. 'Jinty Mutch is to be startin' at the Infirmary in Aberdeen in October. She'd tell't Frankie that she wanted to be a nurse so she could help the wounded soldiers, but, my God, I hope the war's ower afore she finishes her trainin'.'

'Oh, I hope so, but I'm pleased for her. She was aye a clever lassie, Jinty, an' I'm sure she'll . . .'

A knock on the porch made her stop, but before Jess could stand up, the kitchen door opened and Mysie jumped up with a squeal. 'Doddie! You never let me ken you were comin'.'

'I didna ken mysel',' he laughed. 'We was just tell't we was on leave an' that was it.'

'I've got some things to dae ootside,' Jess muttered, rising and going out as quickly as she could. The young man and woman melted together, no words necessary to express their feelings, but at last Doddie said, 'I didna ken you'd be at Downies, Mysie. I was thinkin' I'd ha'e to come to the Big Hoose to see you.'

'It's my day aff, an' I've to go back the nicht.'

'Maybe Meggie'll bide wi' Sandy some other nichts?'

'Aye, will she, for she's got a lad hersel' noo, an' she kens what it is to be in love. Oh, Doddie, I've missed you.'

They made up for lost time as much as possible until Jess's voice, louder than usual, warned them that the world was about to intrude on their reunion, and when Jake came in, he held out his rough, weatherbeaten hand. 'It's good to see you again, Doddie, man.'

'It's good to be back, Jake.' After suppertime, Doddie walked with Mysie to Burnlea House, wheeling the bicycle for her, and she couldn't help smiling when he stopped before they came to the gates and laid it down on the grass. She didn't have to be pulled down like Meggie, and lay next him willingly, aching for his love, responding to it as passionately as it was given.

For the whole of Doddie's leave, the kitchenmaid made Mysie go out with him every night – she didn't need much persuading – and they strolled arm-in-arm until mounting desire made them lie down, the harvest moon smiling down on them through the flickering leaves of the silver birches scattered round the grounds as if bestowing a blessing for the future.

It was on his last night that Mysie was made uneasily aware that their future might not be as rosy as she imagined. They had reached the farthest corner of the wall

161

surrounding the house and gardens when Doddie stopped to light a cigarette, a new habit he had picked up while he was away, and she didn't object because she quite liked the manly smell of the tobacco.

After drawing in deeply, he threw the match on the ground and stood on it. 'I canna stop thinkin' o' the time we'll be in oor ain place. I'd like a wee croft aboot the same size as Rowanbrae, an' there would just be you an' me an' Sandy, an' maybe a wee lassie or laddie come time, or maybe baith?'

Her love for him almost overwhelmed her. 'Oh, I wish it was right noo, Doddie. I'm tired o' waitin'.'

'Aye, it must be worse for you than it is for me. I havena had a real hame since I started workin', but . . .' He broke off, looking at her apologetically. 'I'm sorry, Mysie, I ken I was bidin' wi' you for months, but it didna . . . it wasna like a . . . oh, I'm nae meanin' to hurt you, lass, but it was still Jeems Duncan's hoose to me.'

A coldness stole over her. 'Jeems wouldna ha'e come back.'

'You couldna be sure o' that?' His voice was sharp. 'What dae you think happened to him?'

Mysie wondered if she should tell him now, but this wasn't the time nor the place to say that she had killed Jeems. She should maybe give him a hint, though. 'I dinna ken, Doddie. I think he must be . . . dead.'

'What mak's you think that?'

She couldn't bring herself to utter the damning words. 'He hasna . . . naebody's ever spoke aboot seein' him ony place, an' he canna ha'e . . .'

'He maybe doesna want to be seen. Eh . . . Mysie, I've often wondered what it was that you an' him fought aboot? You can surely tell me noo? It's been three an' a half year.'

Her throat constricted. 'It was naething, Doddie. Just a stupid row ower naething.'

'But Rosie Mennie tell't me your face was a terrible mess o' bruises. He wouldna ha'e hit you like that if it was naething. You can tell me, Mysie, I'll nae judge you.'

162

She was growing more and more agitated. 'It was nae-thing, I tell you. You ken what a temper he had. Do you nae mind him hittin' you, an' that was for naething?'

'It wasna for naething. I'd kissed his wife, an' he'd a right to hit me. Eh . . . there wasna ony other man, was there?'

'There wasna . . . I never loved naebody but you, Doddie. I swear to God I never.' Her evident distress made him say, hastily, 'Weel, there's nae sense in dwellin' on what's past. When we've got oor ain croft, it'll be different. We could maybe go sooth, to Laurencekirk say, or up north Elgin way. Nae a soul would ken we werena lawfully wed, an' if Jeems ever did come back to Burnlea, he wouldna ken where to look for us.'

'I'll nae care where it is, as lang as we're thegither.'

'We'll be the happiest man an' woman in the world . . .' His voice thickened. 'Oh, Mysie, my ain dear love.'

She gave herself to him thankfully when he stubbed out his cigarette and pulled her down on the mossy grass, forgetting everything in the joy of their union. Long after it was over, they still clung to each other, not kissing, but each taking comfort from the other for the imminent parting.

At last, Mysie whispered, unwillingly, 'It must be awfu' late, Doddie. I'll hae to go in.'

'I dinna ken when I'll see you again, or how I'm goin' to live withoot you.' But he jumped up to help her to her feet, and they walked hand in hand to the servants' door. 'Weel, this is goodbye, Mysie, but never forget I love you.'

'An' I love you.' Her voice was choked with emotion. As he kissed her, tenderly and lovingly, she tried to push away the thought that it would be the last kiss for a long time, and was actually glad when he tore himself away and walked round the corner of the house. She couldn't have stood much more.

In bed, she relived every minute of the time he'd been with her, lingering over the memory of his kisses and love-making, then she reluctantly turned her mind to what they had talked about. It was almost as if Doddie knew what she had done and had tried to make her confess, but how could he know – unless he had been there? Then he had said that Jeems would never find them if they went far enough away. She hadn't realised the importance of that statement until now. He surely wouldn't have spoken about Jeems still being alive if he had been the one who killed him? Not unless it was just a bluff. Was it because he *was* guilty that he hadn't felt at ease in Rowanbrae? She was practically certain that she hadn't been responsible . . . and Doddie was the only other person who'd had any cause to put Jeems out of the way. She loved him with all her heart, in spite of her doubts, but for the rest of her life she would be wondering about that, and likely, if he were innocent, he would wonder when Jeems would track them down. How could their life together be happy with that hanging over them? How could their dreams ever be fulfilled?

Chapter Sixteen

The realisation that she was expecting Doddie's child came as a bittersweet shock to Mysie – bitter because she would have to give up her job; sweet because she had longed to give him a son of his own – but she should have known what those moments of uninhibited passion would lead to, and it would be best not to tell her employer until she could no longer hide it.

Unfortunately, she reckoned without Sandy. Upset at seeing her sick every morning, he asked Mrs Phillip if his mother was ill. She reassured him by saying, 'All women have to suffer sickness from time to time,' but watched her cook speculatively over the next few days. The dark-circled eyes and the pinched face were enough to confirm her suspicions, and Mysie's guilty expression only endorsed them. 'You're pregnant, aren't you?' she demanded one morning when Meggie was out of earshot.

This put an end to Mysie's hopes of working for as long as she could. 'I was meanin' to tell you in a wee while, Mrs Phillip, but I'll leave the day if you want, or I could bide till you get another cook.'

'I don't want you to leave at all – you are the best cook I ever had – but I think that you should go away from Burnlea to save people knowing about this.'

'I dinna care aboot other folk . . . but I suppose it would be embarrassin' for you if I bade here?'

Mrs Phillip hesitated. 'Well, yes . . . have you ever heard from your husband since he left you?'

The old fear gripped Mysie again. 'No, nae a thing.'

'That's a pity, because if you had known where he was you could have divorced him, but this means that you will not be free to marry the child's father.'

'No.' What was the point of trying to make out different? It wasn't true, but it was what everyone believed.

Now that Mrs Phillip knew, Mysie saw no reason not to tell Meggie when they were alone. 'You were lucky. It's me that's landed wi' a bairn.'

'Oh, Mysie!' The girl was sympathetic, not triumphant, as she had every cause to be.

'It's my ain fault, I'm auld enough to ken better.' Mysie gave a sad laugh. 'An' here was me tellin' you to watch.'

'Does the mistress ken?' At Mysie's nod, Meggie went on, 'What did she say? Did she gi'e you the sack?'

'She was awfu' nice aboot it, but she would like me to leave afore folk notice onything.'

'What'll you dae?'

'I havena had time to think yet.'

'Look, Mysie, I'll nae tell onybody, nae even my ain mother, for she would tell Jean Petrie, an' she would tell a'body, an' you ken what folk are like roon' here.'

'I ken what they're like,' Mysie said, wryly.

A few weeks later, Mysie had just gone upstairs when

Meggie, back from a visit to her parents, burst into her room without knocking. 'Doddie Wilson's been killed.' In her pregnant state, the abrupt announcement was too much for Mysie, who crumpled in a heap, and Meggie, out of her mind with fear, raced downstairs to the sitting room. 'Oh, Ma'am, Mysie's dropped doon dead.'

Mrs Phillip jumped up, alarmed until she recalled her cook's condition, then, presuming that it was probably a faint, she took the smelling salts out of a cupboard and followed the terrified girl up to the top floor. After wafting the bottle vigorously under Mysie's nose a few times, she was rewarded by a spluttering cough. 'Do you feel better now, Mrs Duncan?' she asked solicitously. 'You gave Meggie a dreadful fright.'

Mysie's eyes were fixed on the girl. 'It's nae true? I was dreamin', wasn't I? Doddie hasna been killed?'

Mrs Phillip's eyes softened even more. 'Ah, so that's it?'

Meggie hung her head. 'I'm awfu' sorry, Mysie, but it *is* true. It was in the day's Press & Journal, for Da let me see it in the list o' Casyou . . . al . . . ities.'

'I'll fetch the newspaper from the morning room, Mrs Duncan, if Chrissie hasn't thrown it out.'

As Mrs Phillip went out, Mysie sat down on the bed to cuddle Sandy, who had been awakened by all the commotion, and Meggie burst into tears. 'Oh, Mysie, I'm sorry for comin' oot wi' it like that. I was that cut up . . .'

'Dinna worry aboot it. I'm sorry I gi'ed you a fear.'

'I thought you'd died o' shock.'

'If that was how shocks took me, I'd ha'e died lang ago.'

'Mam said you'd had your share o' troubles.' Meggie did not repeat Belle's further remark – 'This is a judgement on her an' Doddie for livin' in sin.' – for she had said too much already. When Mysie received the newspaper from Mrs Phillip, she went straight to the end of the Casualty list. 'Corporal William Winpenny, Turriff . . . oh, I mind on Willie Winpenny – he was at the school wi' me. Private George Wilson, Fyvie.' Looking up at her mistress pathetically, she explained. 'He put his father doon as next o' kin, so it's him they'd tell't.'

'I'm so sorry.' Margaret Phillip laid her hand on her cook's shoulder. 'I did not know his surname, and I did not realise that it was your . . . Doddie's death when I read it.'

Meggie was still sniffling. 'My Da said Doddie had tell't him his father bade at Fyvie, that's the road he ken't it was him and nae some other George Wilson.'

'Go and make some tea, Meggie,' Mrs Phillip instructed, 'and take Sandy with you to help you carry the things up here.' Waiting until they went out, she said, 'It *would* be better if you left the area quite soon, Mrs Duncan. I have heard that some of the local women have vile tongues, especially Petrie's wife, and probably the children at school would taunt Sandy about what they heard at home.'

'But I've nae place to go. Jess Findlater hasna room an' ony road, she couldna keep us for naething for months. I'll ha'e to get another job for a while.'

'What about your mother? Where does she live?'

'Oh, I couldna go to my mother.' It was the last thing Mysie would have wanted to do. 'I havena seen her since the day o' my father's funeral – that's mair than eleven year ago. I did write to her for a good while, then she got wed again.'

Incorrectly assuming that Mysie's stepfather had refused to let his wife have anything more to do with her, her employer sat down on a chair, her brow furrowing in deep thought, while Mysie sat on the edge of the bed, wishing that she knew how Doddie had been killed, and wondering mournfully if he'd had time to think about her before he died. Then her mind turned to her mother again, and she felt very thankful that *she* would never know the terrible things her daughter had done.

Mrs Phillip startled her by exclaiming, 'I have the perfect solution. My aunt's cook-housekeeper is leaving shortly, I don't know exactly when, but I am sure she would be delighted to have you. She is eighty and has rather a wicked temper, which is why her housekeepers never remain long with her, but if you could put up with her, it would be a home for you. Even if she only lives for a year or so it would give you time after the baby is born to arrange your own future. I'll be very sorry to lose you – you're such a good cook, and trustworthy, which is more than can be said for your predecessors – but I honestly think that this would be a beneficial move for you, if not for me.'

Mysie, although still in shock about Doddie, was not blind to the pitfalls in this. 'She might object to Sandy, though, an' what aboot . . . ? A' auld wumman wouldna be ower happy aboot me expectin' a bairn oot o' wedlock.'

'I will tell her that your husband has been killed, and I am sure she will be glad to take you in. I am going to Aberdeen on Saturday, so I will suggest it then.'

Another thought occurred to Mysie. 'If I leave, you'll need another cook, so . . . what aboot Meggie?'

'Can Meggie cook?' Mrs Phillip seemed doubtful.

'She's a real good cook, an' I learned her mysel'.'

'That is a good enough recommendation. Meggie it shall be.'

The requested tea being brought in then by Meggie and Sandy, nothing more was said, and when Mysie and her son were left alone, she lay down beside him, still fully dressed. He looked at her sadly. 'Mam, will Doddie never be comin' back?'

'No, my lambie. He'll never be back.' Although her heart was aching, Mysie had accepted it as God's will, and whether it was a punishment on them for what they had done, or if it had been destined for Doddie to die young, it made no difference – he was gone. Cradling her son in her arms, she reflected that, while she had lost the only man she had ever loved, Sandy had lost two fathers, and he was only ten years old.

'Mam, will you nae rage me if I tell you something?'

'No, my loon.' Mysie wished that he would keep quiet. She couldn't make conversation with him, not yet.

'It was me set fire to oor hoose.'

She jerked up. 'You? Oh, God, Sandy, what . . . ?'

'I didna mean it, Mam. I was tryin' to fill the lamp, to let you see I was as good as Doddie, but . . .'

Trembling herself, she held his shaking body, sure that his poor little brain was turned with what had happened, but when he calmed, he told her the truth about the night of the fire. She felt numb when he finished, and he looked up into her face pitifully. 'I wanted to let you see you didna need Doddie, but I never wanted the hoose to burn doon.'

Through ice-cold lips, Mysie murmured, 'I'm sure you didna, an' it was a pure accident, so dinna blame yoursel'.'

The boy gave a sobbing hiccough. 'I wish Doddie could come back, though. I ken noo I did like him. It was just . . . I wanted you to love me best.'

Her throat constricted, and it took a great effort to say, 'It's a' past, my lambie. Lie doon an' sleep like a good loon.'

He shook his head, still agitated. 'But Mam, I . . .'

Having already had more than enough to cope with, she said sharply, 'Lie doon an' sleep. My brain's fair deaved wi' you.'

He closed his eyes and lay still, but it was quite a time before his deep, even breathing told her that he was asleep. Poor little Sandy, she mused, as she undressed, to think he'd had that on his mind all this time. He shouldn't have been messing about with paraffin at all, although she understood his reason for it, but she should have realised at the time how deep his jealousy of Doddie had gone. The fire was really her fault, not Sandy's.

Turning out the lamp, she slid in beside her son, and let her thoughts turn to Doddie again. She would never be sure now whether or not he had killed Jeems, but she would keep loving him until the day she died herself. She would never forget him no matter what happened in the future. The future. It couldn't be worse than the present, and it *would* be best to leave Burnlea, with all its memories,

169

good and bad, and do as Mrs Phillip had suggested, but . . . an eighty-year-old bad-tempered woman?

Mysie sighed in resignation. She had survived worse things than that in her life, and nobody in Aberdeen would know of her previous troubles. She would be Mrs Duncan, mother of one child and expecting another – a woman whose husband had been killed in action, a war widow like hundreds of others – and the sooner the move came, the better.

Because Miss Wallace's housekeeper was working out her month's notice and would not be leaving until the middle of January, Mysie saw the new year of 1918 in at Burnlea House. She had been grateful that Mrs Phillip had not invited any guests for Christmas dinner, because she was sure that she could not have coped – it was only four weeks since Meggie had told her about Doddie's death. Jess Findlater, of course, had been full of commiserations about Doddie and about the expected child, even offering to take her and Sandy in until it was born, and she had been rather hurt when Mysie refused, but had agreed with her that it might not have worked.

As the time for taking up her new post drew nearer, Mysie became more and more apprehensive. It would not have been so bad if she could have gone while she was steeled for it, but having so long to wait, she'd had more time to think, and was not sure now if it was the right thing to do. It wasn't the cooking or the housekeeping that worried her – she had been used to that – it was the city itself . . . and the old lady. Mrs Phillip had said that she had told her aunt that Mysie was expecting a baby, and that Miss Wallace hadn't seemed to mind, but you never knew with women as old as that.

On the early afternoon of the eighth of January, with only a week to go until the big day, Janey came running downstairs and gasped, 'There's a Gordon wantin' to speak to you, Mysie.'

170

Her face blanching, Mysie grabbed the table. Was it possible that the army had made a mistake? 'Is it Doddie?'

'I dinna ken who he is, but the mistress tell't me to put him roon' to the servants' door. That'll be him noo.'

Mysie was rooted to the spot, but Meggie ran to answer the knock, and brought in a broad, stoutish young man who took off his flat bonnet and stood nervously in the middle of the floor 'Mysie?' he said, looking from one to the other.

Mysie nodded, her heart too full of memories to speak. 'I think you'd best sit doon,' the man said, gently. She sank down on the nearest chair. 'If it's aboot Doddie, I ken he's been killed. I saw it in the paper.'

He was obviously relieved that he would not have to break the bad news to her, but before he could speak again, Meggie took it upon herself to say, 'Janey, awa' you go back up that stair an' dinna be so nosey.' She turned to Mysie. 'I'll be in the scullery if you need me.'

There was a moment's silence after the two girls left, then the soldier cleared his throat. 'Me an' Doddie was chums, you see, and' I was wi' him when he . . . I thought you'd like to hear aboot it.' At her nod, he took a chair over to sit beside her. 'I'm Alick Slessor. Me an' Doddie met up when he come back aff leave at the beginning o' September. His battalion had been at Wipers afore, an' a lot of them had been killed, so them that was left was put in oor battalion. Weel, me an' Doddie was on guard duty one nicht, wi' the Bosche's lines just across No Man's Land, an' we started speakin' aboot hame – him aboot you an' Burnlea, an' me aboot Mary, that's my lass, an' Auchbogie. There wasna that big a distance atween where we bade, an' we took to each other right awa', an' after that, ilka time we were thegither, we spoke aboot hame . . . when we wasna gettin' shelled. We was often scared, but there was nae a man among us wasna, though some wouldna admit it.'

He was talking now as if he had forgotten about Mysie, his eyes dark with horrific memories. 'The Bosche was

171

puttin' up awfu' barrages. I've seen some reports in the papers since I come hame that said we could ha'e beaten them if the good weather had kept up, but we hadna the ammunition. The rain an' sleet turned a'thing into mud – naething but mud as far as you could see, an' great muckle shell holes. Of course, the only time you could see them in the dark, was when the Very lights went up, or mair shells burst.'

Mysie said nothing – what was there to say? Alick continued. 'The snaw was even worse, the cauld gettin' right into your bones. Twa o' the officers came roon' one day, in their fine uniforms straight fae tailors in London, an' when a lad complains it was cauld, one o' the officers says, "Get off your jackets, men, and give the horses a rub down, that will keep you warm." Weel, we was near tellin' them to tak' aff their ain jackets, but you canna speak back to an officer, or you'd be put on a charge. Then we were marched to Bourlon Wood, an' once we were dug in, the artillery opened fire, an' so did the enemy's. We had three days o' that, an' on the last day, me an' Doddie was thegither as usual. There was a bit o' a lull, an' one minute, he was speaking aboot you, an' the next minute he was blawn to bits.'

'Oh!' Mysie's agonised cry recalled her presence to him, and he looked at her anxiously. 'God, lass, I'm sorry. I came to br'ak it to you gently, an' I was that carried awa' I've made things worse. Oh, I'm sorry!'

She fought back the tears. 'Dinna be sorry. I was wantin' to ken how he was killed.'

'He didna feel onything – it happened ower quick. At the end o' that day – I'll never forget the date, 25th November 1917 – when they tallied up the casualties, there was 55 officers and men killed, 253 wounded an' 78 missin'.'

They sat silently, Alick Slessor remembering the horrors of the small wood outside Ypres and the comrades who had fallen, Mysie remembering Doddie as he had been in August when he was home.

At last the young man looked up. 'I'd better be goin'.'

'Will you nae wait for a cup o' tea? Meggie'll nae tak' a minute to mak' ane.'

'No, thank you. It was snawin' real heavy when I came in, an' I dinna want to be gettin' lost in a drift.'

Mysie grasped his outstretched hand. 'You've a few mile to go, though, will you manage a' right?'

'My father let me tak' his sledge, an' his horse is weel used to the deep snaw.'

'It was awfu' good o' you to come an' tell me aboot Doddie.'

He gave her hand a firm squeeze as he went out, the telling having been as much of an ordeal for him as it had been for her. When Meggie came through, eager to hear what he'd had to say, Mysie told her as much as she could remember and they sat for a few minutes trying to imagine what it had been like for the men who had fought in that village in Belgium.

At last, the kitchenmaid said, 'Does it nae mak' you feel worse, kennin' how Doddie was killed?'

Mysie wiped her eyes, then gave a contented sigh. 'No, I dinna feel worse, Meggie. I sometimes used to wish the army had sent his body back, so I could ha'e buried it, but I see noo they couldna, an' I feel a lot better for kennin' he died thinkin' aboot me.'

PART TWO

Chapter Seventeen

The little maid who opened the door at Ashley Road looked so timid that Mysie was sure Mrs Phillip's aunt must be a proper tartar, but she gave her name, and added, 'I'm expected.'

Sandy, very quiet since he confessed about the fire, kept close to her as they were taken along the hall and shown into a gloomy room crammed with large furniture and ornaments. At the far side, in a huge chair which practically hid her from sight, an old lady was writing at a beautiful mahogany bureau, but she swivelled round at their entrance.

Waiting for her new employer to speak, Mysie took stock of her. Her yellowing-white hair, very sparse, was drawn severely back from a long angular face, her rather deep-set eyes were a piercing grey and her thin, blue-veined hand, spotted with the brown pigment of advanced age, still held her pen. 'So! You're Mrs Duncan?' she said, at last.

The deep voice came as a surprise. 'Aye, Miss Wallace.'

'You don't look very sturdy, but Margaret, my niece, assured me that you were quite wiry.'

'I'm f-fit for ony k-kind o' hoosework,' Mysie stammered.

'As long as you keep the house clean, I shall be happy. The maid, Gladys, will help with that, but you will have to attend to the ordering of provisions, the cooking, and to me.' The cold eyes turned to the boy. 'This is your son?'

'Aye, Sandy. He's new eleven, an' he sleeps wi' me, so as lang as there's a double bed . . .'

'An eleven-year-old cannot sleep with his mother! It is most indecent, and I will not have indecency in my home.'

'I'm sorry . . . I thought it would save . . .'

'Two rooms have been made ready for you on the top floor, so there is no more to be said.' The old lady laid down her pen to press a bell on the wall behind her, and when the maid ran in, she said, 'Show . . . Sandy up to his room, Gladys. I wish to talk privately to his mother.'

'Yes, ma'am.'

The door had scarcely closed when Miss Wallace turned her penetrating gaze on Mysie again. 'I will make this clear from the start – I am prepared to put up with your son, provided that he is quiet.'

'I'll mak' sure he is. He's nae really a bad loon . . .'

The thin lips tightened. 'And I must insist that both you and he will learn to talk the King's English.'

Mysie felt indignant. 'My mother aye tell't us to keep a good Scots tongue in oor heads, and I've aye spoke like this, though I was learned English at the school.'

The lowering brows descended even farther. 'You were *taught* English, although it certainly does not sound like it, but even if you have always *spoken* in that ridiculous dialect, you will do so no longer, not in front of me, at least. Now, my niece told me that you . . .' she coughed discreetly ' . . . that you are with child. I hope that you are not one of those sickly creatures who will take to her bed at the least excuse and be fit for nothing for weeks?'

'I've had twa . . . *two* loons . . . *sons* already, though Jamie died, an' I worked right up to the day they were born.'

'And afterwards?' There was a hint of amusement in the old lady's eyes now, but Mysie was too anxious to recognise it.

'I was back on my feet the next day.'

'I am pleased to hear it. I had hoped for someone older, but Margaret has great confidence in your ability, and I

176

trust her judgement. Now that we understand each other, Mrs Duncan – I will call you that meantime, it is more fitting in view of your condition – I believe that you will suit me very well.'

'Thank you, Miss Wallace.' Mysie turned and went out into the hall, where Gladys was waiting to show her up to her room.

'That's Sandy's room,' the maid told her, pointing before she ran down the stairs again.

Mysie went into her room to lay down the valise Mrs Phillip had given her for carrying their clothes, then opened the next door. 'Oh, this is a nice room,' she exclaimed, hoping to cheer Sandy up, because he was sitting rigidly on his bed, his mouth drooping and his eyes mournful. 'Do you like it?'

'I dinna like *her*,' he mumbled, pulling a face. 'Do we ha'e to bide here, Mam?'

'Aye, I'm sorry, my loon, but we'll ha'e to.' Mysie caught herself. She was speaking in the Doric again. 'Sandy,' she said, apologetically, 'Miss Wallace wants us to speak English, like in your school books.'

'Will I ha'e to go to a new school?'

'Yes, but I'll need to ask her about it, for there's lots o' schools in Aberdeen. Now, come through and I'll give you your claes . . . clothes, but watch and not crease them when you're laying them by in the drawers. It was good o' Mrs Phillip to give you what her Bobby had grown out of.'

'But I'm as big as him,' Sandy pointed out, as he followed her, 'so they'll be ower little for me as weel.'

'They're all you've got.' She emptied the bag on her own bed and separated his clothes from hers. 'There you go now, and try to speak right in front of Miss Wallace, for I wouldn't want to cross her. She could put us out.'

'Did Mrs Phillip put us oot?'

'No . . . aye. Oh, Sandy, I canna explain. Something happened an' we had to leave.'

'But what . . . ?'

177

'Stop askin' questions, there's a good loon, and go and put your things past. I'll be going down the stairs when I've laid mine away, but I want you to bide up here till I tell you.' He looked at her so forlornly as he went out that she wished with all her heart that things had been different.

When all her own clothes were laid away tidily, Mysie went downstairs, knocked on the sitting-room door and opened it. 'Excuse me, Miss Wallace, but what school will Sandy go to?'

The old lady frowned as she looked up from the letter she was still writing. 'Ashley Road School. It's only a little bit along the street, on the opposite side. You may take your son there while I am having my nap after lunch, and the headmaster will probably tell him to begin on Monday, so he will have the weekend to acclimatise himself to his new surroundings.'

'Thank you, Miss Wallace. Er . . . what do you want me to cook for your luncheon?'

'Luncheon?' The word rang out sarcastically. 'My niece may have fancy ideas nowadays, but she was brought up, as I was, to say "lunch". My father, her grandfather, worked up from the bottom to his managerial position, and he called it "dinner" to the end of his days, although my mother constantly corrected him. Another thing, I know Margaret has "dinner" at seven, but I prefer to have "tea" at five.'

Mysie laughed, feeling easier with her now. 'We used to call that "supper", and we had "dinner" in the middle of the day, but what about today's lunch?'

'Gladys will tell you what is in the larder. I will give you a month's housekeeping allowance at a time, and I expect you to account for every penny. Off you go, because I have lunch at one, but I would like to talk to Sandy on his own.'

Her heart sinking, Mysie ran up to fetch him. 'An' mind an' speak English to her,' she warned him. Sandy was noncommittal when he came into the kitchen later, so she asked, 'What did she say to you?'

'She just wanted to get to ken me, that's a'.'

'Did you mind an' speak right?'

'She never said I wasna speakin' right.'

As Miss Wallace had foreseen, when Mysie took Sandy along to Ashley Road School that afternoon, the headmaster told him to start on Monday. 'What do you think?' she asked, while they were walking back to the house. 'Will you like it?'

'It's awfu' big.'

'They're a' big schools in Aberdeen, but your teacher looked real nice. It was good o' the domin . . . headmaster to show you the class you'd be in.'

'Aye.' He didn't sound too enthusiastic.

Gladys said she went home at seven every evening, so Mysie and her son sat by the kitchen fire until eight o'clock, when she made him go to bed. Alone, she thought of Doddie, of the months they had lived together at Rowanbrae, of the hours he had been with her when he was on leave. She would never be a whole woman again without him. The cruelty of fate made her weep, quietly and hopelessly.

When she recovered, she rose and went over to the sink to wash her face. Miss Wallace rang at nine. 'Help me upstairs,' she ordered, when Mysie went through. 'My legs are so stiff that I can't manage on my own. Is Sandy in bed? I like him, you know. He will put life into the house.'

As long as he behaves himself, Mysie thought, but took the old lady's arm as they mounted the stairs. 'Will I bring up a cup of cocoa or something to you?'

'In about fifteen minutes. I usually read for a little.'

After she had seen Miss Wallace settled, Mysie went to bed herself. She still wasn't sure if she would like working here, but she had burned her boats now.

On the next day, Saturday, Mysie took Sandy with her to buy meat and groceries for the weekend, carefully recording each purchase in the little book the previous housekeeper had used. 'Miss Wallace likes you,' she told her son when the shopping was over. 'What did you say to her?'

'Ach, Mam, I canna mind noo, but she was laughin' whiles, an' she's nae so bad when you get to ken her.'

Mysie left it at that. As long as the old lady could laugh at what he said, everything would be all right.

Everything wasn't all right, however. When Sandy came home from school on Monday afternoon, he had a thick lip and a rip in his jacket. 'You've been fightin'!' Mysie accused. 'Oh, Sandy, can you nae behave yoursel' at a'?'

'The other loons waited in the playground for me, an' they was laughin' at me for the way I speak, so I thumped ane an' him an' some o' the other anes turned on me.'

'Get your face washed and I'll put some ointment on.' Mysie didn't know whether to be angry with him or glad that he had stood up for himself. 'And give me your jacket so I can mend it afore Miss Wallace sees the state you're in, for she said she wanted to see you when you came home from the school.'

He was with the old lady for about fifteen minutes, and came back looking quite pleased with himself. 'She laughed when I tell't . . . told her about the fight, an' she said the only way to get the better o' them was to speak the same as them.'

'You'll maybe take a telling from her then,' Mysie snapped.

'It's funny, though,' he observed, as he sat down. 'Bobby Phillip never laughed at me, an' he spoke like them.'

'Bobby Phillip and you were a pair, and you'll need to behave yourself better here.' He would miss Bobby in the holidays, Mysie mused, but maybe he would make a friend at school.

'Miss Wallace is wantin' to help me wi' my home lessons. She says she was clever when she was at the school, an' she near died laughin' when I said I didna ken schools was invented as lang ago as when she was young.'

Mysie was appalled. 'Oh, you didna say that to her?'

In spite of her fears that the old lady would turn against Sandy for being so outspoken, the next half hour established a pattern. Sandy went to the sitting room every day and did his homework with Miss Wallace sitting beside him at the bureau. His speech, and Mysie's, quickly altered, until they lost almost all their dialect, only a word or two slipping in if they spoke without thinking.

Gladys, always afraid of her mistress, left one day in tears after being scolded for upsetting a tea-tray, and Mabel, the new maid, seemed just as nervous, although Mysie told her that the old lady's bark was worse than her bite. She was nervous herself, however, when Miss Wallace told her to sit down one morning. 'When is your confinement due, Mrs Duncan?'

'Five weeks yet.'

'How are you coping with all the work you have to do?'

'Oh, I'm managing fine. I told you, I worked right up . . .'

'But this is a much bigger house than you had, and . . . oh, I suppose it will be all right, but have you thought of where you will give birth?'

'Where?' Mysie's heart fluttered. Was this her dismissal? 'I hadna thought about that.'

'I have thought about it. You will have your baby here, and I will hire a midwifery nurse for two weeks so that you will have time to recover properly.'

'But I canna pay for a nurse. Is there nae a woman . . . ?'

'I will pay for the nurse. I will also pay for everything the infant will need.'

'But I canna let you do that.'

Miss Wallace shook her head. 'I want to do it. You and your son have changed my life completely. I feel years younger, and I want to repay you.'

'But you give me wages, and it's senseless you paying a nurse for two weeks when I . . .'

'If there is one thing which annoys me, it is kindness being thrown back in my face.'

181

'I'm sorry. I didna mean to . . . oh, Miss Wallace, it's very good of you.'

Mysie had another weep that night. After all those wicked things she had done, she didn't deserve kindness like this. If Miss Wallace ever found out that Doddie wasn't her husband, or that he had stabbed Jeems – she was practically sure now that she hadn't done it herself – or that she had buried the body, the old lady would be sure to throw her out. And where would she go with two children to bring up?

Chapter Eighteen

Because Mabel had an afternoon off, Mysie had to answer the doorbell herself at half-past three. When the caller – a tall, very thin man in the uniform of the Scots Guards – saw her, he exclaimed, 'It's Mrs Duncan, isn't it? I didn't expect to find you here. My sister must have lost what little sense she had before she let you go.'

Conscious of her bulky figure, and of the hot flush stealing across her face, she murmured, 'Miss Wallace was looking for a housekeeper, and Mrs Phillip recommended me.'

'Aunt Beatrice was delighted, I'm sure.'

Desperate to get away, Mysie said, 'You'll have to excuse me, Captain Wallace, but I'm in the middle of making the tea. Will you be staying?'

'I hadn't intended to, but the memory of your delicious meals has made me change my mind. Yes, thank you, I will stay.'

'I expect you know your own way to the sitting room.' Her legs shook as she returned to the kitchen. She had forgotten all about him, but Miss Wallace was his aunt, too, of course. Still, even if the old lady told him about Doddie's death, he wouldn't try to flirt with her, not when she was so uncomely. If he did start anything, she would just let him know that she hadn't time to be bothered with that kind of nonsense – didn't even want to be bothered with it – and he would soon stop.

At ten to five, she went to the dining room to set the table for two – when Miss Wallace was alone, she usually ate off the small table in the sitting room – but the old lady heard her and called to her to come through. 'We will have tea in here, Mrs Duncan. I don't think you have met my nephew?'

'I met Mrs Duncan at Burnlea,' he said, smiling to Mysie. 'Has your husband been home on leave lately?'

'Oh, Gregor, I should have told you.' His aunt looked quite upset. 'Mr Duncan was killed in action.'

His smile vanished. 'I'm very sorry to hear that. Many fine men have lost their lives.' His eyes had hardened. 'I feel ashamed sometimes at only having been slightly wounded.'

'You never told me about that,' his aunt scolded.

'I didn't want to worry you, and it was only a scratch.'

'Excuse me,' Mysie ventured, 'I'll have to go. I've left Sandy watching the potatoes don't boil in, and I don't trust him.'

'Yes, yes, off you go,' Miss Wallace said, rather impatiently, then added, 'Gregor will do the carrying for you, since Mabel is not here to help you. I will send him through shortly.' It was the last thing Mysie wanted, and she turned on Sandy in a bad humour when she went back to the kitchen. 'Have you not set our table yet?'

By the time she had dished everything up, she was a little calmer, but when Gregor came in, she pointed to the tray and said, coldly, 'It's all ready.'

'I am really sorry about your husband, Mrs Duncan,' he said, compassionately. 'His death must have been much worse for you when you were expecting his child, and I expect you have not got over it yet?'

'I'll never get over it.' Mysie wished that he would go away. She didn't like speaking about it, for there was always the chance that she would inadvertently say something that would reveal more than she intended.

'It must have been a bad time for you, and I suppose my aunt intimidated you when you first saw her, but she isn't as bad as she would have people believe.'

'I was a bit worried at first, but she's been very good to me, and to Sandy.'

'How old is your son now? I remember Margaret telling me of the tricks he and Bobby played.'

'Sandy's eleven past January.'

The boy spoke up himself. 'I'm in the qualifying class and Miss King says I'll pass the control exam easy . . . easily.'

'I'm sure you will. Now, I'd better take this tray through before my aunt starts thinking she'll never get her tea.'

His old cheerfulness had vanished, Mysie thought, watching him going out. His back wasn't as straight as it used to be, his face was haggard and he didn't tease any more. It was as if he had lost a loved one himself, although she didn't know if he had ever had a wife. It could be the war having an effect on him, though – maybe he had seen one or more of his friends killed, and that would be enough to change any man. The Captain didn't say much when he took back the dishes and collected the dessert, and Mysie couldn't help feeling sad that he was so subdued. She carried the coffee through herself, and was surprised to find that he wasn't there.

Miss Wallace looked up. 'Gregor had to go, he has to meet someone at six, but he said to tell you how much he enjoyed his meal. He usually only visits me once during his leave, so I suppose I shall not see him again this time.'

An unexpected pang of disappointment touched Mysie. 'Doesn't he live near here?'

'Not far, but he has his own life to lead. He was left the house in Forest Avenue when my brother, his father, died, and lives there when he is on leave. A housekeeper looks after it while he is away, but I often wish that he would marry. He led quite a gay life while he was at university, taking home lots of girls but never wanting to settle down with any of them. Perhaps he will meet his heart's desire after the war. He is forty-two now, and seems more serious than he used to be.'

So his aunt had noticed it, too, Mysie thought, hoping that he *would* find his heart's desire after the war. He was too nice to end up a lonely old bachelor.

On the following day, Sandy came home with a note from his headmaster, saying that the boy was capable of going on to a secondary school rather than an intermediate, and enclosing a form to be signed. Mysie showed it to her employer, who said, 'Tick which school you prefer, Mrs Duncan, and sign the form.'

'But I can't afford to buy a uniform for him,' Mysie pointed out, without thinking.

'I will provide his uniform,' Miss Wallace said, firmly.

Mysie looked at the form again. 'Gordon's College and the Grammar School are both private and charge fees.' The old lady frowned. 'I am aware of that, and I will see to the fees, too. Is it to be the Grammar, where Lord Byron was educated, or Gordon's where Gregor went?'

'I can't let you pay uniforms *and* fees,' Mysie protested, amused that Miss Wallace could place her nephew in the same category as the great poet. 'The Central School's free, so he'd better go there . . . if it's good enough.'

'I believe the Central is a very good school, but I feel we should send Sandy to Gordon's, like Gregor.' Mysie put a tick in the appropriate box and signed the form. Miss Wallace had made the decision for her, and Miss Wallace's word was final.

In May 1918, Mysie was delivered of a daughter whom she named after Doddie, but Georgina seemed incongruous for such a tiny scrap, and when Sandy called her Gina one day, the diminutive stuck, being considered by all to be much more suitable. The nurse, the temporary housekeeper and Miss Wallace all drooled over the dark, curly-

185

haired infant, and Mysie sometimes felt that she was only tolerated as a source of food for Gina.

Miss Wallace wasn't happy with the woman she had engaged to stand in for Mysie, but she wouldn't allow the new mother to leave her bed for two weeks after the birth, and only let her do light work for the next two. Mysie wasn't pleased with this arrangement, but wisely kept that to herself. The old lady was only trying to be kind.

As it happened, Miss Wallace didn't have to pay Sandy's fees for Gordon's College after all – he won a bursary – but she paid for all the books that were prescribed, his jotters and pencils, and provided the money for Mysie to buy his uniform.

In late August, when Sandy was dressed for his first day, he looked so smart that his mother's heart swelled with pride. He was taller than she was, and already looked like a young man, though he wasn't yet twelve. She had often wondered about her recent good fortune, but never so much as on that day. In her previous life, she had become so used to being buffeted by fate that it was hard to believe what had happened since the night, not quite ten months ago, when she learned of Doddie's death. Perhaps the tide had turned for her, the tide of catastrophes and heartache that had beset her for years. Perhaps God had felt He had punished her enough and was trying to make up for what He had done before.

Sandy's homework took longer now he was at secondary school. 'I had forgotten how to do algebra,' Miss Wallace told Mysie after one rather gruelling session, 'but Sandy kept me right. He is very bright, there is no getting away from that.'

'I don't know where he gets his brains,' Mysie remarked, then added, 'though I was quite good at school myself.'

There had been a succession of maids to help Mysie since she came to Ashley Road. Some had stayed longer than others, but all had left because of Miss Wallace's sharp tongue. Mysie herself was often at the receiving end, but she was much more perceptive than the girls and recognised that it was the old lady's worsening arthritis that made her so irritable. Miss Wallace still supervised Sandy's homework, smiling when she told his mother if there had been any contretemps, although that didn't happen very often. He had buckled down to serious study since he had started at Gordon's and seemed to be quite popular, if his chattering about what went on in the school playground was anything to go by. Miss Wallace absolutely doted on Gina, and early in October, when the baby was only five months old, she sprang a surprise on Mysie. She began by saying, 'Mrs Duncan, you have been here for a year now. Do you ever miss your friends in Burnlea?'

'Jess Findlater's the only one I miss. She was my nearest neighbour and my best friend, and we write now and then.'

'Why not visit her? I could look after Gina, and Pearl could make a salad for my lunch. Think about it, then write to your friend to find out which day would suit her best.'

Somewhat taken aback, Mysie considered the suggestion for a moment. 'I don't think Jess . . . she's like all the other crofters' wives, she doesn't have much spare time.'

'She could surely spare an hour or two for an old friend?'

'She'd likely be happy to see me.'

'Well then. Write today and let me know what she says.'

Mysie thought it over all evening, and decided against it. Returning to her old home area would bring everything back, everything she had tried so hard to forget. At Ashley Road she was Mrs Duncan, a widow with two children, but at Burnlea she would always be Mysie, wife of Jeems, who had lived in sin with Doddie Wilson. She had a different kind of life now, a better life . . . a life of deceit. She would only have to make one little slip to set Jess wondering what had really happened on that awful night in January 1914.

When her employer rang at nine, Mysie went through and told her what she had decided. 'I don't want to go to

Burnlea. It's not a good thing to go back to a place where you've known deep sorrow as well as great happiness.'

Miss Wallace gave her an odd look. 'It is up to you, Mrs Duncan, but I . . . oh, I think we could dispense with that formality now. What is your Christian name?'

About to say that it was May, Mysie remembered that, apart from her schoolteachers, only one person had ever called her that, and she didn't want to be reminded of the cause of all her troubles. 'I was always called Mysie.'

The aristrocratic nose wrinkled. 'Mysie? I presume that is a distortion of Maisie?'

Mysie had never thought of it like that. 'I suppose so.'

'I cannot understand your reluctance to visit your friends, Maisie. I thought you would have jumped at the chance to go back and revive memories of your dear husband.'

Mysie's insides gave a jolt. Her dear husband? If the old lady only knew what she had thought of her husband! 'No, I've made my mind up,' she said, louder than she meant.

'Very well. I will not pry into your affairs any longer.'

A great relief swept over Mysie because the subject had been dropped, but when she went back to the kitchen after helping Miss Wallace to her bedroom, she wrote a long letter to Jess to ease her conscience.

An answer came three days later. 'Burnlea is a sad place just now,' Jess had written. 'Robbie and Jackie Duff has both been killed. You maybe do not know about Jackie, he was away working near Peterhead before you came here, but he enlisted after Robbie. Belle says Rab is near demented, though I some think she is not much better. Jean Petrie is very quiet. I suppose she is minding about Denny. I was pleased to get your letter, and I am glad you are still getting on fine. Gina will be growing big now. Give my love to Sandy, and tell him to keep working hard at the school.'

Mysie laid down the two sheets of paper, thankful that she had refused to take up her employer's suggestion. If she had gone to Burnlea, she would have been in the middle of all that mourning, and she was done with mourning.

When the Armistice was signed in November, Miss Wallace and Mysie wept together with happiness that the strife was over. 'I always worried about Gregor,' the old lady admitted, 'but he has survived and will soon be coming home for good.'

Mysie dabbed at her eyes. 'I was worried that the war would carry on for years and Sandy would have to go and fight, but I wish it had finished a month ago – that's when a woman I knew in Burnlea lost both her sons.' She thought sadly of the other men she had known who would never come home: Davey Robertson, Denny Petrie and, more special than any of them, Doddie.

Just before Christmas, Miss Wallace had some good news to tell Mysie. 'Gregor's coming home for a few days. He has not been discharged yet, but he has to attend to some matters in Edinburgh, and will arrive in Aberdeen on Christmas Eve, so I think we should have a proper celebration.'

'Turkey and all the trimmings?' Mysie laughed, recalling her first Christmas at Burnlea House.

'Yes, if it is possible, and I will invite Margaret and her family. Oh, and you and your children must join us.'

Mysie was shocked. 'Oh, no, Miss Wallace! For one thing, I wouldn't have time to sit down, and for another, it's . . . it's not the done thing for servants to . . .'

'I do not care about that,' the old lady smiled, 'and I could engage someone to serve . . .'

'I'd rather not. I wouldn't feel right.' Having patronised only one butcher since she'd taken over as housekeeper, Mysie had no difficulty in obtaining a turkey, and set about preparing a feast fit for the returning hero. It was good to be catering for so many people again.

After the Christmas dinner, both Mr and Mrs Phillip came to the kitchen to tell her how much they had enjoyed it. 'My aunt says she is grateful that I passed you on to her,' Mrs Phillip added. 'I knew anyway, because you and your family are all she ever writes about in her letters.'

Mysie could detect a hint of jealousy in her ex-employer's voice, but told herself that she was imagining things because she was hurt that the Captain hadn't come himself to thank her for the effort she had made for his benefit. 'Miss Wallace has nothing else to write about, and I'm happy here,' she said.

'I'd have liked to see your daughter – Gina, isn't it? – but I expect she's sleeping by now?'

'Yes, Gina's sleeping, and Sandy has just gone upstairs.'

'Bobby is still full of energy, but it's time we got Beatrice home to bed. She is quite tired. Goodbye, Mrs Duncan.' Mrs Phillip pulled the fur collar of her coat up as she swept out, but the laird – as Mysie would always think of him – lingered for a moment. 'I think that my wife is a trifle put out that her aunt thinks more of your Gina than of our Beatrice, but she will get over it.'

'I hope so,' Mysie said. 'I'd hate to think I was causing any trouble between them.'

The man's eyes danced as he grinned, letting Mysie see where Bobby had inherited his mischievous temperament. 'There has often been trouble between them. There is a nasty streak in Margaret somewhere.'

'I'd never have thought that,' Mysie said, as he turned to go. 'Mrs Phillip was always very kind to me.'

'She can be, when it suits her, but if anyone upsets her, woe betide him – or her.'

On Boxing Day, while Mysie cleaned up the sitting room, Miss Wallace amused herself by watching seven-month-old Gina trying to pull herself up by holding the leg of a chair then falling down with a bump. 'What a clever girl,' the old lady said each time, standing her on her feet again and hugging her.

'You'll tire yourself out,' Mysie scolded. 'She's too heavy for you to be lifting like that. Come on, Gina, I'm taking you back to the kitchen.'

'Oh, leave her here, Maisie. I love watching her.'

'Just for a little while, then.'

To help his mother because they were between maids at the time, Sandy volunteered to set Miss Wallace's small table for lunch. 'She's playing with Gina like she was a little girl playing with a doll,' he said, in disgust, when he came back. 'Kissing her and cuddling her.'

'And Gina laps it up.' Mysie sighed as the doorbell rang. 'Answer the door for me, Sandy. My hands are all floury.'

'It was Captain Wallace,' he told her in a minute.

'You'd better go and take Gina out of their way, and ask if he's staying for lunch. It's just leftovers from yesterday.'

Gregor wasn't staying, and Miss Wallace said to leave Gina, much to Mysie's relief, for she was behind schedule already. She shouldn't have started baking, but Miss Wallace loved home-baked bread. She was pounding the dough for the second time when a quiet voice startled her. 'Are you taking your anger out on that? I can almost see sparks flying from your eyes.'

'I'm not angry, Captain Wallace,' she snapped, not looking round at him, for she hadn't time to talk.

'You're giving a very good impression of it.' Giving a laugh, he placed his hand over hers.

'I'm in a hurry,' she explained. 'I want to set this dough to prove before lunch, so would you please leave me in peace?' She tried to pull her hand away, but his grip was too strong.

'I came to thank you for yesterday's lovely meal.' He turned her hand palm up and stroked it. 'I should have done it last night but I had an appointment, and when Aunt Beatrice told me just now that you did it specially for me, I was very touched. Could it possibly be that you like me a little bit?'

Mysie was flustered. She didn't want to encourage him if he was flirting, but her hand was tingling from his touch, and he was rather nice. 'I don't dislike you,' she hedged.

'That's something, I suppose, but I'd better leave you

now – in peace.' He brushed the nape of her neck lightly with his lips before he went out.

Kneading her dough again, Mysie did feel angry. What right had the man to come in here upsetting her? What right had he to kiss her like that without any warning – and in front of Sandy? She shot a suspicious glance at her son, but he was so busy reading that he probably hadn't noticed. Brushing some strands of hair out of her eyes, she decided that the Captain's neck-kiss had meant nothing to him . . . but it had felt good, all the same.

Chapter Nineteen

Having been discharged from the Scots Guards in June 1920, ex-Captain Wallace came to Ashley Road every week to visit his aunt, popping in to talk to Mysie as he was leaving. She grew used to his gentle teasing – in fact, she rather enjoyed it – but occasionally, when she caught him looking at her wistfully, she wondered if it was more than just plain teasing.

'I've organised myself now,' he said, one day in August. 'I couldn't decide whether or not to go back to what I was doing before the war, but I've made up my mind now.'

'What did you do?' Mysie asked, remembering that his aunt had once said he had been at university.

'I worked with a firm of solicitors, but I didn't feel like going back. I've been in a position of authority too long to knuckle down under a boss, so I am starting up on my own.'

'That's good.'

'I won't be able to tell for some time if it's good or not,' he laughed. 'It all depends on the great public.'

'Oh, I'm sure you'll be a success.'

'I'm glad you have faith in me, Mrs Duncan, because I am not too sure about it myself. How would you feel about trusting me with your innermost secrets, if you had any? Do I give you the impression of a man who is capable of unravelling other people's problems?'

Her heart pounding guiltily, Mysie said, 'I'd say you were quite capable.' But he could never unravel her problem, she reflected. Even the most competent, highly-qualified solicitor in the world would not be capable of doing that.

'Have you anything to hide, I wonder?' he persisted, cocking his head to one side. 'I get the feeling that you have.'

'Stop teasing me,' she mumbled, terrified that her eyes would give her away.

'Yes, I'm sorry. I shouldn't do it, but I can't help it. You always look so fetching when you're confused. I want to gather you in my arms and . . .'

'Oh, you're doing it again!' She averted her crimson face.

'I wasn't teasing that time,' he said, gently, 'and I think it is time I left, before I say anything else.'

Sandy came home from school as Gregor left, so Mysie had no time to worry about what he had already said.

Over the next few months, Miss Wallace's legs stiffened even more, her temper becoming correspondingly shorter, and it was fortunate that fifteen-year-old Maudie Low, the current maid, did not easily take offence. When the old lady barked at her, she just laughed and said, 'Now, now, Miss Wallace, watch your blood pressure,' and her employer would just give a wry smile.

'That Maudie is a pert one, Maisie,' she observed, one day, 'but I can't help admiring her spirit.'

Mysie nodded. 'And she's a good worker. I hope she doesn't leave in a couple of months like the rest of them.'

'Do not be too hard on her, then.'

Mysie smiled. It wasn't her fault that the others had left, but she couldn't say that to her crotchety employer. As she went into the hall, the front doorbell rang so she turned to answer it before going back to the kitchen. It was Gregor, who hadn't visited for a few weeks. 'Good afternoon, Mrs Duncan.'

'Good afternoon, Captain Wallace.'

'Not captain,' he corrected. 'I'm plain Mr Wallace, as you very well know, but I would prefer you to call me Gregor.'

Still smiling, she let him in and closed the door. 'Your aunt's in the sitting room, *Mister* Wallace.'

'You're very stubborn. We've known each other for at least four years, yet you're as distant as ever.'

'Not distant, surely? Remembering my place, that's all.'

Twisting his mouth into a frown, he walked into the sitting room, Mysie following to take Gina out of the way. She would never feel on equal terms with him, and that was how it should be.

As he always did, he went to the kitchen before he left, and sat down by the fire to watch Gina play with her dolls. 'I've been very busy lately,' he sighed. 'Setting up an office needs a bit of organising, and I couldn't face my aunt for a while. She is not the most relaxing of women, as you must know, Mrs Duncan. You must get very tired of her, day in, day out.'

'No, I don't. She's been very good to Sandy and me, and she treats little Gina like her own child – spoils her, in fact.'

He laid his hand over hers so quickly that she didn't have time to move it. 'I would treat your children as mine, if you would only let me.'

It took her by surprise though she had sometimes suspected that his teasing covered deeper feelings, but he believed that she was a widow, free to do as she liked, and she couldn't tell him it wasn't that simple. In any case, she didn't love him – she could never love anyone else after Doddie. Looking up, she found him regarding her questioningly. 'If I didn't make myself clear,' he said, softly, 'I was asking you to marry me, and I am still waiting for an answer.'

194

Her eyes dropped again. 'You know I can't marry you. I'm your aunt's housekeeper, what would she say?'

'She could say what she liked, it wouldn't change my mind, and in any case, I don't think she'd be against it. She thinks a great deal of you.'

'And I think a lot of her, so I wouldn't want to upset her. I'm sorry, Mr Wallace, but . . .' She was stopped by a great gust of laughter.

'Oh, my dear girl. It's so ridiculous. I have just proposed to you, yet we still don't call each other by our first names. I've heard Aunt Beatrice calling you Maisie. Won't you allow me the same privilege?'

'I can't stop you, Mr Wallace,' she faltered.

'I can't call you Maisie if you still call me Mr Wallace.'

His eyes were dancing now, and she had to smile. 'Come on, then, Maisie. Let me hear you say my name.'

'Oh . . . Gregor, you're an awful torment.'

'Not at all, just in love, but I can see I've embarrassed you. How is Sandy getting on at school?'

Relaxing, she said, 'Quite well, I think. All his teachers gave him very good reports.'

'I'm pleased to hear that, because I have plans for him.'

'Plans?'

'I won't tell you yet, but Aunt Beatrice approves.'

'Can you not give me some idea?'

'Not an inkling. Have patience, my dear Maisie.' He stood up and swung her little girl up in his arms. 'I'll take you to the door with me, Gina, if you promise to wave goodbye to me.'

He *was* nice, Mysie thought, as he carried her chuckling daughter out, but his proposal couldn't have been serious. A man like him, a solicitor in his own firm, would never dream of marrying a servant. No, it was just the way the gentry had, joking about everything.

Gina came running in from the door. 'Will Thandy be home thoon? He promithed to buy me a thugar mouth today.'

'You're getting spoiled, little madam,' Mysie scolded,

195

for everyone in the house, and even those who visited, petted the lisping toddler and gave her whatever she asked, and it wasn't good for her. She would have to learn that the world didn't revolve around her.

Just before Christmas, Miss Wallace fell as she was dressing, and when her doctor was leaving, he told Mysie that it could have been a slight stroke. The old lady believed that it was the fall which had affected her legs and asked Mysie if she would mind sleeping in the room adjoining hers – the dining room – until she felt better. It entailed some rearranging of furniture, but Gregor helped, and they were all much easier in their minds when the housekeeper was within call. Eighty-four now, Miss Wallace had been doddery on her legs for a year or more, and Mysie had often felt anxious when she heard her walking about. The fall – or stroke – took a heavy toll on the old lady, and even when she was fit enough to be out of bed, she couldn't walk without someone supporting her, so her doctor advised her to buy a wheelchair. It made Mysie sad to see her tied to a chair, and it meant a lot of extra work, but Beatrice Wallace's spirit was unbroken and her tongue was as sharp as ever, except to the children. 'Come up on my lap,' she would say to Gina, and the little girl would give a gurgling laugh and wriggle around until she found the most comfortable position on the knobbly knees. To Sandy, too, the old lady's manner was gentle. As soon as he went in to do his homework, she propelled her wheelchair nearer to the bureau. She talked to him as if he were an adult each time he turned spontaneously to discuss something he wasn't sure of.

Mysie couldn't get over the change in her son since they had come to Aberdeen. He was much older, of course, and probably had more common sense than when he got up to mischief with Bobby Phillip. Perhaps his high spirits had been a means of seeking attention, or had they covered his guilt about the fire? He was different, whatever it was, and now spoke perfect English, with no trace of the dialect that had caused him to be ridiculed when he first went to Ashley Road School.

Because of Miss Wallace's infirmity, Mysie hardly ever left the house – the tweed skirts and jumpers she had bought before would last for years yet, and Maudie could be trusted to buy in the provisions – but, after several months, Mysie began to long for even a short respite from duty, something to brighten at least one day. The letter from Jess Findlater late in July, therefore, seemed to be just what the doctor ordered.

'Dear Mysie, Jake says he is tired of hearing me saying how long it is since I saw you, and he told me I should go to see you. Will this Saturday be all right for you? If it is, do not bother to write. I will get the one o'clock bus into the town, and the half past five bus back. Jake sends his love. Your friend, Jess.'

'I look forward to meeting your friend when she comes,' Miss Wallace remarked, when Mysie asked if she could have a visitor. 'Only for a little time, of course, because I know you will want to be alone with her to catch up on all her gossip.'

'Jess will have plenty to gossip about. You'll like her, even though she speaks as broad as I did when I came here first.'

'It will be a diversion for me. I have very little to amuse me these days. It will be Maudie's afternoon off, which is all the better, and you can just give me something quick for tea after your Mrs Findlater leaves.'

When Jess appeared on Saturday, the two old friends clasped hands tearfully – they hadn't seen each other for three years – then Mysie led her in to the sitting room to get the ordeal of meeting Miss Wallace over before they let their hair down in the kitchen. At first, Jess appeared to be uncomfortable in the 'lady's' presence, but was soon telling her about Jean Petrie and her malicious tongue, about Andra White, the miller, and all the other people in Burnlea. 'They got a shock when they saw Mysie first, for

197

she didna look auld enough to be onybody's wife, never mind a ugly auld stick like Jeems.'

Mysie's blood turned to ice. When Miss Wallace asked about her husband, she had described him as young and handsome, and there was nothing wrong with the old lady's memory. What on earth would she make of this? Her friend's patent unease made Jess realise that she had put her foot in it, and she did her best to put things right. 'I was just jokin' aboot him bein' a ugly auld stick, for we used to say some awfu' things to each other just in fun. His name was . . . James George Duncan, an' we'd aye ken't him as Jeems, but Mysie aye called him Doddie. It was a kind o' pet name she had for him, you see.'

Grateful to her for trying, Mysie could see that the rather lame explanation hadn't fooled Miss Wallace, who said, suddenly, 'I feel quite tired. Take Mrs Findlater to the kitchen, Maisie, and remember to offer her a cup of tea.'

'I'm sorry if it was my lang tongue that tired her oot,' Jess said, as they went along the hall. 'I never ken when to haud it. Did she nae ken you was wed to Jeems?'

Mysie shrugged and sighed. 'Mrs Phillip tell't her Doddie was my man, an' I didna see ony reason to tell her different.'

'I think she believed what I said aboot his name bein' James George though, so likely nae harm's been daen.'

The subject had to be dropped when they entered the kitchen, where Sandy was sitting in a corner with his head as usual buried in a book, and Gina was kneeling on the hearthrug building up her wooden blocks. 'She's got Doddie's nose, Mysie,' Jess exclaimed, delightedly, as the little girl giggled and knocked the pile over again. 'She's a wee darlin' an' I could tak' her hame wi' me – nae bother.'

'She's gettin' spoiled, an' she's got a temper, for as young as she is.'

'A' bairns ha'e tempers, an' naebody could help spoilin' her, the little lamb. An' Sandy, what a big loon you've grown.'

'I'm fourteen and a half,' he said, offhandedly, without even bothering to look up.

'I'm sorry, Jess,' Mysie said, 'but he's ower ta'en up . . .'

'Dinna worry aboot that, lass. Let the laddie be. I'm nae easy put oot, as you should ken.'

Over their cup of tea, Jess gave Mysie all the latest news from Burnlea. 'Jinty Mutch is goin' steady wi' a doctor she met in the Infirmary, and Kirsty's been seen oot wi' ane o' the men fae Waterton. Oh, an' Effie Petrie's gettin' wed to a lad she met at her work in the toon. It's a rush weddin' though, for she's expectin'.'

Mysie laughed. 'What's her mother sayin' aboot that?'

'Och weel, you ken Jean. It's nae a scandal when it's at her ain door. She just says, "He's a fine man an' they were waitin' till they got a hoose afore they got wed, but you canna blame them for lettin' their feelin's run awa' wi' them." '

Jess had imitated Mrs Petrie's clipped tones well, and Mysie could just picture the woman trying to defend her daughter. 'Effie was a nice wee lassie, an' I hope things work oot for her. Did Gavin Leslie ever come back to Fingask?' She turned quickly to take her daughter's hand away from the cakestand. 'No more, Gina. You've had enough biscuits.'

The toddler scowled. 'Me hungry.'

'It'll soon be teatime.'

As soon as Mysie's attention was off her, Gina's hand crept out again and whipped a perkin off the bottom plate, and Jess, who had been waiting to answer Mysie's question, pretended she didn't see. 'You was askin' aboot Gavin Leslie. No, he never come back, but I dinna ken if he was killed, or if he was just bidin' awa' fae Freda Mutch.'

Without warning, a great nostalgia swept over Mysie. 'Oh, I wish I was back in Burnlea. I wish Rowanbrae had never . . .' Horrified at what she had nearly said in front of Sandy, she stopped and swallowed. 'It's seein' you again, Jess. I'm happy here, for Miss Wallace has been awfu' good to us.'

'Poor auld wumman, tied to that chair a' the time. But tell me, does her nephew still come to see her?'

'Aye, he comes every week.'

'What's he like?'

'He must be aboot forty-five, an' he's tall, awfu' thin, an' nae very good-lookin', but he thinks the world o' Miss Wallace.'

'Has he got a wife?'

Mysie coloured in spite of herself. 'No.'

Jess waited, the blush whetting her curiosity, but after a moment, she realised that nothing more was to be forthcoming. 'I clean forgot to tell you, though. Meggie Duff an' Drew White got wed in April, an' him aboot ten year aulder than her, but they're biding at the mill, for Andra hasna been awfu' weel.'

'Oh, I'm pleased for Meggie, for she was awfu' ta'en wi' Drew when I was workin' wi' her.'

'Drew made her gi'e up her cook's job, of course, but her an' Pattie get on fine, an' she's real good wi' Nessie. They're goin' to ha'e to put *her* awa', for she's worse than ever she was. There's nae a man safe if he goes near her, for . . .' Jess broke off as the door opened.

'Oh, I'm sorry, Maisie.' Gregor hesitated and stepped back. 'I didn't know you had company.'

'Come in, Gregor,' Mysie smiled. 'This is a very dear friend of mine from Burnlea. Jess – Miss Wallace's nephew.'

He held out his hand. 'I'm very pleased to meet you, Jess. I'm sorry, but Maisie didn't tell me your surname.'

'Findlater,' Jess said, rather flustered, 'an' I'm pleased to meet you, as weel. I've ken't Mysie for aboot sixteen year, an' we havena seen each other for a lang time, so we've just been ha'ein' a right good gossip.'

'A good gossip is what Maisie is needing, she's been working too hard for months. My aunt can be a real slave-driver.'

'I don't mind, and she's not as bad as that,' Mysie protested, slipping back into English automatically.

'I don't know what Aunt Beatrice would do without her,' he told Jess. 'Nor without the children. I'm sure they are what keeps her going.'

'Aye, they're fine bairns.'

'They're part of the family, and Maisie, too, Mrs Findlater.'

Jess noticed the affection in his eyes as he looked at Mysie, and asked, when he went out, 'Is there a romance in the air?'

Mysie blushed again. 'No, naething like that, an' he doesna ken half the truth aboot me. If he did, he wouldna ha'e . . .'

The abrupt stop told Jess that Gregor had already revealed to Mysie how he felt about her. What a chance for her – she'd be daft not to accept him if he proposed marriage, for she'd be settled for the rest of her life, her and her bairns . . . but maybe she didn't feel the same way about him. Oh, well, Jess thought, this was something to tell Jake. After Jess left, Mysie scrambled some eggs, wondering how she could parry the questions that were bound to be asked when she took in Miss Wallace's tea. It might be better to confess everything, with one crucial omission, and she could only hope that she would not be dismissed for being so deceitful.

Gregor, having gone back to talk to his aunt in the hope of getting Mysie alone later, was still there when she carried in the tray, but that didn't stop the old lady from saying, her eyes hard, 'You have a very loyal friend, Maisie.' Doubly ashamed because of the man's presence, Mysie mumbled, 'Yes, Jess would do anything for me.'

'Even lie for you?'

'She thought she was helping me, but it *was* a lie. Doddie wasn't my husband. His name was Wilson, and he was the finest man I ever knew. After Jeems . . . left me, Doddie came to the croft to help me for months before he came to stay.'

The grey eyes glittered. 'You lived as husband and wife?' Gregor stood up angrily. 'No, Aunt Beatrice. You've no right to ask her that. It's none of our business what Maisie did before she came here.'

'I don't mind telling you.' Mysie was resigned to exposing her past life now, and it was probably just as well that Gregor would learn the truth at the same time.

'Don't say anything else,' he warned. 'There's no need.'

'Yes, there is. I should have been honest from the day I came here. Yes, we lived as husband and wife, though everyone knew we weren't. We'd only a few months together before our house burned down, and Doddie enlisted in the Gordons, and he went away just days later. That was in February 1915, and he was going to take Sandy and me away after the war to a place nobody would know we weren't married, but he was killed at the end of November, 1917, and I was expecting his child.'

Miss Wallace's face had relaxed a little, so Mysie went on. 'Doddie was the only man I ever loved, and I still love him.'

'So you didn't love your husband? Why did you marry him, if he was an ugly old stick, as your friend said?'

This was something Mysie *did* mind talking about, but it was as well to explain it, too. 'My father sold me to Jeems for thirty pounds when I was hardly sixteen.' The shocked silence made her hurry on. 'He was drunk, of course – he was always drunk – and my mother tried to make him change his mind.' She stopped, remembering that awful day in 1905. How could these people understand what life had been like for the Lonies at that time? How would Miss Wallace have dealt with a drunken husband? It was useless to try to explain any more. 'I'm very sorry I didn't tell you before, but I'll pack my things, and Sandy's, and we'll leave tonight.'

But when Mysie looked up, her eyes brimming with tears, she saw that Miss Wallace was drying her own eyes with her handkerchief. 'I do not want you to leave, Maisie. I should not have judged you before I knew the circumstances. I had no right to ask, it was none of my business, and I am very sorry if I have upset you. Gregor, you had better see her back.'

Silently, Gregor followed Mysie out, but when they reached the kitchen, where Sandy was still studying, he said, 'Sandy, I want to talk to your mother in private for a few minutes, so would you please take Gina into the scullery and close the door? I'll let you know when to come back.'

Sandy stood up with bad grace, took Gina's hand and stamped out carrying his book. When the scullery door banged behind them, Gregor turned to Mysie, who was trembling apprehensively. 'Please sit down, my dear. You must feel terrible – that was a dreadful ordeal for you.'

'I don't know what you must think of me,' she wailed.

'I think exactly the same of you as I did before. If I had known what my aunt meant to say, I'd have tried to prevent it, but I'm glad I know. It has explained quite a lot to me. How long is it since your husband left you?'

'It was January 1914.'

'Didn't you know that you could have him presumed dead after seven years? This is July 1921, so it's seven and a half.'

Mysie didn't need to presume that Jeems was dead. His body might be found if another search was made, although the police hadn't found it after the fire. 'What difference would that make?' she asked, timidly.

'You would be free . . . free to marry again.'

'I don't want to marry again.'

'You might, one day.'

She knew what he meant, but she could never marry him. She liked him, and he'd been very understanding, but she didn't love him. In any case, if he ever found out that Jeems was lying under the byre at Rowanbrae, he would think that she had killed her husband, and there was no way to prove otherwise. Aware that Gregor's eyes were on her, she said, 'No, I'm quite sure I'll never want to marry again.'

Shaking his head, he stood up. 'Put your past life out of your mind, Maisie. I'll never mention it again, and neither will my aunt. We will go on as before, and we will still be friends, though I hope that we can be more than that some day.'

Before he left, Gregor called to Sandy that he and Gina could come back, so Mysie had no time to think until she was in her own room. There was no romance, whatever Jess believed. It was Doddie she loved, even four years after his death, even though he had killed Jeems. He had done it because he loved her, but why hadn't he confessed to her? If he had, they could have been married . . . no, it would still have been impossible, since everyone else had thought that Jeems was still alive.

Why did Jeems have to go to the Turriff Show that day? Why did her father force her to marry him? Wishing with all her heart and soul that she could change the past, it suddenly hit her how foolish she was. If she hadn't married Jeems and gone to live at Rowanbrae, she would never have met Doddie, would never have known those few short months of bliss, would never have had his child.

Giving up the struggle to fathom things out, Mysie put up a silent prayer of thanks that Miss Wallace had not thrown her out, then turned over to try to get some sleep.

Chapter Twenty

1925

Having worked at Ashley Road for seven years, Mysie knew all the visitors and was surprised when Miss Wallace said, 'I am expecting a Mr Coutts and his two . . . friends at two o'clock this afternoon.' She gave no further explanation, which made Mysie all the more curious when she admitted the two men and the forbidding-looking middle-aged woman, all soberly dressed.

After an hour with no sign of them leaving, Mysie grew very anxious. The old lady was easily tired these days, and even Gregor and his sister didn't stay as long as this, not that Mrs Phillip came often. Not normally inquisitive, Mysie hung around the hall waiting, and when the sitting room door opened, she moved forward to show the callers out. The young man and the woman smiled absently as they passed her, but the older man turned as he came through the door to look back into the room. 'That is everything in order now, Miss Wallace, but remember, if you should change your mind . . .'

'I will not change my mind!' The emphatic retort made Mysie smile. Miss Wallace's temper had not improved over the years.

As he walked past her, the man – probably the Mr Coutts – said, 'Good afternoon, Mrs Duncan. Your employer's mind is still as clear as ever, and she knows what she wants.'

'Yes, sir.' Shutting the door, she wondered how he had known her name, and presumed that Miss Wallace had mentioned it in passing. Some people were quick at noticing things like that.

Still curious as to who Mr Coutts was and what business he had been doing here – it must be business though he hadn't looked like a tradesman – she tapped at the door of the sitting room and went in. 'Are you all right, Miss Wallace? I hope your visitors weren't too much for you?'

A hint of a crafty smile crossed the old lady's face. 'My visitors were here at my request, but I do feel rather tired. Perhaps you would be good enough to take me to my room?'

'Yes, of course.' Mysie could see that Miss Wallace did not intend to tell her anything, and, of course, there was not the slightest reason why she should.

A particularly nasty cold had made the old lady take to

bed, but when Mysie went into her bedroom one afternoon, she found Gina dancing in time to the old lady's hand-clapping. 'Gina!' she exclaimed angrily. 'You'll tire Miss Wallace out.'

The seven-year-old came to a halt and looked sullenly at her mother, but Miss Wallace said, 'Do not scold her, I was enjoying it. But perhaps you had better go now, Gina, my dear. I am still a bit weak.'

When the girl ran out, the old lady said, 'She would like to learn how to dance properly, and I think you ought to arrange for her to have lessons, Maisie. She is very graceful.'

'It's time she learned that she can't have everything she wants. Now, do you need anything before I go? Maudie bought some nice haddock from the fishmonger when she was out this morning, so I can poach it or bake it in egg for your tea . . . unless you would rather have something else?'

'I am not hungry, Maisie. A cup of tea will be sufficient.'

'You don't eat enough to keep a sparrow going. You'll have to eat properly, or you'll never get over this cold.'

'One doesn't need to eat so much as one grows older.'

'You need more than a cup of tea.'

Mysie closed the door softly, her anxiety for her employer deepening. Miss Wallace was so frail she looked as if a puff of wind would blow her away, her head was inclined to shake and even her voice had lost its bite. Maybe it was just the effects of the heavy cold she had, but it was worrying.

The minute Mysie went into the kitchen, Gina pounced on her. 'When can I start my dancing lessons?'

'You're not having any dancing lessons.'

'But Miss Wallace said . . .'

'Never mind what she said. She's very old and doesn't know how much things like that cost.'

Stamping her foot, Gina cried, 'She's got plenty of money, and I'm sure she doesn't care what things cost. She wants me to learn how to dance properly.'

206

'That's enough! I said no, and I mean no.'

'You never want me to get anything!' Gina's bottom lip stuck out pettishly. 'I wish Miss Wallace was my mother. She would never be as nasty to me as you are.'

'She doesn't know you like I do, so stop carrying on. You are not getting dancing lessons and that's final!'

Tossing her head, the little girl thumped down in a chair. 'All the girls in my class at school get dancing lessons,' she mumbled, but Mysie pretended not to hear. She shouldn't have entered into an argument in the first place, and she would have to be firmer, before her daughter got out of hand altogether. It was a pity that Miss Wallace had insisted on putting her in a private school, for she was getting ideas above herself, and her mother had enough to worry about without that.

When Gregor called in – as he did every day on his way home now – and learned of Mysie's concern for his aunt, he said, 'She's eighty-eight and we can't expect her to be as sprightly as she used to be. She's lucky having you to look after her, Maisie. I only wish I had the same luck.'

She looked away. Although he had never mentioned marriage again, he often came out with things like that, and it still made her feel uncomfortable. 'She didn't eat any of her tea, and she'll die if she doesn't eat.'

'Perhaps she would be quite happy to die.'

Shocked, she looked back at him again quickly. 'Oh, no! It's not as if she has nobody of her own. She's got you and your sister.'

'And you and Sandy and Gina. I'm sure she thinks more of you and your family than she does of Margaret and me.'

'She thinks the world of you and your sister.'

'One day, you'll find out that I am right.' Leaning forward, Gregor planted a kiss on her cheek.

She was too dismayed to say anything, and the enigmatic look he gave her as he went out puzzled her. There had been the usual disquieting affection in it, the affection she could never return, but there had been something different about it, as if he knew something that she didn't, or thought he did.

She was still pondering over this when Sandy came home. At eighteen, he was much taller than he had been at twelve, and his body had broadened out. His light brown hair was darkened by the pomade he used nowadays to tame it, and his deep voice always came as a surprise to her. He was in his first year in Law at Aberdeen University, and was more reserved than he had been before. Whilst Mysie was grateful to Miss Wallace for giving him this opportunity, she was a little afraid that he would come to despise his mother for the lowly position she held, but so far, there had been no sign of that.

'You'll never guess who I ran into today?' he said, sitting down at the kitchen table, and before she could answer, he went on, 'I was crossing the quad and there was Bobby Phillip going the other way. I haven't seen him for nearly eight years, but we recognised each other right away. This is his second year.'

'Fancy that,' Mysie said, busy dishing up.

'He goes to the Tivoli every week with some friends, and he asked if I'd like to go with them tonight, so could you . . . ?'

Mysie had experienced a moment of unease at the thought of the old alliance being resurrected, but Sandy had changed, so perhaps Bobby had quietened down, too. 'You want your pocket money early, is that it?'

'If you can, please. I don't suppose I'll be making a habit of this, but Bobby says the Tivoli is good relaxation after studying hard for five days a week.'

Considering that he couldn't get into any trouble by going to a theatre, Mysie gave him a half-crown out of her purse. 'I hope that's enough?' She didn't spend much on herself, and Miss Wallace hardly allowed her to pay for anything that Sandy and Gina needed, but two-and-six was always two-and-six.

'Oh Lord, it's more than enough. Thanks.'

'Why does Sandy always get what he wants and I don't?' Gina asked, petulantly.

Sandy's glance was scathing. 'Because I'm older.'

'But that shouldn't make any difference.'

'Maybe Mother doesn't love you as much as she loves me.'

'I don't care if she doesn't, then.' The girl's eyes flashed. 'Miss Wallace loves me better than you.'

Mysie stepped in now. 'I love you both the same and so does Miss Wallace, so stop being so silly, Gina.'

Later, after everything had been tidied away, and the oldest and the youngest members of the household had been settled for the night, Mysie sat down. There was always darning to do, for both her children were hard on their socks. Pushing the wooden mushroom into the toe of one of Sandy's, she recalled what Gregor had said about his aunt and wondered what would happen to her when Miss Wallace did die. She would have no home, no job, no money to keep Sandy at university nor Gina at the Girls' High. It was too awful to think about. The poor woman wouldn't live for ever, of course, and it would have to be faced some time, but surely not for years yet?

Sandy had told her that he was going to the first house of the Tivoli, but it was well after ten before he came home. 'It was marvellous,' he burst out. 'Dancers, acrobats, comedians, everything, and we went to the Criterion afterwards.'

'That's a bar, isn't it?' Mysie looked aghast. 'You're far too young to be going into a . . .'

'I'm not, and we only had a beer each. I didn't like to say anything, but I didn't like it all that much.'

'I should hope not. Oh, Sandy, what were you thinking of?'

'The Criterion's respectable enough, and Bobby's asked me to go with them again next week.'

Knowing that forbidding him to go would only make him more determined, Mysie sighed. 'As long as you stop at one drink, then. Now, be quiet when you go upstairs.'

Before she went into her own room, she peeped in to check on her employer and was pleased that she was sleeping peacefully. If the poor woman got one good night's rest, her appetite might pick up and her health would improve.

When Mysie took in Miss Wallace's breakfast the next morning and saw her lying in exactly the same position, she laid the tray down on the chest of drawers and hurried across the room in consternation. Her fears were justified – when she touched the woman's brow, it was ice cold. Realising that the old lady could have been dead when she looked at her the night before, Mysie panicked and raced downstairs in such a state that Sandy had to calm her before she could tell him what had happened.

He took charge then. 'I'll telephone the doctor first, and I suppose you want me to let Mr Wallace know? He always seems to be hanging around you.'

When Gregor arrived Mysie was still in shock. 'If I'd only made sure she was all right last night . . .'

Scarcely realising what she was doing, she let him take her in his arms and cried against his shoulder, as he murmured, 'Don't upset yourself like this, Maisie, dear – it wouldn't have made any difference, and we should be thankful that she died peacefully.'

At last, catching sight of Sandy's disapproving expression, she pulled away. 'I'm sorry, Gregor, but it was such a shock finding her like that. Oh, there's the doctor.'

'I'll go. You had better sit down, my dear.'

Over the next few days, Mysie kept herself from thinking by scrubbing and polishing until she was fit to drop, paying no attention to Gregor, Sandy or Maudie, who all told her to take it easy. 'I must get everything clean for the funeral,' she half-sobbed. 'You know Miss Wallace would hate people to see the place if it wasn't clean.'

Gregor did push her into a chair at one stage. 'It was clean enough before,' he said, gently, but she was on her feet again in a few minutes and he let her carry on.

On the day of the funeral, she prepared sandwiches, washed already-spotless dishes and arranged furniture to make room for extra chairs for the mourners. Twenty minutes before the service was due to begin, she went upstairs to dress, putting on a parson grey skirt and a dove grey jumper because she had nothing black to wear. People had started to arrive before she came down again, so she showed them into the sitting room as Maudie let them in. At three o'clock, when the minister began speaking over the open coffin, she stood at the back, near the door, so upset that she hardly heard a word. Beatrice Wallace may not have been most of her maids' idea of a good employer, but her housekeeper, for one, could vouch that her sharp tongue and short temper had masked a heart of pure gold.

As the flat voice droned on, Mysie was remembering the old lady's kindnesses to her – paying for everything at the time of Gina's birth; sending her son and daughter to good schools and buying their uniforms and other clothes; and, more generous than anything else, keeping her on despite her confession after Jess had unwittingly revealed her secret. She hadn't confessed everything, of course – she could never bring herself to do that – but most women would have sacked her on the spot, and Miss Wallace had never mentioned it again and had treated her the same as she had always done.

The throat-clearing and shuffling of feet made Mysie aware that the eulogy was over, and before the under-takers had even begun to screw down the coffin lid, she had gone back to the kitchen. The funeral tea would have to be served when those who were going in the cortege to Allenvale Cemetery returned to the house. It wasn't like in the country, of course, where the men – and any women who wished – walked behind the hearse to the kirkyard, in some cases a distance of several miles; in Aberdeen they had motor cars to transport them in comfort.

In a few moments, Mrs Phillip came in, looking very smart in a black coat and hat with just a touch of colour provided by a purple feather. 'It's the end of an era, isn't

211

it?' She lifted a cup idly then laid it down again. 'What will you do now that my aunt has passed on, Mrs Duncan?'

Mysie had not allowed herself to think about it. 'I'll have to find another job. Other ladies must need housekeepers.'

'I am willing to provide a reference if you need it.'

'Thank you very much, Mrs Phillip. I'll remember that.'

'One thing I ought to mention, however – I cannot possibly let you have your old job back. I have found an exceptionally good cook meantime, and . . .'

'Oh, I never even dreamt you would take me back.'

A slight sigh escaped the painted lips. 'I thought I should make it perfectly clear. Well, I suppose I must go and talk to all the old ladies who are still in the sitting room. I trust that you have everything organised here?'

'Yes, everything's ready.'

On her way to the door, Mrs Phillip turned round. 'Mr Coutts will be reading the will afterwards. This place will likely have to be sold, since my brother and I both have houses of our own, so I would advise you to find new employment as soon as you can, both of you.'

So that's what Mr Coutts was, Mysie thought – a solicitor. When he was here that day, about seven or eight weeks ago, he must have been helping Miss Wallace to make out her will, and the other two people would have been there as witnesses, likely a clerk and clerkess. As the sound of Mrs Phillip's footsteps receded, Maudie whispered, 'I wouldn't like to get on her wrong side. She sounds a right tartar to me.'

'She's not really. She was good to me, and she recommended me for this job.' Thinking that the maid might wonder why she had ever left Burnlea House, Mysie cast a quick glance at her, but Maudie was filling another milk jug.

When the cars returned, and while she and Maudie made sure that everyone had something to eat and drink, Mr Coutts drew Mysie aside. 'Mr Wallace and Mrs Phillip are to be remaining behind for the reading of the will, and I want you and Miss Low to be present, too.'

Knowing that Gregor and his sister had no other relatives left alive, Mysie had taken it for granted that their aunt's estate would be divided between them, but supposed that the old lady had left Maudie and her a little memento. She was glad, for it would be nice to have something to remember her by.

It was fully an hour later before the chattering neighbours and friends left and Gregor rang the bell. Going along the hall, Maudie nudged Mysie and whispered, 'I hope Miss Wallace has left me the little clock on her dressing table. I think she knew I always liked it.'

Mysie said nothing. Whatever she got, she would treasure it for the rest of her life. In the sitting room, she sat on the edge of a seat and twisted her hands nervously as Mr Coutts laid a document on the table. 'As you all know,' he began, looking round them with a faint smile, 'Miss Wallace knew her own mind. This will, drawn up only two months ago, revokes her previous will, and she insisted that it be made out the way she dictated so that no confusion would arise over complicated legal terms – her words, not mine. However, you are free to ask me at any time about anything you cannot understand.'

'I am sure we will understand if Aunt Beatrice dictated it,' Margaret Phillip said, impatiently. 'Go ahead, Mr Coutts.'

He bent his head to read. 'To Maud Low, who remained with me for longer than any of my other maidservants, and who never grovelled nor snivelled, I leave my dressing table clock, which I know she has always admired, also the sum of £300, which I am sure she will put to good use.' Maud's gasp made him stop briefly to smile to her. 'For the children of my housekeeper, Alexander and Georgina Duncan, I wish the sum of £500 each to be placed in trust until they attain the age of twenty-one.'

'That's just like Aunt Beatrice,' Margaret Phillip observed with a forced smile at her ex-cook, who was so overcome that she could not speak. 'She thought a lot of your children.'

213

'For Robert and Beatrice Phillip, my grand-nephew and -niece, £500 each to be placed in trust until they attain the age of twenty-one.' Observing Mrs Phillip's stony face, the solicitor rushed on. 'To my housekeeper, Maisie Duncan, who looked after me so devotedly and kept my household running so smoothly, and who was like a daughter to me, I give the sum of £2000, with a further £500 to be used to complete her children's education.'

Numbed by the large amount, Mysie was taken aback when Mrs Phillip said, her mouth working spasmodically, 'Congratulations, Mrs Duncan. You and your family have done very well out of my aunt, haven't you?'

Gregor jerked up. 'That is uncalled for, Margaret.'

'She must have worked on Aunt Beatrice to get her to change her will, but you are so besotted with her that you can't see the kind of person she is.'

'I am besotted with her,' here Gregor's eyes rested fondly on Mysie for a second, 'but there is no truth in your allegation. Aunt Beatrice would never have allowed anyone to influence her, not even Mrs Duncan, although Aunt was very fond of her.'

Bewildered and hurt, Mysie murmured, miserably, 'I'm sorry, Mrs Phillip. I didn't know . . . if I had, I'd have told her I didn't want it. Please believe me, I didn't know.'

'I'm quite sure you didn't, and I apologise for my sister's rudeness.' Gregor glared at Margaret.

Lowering his eyebrows, which he had raised at Mrs Phillip's outburst, Mr Coutts went on, fully anticipating more trouble. 'To my niece, Margaret Phillip, the sum of £2000 only.'

Her gasp confirmed his fears. 'What about *my* children's education?' she cried, nostrils flaring.

The solicitor shook his head. 'Miss Wallace seemed to think that they were your husband's responsibility.' His attention went to the document again. 'To my nephew, Gregor Wallace, I leave the residue of my estate, including my house.' He looked up again. 'I can assure you all that Miss Wallace knew exactly what she was doing on the day this will was drawn up, and she appointed me as executor with the strict instructions that her wishes were to be carried out to the letter.'

Margaret Phillip glowered at her brother. 'I might have known that you would be the favoured one. I am to get less than her housekeeper, and you are to get everything else.'

In an attempt to pour oil on the turbulent waters, Mr Coutts said, 'I should perhaps warn you, Mr Wallace, that there will not be a great deal left after all the bequests are met and all the expenses settled. And now, if you will excuse me, I must be going, but if you should wish to consult me about anything, I will be only too pleased to advise you.'

Waiting until the solicitor went out, Gregor gave vent to his anger at his sister. 'Well done, Margaret! That was a proper exhibition – God knows what that Mr Coutts must think of us. It took you all your time to visit Aunt Beatrice about once in every six months, and Maisie has been at her beck and call for twenty-four hours a day for years, so what the hell did you expect? That she would leave everything to you? Well, let me tell you, supposing I get nothing, I am very pleased that she showed her appreciation to the person who did most for her.'

'You obviously know nothing about Mrs Duncan's past history,' Mrs Phillip shouted. 'After her husband left her, she lived with another man until . . .'

'I know about that,' Gregor cut in, his hands clenching, 'and so did Aunt Beatrice. Maisie told us that herself.'

Not having expected this, his sister paused a moment before going on, sarcastically, 'And did she tell you why she had to leave Burnlea and come here to work?'

'Yes, she did, and I thought none the less of her.' His voice was lower, his fury calming now that he had got it out of his system. 'You can tell me nothing that I don't already know, but unlike you, I would never have dragged it out again.'

For the past minute or two, waves of nausea had swept

over Mysie, and the angry voices had come to her as if from a great distance. It was almost as if she were hearing a discussion about an unknown person, but the silence after Gregor's last words seemed to have more impact. It penetrated her benumbed brain then that they were talking about her. 'I'm sorry that I'm the cause of you . . .'

'It has nothing to do with you.' Gregor laid his hand on her sleeve. 'None of this was your doing, and if my sister had any sense in her head, she would see that.'

Margaret Phillip raised her head slowly. 'I suppose I should have come to see Aunt Beatrice more often, but I knew that she was being well looked after, and I was always so busy.'

'I'm sure she did not blame you for that. By the way, she once told me she wanted your Beatrice to have her jewellery, as her namesake, so I will hand them over as soon as I can. I believe that they are antique pieces inherited from her mother, and are quite valuable.'

Giving no indication that she was appeased by this, Margaret got to her feet and walked out. Gregor leaned back. 'I am extremely sorry that you were a witness to that, Maisie.'

Mysie frowned. 'I wish your aunt hadn't left me anything. She should have known that it would just cause trouble.'

'Did you ever know my aunt to bother about creating trouble?' Standing up, he noticed that the maid was still there, her eyes round, her mouth gaping. 'I'm glad that you were included in the will, Maudie, but I still have something to discuss with Mrs Duncan. Would you mind leaving us now? Say nothing to Sandy nor Gina about the trusts, because I'm sure their mother will want to tell them herself.'

'Yes, sir . . . no, sir.' The flustered girl almost ran out.

Gregor sat down next to Mysie. 'I'd forgotten about her, but I think she is capable of keeping all this to herself. Don't let what Margaret said worry you, she'll get over it.'

'But she was a relative and I wasn't. I'd have been happy with just an ornament as a keepsake.'

'When my aunt told me that she had made a new will, I hoped she had left you the house, but perhaps she thought that this way you might change your mind about marrying me.'

'Oh!' Mysie looked dismayed. 'You told her about that?'

'I did, but won't you reconsider now, Maisie?'

'I can't, Gregor, I'm sorry.'

'Don't you feel the least bit fond of me?'

'I am fond of you, but not enough to marry you.'

His mouth gave a wry twist. 'Some day, perhaps. But I am truly happy for you and your children, though Sandy's future is assured anyway, provided he passes all his examinations.'

'What do you mean?'

'I intend taking him in with me. Didn't you realise that was why my aunt told him to go in for Law? And Gina can be . . .'

Mysie jumped up, feeling that it was all too much for her. 'Are you staying for tea?'

Perplexed by the sudden change, he said, coldly, 'No, thank you. My housekeeper is expecting me back.'

She could tell that he was hurt, but was sure that she would break down if she didn't go now. 'Goodbye then, Gregor.' She hurried out, and heard the front door close behind him as she went along the hall.

When she went into the kitchen, Maudie started babbling to her about their good fortune, without once mentioning the big difference between the amounts they were to receive, and she waited until the maid ran out of breath before informing her children about the trusts. Gina was too young to understand, but Sandy looked thoughtful. 'There's no strings attached, are there? I can spend that money on anything I want to, once I'm twenty-one?'

'Yes, legally, but I would advise you not to touch it. It's always better to have something at your back for emergencies.'

'Will Mr Wallace be coming here to live?'

Maudie's question startled Mysie. She hadn't thought of the consequences of the terms of the will. 'He didn't say what he was going to do.'

'If he does, he might keep us on.'

Mysie was glad when Maudie went home and Gina went to bed. Sandy was in the sitting room studying and it gave her peace to think. She couldn't work as housekeeper to Gregor, that was one thing definite. He might propose every day in the hope that he would wear her down. But he wouldn't want to move in here. He already had a house . . . and a housekeeper. She would have to find different employment, whatever happened – unless the house *was* sold and the new owners kept her on.

Gregor called the following day. 'You two ladies must be very anxious to know how you stand,' he said, as he took a seat in the kitchen. 'I am sure you will be pleased to know that I have decided to sell my house in Forest Avenue. It's too big for me, and my housekeeper has told me she wants to retire, so I would be very grateful if you both carried on as you have been doing – with an increase in wages.'

Mysie shook her head. 'I'm sorry, I can't stay on as your housekeeper. I intend to look for another position.'

Unable to argue with her in front of Maudie, he turned to the maid. 'Would you be prepared to take over?'

'Oh, Mr Wallace, I'd love to.' She looked from him to Mysie. 'But are you both sure . . . ?'

'Quite sure,' Mysie said, firmly.

Hesitating for only a moment, Maudie said, 'Tom, that's my young man, wants us to get married, but he can't find a house. Would you consider letting us have the two rooms on the second floor, Mr Wallace? You could deduct the rent from my wages.'

Gregor's laugh rang through the kitchen. 'My aunt would have loved this. Yes, Maudie, you may have those two rooms, and as soon as Mrs Duncan leaves, I will engage a new maid and you will become housekeeper.

Meantime, I would be obliged if both of you would clear out anything you think I wouldn't need, and all my aunt's personal possessions. There is no hurry, and you may take anything you like that isn't of obvious great value. Now, Mrs Duncan, I would like to talk to you in the sitting room for a moment.'

He went ahead of her and waited until she closed the wooden venetian blinds, so that she could light the gas mantle. 'Now, Maisie,' he said when she sat down, 'how are you going to find another position?'

'It'll be difficult,' she admitted, 'with Sandy and Gina to think about, but I'm sure I'll find somewhere.'

'You have the solution in your own hands, you know.'

Knowing he meant that she could marry him, Mysie chose to ignore this. 'The only thing is, I might not get another place for a while, and where would I live . . . ?'

'Let me ease your mind. I'll remain at Forest Avenue until you find somewhere else to live. How does that suit you?'

'Thank you, Gregor, and thank you for agreeing to Maudie's suggestion. She'll be a good housekeeper.'

That night, when Sandy returned from the Tivoli with his eyes much brighter than usual, Mysie rounded on him angrily. 'If you think I don't know you've been drinking, you're wrong.'

'You knew we'd be going to the Criterion. We just had one, the same as last time.' A gurgling chuckle belied his words.

'One beer doesn't make you giggle like that,' she snapped.

'I work hard all day, every day, just to please you, so you can't begrudge me a little enjoyment. And Gregor Wallace can come and cheer you up when I'm out. I know he'd like to.'

Mysie turned away. She wouldn't argue with him now – what was the point? He was only trying to rile her by saying that about Gregor, and he would take his own way over going out with Bobby Phillip, whatever she said.

219

Sandy was too old – and too tall – to be smacked, and she could only hope that he never came home fighting drunk like his father, nor became addicted to alcohol like his grandfather.

Chapter Twenty-one

Over the next two weeks, Mysie and Maudie emptied cupboards and drawers, sorting everything into piles, and consulting each other about what Gregor Wallace would want kept. The clothes, of good quality and some hardly worn at all, were collected by the Salvation Army, but everything else was left until Gregor checked it over.

On the first Friday night, Mysie was relaxing by the kitchen fire when Sandy came home, and one glance told her that he'd had too much to drink. His eyes were glazed, and when he said, 'I'll jusht go to bed,' the words were slurred.

From past experience, she knew that it made better sense to wait until a drunk man was sober before reprimanding him, and let him go. He needed a man to straighten him out, but the only man she knew was Gregor, and she couldn't ask him.

Sandy looked sheepish at breakfast time, and when his mother opened her mouth to speak, he forestalled her. 'I know, I know. I was a bit tiddly last night. I'm just a bit worried about you and what we're going to do – I wish I could help a bit more. Anyway, I wasn't as bad as Bobby.'

'Bobby's not my problem,' Mysie burst out. 'If his father knew, he'd get a good telling off, and I've a good mind not to let you go out with him again.'

Sandy grinned. 'How would you stop me? Lock me in?'

'Don't be so cheeky. It's only for your own good. You don't know what happens to some men when they're drunk. My father fell down an old well and drowned himself – not that I cared.'

'I've never seen any old wells in Aberdeen, though there may be some, for all I know. Look, Mother, I just had a few drinks, that's all. I didn't do anything out of place, did I?'

'No, but . . .'

'Well, let it be. All the students drink, and nobody minds.'

'I mind about you, coming home in a state like that.'

'You can't stop me drinking – all my friends would call me a mother's boy if I did – but I promise I'll never fall down any wells. Will that satisfy you?'

Unable to stop a smile, Mysie let it be. She had enough to worry about. She had applied that week for two jobs she had seen in the newspaper, but as soon as she had mentioned Sandy and Gina, she had been turned down. Of course, that was only two, but it was still very disheartening.

Unfortunately, she was turned down for another three jobs during the following week, and when Sandy came home on Friday night, he was inclined to be argumentative, making her spirits sink even farther. She couldn't punish him, she couldn't really keep him in, not at his age, and she would have to put up with it. But it was really upsetting. She would worry about him every time he was out with Bobby Phillip now, for what might they get up to when they were intoxicated?

Her worries intensified on Saturday night, when he came in drunk again. He had sworn to her that he was going out with different friends this time, but where could he be getting the money to drink so much? What little she gave him as pocket money wouldn't stretch to two nights' drinking in addition to paying his seat in the Tivoli, and she wouldn't be able to give him anything if she didn't get a job soon.

Gregor hadn't called at Ashley Road since the day after the funeral, but when he came that Sunday to find out how Mysie was coping, he was shocked when she burst into tears. 'What's wrong? Is it too much for you?'

'It's nothing to do with that,' she sobbed. 'I can't get a job, and I can't live here once you move in.'

'I told you before that you can live here for as long as you want. I won't move in at all. I'll keep on my old house.'

'But it's too big for you, and this is your house, and I can't keep you out of it.'

'I don't mind. Oh, Maisie, you don't have to leave at all.'

A silence fell while she tried to pull herself together. Her homelessness was nothing to do with Gregor, and she shouldn't have said anything; it had only upset him, too. In any case, it was likely worrying about Sandy as much as worrying about a job that was making her feel like this, but she didn't mean to burden Gregor with that, as well. He had done enough for her already.

After a little while, he took her hand. 'When my aunt's will is settled, you'll be able to buy a house of your own.'

'But I would still need to work to get enough money to pay for the rates, and the gas and electric, besides feeding and clothing the three of us.'

'I've been thinking about that. Would you consider starting a boarding house? What you take in from your boarders would cover all your expenses. You are quite used to catering for large numbers, aren't you? With your capabilities as a cook, you'd have them lining up to get a room.'

'I don't fancy having to run after a lot of people coming in at all different times for their meals – though I might have to, if the worst comes to the worst.' Catching a familiar look in his eyes, she added, 'And don't tell me to marry you. You know I won't.'

'It used to be can't,' he said, sadly. 'Why won't you, Maisie? I love you as much as ever.'

'Oh, Gregor. Why don't you forget about me and find somebody else to love?'

'That's something I'll never do, but if it embarrasses you,

I promise never to ask again. One thing, please let me know if you ever change your mind.' He sat thinking for a moment, then exclaimed, 'I've got it! Why don't you open a home bakery? If you sold cakes, bread and meat pies, you would be a sensation, especially if you found the right district.'

That did appeal to her – it would be a challenge. 'Yes, I'd like that, but there's usually just one small room at the back of a shop. Gina could sleep with me, but Sandy needs a room to himself.'

'I'll make enquiries for you, if you like. Some shops are part of a tenement, and when the shop is given up, one of the houses is often left vacant, too.'

'Oh, Gregor, you've put new heart into me!' The light left her eyes again as suddenly as it had appeared. 'But I would need to buy furniture and bedding and dishes and . . .'

'You could easily afford to buy everything you need, but I suppose, with your thrifty mind, you want to keep a nest egg? Well, I was wondering what to do with my goods and chattels when I sold my house in Forest Avenue, so you'd be doing me a favour if you took them off my hands.'

'If I get a small house, there mightn't be enough space . . . oh, I'll make room for as much as I can.'

She didn't realise until later how cleverly he had arranged it, to avoid her thinking he was giving her the contents of his home out of pity. He was always so kind, nothing was too much trouble for him, and she couldn't burden him with any more of her worries.

It took Gregor almost two months to find the small empty shop in George Street with three rooms vacant on the first floor, and as soon as Mysie approved it, he got a painter to decorate it, and furniture removers to transfer his household goods to Mysie's new home. In a little over twelve weeks after it had been first mentioned, the Duncans were installed in a cosy flat over *'Maisie's Cook-shop – Home Baking and Cooked Meats'*.

Mysie was busy from the very first day, and, when Sandy and Gina complained that George Street wasn't the kind of area they could bring their friends, she told them not to be so snobbish. Her customers' accent amused her at times, it was quicker and more clipped than the broad drawl in Burnlea and Turriff, but they were friendly outgoing women who came into her shop two or three times a day because they never seemed to plan ahead. Gina threw a few tantrums about having to sleep in the same bed as her mother, and Mysie felt obliged one day to confide in Gregor. 'I suppose she's missing all the attention she got from your aunt, for I haven't the time to sit down and speak to her, but I can't go on like this.'

He frowned. 'I'll have a word with her when she comes home.'

When the girl marched in a few minutes later – having been at a friend's house for tea – he told her to sit down. 'I know coming here was a big upheaval for you, Gina,' he began, 'but circumstances have a habit of changing. Your mother has to earn a living, and a shop of her own means that she is not dependent on anyone else. I sympathise with you at not having a room to yourself, but . . .'

'I don't have to listen to you – you're not my father.' She jumped up and flounced out.

'If only I were her father,' Gregor said, wistfully, and Mysie felt like running after her daughter and giving her the beating she deserved, but that would probably only make her worse.

Gina did settle down eventually, although she often had a little dig at Sandy. 'It's all right for you, you've got a whole room to yourself, but I don't have any privacy at all.'

Sandy was coming home the worse for drink on several nights a week now, but there was never any mention of him having got into any trouble, and his mother was thankful for that, though she couldn't understand why he was acting like this, nor where he was getting the money.

224

The bar of the Stanley Hotel was small and smoky, but this did not seem to bother the four young students who were obviously enjoying themselves. They had been making a round of several of the public houses near the harbour and were in very high spirits. They were amused by the antics of four raddled women as they made up to different men, and even laid bets amongst each other as to which of the prostitutes would succeed first, but they were a bit taken aback when one came over. 'What the hell's so funny?' she demanded, belligerently.

It was Bobby Phillip who answered. 'Nothing, we were telling jokes, that's all. We weren't laughing at you.'

Mollified, she gave a simpering smile. 'I could gi'e you a good time, if you wanted. An' there's four o' us an' four o' you, so what aboot it?'

Bobby turned to his friends, devilment dancing in his eyes. 'I'm game, if you are.'

The drink they had consumed giving them Dutch courage, the other three nodded, and within seconds, they were all paired off and leaving the bar. Sandy Duncan wondered if the others had done anything like this before – he certainly hadn't, but they were all a year older – and grinned as he jingled the coins in his pocket. Gregor Wallace had slipped him a pound note the other day, as he sometimes did, saying he knew how hard up students always were, but if he knew what some of his money was being spent on, he would have a fit. It served him right for poking his nose in and telling *his* mother to start a shop. If she hadn't been so ready to listen to Gregor, she might have asked her son's advice and they wouldn't be living in George Street now.

'Are you comin' wi' us, lovey?'

The woman's harsh voice broke into his thoughts, and he let her link arms with him. In for a penny, in for a pound . . . though surely she wouldn't charge as much as that.

The shop being so busy meant that Mysie had to work

hard to keep her stocks up. After teatime each evening, she went down to the back shop to bake the bread, buns, cakes, biscuits, meat pies and fruit tarts which sold so well. She boiled or roasted the meats she got at the killing house along the street, and prepared the black puddings and tripe which were the only things some of the families in the area seemed to eat.

Gregor, who came on Sundays for his tea, grumbled that she hardly ever had time to talk to him, and she did feel a little sorry about that, but it wasn't as if he had nobody at Ashley Road. Maudie had turned out to be an excellent housekeeper and a good cook, and he often said that he was better looked after now than he had ever been.

At times, after a particularly trying day, Mysie lay in bed wondering if she was stupid not to marry him. She didn't love him, but she did like him – very much – and she often longed to be held in a man's arms again. She *was* a widow, although most of the people in Burnlea wouldn't think so, and it would be a relief not to have to slave over a stove every evening and all day Sunday.

But Gregor was always there if she needed him, and it was shame, not guilt, about what had happened in her previous life that stopped her from accepting his standing proposal. Shame . . . and fear. Fear that the byre at Rowanbrae would some day yield up its terrible secret.

Chapter Twenty-two

1931

At a very low ebb, Sandy kicked a stone out of his path. He hadn't had any intention of seducing Beatrice Phillip, he'd only been fooling about, but now he'd lost his one true friend. Why did Bobby have to come back to his lodgings early tonight? He didn't usually put in an appearance until after eleven. They had a sort of unspoken agreement – Bobby had given him a key, and had said that he could take a girl there any Wednesday or Friday, and it had worked very well until now.

Reaching his tenement, Sandy crept quietly up the stairs and sneaked into his own room, praying that his mother wouldn't hear. Flopping down on his bed, he closed his eyes and cast his mind back to his first experience of sex. Although it had been with a middle-aged prostitute, it had set up a need, but he had been timid about approaching any of the girls he knew and had carried on buying his pleasures. When he did venture to ask a female student to go out with him, he felt too shy to make any advances until one, bolder than the rest, asked him outright if he wanted to make love to her. He hadn't thought of love in connection with the act, but had complied readily. Now, at twenty-four, he slept with anybody who was willing, students, shop-girls or prostitutes, and enjoyed every minute, especially since he had a warm place to take them.

Tonight had been a mistake, though. Beatrice had been on her way to visit Bobby when Sandy ran into her, and he ought to have told her that her brother wouldn't be in, but a devil had got into him and he had accompanied her to Bobby's room. She had grown into quite a beauty since he'd seen her last – she was eighteen now – and the temptation had been too great, but he'd only got as far as kissing her when Bobby turned up.

Sighing, Sandy reflected that he was lucky to have escaped unhurt; only his feelings had suffered, for Bobby had called him all the names he could think of before he told him to get out and never come back. 'I should have known you could never rise above the trash you come from,' his ex-friend had shouted, finally, and that had hurt more than anything else. His mother wasn't trash, she was as good as Bobby Phillip's mother, and worked a damned sight harder. The trouble was, she involved herself with men too easily. Doddie Wilson had been the first, but now

227

it was Gregor Bloody Wallace. What did she need with another man when she had a son to look after her?

The cook-shop was so busy that Mysie had very little time to worry during the day, but always at the back of her mind lay the thought that Sandy must be stealing money from somewhere to let him go out as often as he did. Waiting for the brawn to cook one night, she sat down on the old chair in the back shop to puzzle it out. She never left her purse in the house when she was in the shop, so she was certain he hadn't been helping himself from that. He had only recently graduated from university and started work for Gregor, and his salary was a mere pittance. Was it was possible that Bobby Phillip had been paying for Sandy's entertainment as well as his own? But Mr Phillip was sensible, he wouldn't have given his son so much pocket money. It was more likely that Bobby had been dipping into Miss Wallace's trust money. He was twenty-five now, so that was four years he could have been using it, and there wouldn't be much left of it now. Then the answer struck Mysie like a thunderbolt. Sandy must have been dipping into *his* trust, that's what it was. All the time she had been working herself to a shadow to keep him at the university, he'd been squandering his inheritance.

After a few minutes, the anger that had boiled up inside her died down. It was his own money, after all, and he hadn't been stealing, but why hadn't Gregor told her? He must have known about it, but he would have realised that she would be upset, so maybe that was why he had kept it from her. She would ask him to tell her the truth when he came on Sunday.

Her mind easier now that she knew her son was not a thief, Mysie let her thoughts turn to Gina, who seemed to be rather more settled. Most evenings, she sat upstairs reading while her mother was cooking in the back shop, but occasionally she went to the pictures with friends from the Girls' High School. She was old enough at thirteen to lend a hand in the house, if not in the shop, but she had never volunteered to do anything, not even a little dusting. Of course, Miss Wallace had spoiled her from the very day she was born, but the old woman had not foreseen what her over-indulgence would lead to.

When the brawn was ready, Mysie put it in the mould and went upstairs, where her daughter was sprawling on the couch in the kitchen reading a lurid love story. 'There's a letter for you, Mother.' Gina gestured towards the mantelpiece.

'It's from Jess Findlater.' Mysie's spirits lifted. 'I wonder if she's coming to see us again? She hasn't been for a while.'

'That country woman?'

The derisive tone made Mysie snap, 'Yes, that country woman, and don't forget I'm a country woman, too.'

'But I can hardly understand a word she says, she's so broad. At least you talk properly.'

'I spoke like Jess when I came to Aberdeen first, but Miss Wallace told me to speak the King's English.'

'I wish we were still in Miss Wallace's house. It was far better than this old hovel.'

'Gina, you are not to say things like that. If I didn't have the shop, you'd have to leave the High School and . . .'

'Spare me the lecture.' Gina started reading again.

Itching to slap her, Mysie opened the letter. 'Oh, that's good,' she said, after a minute or two. 'Jess is coming to see us on Sunday, but she knows how busy I am and she'll only be staying for about two hours in the afternoon.'

'It's my birthday on Sunday,' Gina pouted, 'and I was going to ask if I could have a few friends in, but if she's coming, I'm going out.'

Mysie bit back her anger. She knew quite well that Gina was too ashamed of the address to invite any of her friends to the house. Sandy would probably be out on Sunday, too – he was hardly ever in – and with neither of them there, she and Jess would have the chance to talk freely.

*

Jess had lost weight, and her face was redder than usual after the effort of climbing the tenement stairs. She sank into one of the armchairs at the fireside, looking much older than she had done the previous year, 'An' how's your shop daein'?'

'It's still daein' fine.' Mysie couldn't talk English to Jess. 'I'm fair rushed aff my feet some days.'

'An' is Sandy an' Gina keepin' weel enough?'

'They're oot the day, but they're fine. Sandy's mair at Bobby Phillip's lodgin's than he is here, an' I wish they wouldna drink so much, nae that I ever ken't o' them gettin' into ony trouble.'

'Bobby'll be near ready to be a doctor, will he nae? He'd need to ha'e calmed doon a lot afore that.'

Mysie laughed. 'Gregor says doctors an' ministers are often worse than other men, especially wi' the drink an' the women.'

'Does Gregor still come an' see you?'

'Aye, he comes for his supper every Sunday.'

'Has he . . . eh . . . has he ever asked you to wed him?'

'A few times,' Mysie laughed, 'but I aye said no.'

'Maybe it's just as weel.'

Jess had such a peculiar expression that Mysie felt a twinge of alarm. 'What d'you mean?'

'I thought I'd better come an' tell you mysel'. The laird's sell't some o' his land.'

'Rowanbrae, I suppose?'

'Aye, some man fae near Oldmeldrum's bought it.' Hesitating for a second, Jess burst out, 'He's pullin' doon your hoose an' puttin' up a new ane.'

Wondering why her friend seemed so troubled, Mysie smiled. 'Weel, it was nae use to naebody the way it was.'

'Are you nae worried?'

'Why would I be . . . ?' As the significance dawned on her, she was horrorstruck. 'You think he'll find Jeems?'

'Weel, there's diggers goin', an' you never ken. Jake says there wouldna be naething left, for the lime would ha'e . . .'

Recalling her last glimpse of Jeems, with the trousers round his head showing no lime on them, Mysie wrung her hands. 'I dinna ken what to dae, Jess.'

'They havena touched the byre yet, an' maybe they never will . . . och, I wish I'd never tell't you.'

'I'm pleased you tell't me. It'll nae be such a shock if the bobbies come for me. I aye ken't it would come oot some day.'

'Dinna worry, lass.' Jess leaned over and patted Mysie's hand. 'You can tell them it must ha'e been Doddie that killed him, for naebody can touch him noo.'

'I've thought for years it *was* Doddie that did it,' Mysie muttered sadly. 'I'm sure it wasna me.'

Jess gave a satisfied grunt. 'I've aye thought it wasna you. Weel, if onybody does find him, they'll think Doddie buried him as weel, so we've naething to worry aboot, nane o' us.'

Jess dropped the disturbing subject and brought Mysie up to date with the latest happenings at Burnlea. 'Andra White died in Febuwary – some kind o' blood disease . . .'

'Oh, I'm sorry to hear that.'

'It's hit Pattie real bad, for she's real poorly hersel', an' I think it's consumption. She used to be that fat, but you wouldna ken her noo, she's that thin, poor thing. Meggie's awfu' good to her, though, an' doesna let her dae a hand's turn. Nessie's still in the mental hospital – she'll never get oot noo – an' Drew's aye busy at the mill.'

Sensing that Mysie hadn't yet recovered from her shock about Rowanbrae, Jess tried to find a cheerier topic. 'Mrs Phillip's cook's run aff wi' ane o' the married men fae Fingask.'

'I hope it's nae lang till she finds somebody else, though she doesna mind the cookin' hersel'.' Mysie bore no ill-will at Gregor's sister for what she had said on the day of Miss Wallace's funeral. It had hurt deeply at the time, but it was quite understandable in the circumstances, and she had sent an apology through Gregor when he told her about the cook-shop, and had wished Mysie luck in her new venture, so it was all over and done with.

'I near forgot,' Jess cried. 'Dougal Mennie's sellin' his shop. Rosie says she's nae keen on leavin', but, my God, they must be weel ower seventy, the pair o' them. An' Eck Petrie's retired, an' him an' Jean's bidin' wi' Effie in Strichen.'

This led to reminiscing about the stories Jean Petrie had spread, and how fair Dougal had always been with what he gave them for their butter and eggs, then Jess stood up. 'I wasna forgettin' it was Gina's birthday, an' I've knitted a Fair Isle jumper for her.' She took a parcel out of her bag and laid it on the table. 'Weel, it's time I was goin', or I'll be missin' my bus an' your lad'll be here for his supper.'

Mysie saw her to the foot of the stairs, then went back to consider what was happening at Rowanbrae. Jess had said they could tell the police that Doddie must have killed Jeems, but she would hate to desecrate his memory, even though she fully believed that it had been him. Sadly, her own memories of him were fading – it would be fourteen years come November since he was killed – and she couldn't even picture his face now. It was another face, a revolting dead face, that had returned to haunt her now, and it could be months, years, until the new house was finished. Could she survive the suspense as long as that? And even if the body wasn't found by then, the new occupiers might come across it at some future time.

When Gregor appeared, about twenty minutes later, he could see that Mysie had something on her mind, but decided to let her tell him when she was ready. 'How was your friend Jess?'

'The same as she usually is.' Mysie hoped that her voice was steady. 'She was telling me who had left Burnlea and who had died, and I'll soon not know a soul there. She said Mr Phillip has sold off Rowanbrae, and the man who bought it is pulling down the old house so he can build a new one.'

'Margaret did say something about that, the last time I saw her. Is that what upset you – your old house coming down?'

'I'm not upset . . . well, maybe I am. It's queer to think of strangers living there.'

Gregor shrugged and smiled. 'You can't halt the march of progress, and, anyway, it's a long time since you left it.'

'Yes, February 1915.'

'Over sixteen years ago. When did you go there first?'

'August 1905.'

'So you were only nine and a half years at Rowanbrae, and I thought you told me you weren't happy there . . .' He halted, recalling that she had been happy for the few months her lover had been with her, then said, 'You've been in Aberdeen longer than that. Don't you consider that it's home to you now?'

'It'll be fourteen years in January, but I don't think it will ever feel home to me. I've got country roots.' Looking at him, concerned for her as always, Mysie suddenly realised that she cared for him more than she had ever done. Her whole body ached for his arms around her, arms that would do their best to reassure her but could never banish her fears. 'Oh, Gregor, I wish things could have been different.'

His lined face was very close, and the sadness in her eyes made him bend to kiss her. His tenderness released the emotions she'd been holding back since Jess left, and she clung to him, her lips meeting his in desperation.

At that moment, Sandy walked in unsteadily, his eyes narrowing when he saw his mother extricating herself from Gregor's arms. 'Sorry, am I interrupting something?'

Swallowing in relief that he had saved her from making a fool of herself, Mysie said, 'No, you're not! But fancy coming home in that state when you knew Gregor would be here. Still, it's maybe a good thing that's he's seen you like this at last.'

His face scarlet with embarrassment, Gregor said, 'Do you mean . . . does he often come home drunk?'

'Oh yes, nearly every night, and it's getting worse. I've been nearly out of my mind with worry.'

'Oh, God, Maisie, why didn't you tell me before? It's all my fault. I've been giving him money occasionally, but I never thought for a minute that he would spend it all on drink.'

'So that's where he got it! And I was beginning to think he must have been taking something out of his trust. Why didn't *you* tell *me* before?'

Sandy butted in now, his brain not clear enough to make him guard his tongue. 'I haven't been spending it all on drink, anyway, so there. I sometimes pick up a woman . . .'

'That's enough,' Gregor warned, but Sandy said, truculently. 'Is it a crime to go out with women nowadays? I've been doing it for years, and doing a lot more than kissing, though I'd to pay some of them to let me use their bodies.'

'Sandy!' Mysie exclaimed.

'Have I shocked you?' he giggled. 'What a naughty boy I am – drinking, smoking, having my way with women.'

Gregor's slap wiped the smile off his face. 'You will not talk like that in front of your mother, and there is no need to gloat over your misdeeds.' Turning to Mysie, he said, 'I am deeply ashamed at my part in this. If I had told you about the money, you would have been saved a lot of heartache. Now, Sandy, after you have had your tea, you are coming for a walk with me, to see if that will sober you up.'

About to object, Sandy thought better of it, and sat down at the table. Mysie felt humiliated because Gregor had witnessed her son's disgusting behaviour, but was glad in a way that he had been there to deal with it – she wouldn't have known what to do if she'd been on her own.

As soon as they finished eating, Gregor stood up and Sandy followed him out. Mysie was still clearing up, wondering what was passing between them, when Gina came home. 'That woman is away, is she?'

Mysie kept her temper. 'Jess left a present for you.'

Screwing up her nose, Gina tore the paper off the parcel. 'A Fair Isle jumper? God, I could never go out wearing that!' She picked the offending article up with two fingers and held it well away from her as she tossed it on to the settee.

'Gina, you're an ungrateful little brat!' Mysie's taut nerves snapped. 'Jess spent ages knitting that, and you'll wear it supposin' I've to knock the livin' daylights oot o' you! Sit doon an' tak' your supper afore I tak' my hand roon' your lug!'

The girl's top lip curled. 'You can't hide your origins, can you?' she sneered. 'That's why I can't take my friends here. I don't know what they'd think of you . . . yes, I do. They'd laugh at you, and at me!' She jumped back as Mysie's hand hit her cheek with full force.

For a moment there was an electrifying silence, then Mysie sank into a chair. 'I shouldn't have hit you, Gina, but you asked for it, and I was all strung up anyway, for Sandy came home drunk. Gregor's taken him out to sober him up.'

An angry crimson spot on her cheek, Gina seated herself at the table and lifted her knife and fork. 'You told me to sit down and eat my supper – well, I'm waiting. Where is it?'

Sighing, Mysie rose to take the dish out of the oven. It was useless trying to discipline her daughter, she had let her take her own way for far too long.

When the two men returned, the subdued Sandy muttered, 'The pubs don't open on Sundays, so I'd been drinking at a friend's house, but I shouldn't have spoken to you the way I did. I'm very sorry, Mother, and I'd better go and sleep it off.'

When Sandy went into his own room, Gina said, defiantly, 'I suppose you've given Sandy a good telling off, Gregor? Well, you needn't bother starting on me, I'm going out.'

As the door slammed behind her, Gregor looked puzzled. 'What was all that about?'

'We had an argument and I slapped her face.'

The tremor in her voice stopped him from asking why they had been arguing. 'I'm sure she deserved it. I think I got through to Sandy tonight. I gave him a very strong lecture, and although I can't guarantee that he will stop what he's been doing with girls, I don't think he will talk to you in that manner again. I will not give him any money in future, so he probably won't be able to drink so much, either.'

'Thank you, Gregor. I'm glad you've sorted him out. Just one thing, has he been taking money out of the trust?'

'No, it's still intact, but I honestly feel responsible for his drinking, Maisie. I began giving give him an odd pound or two years ago, when he first started at Varsity. Remembering my own student days, I knew he'd feel out of it if he hadn't the money to keep up with his friends.'

'I should have told you long ago about him drinking,' Mysie said, ruefully, 'but I didn't want you to know I couldn't control my children. Gina gave me the height of impudence tonight, that's why I slapped her, but it didn't have any effect.'

'Do you want me to talk to her when she comes home again?'

'Not tonight, Gregor. I've had all I can take already.'

'Working so hard in the shop is beginning to tell on you, my dear. You should consider employing someone to help you.'

Mysie thought this over when he went home. If she had an assistant, she could cook during the day and spend more time with Sandy and Gina in the evenings. More attention might be all they needed. Gregor was good at solving her problems, but she shouldn't have let him kiss her earlier. It could make him think she was weakening, and marriage was out of the question as far as she was concerned. Her biggest problem, the one she had swept to the back of her mind for so long, had loomed up menacingly again, and there was no way that he could solve it for her.

Chapter Twenty-three
1934–5

'Oh, boy! Just look what's walked in!' The young man gave a low whistle, and his two friends looked round to see what had caused him to be so excited. They were in a bar on the quay, and girls seldom came into these places on their own, but this one seemed oblivious to the attention she was attracting. She was rummaging inside her handbag now with her head down and Sandy Duncan couldn't see her face, but her hair was long and silky-looking, and very blonde. At that moment, she pulled a packet of cigarettes out of the bag and looked directly at him. Her dark eyes held his for an eternity, then she looked away and took out a box of matches.

'She's beautiful,' he murmured in awe, causing the other two to make lewd comments.

'I wouldn't say no to going up a dark alley with her.'

'You wouldn't have the stamina.'

'I'd die happy if I was on top of her.'

'Just look at her tits. I'd love to get my hands on them.'

This was too much for Sandy, who had been growing steadily angrier at them. 'Don't speak about her like that!' He had only noticed her hair and eyes, but taking another glance he saw that her figure was enticingly curvaceous.

Pete, one of the men he had met in another bar some months previously, was eyeing him teasingly. 'Has the love-bug bitten you? I'd leave her alone if I was you, she's not your type.'

'You've no idea what my type is.'

'Well, being an up and coming solicitor, I'd have imagined you'd prefer them a bit classier.'

It always irritated Sandy when Pete sneered that way about his profession, although it was probably jealousy because he wasn't a white-collar worker himself, so he ignored the remark and walked across to the girl. 'Would you allow me to buy a drink for you?'

Her eyelashes fluttered. 'Oh, thanks, you're a pal. A gin an' tonic, if you wouldna mind.'

The harsh, common voice shocked him – she had the face of an angel – but while they were drinking he saw that her hands were red and rough, and guessed that she had to work hard for a living. She told him her name was Libby and refused another drink. 'I'd better be gettin' hame.'

He offered to see her home and they left with the catcalls of his companions ringing in his ears. Once outside, she slid her arm under his and took him over Regent Bridge and along the docks. 'I bide in Torry,' she explained.

She led him to the top floor of a tenement in Menzies Road, and seemed to be surprised that no one was in. 'Oh, my Ma's surely oot, so will you nae come in for a while?'

Despite having been alone in a room with many women before, Sandy felt shy with Libby, and wondered if she would be angry if he kissed her. She sat down on the shabby sofa with her slim legs crossed, her short skirt riding up to reveal smooth thighs above the tops of her stockings, and he could restrain himself no longer. Practically throwing himself on her, he kissed her passionately.

'There's nae hurry,' she murmured, as his hands delved down.

She let him pet her until he was almost begging her to let him take her, then she stopped pushing his hands away. 'Oh, Sandy,' she moaned, 'I've never daen onything like this afore, but you're makin' me . . .' She halted as he tried to force her legs apart, then said, 'We'll ha'e a fag first, eh?'

238

'I don't want to smoke just now.' He waited impatiently until she flung her cigarette end into the fire and turned to him.

On his way home, Sandy reflected, rather ruefully, that she hadn't been as innocent as she had tried to make out. She had taught him a thing or two about prolonging and enjoying love-making – him, who had been the best stag in the herd since he had been about eighteen. Oh God, even knowing the kind of girl she was, he was mad about her . . . and her gorgeous body.

Forty-four years old, and feeling older than that some days, Mysie was glad that she had taken on an assistant three years previously. She could bake and cook during the day – though she had to serve if the shop was busy – and she was free in the evenings. Her original intention had been to spend more time with Sandy and Gina, but they were so seldom in that she had seen little more of them than she had before. Like all mothers, she worried about what her children might be getting up to – Sandy especially. He was twenty-seven now, and there was no sign of him wanting to marry and settle down. Some of her customers had said that he was with a different girl every time they saw him, and one had even hinted that the girls he went with were no better than they should be.

Gina was still at school, and only interested in fashions, hairstyles and make-up. Mysie disapproved of the 'war-paint', but had to admit that it made the girl even more attractive. When she was all dressed up to go out, she looked twenty-one, not sixteen, and Mysie worried in case any boys took advantage of her. Gina 'had all her back teeth in', as Jess would have said, but she was very young and could easily be led astray.

Mysie always found something to worry about, indeed Gregor often teased her that she must have been born worrying. But her terror about what might be found by the owners of the new house at Rowanbrae had been allayed when Jess visited six months ago.

239

'The bungalow's finished,' her friend had told her, 'though it took mair than twa year. Dick Cattanach built it himself – he's a mason to trade – an' he's made a good job o' it. Mary showed me inside one day, an' there's a bathroom, a kitchen *and* a livin' room, an' they've got three bedrooms as weel. They built oot at the front, nae the back, so the byre's been left as it was, an', Mysie, they're usin' it for a shed. Naebody would ever think o' diggin' up the floor o' a shed, so you've naething to worry aboot noo. The Cattanachs are good enough folk, but they're nae my kind.'

Her information had relieved Mysie so much that Gregor had remarked, the next time he came, 'I don't know what has been troubling you for so long, Maisie, but I'm very glad that you've got over it.'

'Yes, I feel a lot better now.' She hadn't told him why and he hadn't asked.

One Sunday afternoon in September, Mysie was sitting on her own as usual. Sandy was making a name for himself as a junior partner, and both Gregor and she were very pleased about that, but he was always out and had recently taken to coming home in the early hours of the morning. It wasn't Bobby Phillip who was keeping him out – Gregor had told her that he had moved some time ago to a practice in Glasgow, though Sandy had never mentioned it – so he must have made other friends. But what kept him out so late, for he never came home drunk now? Gina, too, was often not home until after midnight and wouldn't say where she had been, which was even more worrying, but it was useless trying to speak to her. She had always been a law unto herself.

When Gregor came for his supper, she told him that she was worried about her children, but he just smiled. 'They're young. Sandy will have fallen in love with his current girl, and Gina has probably found a boyfriend.'

'But she's only sixteen,' Mysie wailed. 'She's too young to have a steady boyfriend.'

His eyes twinkled. 'How old were you when you married?'

'That was different. I told you – I'd no say in it, and I'd never been out with any boys before that.'

'It might have been better if you had.' His face sobered. 'I went out with dozens of girls when I was young, but only for a bit of fun and I never loved any of them.'

It was ten past ten, only twenty minutes after Gregor left, when Sandy came in. Mysie was delighted that he was earlier than usual, but his apprehensive expression alarmed her. 'I've something to tell you, Mother, and I don't think you'll be very pleased about it.'

Wishing that Gregor was there for support, she said, 'You'd better get it over, then.'

'I've been going out with a girl since February, and . . . well, she's . . .'

His acute embarrassment told her the rest. 'She's going to have your child?'

Face scarlet now, he nodded. 'Yes, but I do love her and I'm going to marry her.'

Slightly relieved that it wasn't some young tart he'd picked up and didn't give tuppence for, Mysie said, 'Who is she?'

'She's outside. I'll take her in to meet you.'

The girl who came in *was* a tart, Mysie realised with dismay. A painted, brazen tart. How could Sandy love that smirking, common face? This would have to be nipped in the bud, but it would have to be dealt with tactfully.

'This is Libby Baxter, Mother.'

The pride in his voice made Mysie realise that her son was besotted with the creature, and she had to force herself to be pleasant. 'Sandy tells me he wants to marry you?'

'It's just as weel he wants to, for my Da woulda made him if he didna.' The girl's eyes were bold and triumphant, her voice rough and grating. 'An' a' the quines at my work ken.'

'What is your work?'

'I'm a fish gutter, an' I'm nae ashamed o' it.'

241

'No, that's nothing to be ashamed of, but . . .' Mysie chose her next words carefully, 'Sandy has a position to keep up.'

Libby was quick on the uptake. 'You dinna want him to marry me, is that it? You think I'm nae good enough for him?'

'She didn't say that.' Sandy glared at his mother, waiting for her to deny the accusation.

'It's what she meant, though,' Libby sneered.

'Yes,' Mysie said, quietly, throwing discretion to the winds. 'It's what I meant. I'm sorry, Sandy, but . . .' She hesitated, then continued with what she had been about to say. 'You can't marry a girl like this. What will your friends think? What will Gregor say?'

'I don't give a damn what Gregor Wallace says. Anyway, he couldn't condemn me for making love to Libby, when he's been making love to you for years. I know what's been going on, you see, Mother, and it's only because you're past it that you haven't had a child to him.'

Mysie was so incensed that she didn't see Gina coming in. 'Gregor has never touched me in that way, Sandy, and you should be ashamed of yourself for saying such a thing.'

Sandy *had* seen his sister, but was past caring who heard him. 'Maybe Gregor hasn't made love to you, but you can't deny that Doddie Wilson did, and you weren't married to him, either.'

'That was different.'

'No it wasn't. It was exactly the same, and we had to leave Burnlea House because you were expecting *his* child.'

'I loved Doddie.' It was all Mysie could think of to defend herself. 'If he hadn't been killed, he'd have . . . married me.'

'Well, my child isn't going to be illegitimate like Gina.'

Shocked, Gina stepped forward. 'I am not illegitimate,' she shouted, making Mysie spin round and cover her mouth.

'Yes, you are.' Sandy was too provoked to consider any-one's feelings – his mother's or his sister's.

'Is that true, Mother?' The girl's voice was cold.

'I never thought of it like that,' Mysie groaned.

'Is it true?' Gina persisted, her eyes hard and glittering.

'Yes, it's true, but I can explain . . .'

'It's too late for explanations, and in any case, you couldn't say anything to excuse this. You told me once that you were a country woman like Jess Findlater, and how true that was! You are an ignorant, uncouth country woman with no morals! Did your husband know about you, or weren't you married to Sandy's father either?' Gina was beside herself with fury.

'I *was* married to him, though it was against my will, but he walked out and left me.'

'And I suppose that made it all right for you to have a baby to another man? Oh, my God! I hate you!'

Sandy stepped towards her, appalled at what he'd stir-red up in his anger. 'I'm sorry, Gina. I didn't mean to . . .'

'Didn't you? I bet you've been gloating over it ever since I was born, but I'll never speak to you again for flinging it in my face like that.' She moved towards the door. 'I can't stay in this house a minute longer with a brother like you and a mother like . . . her!'

Mysie's legs refused to move, but she flung her arms out as if to hold on to her daughter. 'Gina?'

'Don't talk to me. You're nothing better than a . . . whore! I suppose your husband found out you'd been carrying on with other men, and that was why he walked out on you?'

'I wasn't carrying on with other men.' Recalling why her husband *had* turned on her, Mysie felt sick, but was heartened by the thought that only Jess and Jake had ever known about the young packman who had taken advan-tage of her sorrow over her elder son's death, and they would never tell.

'You don't look very sure about it,' Gina said, caustically.

'I wasn't carrying on with other men,' Mysie repeated.

'It was only after Sandy's father walked out that I let myself love Doddie Wilson. Gina, please try to understand. I loved your father, and he loved me. You were the outcome of our love, and I even named you after him.'

Gina's attractive turned-up nose screwed up even farther in distaste. 'Doddie? How dreadfully common, but my name is my own. Gina. Do you hear me? Gina! I've always thought that my surname was Duncan, but it appears I don't even have the right to that – but I'll soon change it. Campbell has been after me for months like a dog after a bitch in season, and I've kept him at arm's length, so he'll jump at the chance to get me, and his parents have pots of money, so I won't need you.' Whipping round, she stalked out.

As the outside door banged and Gina's heels clattered on the stairs, Libby Baxter looked at Mysie and said, sarcastically, 'An' you thought I wasna good enough for your son, after the carry on you've had? I'm nae bidin' here, either, Sandy, an' you should leave, an' all.'

'Wait downstairs, I'll just be a few minutes.' He turned to his mother as the girl went out. 'I didn't mean to tell Gina,' he said, sullenly, 'but it was time she knew the truth about herself. She'll come back when she's cooled down.' Mysie, shaking now, wasn't so sure of that, but she still had to try to stop her son ruining his life. 'Sandy, you can't tie yourself to that . . . she's not the kind of wife for you, you should know that.'

Sandy's face whitened with anger again. 'I'm going to marry her, no matter what you say. I want to look after her and our child. I'm twenty-seven, Mother, and I've never had a penny of what Miss Wallace left in trust for me, but I'll ask Gregor tomorrow to let me have the whole five hundred, and I'll use it to buy a house and furniture.'

'Oh, Sandy, you can't. You'll live to regret it if you do. She'll drag you down, after all the money Miss Wallace spent on your education so you could have a decent job, not to mention what I've had to . . .'

'That's right. Cast up that you worked your fingers to

the bone to keep me at the Varsity. Well, I didn't ask you to. It was your precious Gregor that planned my life for me. He'd have done anything to get you. He has always wanted you.'

'Gregor has loved me for years,' she agreed, sadly, 'but he never did anything to me that I couldn't have told the world without shame. He's a decent man, Sandy, a genuine man.'

'Meaning I'm not? Well, maybe you're right. I've sown quite a lot of wild oats in my time, and I'm not marrying Libby out of decency, but because I lust for her, and I don't give a damn if that offends you. You're selfish, Mother, do you know that? Selfish to the very core. You don't like seeing anyone happy – you've even kept Gregor Wallace dangling on a string for years. I wonder if he'll think so much of you when you tell him that both your children have walked out on you. Maybe he'll walk out on you, too, and it'll serve you bloody well right!'

Mysie lost her self-control then. 'Go ahead – leave! But don't think you can ever come crawling back here again.'

'I'll never come back, don't worry about that.'

When he had stormed out, Mysie sank into the nearest chair, her stomach churning and her head reeling. She knew now who had kept her son out until the early hours, but what had she done to deserve this? Had she been selfish, like Sandy said? She hadn't thought she was – in fact, she'd considered herself very unselfish. Everything she had done since she came to Aberdeen had been for her children. The trouble was, Miss Wallace had spoiled them, and they'd taken it all for granted. But perhaps she *had* been selfish tonight as far as Sandy was concerned, since he loved the girl? But . . . he had admitted later that he lusted for her, and lust wasn't the same as love. When his lust was satisfied, there would be nothing, and he'd be left with a wife he was ashamed of.

And what about Gina? She was young and impulsive and could easily find herself in trouble. Who was this Campbell she had mentioned? Did she mean to marry him, or did she just intend to sleep with him? Mysie shuddered at this last thought, but how could she criticise when she had done the very same with Doddie? She had loved Doddie, though, and Gina hadn't sounded as if she loved this Campbell, so there was a difference.

Unable to face going to bed, Mysie recalled another occasion when she had agonised in a chair all night. She had felt then, as she did now, that it was the end of the world, but she had survived, and no doubt she would survive this. She didn't know how she got through the next day – even her young assistant asked if she was ill – but she went upstairs at the usual time to prepare supper for three. There was always the chance that Sandy and Gina would come back as if nothing had happened, and if they did, she would make no reference to what had been said the previous night.

Just after six, Mysie was sitting forlornly by the fire on her own when Gregor walked in. He went straight across to her and kissed her cold lips. 'I had to come, Maisie. Sandy's been avoiding me all day, and he looks so upset that I wondered if anything was wrong here?'

She hadn't been prepared for this, and stood up weakly. 'I can give you some supper, there's plenty.'

'I can see you're upset, too. Sit down and tell me about it.'

She sat down, her fingers kneading the arm of her chair. 'I don't really know where to begin, Gregor, but I'd better tell you first that Sandy and Gina both walked out last night.'

He looked thunderstruck. 'Why? What happened?'

He listened sympathetically to her tearful account, then said, 'Was it because of Gina that you always refused to marry me? You told me long ago that she wasn't your husband's, remember, and it made no difference to how I felt about you.'

'That wasn't the reason,' Mysie whispered, her cheeks chalk white. 'I'd better tell you everything, so you'll see I'm not the kind of woman you think I am.'

'You're my kind of woman, so don't tell me anything else just now. You're in no state to think clearly.'

'I want you to know, and it would be better coming from me than from the police.'

'The police? For God's sake, Maisie, what have the police got to do with it?'

'Let me tell you, and don't say anything till I've done.'

Mysie hadn't planned this, and had to ponder a moment before she began at the day of her wedding to Jeems. She didn't try to hide anything, nor to put the blame on anyone else, and the man sat silently, sick at heart but fascinated by her tale. It unfolded slowly – her distaste at Jeems's sexual demands, the meeting with Doddie, Jamie's death, her seduction by the young packman, the unwanted pregnancy, the confession to her husband. Her voice faltered over the terrible quarrel, but she ignored her listener's sharp intake of breath when she told him how Jeems had meant to rip her with the knife.

Reliving each fear-filled moment, she experienced the same horror as she had done at the time, but carried on doggedly – describing her astonishment at finding a different knife in her husband's side when she regained consciousness; her flight to Downies; the secret burial; the aborting of the packman's child; and, finally, the love and comfort that Doddie had given her. She stopped there, because she had already told him and his aunt the rest many years ago.

Her head had been down all the time she was talking, but she raised it now and looked at him pitifully. 'So you see, I'm not worthy of any man's love, and I'll understand if you want to go away and leave me, too.'

His eyes regarded her compassionately. 'Maisie, my dearest, I'll never leave you, no matter what you've done. You've had a terrible life, and you need me to care for you.'

'But does it not worry you that I might have killed Jeems?'

'I don't believe you did, but I wouldn't care if you had.

Oh, Maisie, now that you've told me everything, there's nothing to stop us being married.'

'I'm not fit to be your wife, Gregor, and apart from anything else, it would be the same as Sandy marrying Libby. It would never work. I'm working class and I would drag you . . .'

His kiss stopped her, then he said, 'You are more of a lady than many of the so-called upper-class ladies I know, Maisie. Everything you did was because of circumstances beyond your control. Oh, my dearest dear, I know I said I would never ask again, but . . .'

She laid her finger on his mouth. 'Let me do it this time, Gregor. I've known for a long time now that I love you, and I've dreamt of being your wife, so if you still love me . . . ?'

'Oh, Maisie, I've never stopped loving you since the day I first saw you at Burnlea House. But are you sure that's what you want to do? Is it not because you are emotional about your children leaving you? I don't want to take advantage of that.'

Putting her arms round his neck, she said, 'Maybe that's what brought it to a head, but I do love you, and I want to be your wife more than I've ever wanted anything in my life before.'

For the next ten minutes, they kissed and caressed like shy young lovers, whispering tenderly to assure each other of their undying love, until Gregor firmly disengaged her arms. 'You have made my dreams come true, my dearest, but we still have one big problem to discuss.' Making her sit down, he took the chair on the other side of the fire-place, his face serious now. 'I hate to bring this up again, but we have to consider every aspect. I know how worried you were when Jess told you that your old house was being pulled down – is there any likelihood of your hus-band's body being found?'

Her new-found happiness dissolving, Mysie muttered, 'Jess says no, for the new folk are using the byre as a shed, and nobody would think of digging up the floor of a shed. Nobody would, would they, Gregor?'

'I shouldn't think so. Now, have you any idea at all who could have killed him?'

'Jess said we could blame Doddie if the body was ever found, because nobody could touch him now, but I'm sure she doesn't think it was really him.'

'What about you? Do you think he did it?'

'There was nobody else it could have been – I've been sure for years it wasn't me.'

'Do you think anyone else in Burnlea knows Jeems is dead?'

'They believed me when I said he'd left me, but I think some of them began to think he committed suicide because he thought it was his fault Jamie died.'

'They don't know anything for certain, though, so perhaps we should do as I suggested some time ago and have him publicly presumed dead. That would make it appear that you thought he was still alive, and no one would think you had anything to do with his death if his body is ever found. I'll have that done, then we can be married quietly.'

'I can hardly believe it's all over.'

'You've nothing to be afraid of now, and you can come back to Ashley Road as my wife. Oh, I've waited so long for this.'

He held her to him as she burst into noisy sobs. 'That's right! Cry it all out of your system then banish it from your mind completely.'

When she recovered, Mysie looked up at Gregor questioningly. 'What if Sandy and Gina want to come back to me? Would you be willing to have them living in your house?'

'You know I would, and it's *our* house now. I hope they do come back, but try not to be too disappointed if they don't. Just remember that I love you with all my heart.'

Over the next month, Mysie kept hoping that at least one

of her children would come home, but her hopes were shattered by two wedding announcements which appeared within days of each other in the *Evening Express*. The first read: 'At Torry Church on 12th October, Alexander Duncan to Elizabeth Baxter, both of Menzies Road, Torry.'

Gregor seemed to be genuinely amazed when she read it out to him. 'He didn't tell me about it, Maisie. He doesn't speak to me except to consult me on business, and I didn't want to stir things up by asking him anything. I'm sorry, my dear. I know how you must be feeling.'

'It's not your fault.'

The second intimation was longer. 'On 16th October 1934, at St Mary's Catholic Cathedral, Huntly Street, Campbell Bisset, younger son of Mr and Mrs Douglas Bisset, Patagonia, Cults, to Gina Duncan, Ashley Road.' Hurt that neither her son nor her daughter had given their proper addresses – Sandy had been too stubborn and Gina too snobbish – Mysie had to accept that she had lost them, and was grateful for Gregor's strength to see her through her darkest hours.

In March, Maudie Low, now Mrs Buchan, informed Gregor that her husband had bought a small house. 'He's always wanted us to have a place of our own, and we've been saving for years, but I'll stay on till you find another housekeeper.'

'No, no, that's not necessary. I'm hardly ever here, anyway.' Gregor's cheeks reddened shyly. 'I haven't told you yet, but Mrs Duncan and I are to be married.'

'Oh, that's good news! You're needing somebody, and I used to think you'd a soft spot for Mrs Duncan when she was here.'

He laughed. 'I've had a "soft spot" for her for a very long time, Maudie, since before the end of the war, in fact.'

'Well I never! Why didn't you ask her to marry you before? Oh, I'm sorry! I'm forgetting my place.'

'I did ask her, several times, and I am very happy that she has said yes at long last. I expect she will want to engage her own housekeeper, so there is no reason why you shouldn't move into your own home whenever you want.'

'And there was me worrying about leaving you in the lurch. Well, if you're sure, we'll move out in two weeks.'

Mysie laughed about this when he told her. 'I won't need a housekeeper, Gregor. I'll be my own housekeeper.'

'I don't want you doing anything, my dearest. I can afford a housekeeper, and a maid – more than one, if you like.'

'But I want to do everything for you myself, and the house isn't really big enough to need one maid, never mind two.'

'It would have been better if I'd sold it and kept on the one at Forest Avenue,' he observed, 'but I felt that the house in Ashley Road, being smaller, would be easier to run.'

'Well, I'll easily run it. We don't need a bigger house, not when there's only two of us.'

In April 1935, Mysie became Mrs Gregor Wallace and went to live with him in the house where Gina had been born. No one was there to welcome her – although Maudie had gone back that morning to clean up and to light the fire – but as soon as she walked through the door, the old familiar smell made memories, happy memories, come flooding back. A toddler twisting Miss Wallace round her little finger. A small girl dancing in the bedroom while an old lady clapped her hands. A boy doing his home lessons under a stern, watchful eye. A tall youth in a navy and gold school uniform. Her heart ached more than ever for her two children.

Understanding her melancholia, Gregor tried to cheer her up by talking about the Findlaters, whom Mysie had asked to be their witnesses in the Registry Office. Within minutes, she was laughing along with him as he reminded her of some of the droll remarks Jess and Jake had come out with when they were in the hotel having a special meal afterwards. 'They didn't try to put on a show of manners,' he smiled, 'and I can see why you have always liked them, Maisie. They don't pretend to be anything other than they are – good, solid country folk.'

'They've always been good to me,' Mysie said, earnestly. 'Jess made friends with me the first day I was at Rowanbrae.'

'It probably seemed strange to them that I am a bridegroom for the first time at fifty-nine, but they didn't let it show, and, anyway, I feel quite young today.'

'You'll always be young to me, whatever age you are. And don't forget I'll be forty-six at the beginning of September.'

'You look the same as you did when I thought you were only seventeen, and you said you were twenty-seven, remember?'

'You teased me and said it was really old.'

'Oh, Maisie, after all the years I've dreamt of it, I can't believe that we are actually married.'

Unaccountably, she felt a rush of shyness, but smiled as she said, 'Neither can I, Gregor, dear. But we really are husband and wife now, and . . . why are we wasting time talking?'

PART THREE

Chapter Twenty-four

1935

The kitchen of the small semi-detached house in Marquis Road, Woodside, was festooned with dripping baby clothes, the sink was clogged with potato peelings and tea leaves as usual, and dirty dishes littered the draining board. Sandy Duncan turned on his wife in exasperation. 'Good God, Libby, this place is like a dump. Do you never think of cleaning it up?'

'You ken fine what a handfu' the bairn is.' Ash dropped from the cigarette between the girl's vermillion lips as she spoke.

'You promised you'd change, but you're still a bloody slut.'

'If your hoity-toity clients could only hear you now,' she jeered, 'they wouldna think so much o' you.'

He drew a deep breath. 'Libby, I'm sorry for saying that, but I can't take much more of this. Please, for Sam's sake if not for mine, won't you at least make an effort to be clean?'

Flinging her cigarette butt into the fire, she stood up. 'I will try, honest I will, but . . . Sandy, darlin', you havena kissed me since you come hame.'

He flung his arms round her and kissed her. 'Oh, Libby,' he sighed, as her soft body arched against his. He couldn't stay angry with her for long, and she knew it.

It was some time later before he helped her to tidy up the kitchen, smiling ruefully when she said, 'You wouldna want onybody else but me, would you?'

Their three-month old son chose that moment to tell them he was hungry, and Sandy watched his wife unbuttoning her blouse after he lifted the infant out of the pram. The full breasts with the dark circles round the pink nipples never failed to arouse him, but he had known all along that what he felt for her was purely physical. At other times, he was so irritated by her slovenly ways that he felt like strangling her, but with any luck she would improve when Sam was less demanding. He *was* a handful, but he was the most beautiful baby in the whole world, with his black fuzzy hair and huge blue eyes. He was perfect, Sandy mused, and more than compensated for everything else, including the break with his mother.

Libby, another cigarette in her mouth, watched his changing expressions, fully aware that he had come perilously near to having a proper row with her earlier. She knew that her only hold on him was her body. If he ever tired of her, if he ever found somebody else, he wouldn't think twice about leaving her. Glancing down at her infant, suckling from her as if he'd been starved for the past twenty-four hours, she felt better. Sandy would surely never abandon his son, but it might be best not to give him any cause to quarrel with her again. He might just walk out on her if he was angry.

'Was . . . were . . .' she corrected herself because Sandy often frowned at her manner of speaking, 'were you busy the day?'

'Very busy. You know, I can't understand Gregor. He's been giving me more and more of his clients lately. It's almost as if he were intending to retire, or fade out, but I don't mind. It's extra money for me, and I'm in demand now. People have even been asking for me, and telling me I've been recommended by their friends. I believe I could set up on my own already, but I suppose I should wait a year or so yet.'

'You don't really like Gregor Wallace, do you?' It puzzled

Libby that he was still working with his stepfather when he had fallen out with his mother.

'I don't dislike him, either,' Sandy said, honestly. 'I was upset when he told me they were married, because he'd never mentioned it before, but, after all, he's my bread and butter.'

'Do you never think of making it up with your mother?' It didn't matter to Libby that they'd had nothing to do with the woman for months, but now that she was Gregor Wallace's wife, it might be a good thing to keep in with her.

'I'll never make it up with her. How could you expect me to, after the things she said about you?'

Libby left it at that. She had kept the cutting announcing Gina's wedding, so they could always borrow from her if they ever ran short. Gina's in-laws had a big house in Cults, so they must be rolling in money.

Gina Bisset was quite happy with life. Her husband adored her and gave her everything she asked, so the two wardrobes were packed with beautiful dresses, coats and costumes, dozens of pairs of shoes with handbags and hats to match. The only fly in the ointment was Campbell's mother, who constantly asked, in her supercilious manner, 'And when will we be hearing the patter of tiny feet?' Gina had no intention of having babies, even if the Bissets wanted her to have a son to carry on their name. They couldn't honestly expect her to spoil her figure? She was very proud of her flat stomach and firm young breasts, which she studied in the mirror every morning for any signs of sagging. She was only seventeen, and it should be a long time before that happened, but one never knew.

When it was time to dress for dinner, she laid down her book and ran upstairs. The bedroom had been tidied since she left it in the morning – Campbell had told their maid that she did not have to tidy up after his wife, although Gina considered that it was what the girl was paid for –

and she went out on to the landing to shout, 'Molly, run a bath for me.'

After hauling dress after dress out of both wardrobes, she decided on the navy crepe-de-chine with powder blue ribbon slotted through the embroidered holes round the neck. She didn't look her best in it, but she wasn't going anywhere tonight. Then she rummaged in the dressing-table for her favourite brassiere and suspender belt and left the drawer half open with items of underwear hanging out. In the bathroom, she shook more than half a jar of bath salts into the water before she stepped in and lay back, letting the fragrant steam envelop her. This was the life. She was born to be a lady, no matter what the true circumstances of her birth were. But she did not want to be reminded of that – it was too revolting.

Returning to the bedroom, she fastened the narrow suspender belt and rolled on her stockings. The luxurious sensuousness of the pure silk against her legs cheered her considerably. At school, before her marriage, she had worn thick, black woollen stockings in winter, and white, cotton three-quarter-length socks in summer, and this was so pleasurably different. She smiled as she drew on the frilled French knickers which drove Campbell wild. At first, he had treated her as if she were a fragile doll, which was rather nice, but lately he'd been less gentle, and she liked that better. She had been inexperienced when they married, but it hadn't taken her long to learn how to fire his passions, and it amused her to watch him fighting a losing battle to keep them under control.

She had just gone downstairs, all the discarded dresses left scattered across the bed, when Campbell came home, taking her in his arms and making her heartbeats quicken with his kisses.

When they went into the dining room, he said, 'Gina, I think we should invite some friends in one evening – yours and mine.'

She knew that he was anxious to show her off, but she

didn't want any competition. 'My friends are still at school, but ask yours. I'd like to meet them.'

A week later, Gina was revelling in the admiration of her husband's friends, all bachelors and all around twenty. She could tell that they envied Campbell by the way they ogled her, and before the evening came to an end, she had perfected the knack of knowing when to stop flirting with them. With some, it was sooner than others, but she could recognise the danger point and she didn't want to go beyond that and jeopardise her marriage – not yet, anyway.

When they went to bed, about 1.30 am, Campbell had drunk so much that he was incapable of sustaining his passion, and Gina lay awake beside him, hurt and frustrated, and wishing that she had taken up the slurred, leering offers of one of the guests.

A lump came into Gregor's throat as he looked at his sleeping wife. She seemed so young, so innocent, and yet . . . He had sworn to himself, on the day they were married, that he would forget all about her past life, but sometimes he couldn't help remembering. Every word she had told him was emblazoned on his mind. It wasn't Jeems Duncan that bothered him – she had been forced into that union – it was Doddie Wilson who aroused the jealousy in him. According to Maisie, he had been young and very good-looking and she had loved him desperately.

She still loved Doddie, Gregor felt occasionally. She never spoke about it, but he had noticed a far-away, dreamy look in her eyes if they were out with friends and anyone mentioned having had a relative killed in the war. It was as if she was remembering her lost love, but it was awful to be jealous of someone who had been dead for so many years. He would have fought tooth and nail for his wife if it had been a man of flesh and blood, but he could do nothing against a ghost.

'Gregor.'

He started, not realising that he had fallen into a brown study. 'Yes, my dear?'

'What were you thinking about? You looked so serious.'

'I was thinking how much I love you, and that *is* serious.'

Putting her hand up lazily to stroke his cheek, she said, 'Yes, it is, and I love you, very seriously.' They laughed, but Mysie's heart was full. She *did* love Gregor, with a deeper, more mature love than she had felt for Doddie, but the physical side wasn't so important to her now, and her children occupied her thoughts for most of the time. Gina had been far too young to have her illusions shattered by having her illegitimacy thrown at her. Perhaps she should have been told earlier, but it was hardly something a person could bring up casually, and Sandy hadn't thought before he came out with it so brutally.

Assailed by a desperate longing to know how they were, she said, 'Gregor, are you sure Sandy never tells you anything?'

'Quite sure. I wouldn't lie to you, my dear. He tells me nothing about his home life, and I don't want to ask. If he thinks I'm trying to interfere, he may leave and start on his own, and he's not quite ready for that yet. He seems to be happy enough with Libby, and that's all I can tell you.'

'Oh, I hope he *is* happy – Sandy's the kind who can put on a front, you know. And Gina was too young to be married.'

'She was older than you were when you . . .'

'That was different. She'd been mollycoddled all her life and it must have been a terrible shock to find out . . .'

'Yes, it must have been a shock,' Gregor interrupted, 'but Gina's no hothouse flower. She knows how to get her own way, and, to be quite honest, it's her poor devil of a husband I'm sorry for.'

Summoning up a smile, Mysie thought that, as loving as her husband was, he would never understand.

The rattle of the letter-box made her jump out of bed. 'Oh, what'll the postie think? It's eight o'clock and the curtains aren't open.'

Gregor swung his legs to the floor. 'If you hadn't been so stubborn, we'd have had a maid to open the curtains. Anyway, what does it matter who knows we're still in bed?' His last words were lost on Mysie, who was already halfway downstairs.

'It's from Belle Duff in Burnlea,' she told him, flatly, when he found her in the kitchen reading a letter. 'Jake Findlater's dead.' Although he had met Jake only once – on the day of his own wedding – he felt a wave of sadness sweep over him, and could see by the tears in his wife's eyes how much the man's death had affected her. 'Let me read the letter, my dear.'

'Dear Mysie,' Belle had written, 'Jess asked me to write and let you know Jake is dead. He got a shot of Fingask's tractor to clear one of his parks but he did not know how to work it and it turned over on top of him. She is biding with me just now for she is awful upset and the frunial is on Wednesday. Yours truly, Belle Duff.'

'Poor Jake,' Mysie whispered. 'If I'd known sooner, I'd have gone to comfort Jess, but the funeral's today.'

'I'll drive you,' Gregor said, quickly. 'We'll go as soon as we have had breakfast and got dressed. I'll phone my office to let them know I won't be in.'

In less than an hour, they were on their way, Mysie sitting silently until they turned off the main road and were nearing Burnlea. 'It feels funny coming back here after so long. My stomach's going round and round. Oh, this is Wellbrae we're coming to now, just beyond the church.'

She was running into the house before Gregor got out of the car, and her heart contracted when she saw Alice Thomson and Belle Duff standing one on each side of the seated Jess, who looked old and lost. Her mournful eyes brightening slightly when she saw her old friend, Jess rose stiffly to her feet, and Alice and Belle drew back to let them embrace, but it was some time before they were capable of talking.

'He was only oot o' the hoose for aboot five minutes,'

Jess gulped, 'an' I went to the door to see how he was gettin' on. Oh, Mysie, it was awfu' . . . I saw it an' I couldna dae a thing.'

'Dinna think aboot it, Jess.'

Mysie was aware that no words of comfort or expressions of sympathy would ever put it out of the poor woman's mind.

'I'm very sorry, Jess,' Gregor murmured as he came over to shake her hand. 'I didn't know Jake well, but I liked what I saw of him. If there is anything I can do . . . ?'

'There's naething naebody can dae, but I'm grateful to you for bringing Mysie oot for his frunial.'

Noticing that her eyes were brimming, Gregor turned to Belle. 'What time is the funeral, Mrs . . . ?'

'I'm Belle Duff, an' the minister'll be here at quarter by twelve for the service. You'll tak' a cuppie tea to heat you?'

The churchyard being so near Wellbrae, everything was being done from there, and the mourners, mostly strangers to Mysie, returned there after the minister had said a prayer and the coffin had been lowered into the grave. Belle went over to her when Gregor was speaking to Jess. 'You're lookin' weel, Mysie. I was real pleased for you when Jess tell't me you'd got wed again, but I couldna understand how . . .?' She stopped in confusion.

Mysie knew what the woman couldn't bring herself to put into words. 'Gregor had Jeems presumed dead. You can dae that if somebody hasna been seen for mair than seven year.'

Astonishment made Belle's eyes widen. 'I didna ken that. He must be dead, ony road, for it must be twenty year since he disappeared. We a' thought, at one time, he'd jumped doon the quarry, but Andra White was sure he hadna.'

A tight knot gathered in Mysie's chest at being reminded of the place where Jamie – her beloved Jamie, her firstborn – had been lost, but she said, praying that it was true, 'I dinna think onybody'll ever find oot what happened to Jeems.'

Belle, satisfied now, went off on another tack. 'It was lucky Frank Mutch went to see how Jake was managin' the tractor, or Jess would ha'e went oot o' her mind. She couldna shift it aff o' him hersel', you see, but Frank took her here in his car, an' phoned the bobbies fae Fingask, an' took some o' his men back to Downies wi' him to lift the big brute o' a thing.'

'I'm glad Jess had you to come to.'

'I've asked her to come an' bide here, for she'll nae be fit to work Downies on her ain. Rab's nae very weel, but me an' her could easy manage Wellbrae atween us.'

Before Mysie could say anything, Gregor tapped her shoulder. 'I think I'll call on Margaret while I'm in the district.'

'That's a good idea, and you can tell her she's welcome to visit us any time.' She had long since forgiven Mrs Phillip for the jealousy she'd shown at the reading of Miss Wallace's will. The poor woman hadn't known what she was saying, with her aunt newly in her grave.

'I won't be very long, but it will give you a chance to talk to your old friends.'

The only old friend that Mysie really wanted to talk to was Jess, but Belle steered her round and introduced her to people she didn't know, most of them eyeing her with interest before they moved away. No doubt they knew what had happened to her; the older residents wouldn't have resisted passing on the story of her troubles to all the newcomers. Almost everyone had left before Mysie got an opportunity to go across to Jess, who was talking to another woman Mysie hadn't seen before.

Jess made the introduction. 'This is Mrs Cattanach, Mysie. Mary, this is Mysie Duncan that used to be at Rowanbrae.'

The stranger's long thin face relaxed into a smile. 'Jess speaks aboot you a lot, an' I'm pleased to meet you at last.'

'I'm pleased to meet you.' For some inexplicable reason, Mysie was glad that she'd worn her heavy black coat with the big fur collar. It gave an appearance of a confidence which she didn't feel.

'You'll need to come an' see oor hoose some time, Mrs Duncan.'

Mysie let the error pass. 'Thank you very much, but I'll nae ha'e time the day.'

'Some other time, then. We had the water piped in, an' we've got a bathroom an' a kitchen – a' the conveniences you could think o'. Of coorse, it's a lot bigger than the ane you bade in. It musta been that little you couldna ha'e swung . . .

In spite of her own sorrow, Jess butted in to save Mysie's feelings. 'Oh, aye, it was just as little as Downies, but she's got a great big hoose in the toon, noo, that would mak' three o' yours, Mary. Her man's a solicitor, you ken.'

Having been put firmly in her place, Mrs Cattanach blustered, 'I'm sorry, Mrs Duncan . . . I dinna ken your new name . . . but I didna mean onything . . . it's just my way o' speakin'.'

'That's quite all right, Mrs Cattanach.' Mysie used her town tongue to impress the woman even more, and was childishly glad when the woman coloured and walked away.

'I canna stand folk that's aye blawin' aboot things,' Jess observed. 'I tell't you she wasna my kind.'

While she had been commandeered by Belle, another option for Jess had occurred to Mysie. 'I've been thinkin', you'll likely nae want to bide on at Downies . . .'

'I'd nae manage on my ain, an' ony road, my he'rt wouldna be in it. Me an' Jake was wed for forty year, an' I'm goin' to miss him. Forbye that, I'm near sixty, ower auld for it.'

'I'll ask Gregor when he comes back if you can come an' bide wi' us. We've plenty o' room, an' he's oot workin', so . . .'

'Dinna bother askin' him, Mysie. I ken I'll ha'e to gi'e up Downies, but you ken as weel as me I wouldna be happy in the toon. Belle's asked me to come an' bide wi' her here, an' I'm thinkin' aboot it, for she's nae a bad wumman. I'd ha'e been lost withoot her this week.'

'I suppose she's different since Jean Petrie went awa'?'

'Jean aye egged her on, of course, but we're aulder noo an' I think I could get on fine wi' her.'

'Oh, weel, Jess, it's up to you.' Mysie realised sadly that they were coming to a parting of the ways. She wouldn't feel comfortable coming to Wellbrae, and Jess would likely feel more uncomfortable at Ashley Road.

Apparently, Jess had caught her mood of dejection. 'I was mindin', last nicht, aboot the days lang syne, when you come to Rowanbrae first. What laughs we used to ha'e, me an' you, but it's a' past noo. We canna turn back the clock nae matter how muckle we want to, an', ony road, there's some things that's best forgot.'

They fell silent, remembering those events that were better left in the past, but after a few minutes, Jess said, 'I didna like to ask you on your weddin' day, but . . . did you ever tell Gregor what happened to Jeems?'

'Aye, I did. I near went oot o' my mind the nicht Sandy an' Gina walked oot, so I tell't him every blessed thing, an' he still wanted to wed me.'

'He's a fine, upstandin' man, an' you deserve your happiness, for you had little enough afore. Nae doot you'll worry whiles, but . . . but he'll never be found noo.'

'You're aye so sure, Jess, but what if the Cattanachs want to use the byre for something else . . . ?'

'Oh, did I nae tell you? They've turned their shed into a garage for their car, an' they poured a great thick layer o' cement on the floor. Mary took me roon' to see it one day, an' they couldna ha'e made a better job o' coverin' it up if they'd tried. So dinna worry nae mair aboot that.'

'Oh, Jess, I can hardly believe it. It's the best news I've had for a lang time.'

When Gregor returned from Burnlea House, he was surprised to see his wife smiling radiantly. He had expected her to be very distressed for her old friend, but Jess, too, seemed happier than before, although their final parting was somewhat tearful. He would never understand women, he thought, as he started the car's engine. Even his sister had surprised him that afternoon when he invited her to come to visit them at Ashley Road.

'I can't face . . . Maisie again,' Margaret had said. 'I was so stupid, so jealous, and I'm bitterly ashamed of what I said.'

'You could tell her that,' he had suggested, hopefully. 'I would really like to see you two being friends.'

'We would both be awkward – she was my servant at one time – but you can tell her that I wish you both every happiness.'

Realising suddenly that his wife hadn't spoken since she'd got into the car, Gregor said, 'You're very quiet, Maisie. Did someone say something to upset you?'

'No, I'm feeling sad because Jess will be living at Wellbrae with the Duffs, and I won't see very much of her in future.'

'You haven't seen much of her over the past few years, but I could run you out to visit her any time you wanted.'

'I wouldn't like to visit her at Wellbrae with Belle Duff listening to every word we say, and I'm sure Jess won't want to come to our house. She'd feel out of place.'

'You think it's the end of a friendship, is that it?'

'Yes, I've practically lost the best friend I ever had.'

'You'll always have me, Maisie.'

'But you're my husband, not my friend.'

Her indignation made him smile. 'I'm your friend, too.'

'That's not the same.' Mysie brightened. 'Jess gave me some good news, though. The new people at Rowanbrae have made the shed – my old byre – into a garage, and they've cemented the floor, so I can stop worrying about . . . you know.'

'I didn't realise you'd still been worried about that. Well, that *is* good news, so how about going out for a meal tonight to celebrate?'

'Oh, no, Gregor. I couldn't go celebrating anything on the day of Jake Findlater's funeral.'

'I'm sorry, my dear. It was very thoughtless of me.'

'No, no. You're the most thoughtful man I ever met.'

So thoughtful, she thought, sadly, that he'd actually turned a blind eye on a murder to prevent her being suspected of it. Not many men would do that for a woman, especially if they were solicitors.

Chapter Twenty-five

In the belief that all newly-weds, whatever their ages, would resent anyone intruding on their lives, Gregor's friends had not invited him to their homes since he had been married, not that it bothered him. 'I always knew that I was only welcomed at the dinner parties as an unattached male,' he joked to Mysie one Saturday.

'I'm sure that's not true.'

'I'm sure it is, and they'll have found another bachelor by this time to even their numbers.' He stood up purposefully. 'I'll dry, if you wash, then I'm going to take you shopping.'

'Again? You've bought me so many clothes I won't need to get any more for years.'

His smile vanished. 'I want to make up to you for all the years you had nothing. You deserve the best, my dearest, and I'd give you the moon if I could.'

Mysie chuckled as she gathered the breakfast dishes on to a tray. 'I don't want the moon. I've got you.'

'It's your birthday next week and I'd like to buy a gift for you, a bit of jewellery, perhaps?'

Never having had any jewellery other than her two wedding rings – one a thin, cheap circlet, and the other an expensive broad band – Mysie agreed to this, but made one stipulation. 'Nothing too dear, though.'

Because it was a beautiful August morning, they walked all the way to Union Street. Gregor made straight for the most expensive jeweller he knew, but bowed to his wife's wish when she turned down a beautiful diamond necklace and chose a much cheaper string of pearls. 'I wouldn't know where to put myself if I was wearing diamonds,' she whispered, causing the rather haughty male assistant to stifle a smile.

The padded box wrapped and secreted in Mysie's handbag, they turned to leave and almost bumped into an immaculately-dressed woman who squealed, 'Gregor! I haven't seen you for ages.' She glanced at Mysie, who squirmed in embarrassment. 'This will be your wife? Ben and I are having a do next Friday, so you must take her along so that all the gang can meet her.'

Gregor smiled. 'Thanks, Amy. We'll be delighted.'

Outside out of earshot, he said, 'That's all right with you, isn't it, Maisie? Ben Parker is one of my partners and I used to go there quite a lot.'

She pulled a face. 'I'll feel like I'm on show, but I suppose we'd better go.' She had often wondered where he spent his week-nights before she agreed to marry him, and was relieved that he hadn't been alone with another woman, although she had never really thought he had been.

Tucking her arm through his as they walked on, Gregor said, 'That's something else we'll have to look for now – an evening dress to knock them all cold.'

'An evening dress?' Her heart sank. Not only was she to be on show for herself, she was to be judged on what she wore. 'What kind of dresses do your friends' wives usually . . . ?'

'Oh, I never paid much attention – long, frilly – you know.'

'No, Gregor, I don't know. The only time I've seen ladies dressed up for the evening was at the ball your sister gave in 1916, and fashions have changed a lot in twenty years.'

As they turned into an exclusive gown shop, he said, 'Let the saleslady advise you, she'll know the kind of thing you need.'

The dress she was persuaded to buy was fitted at the waist with a full skirt billowing out under a sash. For some years, she had been accustomed to a shorter length, but when she said that it seemed strange to feel the taffeta round her ankles, she was assured that 'Madam will soon get used to it.'

She tried it on again when they went home, studying herself in the full-length mirror on the wardrobe door. The tiny pink roses embroidered in sprays all over the skirt seemed to stand out more than they had done in the shop, and she turned to her husband doubtfully. 'Do you think it's a bit too dressy?'

'It's perfect. You'll stun them.'

On Friday, when she surveyed her reflection again, she said, 'I'm sure I look like mutton dressed as lamb.'

Gregor kissed the tip of her nose. 'You look good enough to eat, I know that, and a little powder and that sort of thing would put the icing on the cake.'

She had never worn any make-up before, but Gregor had given her a set of Max Factor as an extra birthday gift. She was pleasantly surprised by the result. Her powdered skin was a velvety peach, and the lipstick and the slight touch of rouge gave more colour to her face. 'I wouldn't have believed the difference it's made,' she smiled. 'I feel like a film star.'

'You're the star of my life, my dearest. Now I think it's time we were leaving.'

'Let me check you first.' She walked round him slowly to make sure that there were no threads or hairs on his dinner-jacket, then picked up the beaded bag he had also bought her. 'You're very distinguished-looking in that suit, Gregor. It makes me proud to be your wife.'

'I have been proud to have you as my wife since the day we were married,' he said, earnestly. 'I can't wait to see their reactions when they discover how beautiful you are.'

Mysie's bolstered confidence deserted her the minute they were shown into the Parkers' elegant sitting room in Royfold Crescent, and her stomach knotted at each introduction. The men pumped her hand and said things like, 'Where did Gregor find you?' and, 'You must have been an answer to his prayers,' to which she just smiled nervously, but the women disconcerted her completely. They were all taller than she was, thickly made up, and most of them looked as if they had been poured into their gowns, although a few seemed to have overflowed.

She stood, tongue-tied, until Amy Parker came to her aid by drawing her away from the group. 'Now, what would you like to drink, Mrs Wallace?'

'Whatever you have. Tea or coffee, I don't mind.'

A titter from behind her made her realise her gaffe, but Amy didn't blink an eyelid. 'Would you care for a little sherry?'

Mysie nodded miserably. All the men, including Gregor, took whisky, but most of the ladies asked for drinks she had never heard of, and, as she sipped from her glass, she wished that she hadn't come. The manicured hands around her, nails painted brightly, made her acutely conscious of her own hands, red and rough from housework, and she felt like a fish out of water.

As the evening wore on, and perhaps as a consequence of the three sherries she drank, her awkwardness vanished. She was as good as any of them, working class or not, and what was to stop her enjoying her evening out? Maybe she'd given a bad impression before, in her fear that she would do or say something wrong, but they were talking easily to her now and she to them.

The dinner the maid served up was uninspiring, little more than just palatable, and Mysie's spirits lifted even farther. At least she was a far better cook than Amy Parker. When they reached the coffee stage, Barbara – Mysie couldn't remember her surname – invited everyone present to her house the following month. The Wallaces had been accepted into the coterie.

In the car going home, Gregor patted her knee. 'You came as a shock to them, Maisie. I think they believed I'd been caught by some brassy gold-digger, and you put every one of the wives in the shade.'

'I made a fool of myself over the drinks,' she confessed. 'I said I didn't mind whether I had tea or coffee.' His guffaw made her indignant. 'It wasn't funny. I felt awful, and I don't know what Mrs Parker must have thought.'

'Amy's a good sort – nothing bothers her. But I think you enjoyed yourself, didn't you, in spite of your faux pas?'

'Yes, after a while.'

'That soup was only lukewarm,' Mysie grumbled, as they walked home from a New Year party at Great Western Road – not far enough away to necessitate taking the car. 'The meat wasn't properly cooked and the dessert was far too sweet.'

'No one could be such a good cook as you,' he laughed, 'but I must agree with you. It wasn't very appetising.'

'Did you notice Amy saying it was her turn again after Bet? We've been at all their houses and we haven't had them here.'

'But they all have cooks and maids to do all the work for them. You can't keep jumping up and down when you have guests. Wouldn't you be embarrassed?'

'Not a bit. If they've got cooks, they're not very good, and I'd love to do some real catering again. Oh, please, Gregor?'

'All right. On your own head be it.'

Mysie was in her element over the next few weeks, planning and preparing, and turned on Gregor angrily when he suggested hiring a waitress for the evening. 'I'm quite capable of seeing to everything myself.'

'I wouldn't want them to see you in your apron and cap,' he teased. 'Buy a new dress for the occasion.'

'You always said you fell in love with me when you saw me in my apron and cap at Burnlea House,' she retorted, smiling.

269

'I did, and I don't want to run the risk of any of the other men falling in love with you.'

Although she had three evening dresses now, Mysie did as she was told – she knew that Gregor was trying to prove to all his friends that it wasn't because he couldn't afford it that they didn't have a cook. Waiting for the salesgirl to wrap up the dark green dress she had chosen, she remembered a time when she'd had only one presentable blouse and skirt to her name. She had come a long way since then.

When she showed Gregor the gown, he told her to model it for him, and when she put it on, he drew in breath sharply. 'You look lovely, Maisie. Like a princess.'

It was as if he had kicked her in the ribs, and it was all she could do to restrain herself from lashing out at him with her fists. 'What in the world possessed you to say that?' she shouted, bursting into tears.

Bewildered, he put his arms round her, but she pushed him away. 'Please, my dearest, what did I say wrong?'

She couldn't answer, but when she pulled herself together, she looked at him apologetically. 'I know you didn't mean to hurt me, Gregor, but it wasn't the first time I'd been told I looked like a princess, and you brought it all back.'

'Was it Doddie?' he asked, gently, a pain in his eyes that she had never seen before.

'No, no. It was . . . that young packman I told you about.'

'Oh, my dear, I'm so sorry. I could cut my tongue out. I wish I had known.'

On the night of the dinner, she forced herself to put on the green dress as a penance for reminding her husband of things she was sure he would rather forget, and several of the women commented on how well it suited her. At five minutes to eight, she stood up. 'Dinner will be at eight o'clock. Gregor, pour out the wine while I dish up.'

As she went out, she was savouring the astonished faces of her guests. She supposed that none of the visiting wives had ever had to dish up anything, but she would show them. This was going to be one dinner no one could criticise.

She did show them, and every single one was loud in praise of the meal, Amy Parker even remarking, 'And you did it all by yourself, Maisie? I find it hard to believe that it wasn't the work of a professional cook.'

'My wife *was* a professional cook, Amy.' Gregor announced it with pride, although Mysie had not meant to let them know, in case it shamed him in front of his friends.

Some pencilled eyebrows rose, but Amy Parker said, 'Well I'll be damned. Girls, I think we should do the washing up.'

'Oh, no,' Mysie gasped, but she was pushed aside, and soon her kitchen was full of women, laughing and chattering as they tackled a mound of dishes for the first time in their lives.

When their guests left, all assuring Mysie that they'd had great fun besides having the best meal they'd ever had, Gregor said, 'That was an eye opener for them. I was very proud of you, but I'm sure you must be utterly exhausted.'

'A bit,' she murmured, blissfully, 'but it feels good.'

The newspapers had concentrated on the Coronation for days before the 12th May 1937, giving details about the visiting foreign dignitaries. Libby Duncan read the reports avidly, her interest in the British royal family aroused when it leaked out that the King was involved with Mrs Simpson. The ex-King, she corrected her thoughts, because he had abdicated in favour of his brother. It was a shame that Edward couldn't marry the woman he loved without having to do that, but Libby realised that it would have been most degrading for Britain to have an American divorcee as queen, and the Duke of York would be a good king, in spite of his stutter.

Hearing a key grating in the outside door, two-year-old

Sam went scampering to greet his father, but Libby laid down the newspaper and stood up hastily to set the table. Sandy always got annoyed if his tea wasn't ready.

With their son astride his shoulders, her husband came in singing 'Girls and Boys Come Out to Play' to the accompaniment of Sam's delighted squeals. He didn't come across to kiss her – that had stopped some time ago – but he did say, 'What have you been doing today?' as he swung the boy to the floor.

'We went to the Stewart Park to feed the ducks, didn't we, Sam? And he pushed his go-car round by himself for a while.'

Sandy ruffled the tight brown curls. 'Clever boy.'

'Da-da boy,' the toddler volunteered.

Sandy beamed. 'That's right. You're Daddy's boy.'

He hardly said a word to his wife during their meal, taking up his time by coaxing Sam to eat, but Libby had grown used to this. Sandy had changed. At first, she had thought he was afraid he would make her pregnant again, but she didn't think that now. It was as if his need for her had diminished after Sam was born, but he wasn't quite thirty and should have been at the peak of his manhood. He never invited his colleagues to the house, and she couldn't understand that, either. She had improved her ways and kept the place spotless, so he shouldn't be ashamed of it, and he surely couldn't be ashamed of her, for she hadn't let herself go, as so many young mothers did. She never let him see her without make-up, and she was very careful about her manners.

After the nightly ritual of helping his wife with bathing Sam and putting him to bed, Sandy sat down by the fireside and buried his head in the newspaper. Libby started ironing – she didn't have the chance while Sam was running about – but when she put the ironing board away, she took a deep breath and said, 'Sandy, would you put that paper down so we can speak.'

Laying it on his knee with a sigh, he looked up. 'What do you want to talk about?'

The altering of that one word infuriated her. 'You've always got to prove I don't sp . . . talk proper, haven't you?'

'Is that all you wanted to say?'

'I haven't started yet! I'd like to know why you hardly ever make love to me now? You couldn't get enough before.'

He grimaced wryly. 'Maybe I got too much.'

'Are you blaming me?'

'No, I'm not blaming you. What I meant was . . . maybe I burned myself out.'

'Or maybe you don't love me any more?' Tears of self-pity sprang to her eyes as she plumped herself into a chair and took her handkerchief out of the pocket in her cardigan.

Sandy gave another deep sigh, ashamed of his lack of feeling towards her, but her primitive attempts to arouse him in bed had repelled him for some time. 'I just don't have the same drive nowadays,' he muttered. 'Give me time, Libby, and maybe I'll get over it.'

In bed that night, next to a wife who had clearly taken umbrage at being denied love, and who was lying with her back to him, Sandy thought over his situation. It had taken him less than a year after their wedding to see Libby for what she really was, less than another year for him to tire of her perpetual sexual demands, and the only thing that made him stay with her was his love for his son. At first, he had hoped that she would improve, and give the girl her due, she had tried, but he knew now that his mother had been right. He should never have married Libby.

He was ashamed to ask any of his associates to the house, not that it wasn't presentable these days. It was his wife who wasn't presentable. She still wore gaudy colours and too short skirts. She still plucked her eyebrows and daubed her cheeks with bright red rouge. She still used garish lipstick and peroxided her hair. She held her knife and fork as if they were pens, and crooked her little finger

273

when she was drinking tea. On top of all that, her harsh voice – even though she no longer spoke in the common dialect – grated on his ears. The wives of his friends would laugh at Libby behind her back if they ever met her, and, much worse, they would pity him.

He had often thought of taking Sam away with him, but where could they go? He hadn't been in contact with his mother for nearly three years, and in any case, it was against his nature to admit to her that he had been wrong. He couldn't afford to buy a second house, nor to rent one, because he would still have to maintain his wife. He was stuck with Libby, like being in prison, with no remission for good behaviour.

'Another new dress? You'll land me in the bankruptcy courts, Gina.' Campbell Bisset scowled at his wife.

'Our coffee morning's at Dot's tomorrow,' Gina whined, 'and she's seen all my dresses before.'

'So what? I bet they've all to wear things more than once.'

'*She* does, and you should hear the rest of them laughing at her behind her back.'

'They're a bunch of cats – bored, useless wives, like you.'

'Oh, thank you very much. You've a great opinion of me.'

His eyes softened. 'You know what I think of you. As far as I'm concerned, you'd be the most gorgeous girl in the world no matter what you wore – sackcloth, even.'

'That's more like it, but I can't let my friends see me in any old thing, even if most of them haven't much dress sense. Diane's growing quite fat and the horizontal stripes she wears make her look fatter still. Sylvia often wears red, and with her colour of hair, that's suicidal. Rose has a . . .'

'You win.' Campbell threw up his hands in mock surrender. 'You've got more dress sense than any of them.'

'Well, I have,' Gina said, seriously. 'I'd be mortified to wear some of the things they turn up in.'

Winking suddenly, he grabbed her. 'You know something? I much prefer to see you wearing your birthday suit.'

'Oh, you lecherous brute,' she gurgled.

In his haste, Campbell almost tore off the item which had precipitated their discussion.

Chapter Twenty-six

The outbreak of war came as a blessing to Sandy, who spent the afternoon of the 3rd September 1939 toying with an idea which had come to his mind after Chamberlain's broadcast. No one would be any the wiser about his home situation if he left to join one of the armed services. His colleagues would think he was mad to give up his career, but they would admire him for his patriotism. It was a heaven-sent way out.

Several times over the next three months he almost took the drastic step, but his courage always deserted him at the last minute, and it was well into December before he actually did it. Afraid of Libby's reaction, he didn't tell her until the night before he was to leave, and she flew at him like a madwoman.

'I know you don't care about me, but what about Sam?' she shouted, after exhausting her flow of expletives.

'You'll get an allowance from the Air Force, and you'll get my share from the firm.' He had started up on his own just over a year ago, and had other two solicitors in partnership with him now, so what Libby would receive should be ample to provide for her and Sam.

'You should have told me before this. I had a right to know, and I'd have liked a bit of warning. I know you're dying to get away from me, but don't think you can take

275

up with other women when you're away, for two can play at that game.'

'You're welcome to "take up" with whoever you like,' he said coldly, 'but if you do, I'll claim Sam when I come back.'

'*If* you come back,' she taunted.

'I suppose you'd be pleased if I was killed?'

'I didn't say that, but there's nothing between us now, and I'd like a man who would love me the way I am.'

He felt a pang of shame at having shown his contempt of her so obviously. 'I can't help how I feel, and if you want to file for divorce, I won't contest it, but I'll fight for my son.'

With a venomous glare, she said, 'There's no point in saying anything else, then, is there? I'm going to bed.'

'I'll sleep down here on the settee. I have to catch an early morning train, so I won't disturb you.'

As he undressed, Sandy's only regret was that he would have to leave Sam, but he could do nothing else and perhaps things would be different after the war. Perhaps he himself would have changed, even if Libby hadn't.

Mysie had been unable to put Doddie out of her mind since the war started, the very word 'war' bringing it all back. She *had* loved him, but with fiery passion, not with the deep, satisfying love she felt for Gregor. Doddie and she had been very young, of course, grasping at life as if they were the only two people who had ever been in love, and it might not have lasted if he *had* come home. Poor Doddie. He had even murdered to save her life, but she had never understood why he had left her to dispose of the body. That was why she still wasn't sure that he had done it. That was why she sometimes woke up in a cold sweat in the middle of the night, trying to remember about that second knife.

Hearing her husband's key in the lock, she stood up and went into the hall, but one look at his face told her that something was wrong. 'What is it, Gregor?'

276

'I'd better tell you,' he said, gently. 'I heard today that Sandy is in the Air Force.'

It seemed as if an icy skin formed on Mysie's blood, slowing the flow and making her feel faint. 'Has the call-up started already?'

'Apparently he volunteered and left Aberdeen some time last week. I can't understand him. I gather that his business is building up well, and it's senseless for him to give it up now.'

'Sandy never had much sense.' She shook her head sadly. 'He never stopped to think before he did anything.'

Gregor was relieved that she was taking it so calmly. 'He'll regret it, and if he had asked my advice I would have warned him against it, but I haven't seen him for almost a year.'

'He wouldn't have taken advice, anyway.'

Her legs trembling, Mysie went into the kitchen to dish up the supper. She hadn't seen her only surviving son since the night he and Gina had walked out five years before, but what had made him leave his wife and child? She jumped when Gregor touched her arm – she hadn't heard him following her through.

'Don't be upset, my dear. Perhaps this is a good thing. By the time the war is over, Sandy may have come to his senses, and it wouldn't surprise me if he came home and apologised to you for what he did.'

'Do you really think so?'

The hope in her eyes touched him deeply. 'I can't promise it, but it's a possibility. In wartime, a man comes face to face with himself. It's a time of testing.'

A little comforted, Mysie stretched up to kiss him.

'You're so jealous,' Gina pouted, her eyelashes fluttering. 'Bob and I only sit and talk, or sometimes we put on a record and dance a bit. It's nothing more than that, Campbell.'

'You're playing with fire, my girl, and you won't know how to cope if it gets out of control.'

Gina laughed. 'I can handle Bob, and, anyway, he's had his call-up papers and leaves in ten days. Don't be a spoilsport. I get so bored at nights. You didn't need to join the A.R.P. just because you failed your medical.'

'It doesn't give you the right to take another man.'

'Oh, for God's sake! How often do I have to tell you? Bob and I haven't made love . . . not yet. But if you don't stop being so stuffy, I *will* let him have his wicked way with me.'

Her teasing laughter pained him, but he said no more. Gina would please herself anyway, and ten days would soon pass.

In May, when Mysie was scanning the personal columns, she suddenly put down the newspaper and turned to Gregor in distress. 'My mother's dead, and I didn't know. I should have gone to see her long ago.'

Gregor, almost sixty-six now and stooping a little, took her hand and gripped it. 'I didn't realise she was still alive – you never spoke about her. If only I'd known, I could have taken you to visit her.'

'I should have told you, but I lost touch with her years ago. She married a man . . .' Mysie stopped, guiltily. 'It was my fault. I didn't like the man she married, so I stopped writing to her, and now it's too late.'

'We'll go to the funeral. It says it's tomorrow – I'm very sorry about your mother's death – would you like me to stay at home with you today?'

'No, no. I'll be all right. It's just . . . well, she'd a hard life, and I don't know what happened.'

'You'll find out tomorrow.'

The address in the announcement turned out to be the cottar home of her youngest brother, Pat – the baby she had seen in the cradle at the time of her father's funeral – and she had to explain to him who she was.

'It was Edmund tell't me to put the death in the Aberdeen paper, for we didna ken where you were,' he said, awkwardly, eyeing Gregor with open curiosity.

Mysie guessed that he was wondering who the distinguished-looking man was. 'This is my husband, Gregor Wallace.'

The two men shook hands, then Pat took them inside to meet her other brothers and sisters, but only Edmund, a year older than Mysie, had any recollection of her. It was as if she was meeting complete strangers, and when Jessie, four years her junior, bobbed respectfully rather than shaking hands with her, she felt more ashamed than ever at not having made an effort to visit before.

'Louie Gill died aboot three year after him an' Mother got wed,' Pat told her, 'but she was still cook at Tinterty so she just kept on workin' as lang as she was able. She'd to gi'e it up five year ago, so we took her here, an' Betty's had to nurse her for twa year, for she took a shock, a cebeerial hemridge, the doctor said it was.'

Mysie bit her lip to keep her from crying. 'I'm glad she'd somebody to look after her. I dinna ken what she must ha'e thought o' me, her auldest lassie, never comin' near her.'

Looking uncomfortable, Edmund muttered, 'She thought you was dead. Beldie McPherson, her up at Lethen, she'd a cousin in Burnlea . . . I think her man had the shop at that time . . .'

'Rosie Mennie?' Mysie whispered.

'I never heard her name, but it was her tell't Beldie that your man . . . eh . . . Jeems Duncan had walked oot on you, an' she said Rowanbrae had burnt doon, an' she never said you'd got oot, an' we thought you'd been burnt alive. It was a while till I ken't you was workin' as cook at Burnlea Hoose, an' I kept it fae Mother, for she'd ha'e been upset that you never wrote to her. It was best leavin' her thinkin' you was dead.'

'She often spoke aboot you, Mysie,' Pat put in. 'Mair so the last wee while afore she died.'

Mysie was so overcome with guilt, and with relief that her mother hadn't known of her neglect, that she let herself go in a paroxysm of tears, while the others stood by

279

watching her helplessly. After several minutes she said, 'It's as weel she didna ken the terrible things I've daen, for . . .'

'Maisie!' Gregor's sharp warning made her brothers and sisters look at each other, wondering what she had done that was so terrible, but not daring to ask. At last, Pat said, somewhat enviously, 'Weel, it looks like you're settled comfortable enough noo.'

They made stilted conversation until it was time for the funeral service, but Mysie knew that there was too big a chasm between them ever to be bridged. This would be her last contact with her family, and it was probably just as well.

On the way back to Aberdeen, Gregor said, sympathetically, 'It was an ordeal for you, my dear. We shouldn't have gone.'

'I only wish I'd seen my mother before she died.'

'She thought you were dead, and it would have grieved her more if she'd known what you'd been through.'

'I caused a lot of it myself. Oh, Gregor, do you ever regret marrying such a bad woman?'

'You weren't bad, you were a victim of circumstances, and I'll never regret marrying you. I know you're depressed about your mother, but she was well looked after and you've nothing to reproach yourself with. Now stop fretting, my dear. I'm sure no more tragedies will befall you.'

Mysie doubted if she would ever stop fretting, although her fear had lessened considerably since the byre at Rowanbrae had been converted into a garage, but that secret would always be a link in the chain, the strongest link with her past, and it would never break. Gregor was right about one thing, though. She had lost her father and her first husband – not that she had ever felt anything other than contempt for either of them – her lover, her three beloved children and now her mother. Surely no more tragedies *could* befall her.

Chapter Twenty-seven

After his initial training, Sandy Duncan was given ten days' leave, which he decided to spend in York. On his first day, he took a walk round the city walls, and wondered suddenly what he was doing there. He should be in Aberdeen with Sam . . . but if he went back to Marquis Road he'd have to face Libby again. The thought of his wife made him uneasy. He had been unfair to her, now that he came to think. She *had* tried to improve herself, and he had no fault to find with her housekeeping, nor in the way she looked after their son. It was Libby herself who had annoyed him, but if he'd only had patience, advised her on her clothes and her make up, as well as on her speech, she might have become more like a solicitor's wife should be. She couldn't help her background, and remembering her as she had been when they met, he realised how much she had changed, and it had all been for him.

She had actually loved him, yet he had thought it was only security she was after. In fact, he had sometimes wondered if Sam was his, but one look at the boy had reassured him that he was the father. Before he left, Libby had threatened to 'take up' with other men, but that had been said in the heat of the moment, at a time when she had a legitimate grievance against him for leaving her. She hadn't really meant it, but it was too soon to admit to her that he had been over-hasty.

Coming down the last step off the wall at Lendal Bridge, he decided to wait for a while – six months or a year, perhaps, to be sure he wasn't being sentimental at being so far from home – then he would write to her, under the pretext of asking about Sam. If her reply was friendly, he might go back to see her, and it could work out all right for them in the end.

For the rest of his stay in York, he explored the museums, walked through the Shambles, spent some time in the Minster, found the house where Guy Fawkes had been born, and kept his mind steadfastly off his wife and son.

When his leave was over, he was told he was being posted to Dyce to train as a fitter – less than three miles from his home. Fortunately, his C.O. listened sympathetically to his appeal against it, and he was sent to Leuchars instead.

'We haven't been invited out for a while,' Mysie observed. 'Not that I'm caring, I'm quite happy being at home with you.'

Gregor smiled. 'I'm more than happy to stay at home with you, but I *have* been wondering why we've been more or less dropped from the social round.'

Mysie sat down on the floor beside his chair. 'Do you think I shocked them when they were here? We've just been to the Parkers once since then, and nobody else has invited us.'

'You did shock them – but only into seeing how idle they are. They don't have to lift a finger in their own homes, and they discovered that you had no cook, not even a maid, and yet you produced a magnificent feast.'

'Did I overdo it, Gregor?' Mysie looked at him anxiously.

He kissed her, reassuringly. No . . . well . . . perhaps, but not intentionally. Not only did you show them up as useless wives, you also outshone them with your beauty.'

'Oh, Gregor, you're teasing me again.'

'I mean it. That green dress was made for you, set off all your charms. I could see the other men drooling over you.'

Chuckling, she jumped up. 'Now I *know* you're teasing.'

'Honestly, but you look beautiful to me whatever you wear. Even the very first time I saw you, with that huge white apron hiding your trim figure, and the mob cap covering your lovely brown hair, I thought you were beautiful. When you worked here as housekeeper to my aunt, in a tweed skirt and jumper with a little pinny to keep you clean, I thought you were beautiful. When I saw you in your cook-shop . . .'

She tutted playfully. 'Gregor Wallace, you couldn't have thought I was beautiful when my face was streaked with flour and I was sweating like a pig.'

'I did, my dearest, and every time I look at you, even yet, my heart flutters like the wings of a trapped butterfly.'

'I think there's a bit of a poet in you, Gregor, do you know that? You've a proper way with words.'

'I only speak the truth.'

Mysie lay that night beside her sleeping husband wondering if she had been too stubborn in refusing to employ a maid. Would Gregor prefer her to sit back and do nothing? But she'd be bored stiff sitting down all day – she didn't fancy the coffee mornings his friends' wives indulged in – and a man soon got tired of a bored woman. How had Gina coped with being a wife? It was difficult to picture her with an apron on, never mind cleaning out a fire. But Gina always landed on her feet, so she probably had a maid and a cleaning woman and would be as happy as a sandboy.

Having thought of her daughter, it was natural that Mysie's mind turned to her son. Where would he be now? Gregor had said that Sandy would have six weeks' training before he was posted, and it was six weeks past since he left, so he could be at any one of the dozens of aerodromes scattered over Britain. But they usually got leave after their training, and he must have been home. He must have been in Aberdeen and he still hadn't come to see her.

Trying to ease the ache inside her, she let her thoughts turn again to what Gregor had been saying earlier. Fancy telling her that she was beautiful. He *had* been teasing, of course, but she loved him for it. If only he would let her

283

bob her hair like Amy and the rest. She always felt so old-fashioned beside them, but Gregor said that her hair was her crowning glory. *He* didn't have the agony of brushing out the tangles every morning and sticking in dozens of hairpins to keep it under control. Maybe she should just have it cut some day, without telling him? He couldn't do anything then – but she didn't want to annoy him. She had never been so happy in her life as she was now, and wished that she had married him when he first asked her. If he had been stepfather to Sandy and Gina, they wouldn't have turned out the way they did.

Sandy and Gina. Her thoughts always came back to them, and she wished that she knew how they were. If only she could see them again, to let them know how sorry she was for what had happened that night. Sandy's child must be five years old by this time, and she had never seen it, boy or girl, and probably never would now.

Being without a servant was intolerable to Gina – the house in Bieldside was far too big for her to run. Why did all these girls want to go into the forces? Munitions she could have understood, there was more money there, but Molly had joined the ATS, Iris, who had come after her, had gone into the WAAFs and Rita, shy little Rita, had left three weeks ago to become a Wren. The army, the air force and the navy, not quite in the same order as the popular song. Campbell was impossible these days, too, frustrated at being graded 4F at his medical, but he didn't need to take it out on her as if it were her fault. Everything she did or said was wrong – his shirts weren't ironed properly; he could write his name on the dust on the furniture. At lunch that very day, he had said he couldn't eat the vegetable stew she'd put in front of him though she was sure that she had cooked it long enough, and had sneered, 'I can't understand you. Your mother was a cook, wasn't she?'

To Gina, this was the worst insult he could have thrown at her. 'You'll be sorry you ever said that, Campbell Bisset!'

'I wasn't demeaning her.' He sounded exasperated. 'I meant that she must have been a good cook before she could have run a cook-shop, and I'm surprised that you never managed to pick up even the rudiments of cookery.'

All afternoon, she brooded over his unreasonableness, and as soon as he appeared at night, she said, 'I want a divorce.'

'You know I'm a Catholic, Gina, so there can be no divorce.'

'I just wanted to make sure, for I've a proposition to make. I'll live with you, your wife in everyone's eyes, but we'll have separate bedrooms and I'll live my life as I please. You can please yourself, too, and do whatever you like. Nobody would know. I promise to act like a loving wife in front of your parents and friends.'

His ready agreement surprised her, 'All right, if that's what you want, but I'll make one condition. You'll have to learn how to cook and keep house properly, otherwise I'll throw you out.'

'Always the gentleman,' she sneered.

He let her sarcasm go. 'And there would be no maintenance. You'd have to stand on your own two feet for a change.' After a long pause, Gina said, 'Okay, we have a bargain. I'll cook and clean like a good little wife, wash and iron for you, sew on your buttons, and you let me live my own way.'

The steady ring of the telephone made Mysie jump. She wasn't at all happy about having to answer this new contraption, but she would likely get used to it. Picking up the receiver, she said, loudly, 'Hello?'

'Amy here. May I come to see you – say about two?'

Wondering why Amy Parker wanted to see her, Mysie nodded, then realised that the woman wouldn't see. 'Two would be fine.'

The doorbell rang at exactly two o'clock. 'I hope you don't mind, Maisie, but I'm in a bit of a pickle,' Amy said, as she sat down in the sitting room.

'If I can help you at all . . . ?'

'You can save my life. I can't find a new cook for love or money. I've never done any cooking before and I'm making a bit of a mess of it. Would you . . . give me a few lessons?'

Mysie laughed. 'I'd be glad to, but I was never trained, you know. When I started as a cook first, I'd to depend on an old recipe book my employer gave me.'

'You're better than any of the cooks I've had. Some of the girls are in the same boat as me, and we wondered if you . . .'

'You want me to take a class?' Mysie joked.

'I'm quite serious, and we would pay you for your time.'

'But I can't teach people to cook. I'm not qualified.'

'Please, Maisie?' Amy's eyes were beseeching. 'I have to do something, otherwise Ben's going to rebel at having fried fish morning, noon and night – burned to a cinder, I might add.'

Laughingly agreeing to the proposal, Mysie suggested that those who wished should turn up at Ashley Road at two o'clock the following Wednesday, and Amy left after a cup of tea, her last words being, 'You're a saviour, Maisie, do you know that?'

At teatime, Gregor scowled when his wife told him what she had arranged. 'Don't you have enough to do, without taking all those helpless creatures under your wing?'

'I can spare an hour or two a week,' Mysie said, having been thinking it over ever since Amy Parker went home, 'and I won't let them pay me. It's funny, really, when you come to think about it. Here am I, daughter of a drunken blacksmith, widow of a penniless crofter, telling the gentry how to cook.'

Her husband's scowl deepened. 'They're not gentry. If you researched into their backgrounds, I'm sure you would find that they come of working class stock, perhaps only a generation or two back. You're as good as any of them, Maisie – better.'

'You're biased,' she chuckled. 'From scullerymaid to lec-

286

turer, that's me, and a few other things in between. Don't forbid me to do it, Gregor, for I'm quite looking forward to it.'

His face clearing, he slipped his arm round her waist. 'Oh, Maisie. You're so full of life, so willing to tackle anything. That's why I love you so much. Don't ever change.'

The cookery classes were great fun, Mysie thought, glancing round her kitchen some months later, and she was sure that the other four women enjoyed them as much as she did. In actual fact, the lessons had replaced their coffee mornings, some gossip being relayed – although she wouldn't allow them to say anything malicious about anybody – clothes and new hairstyles discussed, even recipes exchanged.

It had been a bit difficult at first, with food rationed, but it had been an extra challenge, and she believed that she had risen to it. Amy Parker had obviously thought so. 'Maisie, you're a genius,' she had exclaimed, the week after she had been taught how to tenderise meat by pounding it with a wooden potato masher. 'Ben said I must be seducing the butcher to get meat like that – to get meat at all.'

The others had laughed uproariously, but it had been a great boost to Mysie's morale at a time when she was somewhat unsure of her prowess as a teacher. They had progressed from meat to fish and fowl, and soon she would have to demonstrate how to prepare a Christmas dinner. It was all quite exhilarating, and gave her something to look forward to, now that she had almost given up hope of Sandy or Gina ever coming to see her again.

Chapter Twenty-eight

1941–2

It was not that she was tired of giving cookery lessons, Mysie mused, it was just that she was running out of ideas. It was more than a year since she had started, and, although there were no 'classes' during school holidays because some of her 'students' had young children, she still had conducted over fifty and had covered almost every aspect that she could think of. After main courses, she had concentrated on soups and other starters, then, some weeks later, it had been a selection of desserts. Following this, she had gone on to breakfast dishes and snacks before she started on bread, cakes and biscuits. The cakes had been quite a problem, with few fresh eggs to be had, but she had experimented on her own until she found a successful way of using the powdered kind. At present, she was on garnishes and decoration, and had tried out a recipe for making marzipan with soya flour, which wasn't too bad. What else was there? she wondered.

When Gregor came home, he asked, 'How did your class go, my dearest? Did anyone bring an apple for the teacher?'

He often trotted out this old chestnut, but Mysie laughed as usual. 'I'm trying to think what to give them next. I'm sure they could all cope on their own now, for they know as much about cooking as I do.'

'Maybe they do, but I doubt if any of them will ever measure up to you. You have that extra something – ingenuity.'

'They can't expect me to carry on for much longer, can they? There's a limit to everything.'

His eyes twinkled under his greying eyebrows. 'Not to my love for you.'

'Oh, Gregor, be serious. I once suggested stopping but they said they wanted to carry on. I'm really worried.'

'You've been worried ever since I knew you, but all right, I'll be serious. I'm sure they don't expect you to carry on giving them lessons. They enjoy your company, and they'd be quite happy to come here even if there were no classes.'

'Do you think so? I enjoy their company, too.'

'Well, tell them next Wednesday that you are stopping your classes, but invite them to keep on coming every week.'

So 'Maisie's Cookery Classes' came to be known as 'Maisie's Afternoons,' and her worries about them came to an end, but she still had worries of a different kind. Sometimes, when she was trying to get to sleep, she was plagued by her old fear that what lay under the garage at Rowanbrae might yet be uncovered. What if the man wanted to make a pit to look underneath his car? What a shock he would get if he dug up . . . she could still see that face, that horrible unlimed face with the teeth bared in a grotesque grin, and even if she hadn't killed Jeems, she had concealed his body. She would never be free of that guilt.

Her trembling often woke Gregor, who held her tightly until she calmed down, and she would thank God for having such an understanding husband. He knew everything about her, all her secrets, and he still loved her. She was a very lucky woman even if all three of her children were lost to her.

There had been much activity over the past week or two around El Alamein, even the ground crews had been kept at it, but now there was a lull, a brief respite before the next onslaught – Rommel wouldn't give in easily. But all tanks and aircraft were ready, all nerves taut as wound-up springs. Every soldier and airman, whatever his rank, whatever his trade, knew that the following day could be his last, so there was a constraint in their manner towards each other. A few of the more cocky were laying bets on how long it would take to rout the enemy, but mostly they were quiet, reading or writing letters home in the blistering Egyptian sun.

Sandy Duncan lay with his back against the tent, thinking. His life had never amounted to much, and it would be no great loss to the world if he were killed. He had been told that his squadron was being sent overseas before he had ever written to Libby, and, although they had been given embarkation leave, he hadn't been able to bring himself to go home. Instead, he had gone to London with some single blokes who were looking for a good time, and they had danced in Services clubs or gone to entertainments meant for the forces. Some of them had been drunk occasionally, but he hadn't. He had taken a few drinks, but he hadn't forgotten that he was a married man, and he had refused to get involved with any of the willing females who hung around anyone wearing a uniform.

Surprisingly, or maybe not so surprisingly, he had thought of his wife a lot during that leave, and had considered, several times, buying a writing pad so that he could let her know how he felt, how he missed her, how he regretted leaving her, but what good would it have done? He had accepted, even then, that the chances of his being killed would be greater once he left Britain, that he might never return from the journey on which he was about to embark.

His mind turned again to the probability of his death. Not a soul would mourn his passing if he did lose his life. Libby would be free to take another husband, and Sam would lose a father he wouldn't remember. He had only been four when his father left him, and he would be coming up for seven now. He could hardly remember his own father, Sandy reflected, but his mother . . . his mother *would* care if he were killed, provided she knew about it. Her life had never been easy, and some of the things he had done had placed burdens on her that must have been insufferable, but he knew now that she had loved him in spite of everything. How could he ever atone for all the misery he had inflicted on her? Coming to an abrupt decision, he turned to the man sitting next him. 'Alf, may I borrow your writing pad, please?'

Mysie was worried about Gregor's health. He was working far too hard, too long hours, with half the amount of help he'd had before, and, at sixty-eight, he should really be retired. His face was drawn and haggard, his high cheekbones standing out starkly. His eyes lacked their old sparkle, and his movements were much slower. Looking across the fireside, her heart ached with love. 'Gregor, you should go to bed when you've read that newspaper. You're looking very tired.'

'Hmm?'

She smiled fondly. He hadn't taken in a word she had said. 'Gregor! I'm sure they could manage without you for a week or so. Why don't you take a holiday?'

Frowning, he lifted his head. 'A holiday?'

'You need a rest.'

'I'm resting now.'

'A long rest, Gregor. We could go away for a few days.'

Heaving a sigh, he laid his newspaper down on the floor. 'Do you want to go away, my dear?'

'Not me. I'm afraid you'll work yourself into the grave.'

'Nonsense. I am a little tired, but I can't stay off. We are very busy just now. Treble the number of divorces we used to handle before the war.'

'It's the husbands being away – the wives meet other men.'

'I suppose so. I think I'll go up and read the rest of the paper in bed. Do you want a quick look at it first?'

He picked it up, handed it to her and lay back to wait until she read it. The front page held only depressing news about the war, so she turned to the Births, Marriages and Deaths. She always tried to read that, in case someone she knew, or used to know, had died. Her sharp gasp of dismay made her husband sit up. 'What . . .?'

'Sandy's been killed.'

Forgetting his exhaustion, he jumped out of his chair and she rose to be clasped in his arms. 'Oh, Gregor,' she sobbed, 'I wish I could have seen him before he went away to the war. I wish we could have made up our differences. Now I'll never know if he'd forgiven me for what I said.'

'Hush, my dearest. I'm sure he had forgiven you long ago, but being Sandy, he wouldn't have liked to climb down.'

'But that's both of my sons dead now. I know I really lost Sandy years ago, but I always hoped . . . it's a lot worse now. If only Gina would come back . . . it wouldn't compensate for Sandy's death, but it would help me to bear it.'

'Will I contact her in-laws to find out where she lives, and then ask her to come to see you?'

'Oh, yes, Gregor, please! She might listen to you, but I'm sure she wouldn't listen to me.'

'I'll phone the Bissets now, and if I get Gina's address, I'll go to see her first thing in the morning.'

Leaning against him, Mysie whispered, 'I don't know what I would do without you, Gregor.'

'I'm sure you would cope better than I would without you.'

In bed, she talked far into the night about Sandy – what he had said and done when he was a small boy; his deep jealousy of Doddie which had resulted in the fire; the mischief he had got up to with Bobby Phillip during their school holidays; his homework sessions with Miss Wallace; his wildness when he was at the university; the nights he stayed out so late – and her husband held her closely in his arms, letting her relive her son's life to ease her sorrow.

Mrs Bisset had given Gregor the address he wanted, and when he set off for Bieldside in the morning, he said, 'Don't expect too much of Gina, Maisie. You know how strong-willed she is, and I can't promise anything. I can only try.'

'I know, and I won't blame you if you can't persuade her to come to me, but I'll be praying that you can.'

Too keyed-up to do anything except wait for her daughter to ring the doorbell, Mysie sat in the sitting room for nearly two hours, jumping up hopefully each time she heard a car coming and growing increasingly despondent when every vehicle whizzed past. When the telephone jangled at twenty past ten, she ran to answer it, snatching up the receiver and almost dropping it with excitement. 'Hello,' she said, breathlessly. 'Is that you, Gina?'

'Oh, Maisie, I'm sorry.' Gregor's voice sounded flat. 'She won't come, no matter what I said. She didn't even seem to care that Sandy had been killed, and I was there for about an hour trying to make her see sense. I thought I'd better let you know as soon as I came to the office, so that you wouldn't keep hoping.'

'Thank you. You did your best.' Mysie forced the words out.

Sick at heart, she prepared lunch then baked bread, scones and pancakes to keep herself occupied. She heard the second post coming through the door at ten past twelve, but ignored it. The letters were usually for Gregor, anyway.

Gina tipped the tin of tomato soup into a pan. How dare that man come inside her house at nine o'clock in the morning and lecture her. She had still been in bed, and had wondered who was at the door at such an unearthly hour. She had actually smiled when she opened it, because she really had no quarrel with Gregor. Well, she hadn't had, not until he told her why he was there. If he'd only taken no for an answer, it wouldn't have been so bad, but he had stood in the lounge arguing with her, telling her how selfish she was, and how badly she had hurt her mother. Good God! Did nobody ever remember how hurt *she* had been at the time?

Turning from the cooker to get a spoon, she noticed that she had left the empty tin on the table and hastily disposed of it in the rubbish bin, thrusting it well down under some papers out of sight. If Campbell saw it, he would create merry hell about her using tinned soup.

When her husband came in for lunch, she told him about her unexpected visitor and how Gregor had pleaded with her to make up with her mother. 'She had sent him, of course. She'd been feeling guilty about Sandy now that he's dead, and she'd wanted to ease her conscience by apologising to me.'

'Your mother has nothing to apologise for,' Campbell said, quietly, having been told the whole story on the night Gina came knocking on his parents' door in great distress. 'All she did was to love her son enough to try to prevent an unsuitable marriage, and as far as you're concerned, you were the result of her loving a man other than her husband. And don't pretend you're shocked by that, because you're much worse. I have no idea how many men you have taken here, and you're bloody lucky that you've never been pregnant by any of them.'

'Not lucky,' Gina sneered. 'Careful. I should have known you wouldn't see my side of it, but you don't know what it's like to find out you're illegitimate. It's something you can't get over, and I never forgave Sandy for the way he told me.'

Campbell sighed. 'I suppose it was a shock to you, but you did get over it, and it wasn't your brother's fault. He was angry at his mother and lashed out at her. If you don't want to see her, don't go, but stop harping on at me about it. I've invited my parents to dinner tomorrow night and I want you to be on your best behaviour. You won't need to worry about what to give them, because a farmer I know has promised me a nice piece of pork. He's delivering it in the morning.'

'You might have asked me before you invited them,' Gina burst out. 'I'm going out with James tomorrow night.'

'You'll have to phone him and cancel it, then.'

Seething inside, Gina gave in. When they made their bargain, Campbell had said he would put her out if she didn't keep her promise, and she couldn't face being homeless and penniless, not now – not after all the fun she'd been having recently.

When Gregor came home for lunch at ten past one, he brought the post in with him and laid it down beside his place at the dining room table. 'I'm sorry I couldn't make Gina . . .'

'I didn't really think she would listen – she's always been self-centred. Don't worry, I've got over the disappointment. Sit down and read your mail till I bring through the dinner.'

When she laid down the two steaming plates, he handed her a fat envelope. 'This one's for you.'

Mysie didn't recognise the handwriting, and because there was no postmark during wartime to say where it had been posted, a vague apprehension stole over her. She turned the letter over in her nervous hands and looked fearfully at her husband. 'I don't want to open it, Gregor. There's something . . . I've got a queer feeling about it.'

'Would you like me to read it for you?'

She gave it back and watched him slitting it open with his paper-knife. He read the single sheet first, without saying a word, then held out a second envelope which had been enclosed inside it. 'It's from Sandy,' he said gently, then jumped up in alarm as his wife swayed and sank to the floor.

Chapter Twenty-nine

'Are you quite sure you don't want me to stay at home today?' His wife's wan face and dark-circled eyes had made Gregor have second thoughts about leaving her alone.

Mysie shook her head. 'I told you – I'll be all right.'

'But you didn't sleep a wink last night.'

'And I didn't let you sleep, either. You must be tired, but don't stay off work just for me.'

'I'm not tired, but I haven't many appointments today, and I could quite easily cancel them.'

'Off you go. I'm over the worst.'

When her husband went out, Mysie cleared the table and ran hot water into the washing-up bowl. She had to keep busy. If she didn't, she would give way altogether. But, as she plunged her hands into the suds, she couldn't help thinking about the letter. Before Sandy had written to her, he must have had a premonition of what was going to happen to him – the next day, as far as she could make out. He had addressed the envelope to her, but had marked it 'To be posted only in the event of my death,' and someone must have gone through his belongings afterwards and found it. According to the pilot who sent the little note along with it, he had been coming back to Britain and the commanding officer of Sandy's squadron had given him the letter and told him to post it when he landed.

Lifting her arm to wipe a tear away with her sleeve, Mysie wished that the pilot had given her his address, so that she could have written to thank him. She had told Gregor that she was over the worst, but she still felt empty, as if the bottom had dropped out of her world. She was thankful that Sandy had written, but why, oh why, hadn't he come to see her before he went away? And Gina's refusal to see her made it even worse. Her daughter must have known how his death would affect her.

When the doorbell rang, Mysie considered not answering it – she couldn't face anyone today – but it rang again, and again before she dried her hands. She had believed that her heart was so numb it would never feel anything again, but it jolted and sank when she saw who the caller was.

296

'I had to come to tell you how sorry I am,' Amy murmured, 'but if you'd rather not talk about it . . .'

'It's all right.' Mysie opened the door wider, praying that the woman wouldn't stay long.

As she sat down, Amy said, 'Ben phoned me as soon as Gregor told him your son had been killed. I did see the announcement in the newspaper, but I didn't connect it with you. I hadn't realised you had any family. Have you more than one child?'

Mysie had to force herself to answer. 'I had two sons and a daughter, but Jamie . . . died when he was just a boy.'

'Oh, God,' Amy exclaimed, compassionately. 'How awful to lose both of them. Does your daughter live anywhere near?'

'No.' It wasn't strictly true, but Mysie couldn't say any more, and she was sure that Amy Parker was too well-bred to ask any questions although she was obviously longing to find out why Gina wasn't there at this time.

There was a short silence, then Amy stood up. 'I shouldn't have come, I'm sorry. You must be heartbroken.'

'Yes, I am, but it was very kind of you to . . .'

'I'll let the girls know that you won't be expecting us this Wednesday, but is it all right for next week?'

A voice was screaming inside Mysie's head – not next week or any other week – and it was a moment before she could answer. 'I don't think I . . . I can't carry on with my afternoons. I wouldn't feel . . . I . . . I , . .' She was unable to continue.

'I quite understand, my dear. It will probably take you a long time to get over this. Don't bother to get up, I'll see myself out.'

As the outside door closed quietly, Mysie covered her eyes with her hands, but she wasn't weeping. She had wept enough tears the last two nights to have launched a battleship, and she was beyond that now. She was imprisoned in a vacuum, with nothing but grief and pain to keep her company.

Gregor found her like that half an hour later, Amy Parker having telephoned him to tell him that Maisie was on the verge of a breakdown and that he should go to her at once. He said nothing as he knelt beside his wife and put his arms around her, but was shocked when she lowered her hands and turned her head towards him. Her eyes – her lovely, lively, blue eyes – were absolutely vacant.

He kept holding her, getting no response, until one of his legs got cramp and he had to stand up to flex it. Mysie gave a little mew that tore at his heart, and he took her hands to pull her to her feet. 'You should be in bed, let me take you upstairs.' He was afraid that her legs wouldn't carry her, but she plodded beside him like a robot as he guided her to their bedroom, and stood still until he undressed her and put on her nightdress. Then he helped her into bed, and she lay down on her back, staring at the ceiling.

Sitting down on the edge of the bed, he stroked her forehead over and over again, not stopping until long after her eyelids drooped and closed. Once he was certain that she was asleep, he kicked off his shoes and lay beside her. However long it was before she awoke, he would be there for her to turn to.

Exhausted himself, Gregor, too, soon fell into a deep sleep, but was instantly alert when he felt a movement at his side. His wife, however, had not wakened, so he twisted his head to look at the clock, and was surprised to see that it was past nine – ten hours since he'd put her to bed.

Mysie slept for almost twenty-three hours, and her husband, still in his office suit, was lying with his arm over her when she opened her eyes.

'How do you feel, my dearest?' he asked, thanking God that she was looking lovingly at him, not staring through him as she had done the day before.

'I feel as if I'd been pulled through a hedge backwards,' she tried to joke, then noticed that he was fully clothed.

'Did you put me to bed? Why aren't you in your pyjamas? How long have I been sleeping? What time is it?'

'That's my Maisie come back to me,' he smiled. 'To answer your questions – yes, I put you to bed and I didn't want to leave you even to put on my pyjamas, though I did have to go to the bathroom a few times. You have been sleeping since just after eleven yesterday forenoon, and it is now five to ten. Another hour and you'd have had a complete round of the clock.'

'And you've been lying beside me all that time? You haven't had anything to eat since – since yesterday morning?' She sat up and swung her feet to the floor. 'I'll go down and make a late breakfast, and we can have a late lunch, and . . .'

'I'll make something. Get back to bed, my dear. You're not fit to be doing anything.'

'I'm all right, Gregor, honestly. When I woke up at first, I didn't remember anything for a minute, but when I did, I didn't feel as bad as I did when Amy was here.'

'I shouldn't have left you alone, but you were so determined.'

'I was stupid.' She smiled sadly. 'I thought I could cope with it, and I might have, if Amy Parker hadn't come round, not that she said anything out of place. It hit me after she went out. Now, you go and take a bath to freshen yourself, and I'll have breakfast ready by the time you come down. I'll leave my bath until after we've eaten, that'll give the water time to heat again, so I'll put on my dressing-gown just now.'

On her way out, she turned her head to him. 'Oh, Gregor, I love you more than any other woman ever loved before.'

He didn't move for a moment, storing her words deep inside his heart, to treasure for as long as he lived.

Mysie did not resume her social afternoons, and when Gregor asked her, about six months later, why she was still keeping herself apart from her old 'pupils', she said,

'I'm ashamed to face them again, for I'm sure none of them would have given way to their feelings like I did in front of Amy. If the same thing had happened to them, they would have carried on with a stiff upper lip, and nobody would ever have known the agony they were feeling inside.'

'But your case was different,' Gregor reminded her. 'You have had so much sorrow in your life, and you have never recovered from Sandy and Gina leaving home, then getting his letter the day after you learned of his death – it's no wonder you were affected like that. It was all too much for you.'

Mysie sucked in her lips for a moment. 'Yes, I suppose my case was different . . .'

'It's all over now, my dearest. Try to forget about it. Now, will we divide the newspaper between us, or . . . ?'

'You read it, Gregor, and you can tell me if there's anything important in it. I want to bake a few scones and oatcakes to fill my tins again. We seem to go through an awful lot.'

Grinning, he corrected her. 'You mean I go through an awful lot. What do you expect when they're so delicious?'

'I'm not complaining. I'm glad you enjoy them.'

Gina Bisset dressed carefully. She wasn't doing it to please Campbell, but there could well be an attractive, available man at this party tonight, and if she played her cards right . . . Hannah and Harry usually had quite a few guests, sometimes new people Harry had come in contact with, and that was the only reason she had agreed to go with her husband. They had been living like strangers for quite a while – even his parents had eventually noticed and been distant towards her – but they had their barneys, too. It was like being on a seesaw, the ups of her little flings with the various men she went out with far outweighing her downs with Campbell.

He had made lots of money through the black market, and she often wished that the war would go on for ever, though it made her feel guilty. Anyway, she thought, as she made up her face, their bank balance should be quite healthy and the house in Bieldside was modern and labour-saving. A woman came twice a week to do the heavy cleaning, and a daily did the cooking as well as keeping the place tidy, and it was marvellous to have such a beautiful home to show off when anyone visited.

When Campbell came home, she was ready waiting, but his face lengthened when he saw her in her new cocktail gown. 'You'd better take your glad rags off, Gina, we won't be going to the party tonight.'

'If you think it's funny to say things like that . . .'

'I'm not joking. I'd a phone call today asking me to go to see my accountant, and he's just told me I'm on the verge of bankruptcy.'

'You can't be. You're still busy, aren't you?'

'We're still working hard, but there's no money coming in.'

'What do you mean?'

'I mean our customers haven't been paying.'

'Can't you force them to pay?'

'He says they're in the same boat. There's nothing I can do . . . unless I can borrow a few grand from somewhere. Once you give me something to eat, I'm going over to ask my father, that's why the party is out.'

'But what will you tell Hannah and Harry?'

'Bugger Hannah and Harry!'

It was the first time Gina had ever heard him speaking like that, and she knew then, with a sinking heart, that things were very serious indeed. 'Do you think your father will . . . ?'

'If he doesn't, I'm sunk.'

Without warning, Gina felt a slight tug at her heartstrings. Poor Campbell, she had treated him very badly, and any other husband would have thrown her out for the way she had carried on. 'I hadn't prepared anything, seeing we were supposed to be going out, but I can give you beans on toast, if that's okay?'

'I'm not really hungry, but I thought I should eat something to buck me up a bit.'

'I'd better change, I don't want to dirty this dress.' She ran upstairs to put on a skirt and blouse, then went down to open a tin of beans in the kitchen.

Campbell came in behind her. 'I'm really sorry, Gina.'

Her normal reaction would have been to laugh in his face, but she didn't feel normal any more. 'It can't be helped. Maybe your father *will* stump up.'

'I don't set much store on it.'

When he left, Gina washed up thoughtfully. If old man Bisset refused to help, what would happen to Campbell? If she hadn't been so stupid, their marriage might have succeeded, but she had wanted excitement. They had both been too young to settle down, of course, and hadn't considered each other's feelings, though she had probably been more selfish than he was.

When she heard the car drawing up outside, she ran to the door. 'Well?'

His shook his head dejectedly as he came in. 'No go, he's having difficulties too.'

'Oh, God, Campbell, what'll you do?'

'Go through the bankruptcy court, I suppose.' His shoulders slumped. 'I never thought it would come to this, and I suppose you want to leave the sinking ship?'

Something snapped inside Gina then, and she threw her arms round him. 'I don't want to leave you. I've been a stupid bitch, for I know I love you. If you'd been more masterful, I wouldn't have done what I did.'

He looked at her in amazement. 'Did I hear you right? Did you actually say you loved me?'

'Yes, yes, yes, and I only hope there's a little love left somewhere in your heart for me.'

His mouth came down softly on hers. 'I never stopped loving you, my darling. I always hoped that you would come to your senses and be a proper wife to me again. If you do, I don't care about being bankrupt. We'll start again from the bottom.'

After a few moments, she drew away from him. 'We might not have to. How much money do you actually need?'

'Five thousand would see me through until I get back on my feet. Why? Do you know where you could get it?'

'I might,' she said, cautiously. 'If you just give me time to think properly.'

'Time's something else I don't have much of, my creditors are snapping at my heels.'

'I'll let you know tomorrow night. Will that do?'

'I suppose I could fob them off with promises for a day or so, but who are you going to tap?'

'Don't ask.'

Much later, Gina lay wide awake beside her husband, who was deep in the sleep of the sexually replete, but her brain was too active to allow her to drift off. Would Gregor Wallace lend her the money after what she had said to him only a year ago, after Sandy was killed? He had never given any sign of being a vindictive man, but it was difficult to tell how any person would react in such a situation. She couldn't ask any of her friends – she doubted if they would have enough money anyway – and Gregor was the only one she could turn to. She would have to make him promise not to let her mother know, for she didn't want *her* gloating over Campbell's misfortune – but she could surely turn on enough charm to win Gregor round?

At nine o'clock the following morning, Gina telephoned to make an appointment with her mother's husband. 'Mr Wallace only comes in for an hour or so every afternoon now,' the girl on the switchboard told her. 'I can put you through to Mr Martin or Mr Parker, if you like. They deal with mostly everything since Mr Wallace retired.'

'No, thank you. It's Mr Wallace I have to talk to.' Gina was dismayed by the information. She hadn't realised that Gregor was old enough to retire, but he must be about seventy now.

'I could give you his home address,' the girl offered.

'No, it's personal and I don't want to bother him at

home – but I must see him. Look, if I come in this afternoon about three, is there any chance that he'd be there?'

'He usually comes in about two, so I'll tell him you wish to see him, but I can't promise anything.'

'I understand, and thank you very much.' Laying down the receiver, Gina wished that she didn't have to wait. She might lose her courage by afternoon.

After lunch, she dressed in her grey wool costume with black accessories – they had cost a small fortune and she wanted to impress Gregor – then went out to catch a bus into town. If she could have used some of Campbell's petrol ration in her small car it would have been quicker, but the garage would not give her commercial fuel, which was coloured pink to prevent such private use.

It was only ten to three when she arrived, and she walked round Bon Accord Square twice so that she wouldn't be early, but at last she went up the steps. She was shown immediately into Gregor's office, and was surprised at how much older he looked, his hair almost white, his face gaunt and grey.

He smiled warmly and stood up, holding out his hand. 'Gina! I wondered who this lady was who was so desperate to see me. This is an unexpected pleasure.'

She ignored his hand. 'It's not pleasure at all, Gregor. It's purely business.'

'I'm afraid I don't attend to much business these days, but how can I help you?'

After hearing her request, he sat twiddling his thumbs for a moment or two, then said, 'What collateral are you offering? It's rather a large sum of money, and I must protect myself.'

Gina hadn't foreseen this, but recognised the necessity for it. 'We have a large house in Bieldside, a Rover car and a small Austin. And your money will be safe enough. Campbell is a good businessman.'

His smile held no humour. 'Not good enough to keep him from bankruptcy, apparently. However, I will trust you, Gina. Shall I make the cheque out to you or to your husband?'

'You'd better make it out to Campbell, it's for his company.' As she watched him take his cheque book out, she remembered the other part of her errand. 'By the way, I want your promise that you will never tell my mother anything about this.'

He screwed the cap back on his fountain pen. 'Ah, that's a different matter.'

Feeling alarmed, she said, 'Why? I don't want her to know.'

'Your mother and I have no secrets from each other, and it so happens that I intended making *you* promise something before I handed over the cheque.'

'What was that?'

'Your solemn oath that you will go to see her and apologise for all the heartache you have caused her.'

'Oh, Gregor, you can't seriously expect me to do that? You know how I feel about her.'

'No apology, no cheque.'

He made to place his pen in the tray, but Gina said, 'Wait. Give me time to think about it.'

'Take all the time you need.' With a slight smile, Gregor leaned back in his chair.

Desperate for Campbell's sake, Gina let her mind tick over. Would it be so terrible to do as Gregor asked? It shouldn't be too difficult to keep up a pretence in front of her mother for an hour, as long as Gregor kept silent about Campbell's failure. It was worth a try. 'Could we make a bargain?'

'It depends, Gina.'

'I promise to apologise to my mother if you promise never to tell her you've had to help me out of a hole.'

He frowned. 'You're asking rather a lot of me, but . . .' He tapped his pen a few times on his desk. 'I know that it would make my wife very happy to see you, and her happiness means more to me than anything else. All right, Gina.' He opened the chequebook. 'I promise to keep quiet about your husband's financial problems, if you promise to go to see her tomorrow afternoon.' Bending his head to write, Gregor said, 'If you don't, I can quite easily stop this cheque.'

Her eyes blazing, Gina burst out, 'I bet you would, too, but let me tell you, if you ever mention one word of this to her, I'll create such a row that she'll never forgive you.'

Lifting his eyes for a second, he said, 'So now we understand each other.' After blotting the cheque, he tore it out and handed it to her. 'I trust that this will allow your husband to continue in business. If not, you need not bother coming to me again. I will have a contract drawn up, in which he will agree to pay me back this amount within . . . five years, and you will ensure that he signs it as soon as he receives it and returns it to me here.'

'He will.' Gina placed the cheque inside her handbag and stood up. 'I promise to go tomorrow, and thank you, Gregor.'

His eyes were cold. 'I did it for your mother's sake, not yours. She is a far better woman than you will ever be.'

Stung, Gina retorted, 'She wasn't always a good woman.'

'I know exactly what she did when she was younger, more than you do, probably, but it was done out of love, not spite nor hate. She has never hurt anyone intentionally in her life.'

Gregor remained sitting after Gina left. If he had known who had made the appointment, he would not have kept it. He certainly should have refused to give her what she asked – a spell on the bread line was what that young lady needed to make a better person of her. But it was Maisie he had thought of, Maisie he had done it for, and if Gina kept her promise it would even be worth losing the five thousand pounds . . . *if* Gina kept her promise, which was extremely doubtful. But then he could always stop that cheque.

It was a miserable, blustery day, and Mysie was feeling

quite miserable herself. She wished that Gregor would stop going to the office, even if it was only for an hour or two every day. He'd looked so peculiar when he came home yesterday that she'd asked him what was wrong, but he had said there was nothing. Knowing him as she did, however, she could tell that something was bothering him, and had been hurt that he hadn't confided in her. It wasn't like him to be so secretive.

When the doorbell rang, she took her time about answering it. It was probably a door-to-door salesman of some kind and she couldn't be bothered with that this afternoon. But it wasn't a man at all – it was a well-dressed young woman with a beautifully made-up face that reminded her of . . . 'Gina?' she asked, scarcely able to believe it.

'May I come in?' There was no warmth in the words.

Taking her hand off the doorpost, Mysie was astonished that she could stand without support. 'Yes, of course.'

In the sitting room, they stood looking at each other warily for a moment, then Mysie said, 'Sit down, Gina.'

'I won't sit down, thank you. I only came to see how you were and to tell you that . . . I'm sorry for . . . I'm . . .'

She got no further. Her mother's arms were held out towards her, and she went into them in the same way she had done when she was a small girl. Recalling the comfort she'd been given then, in spite of her tantrums and misbehaviour, she was overwhelmed by a rush of love, of regret, of guilt for having stayed away. 'Oh, Mother,' she sobbed, 'it's been such a long time, and I'm truly, truly sorry.'

'Gina, don't apologise. I've prayed and prayed for you to come back to me, and nothing else matters now that you have.' Mysie led her daughter over to the settee and sat down beside her. 'That's both my prayers answered now,' she said, softly. 'Before he was killed, Sandy wrote and apologised, too.'

Gina gulped. 'I *was* sorry about Sandy, even though I told Gregor I wasn't. I realise now that he didn't mean to hurt me when he said I was . . .'

'It was all my fault that night,' Mysie said, tearfully.

'No, it wasn't. It was nobody's fault, really, but I was too young to understand.'

They sat silently then, Gina gripping Mysie's hand. Before she came, she had thought of this visit as being a price she had to pay to ensure Campbell's solvency, but it had turned out differently. She wanted her mother's love now, needed it, and she couldn't keep up a pretence any longer.

When Gregor came home, he was amazed to find his wife with her arm round her daughter's shoulders, both weeping softly. He hadn't been prepared to find Gina still there – he hadn't really believed that she would come at all – and was at a loss as to how to deal with the situation. 'Gina. What a surprise,' he said, lamely.

'She's told me everything, Gregor,' Mysie murmured, drying her eyes. 'How you trapped her into coming to see me, so don't pretend you didn't know she'd be here.'

'I thought she'd be gone by this time.'

Gina looked round at him. 'It's you we've to thank for us making things up, Gregor. Your trap was loaded, wasn't it? You must have guessed what would happen.' Turning to Mysie, she said earnestly, 'I'd been so busy grabbing what I could out of life, that I never gave a thought to what you were going through, Mother.'

Mysie stood up. 'Well, it's all over. Everything's all right now, so just sit there and talk to Gregor while I make a pot of tea.'

When she went out, Gregor said, gently, 'You have my heartfelt thanks, Gina. You've done much more than I asked.'

She smiled wryly. 'I didn't plan to let it go as far as this. It just . . . sort of happened.'

'Well, I'm so grateful that we'll forget about that contract. Your husband can take his own time to . . . no! I don't want to be paid back at all.'

'He'll pay you back,' Gina declared, looking slightly offended. 'I don't want to be accused of being a beggar on top of all the other bad things I've been.' Her mouth relaxed abruptly. 'I know I've been a poor specimen for years, thinking of nobody but myself, but I swear I'll turn over a new leaf now.'

'Good for you. I see you do have something of your mother in you, after all, and that's the highest compliment anyone could ever pay you, believe me.' Gregor sat back, beaming.

When Mysie carried in the teatray, she could see that both Gina and Gregor looked very smug, as if they had come to some big decision together. She did not know what they had been talking about, and she didn't care.

After filling the three cups, she lifted hers high up in the air. 'It's maybe not the done thing to drink a toast in tea, but who cares? Here's to us – to you, my darling Gregor, for loving me so much over all the years; to you, dear Gina, for coming home again and healing the rift in my family; to me, because I feel that my life has come full circle and I am truly happy at last.'

She sipped daintily for a moment, then ordered, 'Go on, drink the toast, just to please a sentimenal old woman.'

The other two cups were raised and two voices, one holding the suggestion of a sob and the other deep and resonant, said, 'To us.'

PART FOUR

Chapter Thirty

1982

'I wish you'd go and sit down, Mrs Wallace.' Gina's current housekeeper was mildly irritated with the old woman. 'You're not fit to be standing so long.'

Her faded eyes flashing, Mysie snapped, 'I'd pared tons of potatoes long before you were even born, Marion, likely before your mother was born, and I'm not stopping now.'

'But Mrs Bisset said I shouldn't let you do anything.'

'My daughter's a fusspot. I'm as strong as a horse. Get on with your own work and let me get on with this.'

Marion Miller shrugged and took the canister of flour out of the cupboard. She'd be glad to sit down if she was given the chance, and she was only forty-one. God knows what she'd be like when she was ninety-three, like her employer's mother.

She had weighed out all the ingredients for the pastry she was making for the apple pie, and had just started to rub the butter into the flour when the shrill voice spoke again. 'Hold your hands well above the bowl when you're doing that. It lets the air in, and that's what makes pastry lighter – that, and not using too much water.' Mysie tutted disapprovingly. 'Girls nowadays have no idea how to do things properly.'

Saying nothing, Marion did as she was told. Mr Bisset had told her, not long after she started working for them, that his mother-in-law had once been a cook, and that she'd run a cook-shop at one time, too, but that must have

311

been in the year dot and her ideas were old-fashioned. Just the same, it was wiser not to get on her wrong side.

'That's more like it,' Mysie said, as she passed on her way out, 'and don't handle it too much when you're rolling it out. I'm going to tidy the lounge now.'

Some of these girls would never learn, she thought. What did she need with a housekeeper, anyway? She'd managed perfectly well, ever since she came to Bieldside, with just the charwoman coming in twice a week to do the heavy cleaning. Of course, it was that little dizzy spell she'd had a few years ago that had frightened her daughter. It hadn't really been anything at all – she'd just turned too quickly – but that Mrs Dickie had made a meal of it, phoning Gina and fussing around until she came home from work, worried out of her mind.

'It's a blessing I was here,' the cleaner had told Gina as soon as she set her foot inside, 'or she'd have been a goner.'

Gina had scolded her gently. 'Mother, I've told you hundreds of times to take it easy, and I don't care what you say now, I'm employing a housekeeper.'

Mysie, feeling better by that time, had been sarcastic. 'Am I supposed to sit and twiddle my thumbs all day?'

'It's what you should be doing anyway, at your age.'

'My age has nothing to do with it. I don't feel old, and that's because I've kept going all my life. If I'd let you take in a housekeeper when you first suggested it, I'd have died of boredom by this time.' Mysie had changed her tone. 'I'll just fade away slowly if you stop me doing things.'

'No, Mother, you won't get round me this time.' Gina had been angry. 'I'm employing a housekeeper, and that's final.'

So a woman had started the following week – Mrs . . . ? Mysie couldn't remember her name, but she hadn't lasted long. None of them had lasted long, for they didn't like to be told the right way to do things. This Marion, though, wasn't as bad as the rest. At least she did what she was told without arguing.

Mysie's thoughts stopped abruptly. Why had she come into the dining room? It was the lounge that needed tidying. She'd better not tell anyone about this – they'd think she was going off her head. She turned slowly, not wanting a repeat of the giddiness, and suddenly felt very tired. She'd better take a seat for a while. Maybe she *was* too old to be doing so much.

Lying back in the settee, she let her mind go back over the years to her reconciliation with her daughter. It was only a couple of months later that she was told she was going to be a grandmother. She had been a grandmother long before that, of course, and she would regret to her dying day never having seen Sandy's child. But she'd been so pleased about Gina that she had gone to Wellbrae to tell Jess Findlater. She was very glad that she had, for Jess had died not long after. She had thought her old friend was much thinner, especially about the face, but she had never dreamt that it was cancer. She had been very upset at the funeral, but Gregor had helped her to get over it, though it had taken a long time. It was really Alexander's birth that brought her out of her depression.

Poor wee Alexander. Gina had called him after Sandy, and he had been the light of Gregor's life, and hers, from the day he was born. They had worshipped him, and they'd come to Gina's house every day to take him out, in the pram until he was old enough to walk himself. He'd been such a bright boy, drinking in everything she told him about the different trees, and the wild flowers, and the birds. He could name them all without any help in no time at all, and he'd been so pleased when they told him he was very clever. He had only been four and a half when the tragedy struck. Meningitis. Gina had not been able to have any more children.

She was still almost certain that it was Alexander's death that had started Gregor's health deteriorating so quickly. It had affected him as badly as it had affected her, but he had been a great comfort to her. She would never have got over it if he hadn't been there, but only a couple of months later, he'd begun to forget things, to be bad-tempered, and he had never been like that before. It was a year or so after that before he grew senile altogether, not able to do a single thing for himself, and she had nursed him day and night for seven long years. Not that she minded, for he would have done the same for her if their positions had been reversed. Gina, of course, had wanted her to get a proper nurse in, but she had stuck to her guns. It was her place to look after her husband.

By the time Gregor died she was so worn out that she didn't even feel like arguing when Gina told her to sell the house and come to live at Bieldside, and it had taken her a month or two to get her strength back. She might have known that they wouldn't get on, together all day like that, and it was probably because she had interfered too much that Gina had taken a job. Her daughter had done very well, and was now an active partner in a pair of boutiques, as they called dress shops now – out all day, though she came back at dinnertime.

When Gina came home for lunch, she was alarmed at being told that her mother had been asleep in the lounge for an hour and three-quarters. Hurrying through, she made up her mind to be firmer. This couldn't go on. 'Mother,' she said gently, 'it's time for lunch.'

'Already? I just shut my eyes for a minute.'

'Marion said you'd been sleeping for nearly two hours.'

'Oh no, I couldn't have been.'

'Oh yes, you were. I've let you have your own way ever since you came here, but I'm putting my foot down now. You are not to do any housework in future. I'd have thought you would have had enough of it, anyway. You've been here for over twenty-two years, and you kept house for seventeen of them, so . . .'

'I didn't do the heavy work, there was always a cleaner.'

Gina felt her anger rising. 'Don't quibble. You didn't

314

even stop working when I did get a housekeeper in. Goodness knows what they must have thought of me for letting you go on the way you've been doing, and it's got to stop. I mean it.'

Mysie frowned and made to stand up, but her legs wouldn't take her weight and she sat back heavily. 'Oh, Mother.' Gina was concerned now. 'You're not fit, and I'm only doing it for your own good.'

'You can't expect me to sit about all day doing nothing,' Mysie muttered, but she knew in her own heart that what her daughter said was true. She wasn't fit any longer.

'You could knit, or take up embroidery, or read books. Oh, there's plenty of things you could do to pass the time.'

'Pass the time? Aye,' Mysie observed, mournfully, 'that's all I'll be doing from now on, I suppose – passing time. Well, maybe it'll not be for much longer.' Letting her daughter help her to her feet, she went through to the dining room.

Mysie took to lying in bed later in the morning, watching television in the lounge all forenoon and having a nap in the afternoon. In spite of this, she often felt ready for bed in the early evening and went upstairs at eight. 'I'm stiffening up,' she informed Gina one day. 'All this sitting about's not good for me.'

Her daughter had noticed that she was very unsteady on her feet, but had assumed that it was just the ageing process. 'It would be a lot worse for you if you were on your legs all day. Do you want me to get the doctor in to have a look at you?'

'He'd laugh at me.' Mysie hadn't much faith in doctors.

Gina talked things over with her husband that night. 'Do you think I should stop going to the shop and stay at home to look after her?'

After considering briefly, Campbell said, 'I don't think she'd be happy about that, and she would still be sitting all day. Her arthritis is getting worse, and she'll soon be off her feet altogether. Anyway, you would just get on

315

each other's nerves again, and that's why you went out to work in the first place.'

'I would never forgive myself if anything happened to her and I wasn't here.'

'Forget it, Gina,' he advised. 'Nothing's going to happen to her for a long time yet. I know she's old, and her legs are a bit dodgy, but her heart is as sound as a bell. You should be retiring next year, in any case, shouldn't you.'

'Don't remind me that I'll be sixty-five on my birthday,' she pouted. 'Anna and I are the same age – we were in the same class at school – and we're going to have to discuss what to do with the shops soon, but we haven't mentioned it yet.'

'You should have packed it in when you were sixty.'

'Anna didn't, but I suppose we will have to sell them.'

Although the subject wasn't mentioned again, Mysie knew that it had only been shelved. Within herself, she knew that her legs were . . . on their last legs – she chuckled at the thought – and that it was just a matter of time before she would be as dependent on someone else as Gregor had been on her during the last few years of his life. It was inevitable. Her body would give up gradually, bit by bit, and she'd be very fortunate if her brain lasted as long as her heart. Gregor's hadn't.

She would hate for Gina and Campbell to have to put up with a senile old woman, dribbling at both ends . . . it was quite unthinkable. But it had to be thought about, planned for.

Two days later, she voiced her idea after they had finished their evening meal. 'I want to go into a home.' Their wary, shocked expressions told her that they thought she had gone over the edge. 'I'm not mad, I know what I'm saying. I want to go into a home. I've given it a lot of thought, Gina, and I don't want you to be tied to the house looking after me.'

Gina found her voice at last. 'But I wouldn't mind . . .'

'I know what it's like, remember, and it wasn't so bad for me, because I loved Gregor with all my heart.'

'But I love you, Mother, and I'm quite prepared to stop work to be here with you . . . I should have stopped long ago.'

'My mind's made up. The places they have nowadays, private nursing homes they're called, they're not like the places the old folk were put into long ago. They were more like lunatic asylums, but the new ones are like . . . hotels, and there's people to look after you, day and night, if you need it. And because they're run privately, you can move if you don't like the first one you go to. I've read all about them.'

Campbell spoke now. He hadn't wanted to interfere before, but he could see that Gina was on the verge of tears. 'Look, Mother, if you've made up your mind, I wouldn't think of trying to make you change it, but you've lived here for so long that I'd have thought you would consider it your home.'

Mysie held up her hand. 'I've outlived my usefulness, and it's time I was moving on.'

'Oh, Mother,' Gina burst out, 'you don't have to move on. I'll stop working right now and I'll be here every day with you.'

'And that's just what I don't want,' Mysie said, firmly, and turned to her son-in-law. 'Campbell, if you understand what I'm getting at, will you please explain to Gina?' She rose unsteadily and picked up the walking stick she had lately been forced to use. 'I want no more arguments, and I'll be in the lounge if you want me.'

Making her laborious way through, she smiled to herself as she heard Campbell quietly calming the now hysterical Gina. He would likely be reminding her about the terrible life his own mother had given his unmarried sister until old Mrs Bisset died. The old lady had been inclined to be violent, so that might help Gina to see what her mother was afraid could happen.

Resigned to following Mysie's wishes, Gina drove her to inspect several private nursing homes over the next few weeks. Most of them seemed quite pleasant, but the younger woman always had faults to pick, and it wasn't until they found Sunnyfields that Mysie put her foot down. 'I like this place,' she told her daughter. 'But you'd better find out what they charge.'

Back in the car, she said, 'It's too much. I'd never dream of paying that every week.'

Gina turned to her seriously. 'You don't need to worry about the financial side of it, Mother. You've never touched Gregor's money, nor what you made off the house in Ashley Road, and it's been gathering interest all this time.'

'I wanted to have something to leave you when I die,' Mysie protested, rather plaintively.

'I don't need anything, Mother. Campbell and I are quite comfortably off, as you should know. I can't understand why you're so set on going into a home, but if Sunnyfields is where you want to go, I'll arrange it for you.'

'I'd like to think it over a bit longer.'

Mysie thought it over that night. She had liked the place, recently built on the outskirts of the city, and all on one level. It was set in its own grounds, and it would be like living in the countryside again. The single rooms were light and airy, but you didn't have to be cooped up there all the time. There was a common room where the residents could sit and talk to each other, a TV room if you felt so inclined, a dining room for those fit enough to get to it, and those who weren't had their meals served in their rooms. Best of all, there was a welcoming feeling as soon as you went through the door, and Mrs Warrender, the woman who ran it, was very pleasant. She was a woman of between forty and fifty, stout and motherly with a gentle manner. Yes, Mysie decided, she would like to live there, even if the fees were exorbitant. If Gina didn't need her money, what else was there to do with it?

The arrangements were made very quickly, and within

three weeks, Mysie was installed in Sunnyfields Private Nursing Home, with Gina's solemn promise that she and Campbell would visit her every Sunday.

Chapter Thirty-one

1984

There was something vaguely familiar about the young man who had rung her doorbell, Gina thought, although she was almost certain that she had never seen him before. 'Yes?'

'Mrs Bisset? You won't know me, but I'd like to talk to you for a few minutes, if you don't mind. I'd better explain that my name is Ewan Duncan and I'm . . .'

'Ewan *Duncan*?' Now she knew why he'd looked familiar. 'You must be Sandy's son? No, you can't be – you're too young.'

'I'm your brother's grandson,' Ewan said, quietly. 'May I come in?'

'Of course.' Smiling, Gina showed him into the lounge. 'How did you find me? How did you even know about me?'

'My grandmother remembered that she had cut the announcement of your wedding out of the newspaper. Don't ask me why.'

'Sandy's wife kept that all this time? That's fifty years ago. But it still doesn't explain how you found me.'

'I went to your in-laws' house to ask where you lived now, but, as you'll know, they died some time ago and it was your husband's brother who inherited the house. He gave me your address, so here I am.'

'Yes, so here you are.' Gina was still perplexed as to the purpose of his visit. 'Why were you so keen to find me?'

His manner became guarded. 'I wanted to know more

about my family history, that's why I asked my grand-mother, and . . .'

'She told you I was the skeleton in the cupboard?' Gina gave a rippling laugh. 'What do you want to know about me? There's nothing interesting, apart from the fact that I was born on the wrong side of the blankets.' She could joke about it now.

'It's not really you I wanted to find out about. You see, I've bought a house in Burnlea, and I discovered that it had been built on the site of an old croft. When I mentioned to my grandmother that it was called Rowanbrae, she said she was sure that was where my grandfather had been born. This made me a bit curious, and when I looked up the Evaluation Rolls I learned that several James Duncans had leased it. Going by dates, the last of them must have been my great-grandfather, but apparently my grandfather had never told Grandma anything about his early life. I was a bit disappointed when I heard that, but when she told me that he'd had a sister, and gave me the clipping, I decided to come and ask if you knew anything about the croft, or about a possible fire?'

'A fire?'

'It seems the crofthouse was unoccupied for some time, and I presume it had either been abandoned as unprofit-able, or left derelict, perhaps burned down, accidentally or intentionally.'

Gina's eyebrows lifted. 'You've really been digging things up, haven't you?'

Unwilling to reveal what he *had* dug up, Ewan grinned self-consciously. 'I was fascinated by it, but I haven't found out very much yet. As far as I can make out, no one lived there from some time after 1910, until the bungalow was built early in the thirties, the feu having been sold by the Phillips, who owned all Burnlea at that time. The rest of their estate was sold in 1962, but I don't know if they had both died and one of their family disposed of it, or if they had family at all.'

'I know they had a son,' Gina butted in. 'Sandy used to

be quite friendly with Bobby Phillip at one time, but I was too young to pay any attention to what was said about him.'

'It doesn't matter – I don't suppose he could tell me what I want to know, anyway. Burnlea is quite a township now, but I'm just trying to find out about the original Rowanbrae croft – as a matter of interest. Can you help?'

Gina sighed. 'I'm sorry, I don't know anything about it. I was born in Aberdeen, you see, and my mother never spoke about the croft.' She sat up eagerly. 'But you could go and ask her. I'm sure she would tell you everything you want to know.'

Ewan felt his pulse quickening. 'Your mother's still alive?' It was a stupid question, he realised, as soon as he asked it, but Mrs Bisset looked to be over sixty although she was made up to the teeth, and he hadn't thought of asking before.

'Mother's still going strong. It was her own decision to move into the home two years ago. She's ninety-five now.'

'Is she still quite . . . ?'

'She's perfectly compos mentis, if that's what you mean. Her legs are crippled with arthritis, but her brain's still as clear as ever. I'm sure she'd be pleased to answer your questions.'

'Which home is she in?'

'Sunnyfields. Do you know it?'

'Yes, I do. Would it be all right if I went this afternoon?'

'You can't wait to get going, can you?' Gina chuckled. 'Well, my husband and I visit her every Sunday, so I expect she'll be pleased to have someone on a Saturday for a change.'

'Great!' Ewan made to rise, but Gina motioned to him to keep sitting. 'I never knew if Sandy's child was a girl or a boy, but he must have had a son, if your name's Duncan, too?'

'Yes, my father's name's Sam.' Impatient to carry on with his quest, he stood up abruptly. 'You've been a great help, Mrs Bisset, thank you very much for listening to me.'

321

'I'm your Aunt Gina . . . well, I would really be your father's aunt, of course, so you'd better just call me Gina.'

'Dad'll be surprised when I tell him. I'm sure he doesn't know anything about you.'

Gina smiled as she got to her feet. 'It's quite exciting to learn I've got relatives I didn't know existed, we must have a meeting some time to get to know each other. Oh, it's a good thing I remembered. My mother married again, and her surname is Wallace now. Did your grandmother ever remarry?'

'No, she didn't.' Too keyed up to discuss anything else, Ewan stood up and took his leave quickly. He started his car and drove off in the direction of the city, but when he found a suitable spot he drew in to the side to think. It had never occurred to him that his great-grandmother might still be alive! Gina had said that her brain was still quite clear, but what about her memory? Hopefully, she would be like most old people and remember the distant past more clearly than the recent past.

Glancing at the clock on the dashboard, he saw that it was only ten to twelve – too near lunchtime to go to Sunnyfields – and he didn't fancy going home to Angie to make small talk with her and her parents, he was far too excited. The sensible thing would be to go in somewhere for a meal, but he wanted to be alone. Remembering having seen a Chinese carry-out in Holburn Street, he drove off again, and within fifteen minutes, he was sitting on a bench in the Johnstone Gardens – a small haven of peace off Queen's Road which was not so crowded as the other public parks – eating sweet-and-sour pork from one foil dish, and special fried rice from another. By his side sat a can of Coke he had bought in a grocer's shop to quench his thirst.

Lighting a cigarette, he wondered what he would say to the great-grandmother he was going to see. He could hardly come right out and ask her about the skull he'd found – the poor old dear would probably drop dead with shock. He would have to be very careful and take it step by step, but how?

At five past two, he was shown into the large, airy common room at Sunnyfields, the young nurse telling him, 'That's Mrs Wallace in the chair next the rubber plant.'

He was rather disappointed at how old she looked. She was gazing out of the window; her face was very wrinkled and her skin had a transparency about it. Her hair was done up in some kind of coil at the back, but it was pure silver, with no trace of yellow. Walking past several old people who smiled vacantly at him, Ewan was very relieved when her rheumy eyes turned on him with a normal curiosity. 'Hello, Mrs Wallace,' he said brightly. 'May I talk to you for a while?'

'Sit down here beside me.' Mysie patted the empty chair next to her. 'I don't remember who you are, but my memory's not as good as it used to be.'

'You don't know me,' he assured her. 'My name is Ewan Duncan and I'm your son's grandson.'

Mysie's hand went to her chest, but her voice didn't waver. 'Sandy's grandson? My goodness, what a surprise.'

'My father's name is Sam, and he was born in . . .'

'It must have been 1935. It was the year I married Gregor, that's why I remember. Is your grandmother still alive?'

'There's nothing wrong with your memory, and yes, she is.'

'You're very like Sandy, now that I come to think about it. You've the same hair, the same eyes – you even walk like him. I should have guessed who you were.'

He told her the same as he'd told Gina, but Mysie gave a low sardonic laugh when he said that he had bought the bungalow at Rowanbrae. 'So the Cattanachs had to sell it?'

'I bought it from people called McGregor, so the Cattanachs must have given it up before that.'

The old lady seemed childishly pleased. 'Pride always goes before a fall.'

'It's not that house I'm interested in, though, it's the

croft that was there before. Can you tell me anything about that? Why was it abandoned? Was there a fire?'

Mysie nodded. 'Aye, that's right, there was a fire.'

'I guessed it must be that. How did it start?'

'We thought it was a bit of peat that fell on the rug.'

Her sudden wariness made him wonder if she had a reason for not wanting to talk about it. 'Was anyone inside at the time? Was anyone . . . hurt?'

'There was just Sandy and me there, and we both got out.'

He wasn't progressing very quickly, Ewan thought. Maybe he shouldn't have come? How could this old lady tell him what he wanted to know? Still, now that he was here, he'd better keep on. 'Did anybody you knew ever disappear? I mean, disappear and never turn up again?' Noticing that she looked more wary than ever, he was sure there was a mystery of some kind to be uncovered. He was on the right track, if only she would come clean and tell him everything she knew.

'Aye,' Mysie said, uneasily. 'You could say that, I suppose. You see, Sandy's father walked out on us, and nobody ever knew what happened to him.'

This was more like it, and Ewan jumped in with both feet. 'I could probably help you there. I'm having an extension built at the back of the house – a sort of utility room, you know – and the garage had to come down – it was a ramshackle wooden thing, anyway. I got the loan of a drill to break up the old cement floor first, and I nearly fell in a heap when I came across a skull.' He stopped, watching his great-grandmother closely for signs of distress.

Mysie, however, was made of stronger stuff, and not a flicker of her inner turmoil appeared on her face as she wrestled with her conscience for a few minutes before saying softly, 'Well, well! So it was my own great-grandson that dug him up, after all these years. That's irony for you.'

Ewan was thunderstruck. Surely it couldn't have been

324

this frail creature who had murdered . . . ? 'I'm sorry, I shouldn't have told you about it.'

'No, lad, I'm pleased you did.' Mysie cast a quick glance round the room, where several visitors were now talking to the other residents of the home. 'I'd like to tell you the whole story, get it off my chest, but not here, not when there's so many old wives with nothing to do but listen to other folk's conversations. You'd better help me to my own room.'

Gripping her elbow as she got her walking stick ready and rose shakily to her feet, Ewan felt himself trembling. Gina had said that she was the skeleton in the family cupboard, but her mother was about to tell him about a real skeleton, or all that remained of it.

When they entered her room, Mysie thumped into a seat with a sigh. 'It's a relief to me that it was you that found him, but it'll be hard for you to believe what I'm going to tell you.'

She waited until he drew over a chair and sat down beside her. 'You said you were interested in your family history, so I'll start at the beginning, when I met Jeems Duncan first.'

While the story unfolded, Ewan wished that he had thought of taking a tape recorder with him – nobody would ever believe it if he told them this. Mysie, reliving the past, reverted to the dialect she had spoken then and kept nothing back, remarking, when she told him about the meal and ale, 'An' that was the nicht I fell in love wi' Doddie Wilson. He was a good, decent man, an' I've aye regretted thinkin' it was him that killed Jeems. But I'm gettin' ahead o' my story.'

She talked candidly about what had caused the quarrel with her husband and what he had done in his temper. 'I was near sure it wasna me that used that second knife, an' Doddie was the only other person I could think on. Weel, I found oot, years after, that it wasna me . . . or Doddie.' Her eyes, which had been on her hands all the time she was speaking, lifted and focused on Ewan. 'But

I'd best nae tell you who it was, nae yet. I'll wait till I come to the time I learned mysel', for a lot happened in between.'

'Whatever you think,' he murmured, astounded that any woman could have come through so much. 'But I don't want you to tire yourself out. I could come back another day to hear the rest.'

'No, you'd best let me finish as lang as I'm into the swing o' it. There's nae that much left to tell.'

In spite of this assurance, the soft voice carried on for a further twenty minutes, detailing all the events right up to her leaving Burnlea, the dialect disappearing as she related what had happened to her after she came to Aberdeen as housekeeper to Miss Wallace. When Ewan learned the reason for his grandfather's quarrel with her, he understood why his family had never had any contact with her, but could not associate Libby, the common tart she had just described, with Beth, the grandmother he loved. She had certainly changed.

'When Gina found out she was illegitimate,' Mysie continued, 'she was so shocked she walked out, and Sandy left the house for good just minutes after her. That was when I agreed to marry Gregor, and it was him that helped me get over it. And I don't know what I'd have done without him when I saw Sandy's death in the paper in 1942. I was demented, and wished with all my heart that he had come to see me before he went off to the war. Then his letter came. I was only to get it if he was killed, so his officer gave it to a pilot to post in England. I still have it in my handbag there . . .' She stopped abruptly, then sighed. 'I think you'd better read it for yourself.'

Ewan passed over the rather dilapidated brown leather bag, and she took out an envelope, discoloured and crumpled from years of handling. 'Read it out to me,' she instructed.

'Dear Mother,' he read, 'I am writing this to tell you that I bitterly regret quarrelling with you. You were not mistaken in what you thought about Libby, she was everything you said she was and I joined the Air Force to get away from her. It was only later that I realised how much she had changed from the time I met her, and if I come through the war, I might try to patch things up with her.'

Glancing up briefly, Ewan saw that his great-grand-mother's lips were forming the words along with him, showing that she knew the letter off by heart, and he had to swallow before he carried on reading. 'But now that I've made a start, I want to unburden my soul completely before I meet my Maker, though I doubt if He will accept me into heaven after the awful things I've done, because the fire wasn't the worst. I should have told you at the time, but I was very young, and very scared. Brace your-self, Mother, this is going to be a terrible shock. It was I who killed my father.'

Gasping, Ewan looked up again, but Mysie said, 'Aye, that's a surprise to you, but go on.'

'I heard him fighting with you and I went to the door of the kitchen and saw he had a knife in his hand. I thought he was going to kill you, so I crept over and picked another knife off the floor, but he jabbed at you before I was close enough to stop him. He didn't know I was there, and I thought you were dead, so I lifted my arm to stick the knife in him. Being so young, I didn't have any great strength, so if he hadn't heard me just at that minute, he would likely only have had a small cut, but he did hear. He whipped round as my hand came down, and it was the force of his own body that made the knife go in right up to the hilt. I was only seven, remember, but I knew that I had killed him. Not knowing what else to do, I went back to bed, and when I heard you moving about again, and coughing, I knew you were still alive, so I fell asleep with an easier mind, although I was too fright-ened to say anything the next day. I tried to tell you on the night you learned that Doddie had been killed, but you wouldn't let me.'

'Aye,' Mysie murmured. 'That was when he said it was him filling the oil lamp that caused the fire and I was too

327

upset to listen to him when he wanted to tell me something else.'

Bending his head again, Ewan read the rest of the letter. 'I have often wondered where you hid the body, and you must have wondered who killed him. I did not really mean to, but I am not sorry I did, because he didn't deserve to live after the way he used to treat you. As I grew older, that night often came back to haunt me, and I suppose that's really why I began drinking so much, which is another thing I have to apologise for. Be that as it may, I trust you will forgive me for not telling you all this before. I pray that you never have to read this letter, but if you do, please remember that what I did that night was out of love for you, and that I still love you as much as ever. I will always be – your loving son, Sandy.'

As Ewan replaced the faded pages in the envelope, the lump in his throat almost choking him, Mysie looked quizzically at him. 'I suppose you'll be so shocked now, you'll be wishing you had never tried to find out your family history?'

He couldn't speak just yet, and pretended to consider. 'I am shocked,' he admitted, after a moment. 'I'm shocked that you had such a terrible life, but I'm very glad you have told me exactly what happened, and I don't condemn you nor your son. God Almighty, Great-grandmother, I don't know how you didn't go off your head after some of the things that happened to you.'

'I don't know myself, laddie, but would you mind not calling me Great-grandmother? It makes me feel really ancient.' She gave a throaty chuckle. 'I'm not a hundred yet . . . though it'll not be long. Gregor used to call me Maisie, but you could call me Mysie, if you like. Nobody's called me that for a long time – not since Jess Findlater died – and I quite like it.'

'Okay, Mysie it is. May I come back to see you? I promise never to bring any of this up again.'

'I'd love to see you again, but before you go, will

you . . . will you have to tell the police about what you found?'

'No, it would only cause a furore, and I won't tell anyone else, either. I'll dig the thing well down, and cover it with fresh cement. Nobody will ever find it again, Mysie, I swear.'

'Oh, that's a weight off my mind. Bless you, Ewan.'

When he left, Mysie leaned back and closed her eyes. Fancy it being Sandy's grandson that found Jeems. She had known he was bound to be unearthed some day, but she had begun to think that she was safe enough – that it wouldn't be in her lifetime. She had been proved right about one thing, though – the head hadn't been limed. Thank goodness her great-grandson would be the only one to know the truth about that traumatic night in 1914. Gregor had known, of course, he'd had to read Sandy's letter to her, but she had trusted Gregor. He had seen her through a lot, brought her back to life after Sandy was killed, for his letter had had an even worse effect on her than his death. She'd been horrified to think that her young son had been a witness to his father's insane rage; sick at picturing the child thrusting a knife into the man.

She had almost gone out of her mind then, and it had taken her much longer to get over than any of the other things that had happened to her. The other things. Being sold to Jeems for thirty pounds; losing her dear Jamie down the old quarry; discovering that she was expecting a packman's child; finding Jeems and burying him; aborting that same night; the fire; Doddie being killed; Sandy and Gina leaving her; poor little Alexander. But Gregor had also seen her through that last two. Dear Gregor. She was grateful that she had been able to repay his devotion by nursing him in his last years, and it shouldn't be long now before they were together again – for ever.

At five o'clock, the young nurse went to help Mrs Wallace to the dining room, and was quite surprised to find her sleeping. Some of the old folk slept nearly all day and

329

wandered about all night, but Mrs Wallace wasn't like that. She was always alert, but her visitor had stayed quite a long time, and she must have been tired out, poor soul.

'Wakey, wakey!' the girl sang out, and it wasn't until she had shaken the old lady several times that she turned and ran to the office. 'I think Mrs Wallace has died in her chair,' she burst out when she opened the door.

Knowing how quick some of the young girls were in jumping to the wrong conclusion, Mrs Warrender went with her to check it out, but it was true. 'I'll have to get the doctor to write out a death certificate.'

'She was a dear old thing,' the girl remarked sadly. 'I'm glad she died peacefully with a smile on her face.'

Mrs Warrender gave a long sigh. 'Yes, it's not so bad when they go like that, some of them have a terrible struggle. And Mrs Wallace has had a good innings, remember, she'd have been ninety-six on her birthday. Of course, she was very well off, and I suppose she'd had things easy all her life.'

The girl nodded. 'Yes, I suppose so. Some people have all the luck, haven't they?'